Thomas Babington Macaulay

The Miscellaneous Writings, Speeches and Poems

Vol. IV

Thomas Babington Macaulay

The Miscellaneous Writings, Speeches and Poems
Vol. IV

ISBN/EAN: 9783337206642

Printed in Europe, USA, Canada, Australia, Japan

Cover: Foto ©Andreas Hilbeck / pixelio.de

More available books at **www.hansebooks.com**

THE

MISCELLANEOUS WRITINGS

SPEECHES AND POEMS

OF

LORD MACAULAY

IN FOUR VOLUMES

VOL. IV.

LONDON
LONGMANS, GREEN, AND CO.
1880

CONTENTS

OF

THE FOURTH VOLUME.

———◦◦———

INTRODUCTORY REPORT

UPON THE

INDIAN PENAL CODE.

VOL. IV.   B

INTRODUCTORY REPORT

UPON THE

INDIAN PENAL CODE.

———◦◦———

TO THE RIGHT HONOURABLE GEORGE LORD AUCK-
LAND, C.G.C.B., GOVERNOR-GENERAL OF INDIA IN
COUNCIL.

MY LORD,

THE Penal Code which, according to the orders of
Government of the 15th of June, 1835, we had the
honour to lay before your Lordship in Council on the
2nd of May last, has now been printed under our
superintendence, and has, as well as the Notes, been
carefully revised and corrected by us while in the
press.

The time which has been employed in framing
this body of law will not be thought long by any
person who is acquainted with the nature of the
labour which such works require, and with the
history of other works of the same kind. We
should, however, have been able to lay it before
your Lordship in Council many months earlier, but
for a succession of unfortunate circumstances against
which it was impossible to provide. During a great
part of the year 1836, the Commission was rendered
almost entirely inefficient by the ill-health of a majority of the members; and we were altogether de-

B 2

prived of the valuable services of our colleague Mr. Cameron, at the very time when those services were most needed.

It is hardly necessary for us to entreat your Lordship in Council to examine with candour the work which we now submit to you. To the ignorant and inexperienced the task in which we have been engaged may appear easy and simple. But the members of the Indian Government are doubtless well aware that it is among the most difficult tasks in which the human mind can be employed; that persons placed in circumstances far more favourable than ours have attempted it with very doubtful success; that the best codes extant, if malignantly criticised, will be found to furnish matter for censure in every page; that the most copious and precise of human languages furnish but a very imperfect machinery to the legislator; that, in a work so extensive and complicated as that on which we have been employed, there will inevitably be, in spite of the most anxious care, some omissions and some inconsistencies; and that we have done as much as could reasonably be expected from us if we have furnished the Government with that which may, by suggestions from experienced and judicious persons, be improved into a good code.

Your Lordship in Council will be prepared to find in this performance those defects which must necessarily be found in the first portion of a code. Such is the relation which exists between the different parts of the law, that no part can be brought to perfection while the other parts remain rude. The penal code cannot be clear and explicit while the substantive civil law and the law of procedure are dark and confused. While the rights of individuals and the powers of public functionaries are uncertain, it cannot always be certain whether those rights have been attacked, or those powers exceeded.

Your Lordship in Council will perceive that the system of penal law which we propose is not a digest of any existing system, and that no existing system has furnished us even with a groundwork. We trust that your Lordship in Council will not hence infer that we have neglected to inquire, as we are commanded to do by Parliament, into the present state of that part of the law, or that in other parts of our labours we are likely to recommend unsparing innovation, and the entire sweeping away of ancient usages. We are perfectly aware of the value of that sanction which long prescription and national feeling give to institutions. We are perfectly aware that lawgivers ought not to disregard even the unreasonable prejudices of those for whom they legislate. So sensible are we of the importance of these considerations, that, though there are not the same objections to innovation in penal legislation as to innovation affecting vested rights of property, yet, if we had found India in possession of a system of criminal law which the people regarded with partiality, we should have been inclined rather to ascertain it, to digest it, and moderately to correct it, than to propose a system fundamentally different.

But it appears to us that none of the systems of penal law established in British India has any claim to our attention, except what it may derive from its own intrinsic excellence. All those systems are foreign. All were introduced by conquerors differing in race, manners, language and religion from the great mass of the people. The criminal law of the Hindoos was long ago superseded, through the greater part of the territories now subject to the Company, by that of the Mahomedans, and is certainly the last system of criminal law which an enlightened and humane Government would be disposed to revive. The Mahomedan criminal law has in its turn been superseded, to a great extent, by the British

Regulations. Indeed, in the territories subject to
the Presidency of Bombay, the criminal law of the
Mahomedans, as well as that of the Hindoos, has
been altogether discarded, except in one particular
class of cases ; and even in such cases, it is not im-
perative on the judge to pay any attention to it.
The British Regulations, having been made by three
different legislatures, contain, as might be expected,
very different provisions. Thus in Bengal serious
forgeries are punishable with imprisonment for a
term double of the term fixed for perjury : [1] in the
Bombay Presidency, on the contrary, perjury is
punishable with imprisonment for a term double of
the term fixed for the most aggravated forgeries : [2]
in the Madras Presidency, the two offences are
exactly on the same footing.[3]   In the Bombay Presidency the escape of a convict is punished with
imprisonment for a term double of the term assigned
to that offence in the two other Presidencies ; [4] while
a coiner is punished with little more than half the
imprisonment assigned to his offence in the other
two Presidencies.[5]   In Bengal the purchasing of
regimental necessaries from soldiers is not punishable except at Calcutta, and is there punishable with
a fine of only fifty rupees.[6]   In the Madras Presidency it is punishable with a fine of forty rupees.[7]
In the Bombay Presidency it is punishable with imprisonment for four years.[8]   In Bengal the vending

[1] Bengal Regulation XVII.
of 1817, section IX.

[2] Bombay Regulation XIV. of
1827, sections XVI. and XVII.

[3] Madras Regulation VI. of
1811, section III.

[4] Bombay Regulation XIV. of
1827, section XXIV., and Regulation V. of 1831, section I.
Bengal Regulation XII. of 1818,
section V. clause 1. Madras Regulation VI. of 1822, section V.
clause 2.

[5] Bombay Regulation XIV.
of 1827, section XVIII. Bengal
Regulation XVII. of 1817, section IX. Madras Regulation II.
of 1822, section V.

[6] Calcutta Rule, Ordinance
and Regulation, passed 21st August, registered 13th Nov., 1821.

[7] Madras Regulation XIV. of
1832. section II. clause 1.

[8] Bombay Regulation XXII.
of 1827, section XIX.

of stamps without a license is punishable with a moderate fine; and the purchasing of stamps from a person not licensed to sell them is not punished at all.[1]   In the Madras Presidency the vendor is punished with a short imprisonment; but there also the purchaser is not punished at all.[2]   In the Bombay Presidency, both the vendor and the purchaser are liable to imprisonment for five years, and to flogging.[3]

Thus widely do the systems of penal law now established in British India differ from each other : nor can we recommend any one of the three systems as furnishing even the rudiments of a good code. The penal law of Bengal and of the Madras Presidency is, in fact, Mahomedan law, which has gradually been distorted to such an extent as to deprive it of all title to the religious veneration of Mahomedans, yet which retains enough of its original peculiarities to perplex and encumber the administration of justice.   In substance it now differs at least as widely from the Mahomedan penal law, as the penal law of England differs from the penal law of France.   Yet technical terms and nice distinctions borrowed from the Mahomedan law are still retained. Nothing is more usual than for the Courts to ask the law officers what punishment the Mahomedan law prescribes in a hypothetical case, and then to inflict that punishment on a person who is not within that hypothetical case, and who by the Mahomedan law would be liable either to a different punishment, or to no punishment. We by no means presume to condemn the policy which led the British Government to retain, and gradually to modify, the system of criminal jurisprudence which it found established in these provinces. But it is evident

---

[1] Bengal Regulation X. of of 1816, section X. clause 10.
1829, section IX. clause 2.   [3] Bombay Regulation XVIII.
[2] Madras Regulation XIII. of 1827, section IX. clause 1.

that a body of law thus formed must, considered merely as a body of law, be defective and inconvenient.

The penal law of the Bombay Presidency is all contained in the Regulations; and is almost all to be found in one extensive Regulation.[1] The Government of that Presidency appears to have been fully sensible of the great advantage which must arise from placing the whole law in a written form before those who are to administer and those who are to obey it; and, whatever may be the imperfections of the execution, high praise is due to the design. The course which we recommend to the Government, and which some persons may perhaps consider as too daring, has already been tried at Bombay, and has not produced any of those effects which timid minds are disposed to anticipate even from the most reasonable and useful innovations. Throughout a large territory, inhabited to a great extent by a newly-conquered population, all the ancient systems of penal law were at once superseded by a code, and this without the smallest sign of discontent among the people.

It would have given us great pleasure to have found that code such as we could with propriety have taken as the groundwork of a code for all India. But we regret to say that the penal law of the Bombay Presidency has over the penal law of the other Presidencies no superiority, except that of being digested. In framing it, the principles according to which crimes ought to be classified and punishments apportioned have been less regarded than in the legislation of Bengal and Madras. The secret destroying of any property, though it may not be worth a single rupee, is punishable with imprisonment for five years.[2] Unlawful confinement, though it may

---

[1] Bombay Regulation XIV. of 1827.

[2] Regulation XIV. of 1827, section XLII. clause 2.

last only for a quarter of an hour, is punishable with imprisonment for five years.[1] Every conspiracy to injure or impoverish any person is punishable with imprisonment for ten years;[2] so that a man who engages in a design as atrocious as the Gunpowder Plot, and one who is party to a scheme for putting off an unsound horse on a purchaser, are classed together, and are liable to exactly the same punishment. Under this law, if two men concert a petty theft, and afterwards repent of their purpose and abandon it, each of them is liable to twenty times the punishment of the actual theft.[3] All assaults which cause a severe shock to the mental feelings of the sufferer are classed with the atrocious crime of rape, and are liable to the punishment of rape, that is, if the Courts shall think fit, to imprisonment for fourteen years.[4] The breaking of the window of a house, the dashing to pieces a china cup within a house, the riding over a field of grain in hunting, are classed with the crime of arson, and are punishable, incredible as it may appear, with death. The following is the law on the subject: "Any person who shall wilfully and wrongfully set fire to or otherwise damage or destroy any part of a dwelling-house or ˙building appertaining thereto, or property contained in a dwelling house, or building or inclosure appertaining thereto, or crops standing or reaped in the field, shall be liable to any of the punishments specified in Section III. of this Regulation."[5] The section to which reference is made contains a list of the punishments authorised by the Bombay code, and at the head of that list stands "Death."

But these errors, the effects probably of inadvertence, are not, in our opinion, the most serious faults

[1] Regulation XIV. of 1827, section XXXIII. clause 1.
[2] Regulation XVII. of 1828.
[3] Regulation XIV. of 1837, section XXXIX.
[4] Regulation XIV. of 1827, section XXIX. clause 1.
[5] Regulation XIV. of 1827, section XLII. clause 1.

of the penal code of Bombay. That code contains enactments which it is impossible to excuse on the ground of inadvertence—enactments the language of which shows that when they were framed their whole effect was fully understood, and which appear to us to be directly opposed to the first principles of penal law. One of the first principles of penal law is this, that a person who merely conceals a crime after it has been committed ought not to be punished as if he had himself committed it. By the Bombay code, the concealment after the fact of murder is punishable as murder; the concealment after the fact of gang-robbery is punishable as gang-robbery;[1] —and this, though the concealment after the fact of the most cruel mutilations, and of the most atrocious robberies committed by not more than four persons, is not punished at all.

If there be any distinctions which more than any other it behoves the legislator to bear constantly in mind, it is the distinction between harm voluntarily caused and harm involuntarily caused. Negligence, indeed, often causes mischief, and often deserves punishment. But to punish a man whose negligence has produced some evil which he never contemplated, as if he had produced the same evil knowingly and with deliberate malice, is a course which, as far as we are aware, no jurist has ever recommended in theory, and which we are confident that no society would tolerate in practice. It is, however, provided by the Bombay code that the "unintentional commission of any act punishable by that code shall be punished according to the Court's judgment of the culpable disregard of injury to others evinced by the person committing the said act, but the punishment for such unintentional commission shall not exceed that prescribed for the offence committed."[2]

[1] Regulation XIV. of 1827, section I. clause 1.

[2] Regulation XIV. of 1827, section I. clause 3.

We have said enough to show that it is owing not at all to the law, but solely to the discretion and humanity of the judges, that great cruelty and injustice is not daily perpetrated in the Criminal Courts of the Bombay Presidency.

Many important classes of offences are altogether unnoticed by the Bombay code ; and this omission appears to us to be very ill supplied by one sweeping clause, which arms the Courts with almost unlimited power to punish as they think fit offences against morality, or against the peace and good order of society, if those offences are penal by the religious law of the offender.[1] This clause does not apply to people who profess a religion with which a system of penal jurisprudence is not inseparably connected. And from this state of the law some singular consequences follow. For example, a Mahomedan is punishable for adultery : a Christian is at liberty to commit adultery with impunity.

Such is the state of the penal law in the Mofussil. In the meantime the population which lives within the local jurisdiction of the Courts established by the Royal Charters is subject to the English Criminal Law, that is to say, to a very artificial and complicated system,—to a foreign system,—to a system which was framed without the smallest reference to India,—to a system which even in the country for which it was framed is generally considered as requiring extensive reform,—to a system finally which has just been pronounced by a Commission composed of able and learned English lawyers to be so defective that it can be reformed only by being entirely taken to pieces and reconstructed.[2]

[1] Regulation XIV. of 1827, section I. clause 1.

[2] Letter to Lord John Russell from the Commissioners appointed to inquire into the state of the Criminal Law dated 19th January, 1837.

Under these circumstances we have not thought it desirable to take as the groundwork of the code any of the systems of law now in force in any part of India. We have, indeed, to the best of our ability, compared the code with all those systems, and we have taken suggestions from all; but we have not adopted a single provision merely because it formed a part of any of those systems. We have also compared our work with the most celebrated systems of Western jurisprudence, as far as the very scanty means of information which were accessible to us in this country enabled us to do so. We have derived much valuable assistance from the French code, and from the decisions of the French Courts of Justice on questions touching the construction of that code. We have derived assistance still more valuable from the code of Louisiana, prepared by the late Mr. Livingston. We are the more desirous to acknowledge our obligations to that eminent jurist, because we have found ourselves under the necessity of combatting his opinions on some important questions.

The reasons for those provisions which appear to us to require explanation or defence will be found appended to the Code in the form of Notes. Should your Lordship in Council wish for fuller information as to the considerations by which we have been guided in framing any part of the law, we shall be ready to afford it.

One peculiarity in the manner in which this code is framed will immediately strike your Lordship in Council,—we mean the copious use of illustrations. These illustrations will, we trust, greatly facilitate the understanding of the law, and will at the same time often serve as a defence of the law. In our definitions we have repeatedly found ourselves under the necessity of sacrificing neatness and perspicuity to precision, and of using harsh expressions because we could find no other expressions which would convey our whole meaning, and no more than our whole meaning. Such definitions standing by themselves might repel and perplex the reader, and would perhaps be fully comprehended only by a few students after long application. Yet such definitions are found, and must be found, in every system of law which aims at accuracy. A legislator may, if he thinks fit, avoid such definitions, and by avoiding them he will give a smoother and more attractive appearance to his workmanship ; but in that case he flinches from a duty which he ought to perform, and which somebody must perform. If this necessary but most disagreeable work be not performed by the lawgiver once for all, it must be constantly performed in a rude and imperfect manner by every judge in the empire, and will probably be performed by no two judges in the same way. We have therefore thought it right not to shrink from the task of framing these unpleasing but indispensable parts of a code. And we hope that when each of these definitions is followed by a collection of cases falling under it, and of cases which, though at first sight they appear to fall under it, do not really fall under it, the definition and the reasons which led to the adoption of it will be readily understood. The illustrations will lead the mind of the student through the same steps by which the minds of those who framed the law proceeded, and may sometimes show him that a phrase which may have struck him as uncouth, or a distinction which he may have thought idle, was deliberately adopted for the purpose of including or excluding a large class of important cases. In the study of geometry it is constantly found that a theorem which, read by itself, conveyed no distinct meaning to the mind, becomes perfectly clear as soon as the reader casts his eye over the statement of the individual case taken for the purpose of demonstration. Our illustrations, we trust, will in a similar manner facilitate the study of the law.

There are two things which a legislator should always have in view while he is framing laws; the one is, that they should be as far as possible precise: the other, that they should be easily understood. To unite precision and simplicity in definitions intended to include large classes of things, and to exclude others very similar to many of those which are included, will often be utterly impossible. Under such circumstances it is not easy to say what is the best course. That a law, and especially a penal law, should be drawn in words which convey no meaning to the people who are to obey it is an evil. On the other hand, a loosely-worded law is no law, and to whatever extent a legislature uses vague expressions, to that extent it abdicates its functions, and resigns the power of making law to the Courts of Justice.

On the whole, we are inclined to think that the best course is that which we have adopted. We have, in framing our definitions, thought principally of making them precise, and have not shrunk from rugged or intricate phraseology when such phraseology appeared to us to be necessary to precision. If it appeared to us that our language was likely to perplex an ordinary reader, we added as many illustrations as we thought necessary for the purpose of explaining it. The definitions and enacting clauses contain the whole law. The illustrations make nothing law which would not be law without them. They only exhibit the law in full action, and show what its effects will be on the events of common life.

Thus the code will be at once a statute book and a collection of decided cases. The decided cases in the code will differ from the decided cases in the English law books in two most important points. In the first place, our illustrations are never intended to supply any omission in the written law, nor do they ever, in our opinion, put a strain on the written law. They are merely instances of the practical application of the written law to the affairs of mankind. Secondly, they are cases decided not by the judges but by the legislature, by those who make the law, and who must know more certainly than any judge can know what the law is which they mean to make.

The power of construing the law in cases in which there is any real reason to doubt what the law is amounts to the power of making the law. On this ground the Roman jurists maintained that the office of interpreting the law in doubtful matters necessarily belonged to the legislature. The contrary opinion was censured by them with great force of reason, though in language perhaps too bitter and sarcastic for the gravity of a code. " Eorum vanam subtilitatem tam risimus quam corrigendam esse censuimus. Si enim in præsenti leges condere soli imperatori concessum est, et leges interpretari solo dignum imperio esse oportet. Quis legum ænigmata solvere et omnibus aperire idoneus esse videbitur nisi is cui legislatorem esse concessum est? Explosis itaque his ridiculosis ambiguitatibus tam conditor quam interpres legum solus imperator juste existimabitur."[1]

The decisions on particular cases which we have annexed to the provisions of the code resemble the imperial rescripts in this, that they proceed from the same authority from which the provisions themselves proceed. They differ from the imperial rescripts in this most important circumstance, that they are not made *ex post facto*, that they cannot therefore be made to serve any particular turn, that the persons condemned or absolved by them are purely imaginary

[1] Cod. Just., Lib. I., Tit. XIV. 12.

persons, and that, therefore, whatever may be thought
of the wisdom of any judgment which we have passed,
there can be no doubt of its impartiality.

The publication of this collection of cases decided by legislative authority will, we hope, greatly
limit the power which the Courts of Justice possess
of putting their own sense on the laws.   But we are
sensible that neither this collection nor any other
can be sufficiently extensive to settle every question
which may be raised as to the construction of the
code.   Such questions will certainly arise, and, unless
proper precautions be taken, the decisions on such
questions will accumulate till they form a body of
law of far greater bulk than that which has been
adopted by the legislature.   Nor is this the worst.
While the judicial system of British India continues
to be what it now is, these decisions will render the
law not only bulky, but uncertain and contradictory.
There are at present eight chief Courts subject to
the legislative power of your Lordship in Council,
four established by Royal Charter, and four which
derive their authority from the Company.   Every
one of these tribunals is perfectly independent of
the others.   Every one of them is at liberty to put
its own construction on the law ; and it is not to be
expected that they will always adopt the same construction.   Under so inconvenient a system there
will inevitably be, in the course of a few years, a
large collection of decisions diametrically opposed to
each other, and all of equal authority.

How the powers and mutual relations of these
Courts may be placed on a better footing, and
whether it be possible or desirable to have in India
a single tribunal empowered to expound the code in
the last resort, are questions which must shortly
engage the attention of the Law Commission.   But
whether the present judicial organization be retained
or not, it is most desirable that measures should be

taken to prevent the written law from being overlaid by an immense weight of comments and decisions. We conceive that it is proper for us, at the time at which we lay before your Lordship in Council the first part of the Indian code, to offer such suggestions as have occurred to us on this important subject.

We do not think it desirable that the Indian legislature should, like the Roman emperors, decide doubtful points of law which have actually been mooted in cases pending before the tribunals. In criminal cases, with which we are now more immediately concerned, we think that the accused party ought always to have the advantage of a doubt on a point of law, if that doubt be entertained after mature consideration by the highest judicial authority, as well as of a doubt on a matter of fact. In civil suits which are actually pending, we think it on the whole desirable to leave to the Courts the office of deciding doubtful questions of law which have actually arisen in the course of litigation. But every case in which the construction put by a judge on any part of the code is set aside by any of those tribunals from which at present there is no appeal in India, and every case in which there is a difference of opinion in a Court composed of several judges as to the construction of any part of the code, ought to be forthwith reported to the legislature. Every judge of every rank whose duty it is to administer the law as contained in the code should be enjoined to report to his official superiors every doubt which he may entertain as to any question of construction which may have arisen in his Court. Of these doubts, all which are not obviously unreasonable ought to be periodically reported by the highest judicial authorities to the legislature. All the questions thus reported to the Government might with advantage be referred for examination to the Law Commission, if that Commission should be a permanent body. In some cases it will be found that the law is already sufficiently clear, and that any misconstruction which may have taken place is to be attributed to weakness, carelessness, wrongheadedness or corruption on the part of an individual, and is not likely to occur again. In such cases it will be unnecessary to make any change in the code. Sometimes it will be found that a case has arisen respecting which the code is silent. In such a case it will be proper to supply the omission. Sometimes it may be found that the code is inconsistent with itself. If so, the inconsistency ought to be removed. Sometimes it will be found that the words of the law are not sufficiently precise. In such a case it will be proper to substitute others. Sometimes it will be found that the language of the law, though it is as precise as the subject admits, is not so clear that a person of ordinary intelligence can see its whole meaning. In these cases it will generally be expedient to add illustrations, such as may distinctly show in what sense the legislature intends the law to be understood, and may render it impossible that the same question, or any similar question, should ever again occasion difference of opinion. In this manner every successive edition of the code will solve all the important questions as to the construction of the code which have arisen since the appearance of the edition immediately preceding. Important questions, particularly questions about which Courts of the highest rank have pronounced opposite decisions, ought to be settled without delay; and no point of law ought to continue to be a doubtful point more than three or four years after it has been mooted in a Court of Justice. An addition of a very few pages to the code will stand in the place of several volumes of reports, and will be of far more value than such reports, inasmuch as the additions to the code will proceed from the legislature, and will be of unquestionable authority; whereas the reports would only give the opinions of the judges, which other judges might venture to set aside.

It appears to us also highly desirable that, if the code shall be adopted, all those penal laws which the Indian legislature may from time to time find it necessary to pass should be framed in such a manner as to fit into the code. Their language ought to be that of the code. No word ought to be used in any other sense than that in which it is used in the code. The very part of the code in which the new law is to be inserted ought to be indicated. If the new law rescinds or modifies any provision of the code, that provision ought to be indicated. In fact the new law ought, from the day on which it is passed, to be part of the code, and to affect all the other provisions of the code, and to be affected by them as if it were actually a clause of the original code. In the next edition of the code, the new law ought to appear in its proper place.

For reasons which have been fully stated to your Lordship in Council in another communication, we have not inserted in the code any clause declaring to what places and to what classes of persons it shall apply.

Your Lordship in Council will see that we have not proposed to except from the operation of this code any of the ancient sovereign houses of India residing within the Company's territories. Whether any such exception ought to be made is a question which, without a more accurate knowledge than we possess of existing treaties, of the sense in which those treaties have been understood, of the history of negotiations, of the temper and of the power of particular families, and of the feeling of the body of the people towards those families, we could not venture to decide. We will only beg permission most respectfully to observe that every such exception is an evil; that it is an evil that any man should be above the law; that it is a still greater evil that the public should be taught to regard as a high and enviable distinction the privilege of being above the law; that the longer such privileges are suffered to last, the more difficult it is to take them away; that there can scarcely ever be a fairer opportunity for taking them away than at the time when the Government promulgates a new code binding alike on persons of different races and religions; and that we greatly doubt whether any consideration, except that of public faith solemnly pledged, deserves to be weighed against the advantages of equal justice.

The peculiar state of public feeling in this country may render it advisable to frame the law of procedure in such a manner that families of high rank may be dispensed, as far as possible, from the necessity of performing acts which are here regarded, however unreasonably, as humiliating. But though it may be proper to make wide distinctions as respects form, there ought in our opinion to be, as respects substance, no distinctions except those which the Government is bound by express engagements to make. That a man of rank should be examined with particular ceremonies or in a particular place may, in the present state of Indian society, be highly expedient. But that a man of any rank should be allowed to commit crimes with impunity must in every state of society be most pernicious.

The provisions of the code will be applicable to offences committed by soldiers, as well as to offences committed by other members of the community. But for those purely military offences which soldiers only can commit, we have made no provision. It appears to us desirable that this part of the law should be taken up separately, and we have been given to understand that your Lordship in Council has determined that it shall be so taken up. But we have, as your Lordship in Council will perceive, made provision for punishing persons who, not being themselves subject to martial law, abet soldiers in the breach of military discipline.

Your Lordship in Council will observe that in many parts of the penal code we have referred to the code of procedure, which as yet is not in existence; and hence it may possibly be supposed to be our opinion that, till the code of procedure is framed, the penal code cannot come into operation. Such, however, is not our meaning. We conceive that almost the whole of the penal code, such as we now lay it before your Lordship, might be made law, at least in the Mofussil, without any considerable change in the existing rules of procedure. Should your Lordship in Council agree with us in this opinion, we shall be prepared to suggest those changes which it would be necessary immediately to make.

In conclusion, we beg respectfully to suggest that, if your Lordship in Council is disposed to adopt the code which we have framed, it is most desirable that the native population should, with as little delay as possible, be furnished with good versions of it in their own languages. Such versions, in our opinion, can be produced only by the combined labours of enlightened Europeans and natives; and it is not probable that men competent to execute all the translations which will be required would be found in any single province of India. We are sensible that the difficulty of procuring good translations will be great; but we believe that the means at the disposal of your Lordship in Council are sufficient to overcome every difficulty; and we are confident that your Lordship in Council will not grudge anything that may be necessary for the purpose of enabling the people who are placed under your care to know what that law is according to which they are required to live.

We have the honour to be,

My Lord,

Your Lordship's most obedient humble Servants,

T. B. Macaulay,

J. M. Macleod,

G. W. Anderson,

F. Millett.

Indian Law Commission,
October 14, 1837.

NOTES.

NOTE (A).

ON THE CHAPTER OF PUNISHMENTS.

FIRST among the punishments provided for offences by this code stands death. No argument that has been brought to our notice has satisfied us that it would be desirable wholly to dispense with this punishment. But we are convinced that it ought to be very sparingly inflicted, and we propose to employ it only in cases where either murder or the highest offence against the State has been committed.

We are not apprehensive that we shall be thought by many persons to have resorted too frequently to capital punishment; but we think it probable that many, even of those who condemn the English statute book as sanguinary, may think that our code errs on the other side. They may be of opinion that gang-robbery, the cruel mutilation of the person, and possibly rape, ought to be punished with death. These are doubtless offences which, if we looked only at their enormity, at the evil which they produce, at the terror which they spread through society, at the depravity which they indicate, we might be inclined to punish capitally. But atrocious as they are, they cannot, as it appears to us, be placed in the same class with murder. To the great majority of mankind nothing is so dear as life. And we are of opinion that to put robbers, ravishers, and mutilators on the same footing with murderers, is an arrangement which diminishes the security of life.

There is in practice a close connection between murder and most of those offences which come nearest to murder in enormity. Those offences are almost always committed under such circumstances that the offender has it in his power to add murder to his guilt. They are often committed under such circumstances that the offender has a temptation to add murder to his guilt. The same opportunities, the same superiority of force, which enabled a man to rob, to mangle or to ravish, will enable him to go further, and to despatch his victim. As he has almost always the power to murder, he will often have a strong motive to murder, inasmuch as by murder he may often hope to remove the only witness of the crime which he has already committed. If the punishment of the crime which he has already committed be exactly the same with the punishment of murder, he will have no restraining motive. A law which imprisons for rape and robbery, and hangs for murder, holds out to ravishers and robbers a strong inducement to spare the lives of those whom they have injured. A law which hangs for rape and robbery, and which only hangs for murder, holds out indeed, if it be rigorously carried into effect, a strong motive to deter men from rape and robbery, but as soon as a man has ravished or robbed, it holds out to him a strong motive to follow up his crime with a murder.

If murder were punished with something more than simple death ; if the murderer were broken on the wheel or burned alive, there would not be the same objection to punishing with death those crimes which in atrocity approach nearest to murder. But such a system would be open to other objections so obvious that it is unnecessary to point them out. The highest punishment which we propose is the simple privation of life ; and the highest punishment, be it what it may, ought not, for the reason which we have given, to be assigned to any crime against the person which stops short of murder. And it is hardly necessary to point out to his Lordship in Council how great a shock would be given to public feeling if, while we propose to exempt from the punishment of death the most atrocious personal outrages which stopped short of murder, we were to inflict that punishment even in the worst cases of theft, cheating, or mischief.

It will be seen that, throughout the code, wherever we have made any offence punishable by transportation, we have provided that the transportation shall be for life. The consideration which has chiefly determined us to retain that mode of punishment is our persuasion that it is regarded by the natives of India, particularly by those who live at a distance from the sea, with peculiar fear. The pain which is caused by punishment is unmixed evil. It is by the terror which it inspires that it produces good ; and perhaps no punishment inspires so much terror in proportion to the actual pain which it causes as the punishment of transportation in this country. Prolonged imprisonment may be more painful in the actual endurance ; but it is not so much dreaded beforehand ; nor does a sentence of imprisonment strike either the offender or the bystanders with so much horror as a sentence of exile beyond what they call the Black Water. This feeling, we believe, arises chiefly from the mystery which overhangs the fate of the transported convict. The separation resembles that which takes place at the moment of death. The criminal is taken for ever from the society of all who are acquainted with him, and conveyed by means of which the natives have but an indistinct notion over an element which they regard with extreme awe, to a distant country of which they know nothing, and from which he is never to return. It is natural that his fate should impress them with a deep feeling of terror. It is on this feeling that the efficacy of the punishment depends, and this feeling would be greatly weakened if transported convicts should frequently return, after an exile of seven or fourteen years, to the scene of their offences, and to the society of their former friends.

We may observe that the rule which we propose to lay down is already in force in almost every part of British India. The Courts established by the Royal Charters and Courts Martial are at present the only Courts which sentence offenders to transportation for any term short of life. In the case of European offenders who are condemned to long terms of imprisonment, we allow the Government to commute imprisonment for transportation not perpetual. But in that case we are of opinion that in general the transported criminal ought not, after the expiration of the term for which he is transported, to be allowed to return to India. This rule and the reasons for it will be considered hereafter.

Of imprisonment we propose to institute two grades, rigorous imprisonment and simple imprisonment. But we do not think the penal code the proper place for describing with minuteness the nature of either kind of punishment.

We entertain a confident hope that it will shortly be found practicable greatly to reduce the terms of imprisonment which we propose. Where a good system of prison discipline exists, where the criminal, without being subject to any cruel severities, is strictly restrained, regularly employed in labour not of an attractive kind, and deprived of every indulgence not necessary to his health, a year's confinement will generally prove as efficacious as confinement for two years in a gaol where the superintendence is lax, where the work exacted is light, and where the convicts find means of enjoying as many luxuries as if they were at liberty. As the intensity of the punishment is increased, its length may safely be diminished. As members of the committee which is now employed in investigating the system followed in the gaols of this country, we have had access to information which enables us to say with confidence that, in this department of the administration, extensive reforms are greatly needed, and may easily be made. The researches of that committee will, we hope, enable the Law Commission hereafter to prepare such a code of prison discipline as, without shocking the humane feelings of the community, may yet be a terror to the most hardened wrong-doers. Whenever such a code shall come into operation, we conceive that it will be advisable greatly to shorten many of the terms of imprisonment which we have proposed.

It will be seen that we have given to the Government a power of commuting sentences in certain cases without the consent of the offender. Some of the rules which we have laid down on this subject will be universally allowed to be proper. It is evidently fit that the Government should be empowered to commute the sentence of death for any other punishment provided by the code. It seems to us also very desirable that the Government should have the power of commuting perpetual transportation for perpetual imprisonment. Many circumstances of which the executive authorities ought to be accurately informed, but which must often be unknown to the ablest judge, may, at particular times, render it highly inconvenient to carry a sentence of transportation into effect. The state of those remote provinces of the empire in which convict settlements are established, and the way in which the interest of those provinces may be affected by any addition to the convict population, are matters which lie altogether out of the cognizance of the tribunals by which those sentences are passed, and which the Government only is competent to decide.

The provisions contained in clauses 43 and 44 are more likely to cause difference of opinion. We are satisfied that both humanity and policy require that those provisions, or provisions very similar to them, should be adopted.

The physical difference which exists between the European and the native of India renders it impossible to subject them to the same system of prison discipline. It is most desirable, indeed, that in the treatment of offenders convicted of the same crime and sentenced to the same punishment there should be no apparent inequality. But it is still more desirable that there should be no real inequality, and there must be real inequality unless there be apparent inequality. It would be cruel to subject an European for a long period to a severe prison discipline, in a country in which existence is almost constant misery to an European who has not many indulgences at his command. If not cruel, it would be impolitic. It is unnecessary to point out to his Lordship in Council how desirable it is that our national character should stand high in the estimation of the inhabitants of India, and how much that character would be lowered by the frequent exhibition of Englishmen of the worst description, placed in the most degrading situations, stigmatized by the courts of justice, and engaged in the ignominious labour of a gaol.

As there are strong reasons for not punishing Europeans with imprisonment of the same description with which we propose to punish natives, so there are reasons equally strong for not suffering Europeans who have been convicted of serious crimes to remain in this country. As we are satisfied that nothing can add more strength to the Government, or can be more beneficial to the people, than the free admission of honest, industrious, and intelligent Englishmen, so we are satisfied that no greater calamity could befall either the Government or the people than the influx of Englishmen of lawless habits and blasted character. Such men are of the same race and colour with the rulers of the country, they speak the same language, they wear the same garb. In all these things they differ from the great body of the population. It is natural and inevitable that in the minds of a people accustomed to be governed by Englishmen, the idea of an Englishman should be associated with the idea of Government. Every Englishman participates in the power of Government, though he holds no office. His vices reflect disgrace on the Government, though the Government gives him no countenance.

It was probably on these grounds that Parliament, at the same time at which it threw open a large part of India to British-born subjects of the King, directed the local legislature to provide against those dangers which might be expected from an influx of such settlers. No regulation can, in our opinion, promote more effectually, or in a more unexceptionable manner, the end which Parliament had in view than that which we now propose.

We recommend that, whenever a person, not both of Asiatic birth and of Asiatic blood, commits an offence so serious that he is sentenced to two years of simple imprisonment, or to one year of rigorous imprisonment, it shall be competent to the Government to commute that punishment for banishment from the territories of the East India Company.

If a person of unmixed European blood should commit an offence so heinous as to be visited with a sentence of imprisonment for seven years or more, we would give to the Government the power of substituting an equal term of transportation for that term of imprisonment, and of excluding the offender, after the expiration of the term of transportation, from the territories of the East India Company. The Government would, doubtless, make arrangements for transporting such offenders to some British colony situated in a temperate climate.

In the great majority of cases we believe that this commutation of punishment would be most welcome to an European offender. But however this may be, we are satisfied that it is for the interest both of the British Government and of the Indian people that the executive authorities should possess the power which we propose to confide to them.

The forfeiture of property is a punishment which we propose to inflict only on persons guilty of high political offences. The territorial possessions of such persons often enable them to disturb the public peace, and to make head against the Government; and it seems reasonable that they should be deprived of so dangerous a power.

Fine is one of the most common punishments in every part of the world, and it is a punishment the advantages of which are so great and obvious, that

we propose to authorize the Courts to inflict it in
every case, except where forfeiture of all property is
necessarily part of the punishment. Yet the punishment of fine is open to some objections. Death,
imprisonment, transportation, banishment, solitude,
compelled labour, are not, indeed, equally disagreeable to all men. But they are so disagreeable to all
men that the legislature, in assigning these punishments to offences, may safely neglect the differences
produced by temper and situation. With fine, the
case is different. In imposing a fine, it is always
necessary to have as much regard to the pecuniary
circumstances of the offender as to the character and
magnitude of the offence. The mulct which is
ruinous to a labourer is easily borne by a tradesman,
and is absolutely unfelt by a rich zemindar.

It is impossible to fix any limit to the amount of
a fine which will not either be so high as to be
ruinous to the poor, or so low as to be no object of
terror to the rich. There are many millions in India
who would be utterly unable to pay a fine of fifty
rupees; there are hundreds of thousands from whom
such a fine might be levied, but whom it would
reduce to extreme distress; there are thousands to
whom it would give very little uneasiness; there are
hundreds to whom it would be a matter of perfect
indifference, and who would not cross a room to
avoid it. The number of the poor in every country
exceeds in a very great ratio the number of the rich.
The number of poor criminals exceeds the number
of rich criminals in a still greater ratio. And to the
poor criminal it is a matter of absolute indifference
whether the fine to which he is liable be limited or
not, unless it be so limited as to render it quite inefficient as a mode of punishing the rich. To a man
who has no capital, who has laid by nothing, whose
monthly wages are just sufficient to provide himself
and his family with their monthly rice, it matters

not whether the fine for assault be left to be settled by the discretion of the Courts, or whether a hundred rupees be fixed as the maximum. There are no degrees in impossibility. He is no more able to pay a hundred rupees than to pay a lac. A just and wise judge, even if entrusted with a boundless discretion, will not, under ordinary circumstances, sentence such an offender to a fine of a hundred rupees. And the limit of a hundred rupees would leave it quite in the power of an unjust or inconsiderate judge to inflict on such an offender all the evil which can be inflicted on him by means of fine.

If, in imitation of Mr. Livingston, we provide that no fine shall exceed one-fourth of the amount of the offender's property, no serious fine will ever be imposed in this country without a long and often a most unsatisfactory investigation, in which it would be necessary to decide many obscure questions of right purposely darkened by every artifice of chicanery. And even if this great practical difficulty did not exist, we should see strong objections to such a provision in a very large class of cases. Take the case of a corrupt judge who has accumulated a lac of rupees by his illicit practices. A fine which should deprive such a man of the whole of his fortune would not appear to us excessive: and certainly we should think it most undesirable that he should be allowed to retain 75,000 rupees of his ill-gotten gains. Again, take the case of a man who has been suborned to commit perjury, and has received a great bribe for doing so. Such a man may have little or no property, except what he has received as a bribe: yet it is evidently desirable that he should be compelled to disgorge the whole. No man ought ever to gain by breaking the law ; and if Mr. Livingston's rule were adopted in this country, many would gain by breaking the law. To punish a man for a crime, and yet to leave in his possession three-fourths of the con-

sideration which tempted him to commit the crime,
is to hold out at once punishments for crime, and
inducements to crime. It appears to us that the
punishment of fine is a peculiarly appropriate punishment for all offences to which men are prompted by
cupidity; for it is a punishment which operates
directly on the very feeling which impels men to
such offences. A man who has been guilty of great
offences arising from cupidity, of forging a bill of
exchange, for example, of keeping a receptacle for
stolen goods, or of extensive embezzlement, ought,
we conceive, to be so fined as to reduce him to
poverty. That such a man should, when his imprisonment is over, return to the enjoyment of three-
fourths of his property, a property which may be very
large, and which may have been accumulated by his
offences, appears to us highly objectionable. Those
persons who are most likely to commit such offences
would often be less deterred by knowing that the
offender had passed several years in imprisonment,
than encouraged by seeing him, after his liberation,
enjoying the far larger part of his wealth.

We have never seen any general rule for the
limiting of fine, which we are disposed to adopt.
The difficulty of framing a rule has evidently been
felt by many eminent men. The authors of the Bill
of Rights, with many instances of gross abuse fresh
in their recollection, could devise no other rule than
that excessive fines should not be imposed. And
the authors of the Constitution of the United States,
after the experience of another century, contented
themselves with repeating the words of the Bill of
Rights.

It will be seen that in cases which are not very
heinous we propose to limit the amount of fine which
the Courts may impose. But in serious cases we
have left the amount of fine absolutely to their
discretion; and we feel, as we have said, that, even

in the cases where we have proposed a limit, such a limit will be no protection to the poor, who in every community are also the many. We feel that the extent of the discretion which we have thus left to the Courts is an evil, and that no sagacity and no rectitude of intention can secure a judge from occasional error. We conceive, however, that if fine is to be employed as a punishment,—and no judicious person, we are persuaded, would propose to dispense with it,—this evil must be endured. We shall attempt in the code of procedure to establish such a system of appeal as may prevent gross or frequent injustice from taking place.

The next question which it became our duty to consider was this :—when a fine has been imposed, what measures shall be adopted in default of payment ? And here two modes of proceeding, with both of which we were familiar, naturally occurred to us. The offender may be imprisoned till the fine is paid, or he may be imprisoned for a certain term, such imprisonment being considered as standing in place of the fine. In the former case, the imprisonment is used in order to compel him to part with his money ; in the latter case, the imprisonment is a punishment substituted for another punishment. Both modes of proceeding appear to us to be open to strong objections. To keep an offender in imprisonment till his fine is paid is, if the fine be beyond his means, to keep him in imprisonment all his life ; and it is impossible for the best judge to be certain that he may not sometimes impose a fine which shall be beyond the means of an offender. Nothing could make such a system tolerable except the constant interference of some authority empowered to remit sentences ; and such constant interference we should consider as in itself an evil. On the other hand, to sentence an offender to fine and to a certain fixed term of imprisonment in default of payment, and then to leave it to himself to determine whether he will part with his money or lie in gaol, appears to us to be a very objectionable course. The high authority of Mr. Livingston is here against us. He allows the criminal, if sentenced to a fine exceeding one-fourth of his property, to compel the judge to commute the excess for imprisonment at the rate of one day of imprisonment for every two dollars of fine, and he adds, that such imprisonment must in no case exceed ninety days. We regret that we cannot agree with him. The object of the penal law is to deter from offences, and this can only be done by means of inflictions disagreeable to offenders. The law ought not to inflict punishments unnecessarily severe; but it ought not, on the other hand, to call the offender into council with his judges, and to allow him an option between two punishments. In general, the circumstance that he prefers one punishment raises a strong presumption that he ought to suffer the other. The circumstance that the love of money is a stronger passion in his mind than the love of personal liberty is, as far as it goes, a reason for our availing ourselves rather of his love of money than of his love of personal liberty for the purpose of restraining him from crime. To look out systematically for the most sensitive part of a man's mind, in order that we may not direct our penal sanctions towards that part of his mind, seems an injudicious policy.

We are far from thinking that the course which we propose is unexceptionable; but it appears to us to be less open to exception than any other which has occurred to us. We propose that, at the time of imposing a fine, the Court shall also fix a certain term of imprisonment which the offender shall undergo in default of payment. In fixing this term the Court will in no case be suffered to exceed a certain maximum, which will vary according to the nature of the offence. If the offence be one which is punishable with imprisonment as well as fine, the term of imprisonment in default of payment will not exceed one-fourth of the longest term of imprisonment fixed by the code for the offence. If the offence be one which by the code is punishable only with fine, the term of imprisonment for default of payment will in no case exceed seven days.

But we do not mean that this imprisonment shall be taken in full satisfaction of the fine. We cannot consent to permit the offender to choose whether he will suffer in his person or in his property. To adopt such a course would be to grant exemption from the punishment of fine to those very persons on whom it is peculiarly desirable that the punishment of fine should be inflicted, to those very persons who dislike that punishment most, and whom the apprehension of that punishment would be most likely to restrain. We therefore propose that the imprisonment which an offender has undergone shall not release him from the pecuniary obligation under which he lies. His person will, indeed, cease to be answerable for the fine; but his property will for a time continue to be so. What we recommend is, that at any time during a certain limited period the fine may be levied on his effects by distress. If the fine is paid or levied while he is imprisoned for default of payment, his imprisonment will immediately terminate, and if a portion of the fine be paid during the imprisonment, a proportional abatement of the imprisonment will take place.

It may perhaps appear to some persons harsh to imprison a man for non-payment of a fine, and, after he has endured his imprisonment, to take his property by distress in order to realize the fine. But this harshness is rather apparent than real. If the offender, having the means of paying the fine, chooses rather to lie in prison than to part with his

money, his case is the very case in which it is most
desirable that the fine should be levied, and he is
the very convict who has least claim to indulgence.
The confinement which he has undergone may be
regarded as no more than a reasonable punishment
for his obstinate resistance to the due execution of
his sentence.   If the offender has not the means of
paying the fine while he continues liable to it, he
will be quit for his imprisonment.   There remains
another case ; that of an offender who, being really
unable to pay his fine, lies in prison for a term, and
within six years after his sentence acquires property.
This case is the only case in which it can, with any
plausibility, be maintained that the law, as we have
framed it, would operate harshly.   Even in this case,
it is evident that our law will operate far less harshly
than a law which should provide that an offender
sentenced to a fine should be imprisoned till the fine
should be paid.   Under both laws imprisonment is
inflicted, under both a fine is exacted.   But the one
law liberates the offender on payment of the fine,
and also fixes a limit beyond which he cannot be de-
tained in gaol, whether the fine be paid or no.   The
other law keeps him in confinement till the money
is actually paid.   It is, therefore, at least as severe
as ours on his property, and is immeasurably more
severe on his person.

In fact, we treat an offender who has been sentenced to fine more leniently than the law now treats
a debtor either in England or in this country.   By
the English law, an insolvent not in trade is kept in
confinement till he has surrendered all his property,
till he has answered interrogatories respecting it, till
the Court is satisfied that he has paid all that he can
pay.   Even when his person is liberated, his future
acquisitions still continue to be liable to the claims
of his creditors.   The law throughout British India
is in principle the same with the law of England.

The offender who has been sentenced to fine must be considered as a debtor, and, as a debtor, not entitled to any peculiar lenity. It will be difficult to show on what principles a creditor ought to be allowed to employ, for the purpose of recovering a debt from a person who is perhaps only unfortunate, a more stringent mode of procedure than that which the State employs for the purpose of realizing a fine from the property of a criminal. If a temporary imprisonment for debt ought not to cancel the claim of the private creditor, neither ought a temporary imprisonment in default of payment of a fine to cancel the claims of public justice.

It is undoubtedly easy to put cases in which this part of the law will operate more severely than we could wish ; and so it is easy to put cases in which every penal clause in the code would operate more severely than we could wish. This is an evil inseparable from all legislation. General rules must be framed ; and it is absolutely impossible to frame general rules which shall suit all particular cases. It is sufficient if the rule be, on the whole, more beneficial than any other general rule which can be suggested. Those particular cases in which a rule generally beneficial may operate too harshly must be left to the merciful consideration of the Executive Government. We are satisfied that the punishment of fine would, under the arrangement which we propose, be found to be a most efficacious punishment in a large class of cases. We are satisfied that if offenders are allowed to choose between imprisonment and fine, fine will lose almost its whole efficacy, and will never be inflicted on those who dread it most.

Closely connected with these questions respecting the punishment of fine is another question of the highest importance, which indeed belongs rather to the law of civil rights and to the law of procedure than to the penal law, but respecting which we are

desirous to place on record the opinion which we
have formed, after much reflection and discussion.

In a very large proportion of criminal cases there
is good ground for a civil as well as for a penal proceeding. The English law, most erroneously in our
opinion, allows no civil claim for reparation in cases
where injury has been caused by an offence amount-
ing to felony. Thus a person is entitled to reparation
for what he has lost by petty fraud, but to none if he
has been cheated by means of a forged bill of exchange. He is entitled to reparation if his coat has
been torn, but to none if his house has been maliciously burned down. He is entitled to reparation
for a slap on the face, but to none for having his nose
maliciously slit, or his ears cut off. A woman is
entitled to reparation for a breach of promise of
marriage, but to none for a rape. To us it appears
that of two sufferers, he who has suffered the greater
harm has, *cæteris paribus*, the stronger claim to
compensation; and that of two offences, that which
produces the greater harm ought, *cæteris paribus*,
to be visited with the heavier punishment. Hence
it follows that in general the strongest claims to
compensations will be the claims of persons who have
been injured by highly penal acts; and that to refuse
reparation to all sufferers who have been injured by
highly penal acts is to refuse reparation to that very
class of sufferers who have the strongest claim to it.

We are decidedly of opinion that every person
who is injured by an offence ought to be legally entitled to a compensation for the injury. That the
offence is a very serious one, far from being a reason
for thinking that he ought to have no compensation,
is *primâ facie* a reason for thinking that the compensation ought to be very large.

Entertaining this opinion, we are desirous that the
law of criminal procedure should be framed in such
a manner as to facilitate the obtaining of reparation

by the sufferer. We are inclined to think that an arrangement might be adopted under which one trial would do the work of two. We conceive that, in every case in which fine is part of the punishment of an offence, it ought to be competent to the tribunal which has tried the offender, acting under proper checks, to award the whole or part of the fine to the sufferer, provided that the sufferer signifies his willingness to receive what is so awarded in full satisfaction of his civil claim for reparation. If the Criminal Court shall not make such an award, or if the sufferer shall not be satisfied with such an award, he must be left to his civil action. But if, in such an action, he recovers damages, the fine ought, in our opinion, to be employed, as far as the fine will go, in satisfying those damages.

The plan we propose would not be open to the strong and indeed unanswerable objections which Mr. Livingston has urged against the plan of blending a civil and criminal trial together. Yet we think it likely that our plan would in a great majority of cases render a civil proceeding unnecessary. We are happy to be able to quote the high authority of Mr. Livingston in favour of the doctrine that every fine imposed for an offence ought to be expended, as far as it will go, in paying any damages which may be due in consequence of injury caused by that offence.

This course seems to be the only course consistent with justice to either party. It is most unjust to the man who has been disabled by a wound, or ruined by a forgery, that the Government should take, under the name of fine, so large a portion of the offender's property as to leave nothing to the sufferer. In general, the greater the injury the greater ought to be the fine. On the other hand, the greater the injury the greater ought to be the compensation. If, therefore, the Government keeps whatever it can raise in the way of fine, it follows that the sufferer who has the greatest claim to compensation will be least likely to obtain it. By empowering the Courts to grant damages out of the fine, and by making the fine after it has reached the treasury of the Government answerable for the damages which the sufferer may recover in a Civil Court, we avoid this injustice.

Nor is this arrangement required only by justice to the sufferer. It is also required by justice to the offender. However atrocious his crime may have been, he ought not to be subjected to any punishment beyond what the public interest demands. And we depart from this principle if, when a single payment would effect all that is required both in the way of punishment and in the way of reparation, we impose two distinct payments, the one by way of punishment, and the other by way of reparation.

The principles on which a Court proceeds in imposing a fine are quite different from those on which it proceeds in assessing damages. A fine is meant to be painful to the person paying it. But civil damages are not meant to cause pain to the person who pays them. They are meant solely to compensate the plaintiff for evil suffered. They cause pain undoubtedly to the person who has to pay them. But this pain is merely incidental; nor ought the amount of damages at all to depend on the degree of depravity which the wrongdoer has shown, except in so far as that depravity may have increased the evil endured by the sufferer. If A., by mere inadvertence, drives the pole of his carriage against Z.'s valuable horse, and thus kills the horse, A. has committed an action infinitely less reprehensible than if he kills the horse by laying poison secretly in its food. The former act would probably not fall at all under the cognizance of the Criminal Courts. The latter act would be severely punished. But the payment to which Z. has a civil claim is in both cases exactly the same, the value of the horse, and a compensation for any expense and inconvenience which the loss of the horse may have occasioned. That A. has committed no offence is no reason for giving Z. less than his full damages; that A. has committed a most wicked and malignant offence is no reason for giving Z. more than his full damages. · If a mere inadvertence cause a great loss, the damages ought to be high. If the most atrocious crime cause a small loss, the damages ought to be low. They are fixed on a principle quite different from that according to which penal laws are framed and administered.

Here then are two payments required from one person on account of one transaction. The object of the one payment is to give him pain, and the amount of that payment must be supposed to be sufficient to give him as much pain as it is desirable to inflict on him in that form. The object of the other payment is not at all to give pain to the payer, but solely to save another person from loss. It does, indeed, incidentally give pain to the payer; but it is not imposed for that end, nor is it proportioned to the degree in which it may be fit that the payer should suffer pain. Surely under such circumstances justice to the payer requires that the former payment should, as far as it will go, serve both purposes, and that if in the very act of enduring punishment he can make reparation, he should be permitted to do so.

We have now said all that we at present think it necessary to say respecting the punishments provided in the code. It may be fit that we should explain why some others are omitted.

We have thought it unnecessary to place incapacitation for office, or dismissal from office, in the list of punishments. It will always be in the power of the Government to dismiss from office and to exclude from office even persons against whom there is no legal evidence of guilt. It will always be in the power of the Government, by an act of grace, to admit to office even those who may have been dismissed. We therefore propose that the power of inflicting this penalty shall be left in form, as it must be left in reality, to the Government.

We also considered whether it would be advisable to place in the list of punishments the degrading public exhibition of an offender on a pillory, after the English fashion, or on an ass, in the manner usual in this country. We are decidedly of opinion that it is not advisable to inflict that species of punishment.

Of all punishments this is evidently the most unequal. It may be more severe than any punishment in the code. It may be no punishment at all. If inflicted on a man who has quick sensibility, it is generally more terrible than death itself. If inflicted on a hardened and impudent delinquent, who has often stood at the bar, and who has no character to lose, it is a punishment less serious than an hour of the treadmill. It derives all its terrors from the higher and better parts of the character of the sufferer; its severity is therefore in inverse proportion to the necessity for severity. An offender who, though he has been drawn into crime by temptation, has not yet wholly given himself up to wickedness and discarded all regard for reputation, is an offender with whom it is generally desirable to deal gently. He may still be reclaimed. He may still become a valuable member of society. On the other hand, the criminal for whom disgrace has no terrors, who dreads nothing but physical suffering, restraint and privation, and who laughs at infamy, is the very criminal against whom the whole rigour of the law ought to be put forth. To employ a punishment which is more bitter than the bitterness of death to the man who has still some remains of virtuous and honourable feeling, and which is mere matter of jest to the utterly abandoned villain, appears to us most unreasonable.

If it were possible to devise a punishment which should give pain proportioned to the degree in which the offender was shameless, hard-hearted, and abandoned to vice, such a punishment would be the most effectual means of protecting society. On the other hand, of all punishments the most absurd is that which produces pain proportioned to the degree in which the offender retains the sentiments of an honest man.

This argument proceeds on the supposition that the public exposure of the criminal has no other terrors than those which it derives from his sensibility to shame. The English pillory, indeed, had terrors of a very different kind. The offender was, even in our own time, given up with scarcely any protection to the utmost ferocity of the mob. Such a mode of punishment is, indeed, free from one objection which we have urged against simple exposure; for it is an object of terror to the most hardened criminal. But it is open to other objections so obvious, that it is unnecessary to bring them to the notice of his Lordship in Council. That the amount of punishment should be determined, not by the law or by the tribunals, but by a throng of people accidentally congregated, among whom the most ignorant and brutal would always on such an occasion be the most forward, would be a disgrace to an age and country pretending to civilisation. We take it for granted that the punishment which we are considering, if inflicted in any part of India subject to the British Government, would consist in degrading exposure, and nothing more. That punishment, we repeat, while it would be a mere subject of mockery to shameless and abandoned delinquents, would, when inflicted on men who have filled respectable stations and borne respectable characters, be so cruel that it would become justly more odious to the public than the very offences which it was intended to repress.

We have not thought it desirable to place flogging in the list of punishments. If inflicted for atrocious crimes with a severity proportioned to the magnitude of those crimes, that punishment is open to the very serious objections which may be urged against all cruel punishments, and which are so well known that it is unnecessary for us to recapitulate them. When inflicted on men of mature age, particularly if they be of decent stations in life, it is a punishment of which the severity consists, to a great extent, in the disgrace which it causes; and to that extent the arguments which we have used against public exposure apply to flogging.

It has been represented to us by some functionaries in Bengal, that the best mode of stimulating the lower officers of police to the active discharge of their duties is by flogging, and that since the abolition of that punishment in this presidency, the magistrates of the lower provinces have found great difficulty in managing that class of persons.

This difficulty has not been experienced in any other part of India. We therefore cannot, without much stronger evidence than is now before us, believe that it is impracticable to make the police officers of the lower provinces efficient without resorting to corporal punishment. The objections to the old system are obvious. To inflict on a public servant, who ought to respect himself and to be respected by others, an ignominious punishment, which leaves an indelible mark, and to suffer him still to remain a public servant, to place a stigma on him which renders him an object of contempt to the mass of the population, and to continue to entrust him with any portion, however small, of the powers of Government, appears to us to be a course which nothing but the strongest necessity can justify.

The moderate flogging of young offenders for some petty offences is not open, at least in any serious degree, to the objections which we have stated. Flogging does not inflict on a boy that sort of ignominy which it causes to a grown man. Up to a certain age, boys, even of the higher classes, are often corrected with stripes by their parents and guardians : and this circumstance takes away a considerable part of the disgrace of stripes inflicted on a boy by order of a magistrate. In countries where a bad system of prison discipline exists, the punishment of flogging has in such cases one great advantage over that of imprisonment. The young offender is not exposed, even for a day, to the contaminating influence of an ill-regulated gaol. It is our hope and belief, however, that the reforms which are now under consideration will prevent the gaols of India from exercising any such contaminating influence ; and, if that should be the case, we are inclined to think that the effect of a few days passed in solitude or in hard and monotonous labour would be more salutary than that of stripes.

Being satisfied, therefore, that the punishment of flogging can be proper only in a few cases, and not being satisfied that it is necessary in any, we are unwilling to advise the Government to retrace its steps, and to re-establish throughout the British territories a practice which, by a policy unquestionably humane and by no means proved to have been injudicious, has recently been abolished through a large part of those territories.

The only remaining point connected with this chapter, to which we wish to call the attention of his Lordship in Council, is the provision contained in clause 61. This provision is intended to prevent an offender whose guilt is fully established from eluding punishment, on the ground that the evidence does not enable the tribunals to pronounce with certainty under what penal provision his case falls.

Where the doubt is merely between an aggravated and mitigated form of the same offence, the difficulty will not be great. In such cases the offender ought always to be convicted of the minor offence. But the doubt may be between two offences, neither of which is a mitigated form of the other. The doubt, for example, may lie between murder and the aiding of murder. It may be certain, for example, that either A. or B. murdered Z., and that whichever was the murderer was aided by the other in the commission of the murder; but which committed the murder, and which aided the commission, it may be impossible to ascertain. To suffer both to go unpunished, though it is certain that both are guilty of capital crimes, merely because it is doubtful under what clause each of them is punishable, would be most unreasonable. It appears to us that a conviction in the alternative has this recommendation, that it is altogether free from fiction, that it is exactly consonant to the truth of the facts. If the Court find both A. and B. guilty of murder, or of aiding murder, the Court affirms that which is not literally true; and on all occasions, but especially in judicial proceedings, there is a strong presumption in favour of literal truth. If the Court finds that A. has either murdered Z. or aided B. to murder Z., and that B. has either murdered Z. or aided A. to murder Z., the Court finds that which is the literal truth; nor will there, under the rule which we have laid down, be the smallest difficulty in prescribing the punishment.

It is chiefly in cases where property has been fraudulently appropriated that the necessity for such a provision as that which we are considering will be felt. It will often be certain that there has been a fraudulent appropriation of property; and the only doubt will be, whether this fraudulent appropriation was a theft or a criminal breach of trust. To allow the offender to escape unpunished on account of such a doubt would be absurd. To subject him to the punishment of theft, which is the higher of the two crimes between which the doubt lies, would be grossly unjust. The punishment to which he ought to be liable is evidently that of criminal breach of trust. But that a Court should convict an offender of a criminal breach of trust, when the opinion of the Court perhaps is, that it is an even chance, or more than an even chance, that no trust was ever reposed in him, seems to us an objectionable mode of proceeding. We will not, in this stage of our labours, venture to lay it down as an unbending rule that the tribunals ought never to employ phrases which, though literally false, are conventionally true. Yet we are fully satisfied that the presumption is always strongly in favour of that form of expression which accurately sets forth the real state of the facts. In the case which we have supposed, the real state of the facts is, that the offender has certainly committed either theft or criminal breach of trust, and that the Court does not know which. This ought, therefore, in our opinion, to be the form of the judgment.

The details of the law on this subject must, of course, be reserved for the code of procedure. But the provision which directs the manner in which the punishment is to be calculated appears properly to belong to the penal code.

NOTE (B).

ON THE CHAPTER OF GENERAL EXCEPTIONS.

THIS chapter has been framed in order to obviate the necessity of repeating in every penal clause a considerable number of limitations.

Some limitations relate only to a single provision, or to a very small class of provisions. Thus the exception in favour of true imputations on character (clause 470) is an exception which belongs wholly to the law of defamation, and does not affect any other part of the code. The exception in favour of the conjugal rights of the husband (clause 359) is an exception which belongs wholly to the law of rape, and does not affect any other part of the code. Every such exception evidently ought to be appended to the rule which it is intended to modify.

But there are other exceptions which are common to all the penal clauses of the code, or to a great variety of clauses dispersed over many chapters. Such are the exceptions in favour of infants, lunatics, idiots, persons under the influence of delirium ; the exceptions in favour of acts done by the direction of the law, of acts done in the exercise of the right of self-defence, of acts done by the consent of the party harmed by them. It would obviously be inconvenient to repeat these exceptions several times in every page. We have, therefore, placed them in a separate chapter, and we have provided that every definition of an offence, every penal provision, and every illustration of a definition or penal provision, shall be construed subject to the provisions contained in that chapter. Most of those explanations appear to us to require no explanation or defence. But the meaning and the ground of the rules laid down in clause 69 and in the three following clauses may not be obvious at first sight. On these, therefore, we wish to make a few observations.

We conceive the general rule to be, that nothing ought to be an offence by reason of any harm which it may cause to a person of ripe age who, undeceived, has given a free and intelligent consent to suffer that harm or to take the risk of that harm. The restrictions by which the rule is limited affect only cases where human life is concerned. Both the general rule and the restrictions may, we think, be easily vindicated.

If Z., a grown man, in possession of all his faculties, directs that his valuable furniture shall be burned, that his pictures shall be cut to rags, that his fine house shall be pulled down, that the best horses in his stable shall be shot, that his plate shall be thrown into the sea, those who obey his orders, however capricious those orders may be, however deeply Z. may afterwards regret that he gave them, ought not, as it seems to us, to be punished for injuring his property. Again, if Z. chooses to sell his teeth to a dentist, and permits the dentist to pull them out, the dentist ought not to be punished for injuring Z.'s person. So if Z. embraces the Mahomedan religion, and consents to undergo the painful rite which is the initiation into that religion, those who perform the rite ought not to be punished for injuring Z.'s person.

The reason on which the general rule which we have mentioned rests is this, that it is impossible to restrain men of mature age and sound understanding from destroying their own property, their own health, their own comfort, without restraining them from an infinite number of salutary or innocent actions. It is by no means true that men always judge rightly of their own interest. But it is true that, in the vast majority of cases, they judge better of their own interest than any lawgiver, or any tribunal, which must necessarily proceed on general principles, and which cannot have within its contemplation the circumstances of particular cases and the tempers of particular individuals, can judge for them. It is difficult to conceive any law which should be effectual to prevent men from wasting their substance on the most chimerical speculations, and yet which should not prevent the construction of such works as the Duke of Bridgewater's canals. It is difficult to conceive any law which should prevent a man from capriciously destroying his property, and yet which should not prevent a philosopher, in a course of chemical experiments, from dissolving a diamond, or an artist from taking ancient pictures to pieces, as Sir Joshua Reynolds did, in order to learn the secret of the colouring. It is difficult to conceive any law which should prevent a man from capriciously injuring his own health, and yet which should not prevent an artisan from employing himself in callings which are useful and indeed necessary to society, but which tend to impair the constitutions of those who follow them, or a public-spirited physician from inoculating himself with the virus of a dangerous disease. It is chiefly, we conceive, for this reason, that almost all Governments have thought it sufficient to restrain men from harming others, and have left them at liberty to harm themselves.

But though in general we would not punish an act on account of any harm which it might cause to a person who had consented to suffer that harm, we think that there are exceptions to this rule, and that the case in which death is intentionally inflicted is an exception.

It appears to us that the reasons which render it highly inexpedient to inflict punishment in ordinary cases of harm done by consent of the person harmed do not exist here. The thing prohibited is not, like the destruction of property, or like the mutilation of the person, a thing which is sometimes pernicious, sometimes innocent, sometimes highly useful. It is always, and under all circumstances, a thing which a wise lawgiver would desire to prevent, if it were only for the purpose of making human life more sacred to the multitude. We cannot prohibit men from destroying the most valuable effects, or from disfiguring the person of one who has given his unextorted and intelligent consent to such destruction or such disfiguration, without prohibiting at the same time gainful speculations, innocent luxuries, manly exercises, healing operations. But by prohibiting a man from intentionally causing the death of another, we prohibit nothing which we think it desirable to tolerate.

It seems to us clear, therefore, that no consent ought to be a justification of the intentional causing of death. Whether such intentional causing of death ought or ought not to be punished as murder is a distinct question, and will be considered elsewhere.

The next point which we have here to consider is how far consent ought to be a justification of the causing of death, when that causing of death is, in our nomenclature, voluntary, yet not intentional, that is to say, when the person who caused the death did not mean to cause it, but knew that he was likely to cause it.

In general we have made no distinction between cases in which a man causes an effect designedly, and cases in which he causes it with a knowledge that he is likely to cause it. If, for example, he sets fire to a house in a town at night, with no other object than that of facilitating a theft, but being perfectly aware that he is likely to cause people to be burned in their beds, and thus causes the loss of life, we punish him as a murderer. But there is, as

it appears to us, a class of cases in which it is absolutely necessary to make a distinction. It is often
the wisest thing that a man can do to expose his
life to great hazard. It is often the greatest service
that can be rendered to him to do what may very
probably cause his death. He may labour under a
cruel and wasting malady which is certain to shorten
his life, and which renders his life, while it lasts,
useless to others and a torment to himself. Suppose
that under these circumstances he, undeceived, gives
his free and intelligent consent to take the risk of an
operation which in a large proportion of cases has
proved fatal, but which is the only method by which
his disease can possibly be cured, and which, if it
succeeds, will restore him to health and vigour. We
do not conceive that it would be expedient to punish
the surgeon who should perform the operation,
though by performing it he might cause death, not
intending to cause death, but knowing himself to be
likely to cause it. Again; if a person attacked by a
wild beast should call out to his friends to fire,
though with imminent hazard to himself, and they
were to obey the call, we do not conceive that it
would be expedient to punish them, though they
might by firing cause his death, and though when
they fired they knew themselves to be likely to cause
his death.

We propose, therefore, that it shall be no offence
to do even what the doer knows to be likely to cause
death if the sufferer being of ripe age has, undeceived, given a free and intelligent consent to
stand the risk, and if the doer did not intend to
cause death, but on the contrary, intended in good
faith the benefit of the sufferer.

We have now explained the provisions contained
in clauses 69 and 70. The cases to which the two
next clauses relate bear a close affinity to those which
we have just considered.

A lunatic may be in a state which makes it proper that he should be put into a strait waistcoat. A child may meet with an accident which may render the amputation of a limb necessary. But to put a strait waistcoat on a man without his consent is, under our definition, to commit an assault. To amputate a limb is, by our definition, voluntarily to cause grievous hurt, and, as sharp instruments are used, is a very highly penal offence. We have therefore provided, by clause 71, that the consent of the guardian of a sufferer who is an infant or who is of unsound mind shall, to a great extent, have the effect which the consent of the sufferer himself would have, if the sufferer were of ripe age and sound mind.

That there should be some provision of this sort is evidently necessary. On the other hand, we feel that there is a considerable danger in allowing people to assume the office of judging for others in such cases. Every man always intends in good faith his own benefit, and has a deeper interest in knowing what is for his own benefit than anybody else can have. That he gives a free and intelligent consent to suffer pain or loss, creates a strong presumption that it is good for him on the whole to suffer that pain or loss. But we cannot safely confide to him the interest of his neighbours in the same unreserved manner in which we confide to him his own, even when he sincerely intends to benefit his neighbours. Even parents have been known to deliver their children up to slavery in a foreign country, to inflict the most cruel mutilations on their male children, to sacrifice the chastity of their female children, and to do all this declaring, and perhaps with truth, that their object was something which they considered as advantageous to the children. We have therefore not thought it sufficient to require that on such occasions the guardian should act in good faith for the benefit of the ward. We have imposed several additional restrictions which, we conceive, carry their defence with them.

There yet remains a kindred class of cases which are by no means of rare occurrence. For example, a person falls down in an apoplectic fit. Bleeding alone can save him, and he is unable to signify his consent to be bled. The surgeon who bleeds him commits an act falling under the definition of an offence. The surgeon is not the patient's guardian, and has no authority from any such guardian; yet it is evident that the surgeon ought not to be punished. Again, a house is on fire. A person snatches up a child too young to understand the danger, and flings it from the house-top, with a faint hope that it may be caught in a blanket below, but with the knowledge that it is highly probable that it will be dashed to pieces. Here, though the child may be killed by the fall, though the person who threw it down knew that it would very probably be killed, and though he was not the child's parent or guardian, he ought not to be punished.

In these examples there is what may be called a temporary guardianship justified by the exigency of the case and by the humanity of the motive. This temporary guardianship bears a considerable analogy to that temporary magistracy with which the law invests every person who is present when a great crime is committed, or when the public peace is concerned. To acts done in the exercise of this temporary guardianship, we extend by clause 72 a protection very similar to that which we have given to the acts of regular guardians.

Clause 73 is intended to provide for those cases which, though, from the imperfections of language, they fall within the letter of the penal law, are yet not within its spirit, and are all over the world considered by the public, and for the most part dealt

with by the tribunals, as innocent. As our definitions are framed, it is theft to dip a pen in another
man's ink, mischief to crumble one of his wafers, an
assault to cover him with a cloud of dust by riding
past him, hurt to incommode him by pressing against
him in getting into a carriage. There are innumerable acts without performing which men cannot live
together in society, acts which all men constantly do
and suffer in turn, and which it is desirable that
they should do and suffer in turn, yet which differ
only in degree from crimes. That these acts ought
not to be treated as crimes is evident, and we think
it far better expressly to except them from the penal
clauses of the code than to leave it to the judges to
except them in practice; for if the code is silent on
the subject, the judges can except these cases only
by resorting to one of two practices which we consider as most pernicious, by making law, or by
wresting the language of the law from its plain
meaning.

We propose (clauses 74 to 84) to except from
the operation of the penal clauses of the code large
classes of acts done in good faith for the purpose of
repelling unlawful aggressions. In this part of the
chapter we have attempted to define, with as much
exactness as the subject appears to us to admit, the
limits of the right of private defence. It may be
thought that we have allowed too great a latitude to
the exercise of this right; and we are ourselves of
opinion that if we had been framing laws for a bold
and high-spirited people, accustomed to take the
law into their own hand, and to go beyond the line
of moderation in repelling injury, it would have
been fit to provide additional restrictions. In this
country the danger is on the other side; the people
are too little disposed to help themselves; the
patience with which they submit to the cruel depre-
dations of gang-robbers and to trespass and mischief

committed in the most outrageous manner by bands
of ruffians, is one of the most remarkable, and at the
same time one of the most discouraging symptoms
which the state of society in India presents to us.
Under these circumstances we are desirous rather to
rouse and encourage a manly spirit among the people
than to multiply restrictions on the exercise of the
right of self-defence. We are of opinion that all the
evil which is likely to arise from the abuse of that
right is far less serious than the evil which would
arise from the execution of one person for overstep-
ping what might appear to the Courts to be the exact
line of moderation in resisting a body of dacoits.

We think it right, however, to say that there is
no part of the code with which we feel less satisfied
than this. We cannot accuse ourselves of any want
of diligence or care. No portion of our work has
cost us more anxious thought or has been more
frequently re-written. Yet we are compelled to own
that we leave it still in a very imperfect state; and
though we do not doubt that it may be far better
executed than it has been by us, we are inclined to
think that it must always be one of the least exact
parts of every system of criminal law.

We have now made such observations as appear
to us to be required on the general exceptions which
we propose. It is proper that we should next explain why we have not proposed any exception in
favour of some classes of acts which, as some persons
may think, are entitled to indulgence.

We long considered whether it would be advisable to except from the operation of the penal
clauses of the code acts committed in good faith
from the desire of self-preservation; and we have
determined not to except them.

We admit, indeed, that many acts falling under
the definition of offences ought not to be punished
when committed from the desire of self-preservation;

and for this reason, that, as the penal code itself appeals solely to the fears of men, it never can furnish them with motives for braving dangers greater than the dangers with which it threatens them. Its utmost severity will be inefficacious for the purpose of preventing the mass of mankind from yielding to a certain amount of temptation. It can, indeed, make those who have yielded to the temptation miserable afterwards. But misery which has no tendency to prevent crime is so much clear evil. It is vain to rely on the dread of a remote and contingent evil as sufficient to overcome the dread of instant death, or the sense of actual torture. An eminently virtuous man indeed will prefer death to crime ; but it is not to our virtue that the penal law addresses itself ; nor would the world stand in need of penal laws if men were virtuous. A man who refuses to commit a bad action, when he sees preparations made for killing or torturing him unless he complies, is a man who does not require the fear of punishment to restrain him. A man, on the other hand, who is withheld from committing crimes solely or chiefly by the fear of punishment, will never be withheld by that fear when a pistol is held to his forehead or a lighted torch applied to his fingers for the purpose of forcing him to commit a crime.

It would, we think, be mere useless cruelty to hang a man for voluntarily. causing the death of others by jumping from a sinking ship into an overloaded boat. The suffering caused by the punishment is, considered by itself, an evil, and ought to be inflicted only for the sake of some preponderating good. But no preponderating good, indeed no good whatever, would be obtained by hanging a man for such an act. We cannot expect that the next man who feels the ship in which he is left descending into the waves, and sees a crowded boat putting off from it, will submit to instant and certain death from fear of a remote and contingent death. There are men, indeed, who in such circumstances would sacrifice their own lives rather than risk the lives of others. But such men act from the influence of principles and feelings which no penal laws can produce, and which, if they were general, would render penal laws unnecessary. Again, a gang of dacoits, finding a house strongly secured, seize a smith, and by torture and threats of death induce him to take his tools and to force the door for them; here, it appears to us, that to punish the smith as a housebreaker would be to inflict gratuitous pain. We cannot trust to the deterring effect of such punishment. The next smith who may find himself in the same situation will rather take his chance of being, at a distant time, arrested, convicted, and sentenced to imprisonment, than incur certain and immediate death.

In the cases which we have put, some persons may perhaps doubt whether there ought to be impunity; but those very persons would generally admit that the extreme danger was a mitigating circumstance to be considered in apportioning the punishment. It might, however, with no small plausibility be contended that if any punishment at all is inflicted in such cases, that punishment ought to be not merely death, but death with torture; for the dread of being put to death by torture might possibly be sufficient to prevent a man from saving his own life by a crime; but it is quite certain, as we have said, that the mere fear of capital punishment which is remote, and which may never be inflicted at all, will never prevent him from saving his life. And *à fortiori*, the dread of a milder punishment will not prevent him from saving his life. Laws directed against offences to which men are prompted by cupidity, ought always to take from offenders

more than those offenders expect to gain by crime.
It would obviously be absurd to provide that a thief
or a swindler should be punished with a fine not exceeding half the sum which he had acquired by theft
or swindling; in the same manner, laws directed
against offences to which men are prompted by fear
ought always to be framed in such a way as to be
more terrible than the dangers which they require
men to brave. It is on this ground, we apprehend,
that a soldier who runs away in action is punished
with a rigour altogether unproportioned to the moral
depravity which his offence indicates. Such a soldier may be an honest and benevolent man, and
irreproachable in all the relations of civil life; yet
he is punished as severely as a deliberate assassin,
and more severely than a robber or a kidnapper.
Why is this? Evidently because, as his offence
arises from fear, it must be punished in such a manner that timid men may dread the punishment more
than they dread the fire of the enemy.

If all cases in which acts falling under the definition of offences are done from the desire of self-
preservation were as clear as the cases which we
have put of the man who jumps from a sinking ship
into a boat, and of the smith who is compelled by
dacoits to force a door for them, we should, without
hesitation, propose to exempt this class of acts from
punishment. But it is to be observed, that in both
these cases the person in danger is supposed to have
been brought into danger, without the smallest fault
on his own part, by mere accident, or by the depravity
of others. If a captain of a merchantman were to
run his ship on shore in order to cheat the insurers,
and then to sacrifice the lives of others in order to
save himself from a danger created by his own villany; if a person who had joined himself to a gang
of dacoits with no other intention than that of
robbing, were at the command of his leader, accom-

panied with threats of instant death in case of disobedience, to commit murder, though unwillingly,
the case would be widely different, and our former
reasoning would cease to apply; for it is evident that
punishment which is inefficacious to prevent a man
from yielding to a certain temptation may often be
efficacious to prevent him from exposing himself to
that temptation. We cannot count on the fear
which a man may entertain of being brought to the
gallows at some distant time as sufficient to overcome
the fear of instant death; but the fear of remote
punishment may often overcome the motives which
induce a man to league himself with lawless companions, in whose society no person who shrinks
from any atrocity that they may command can be
certain of his life. Nothing is more usual than for
pirates, gang-robbers and rioters to excuse their
crimes by declaring that they were in dread of their
associates, and durst not act otherwise. Nor is it by
any means improbable that this may often be true.
Nay, it is not improbable that crews of pirates and
gangs of robbers may have committed crimes which
everyone among them was unwilling to commit, under
the influence of mutual fear; but we think it clear
that this circumstance ought not to exempt them from
the full severity of the law.

Again, nothing is more usual than for thieves to
urge distress and hunger as excuses for their thefts.
It is certain, indeed, that many thefts are committed
from the pressure of distress so severe as to be more
terrible than the punishment of theft, and than the
disgrace which that punishment brings with it to
the mass of mankind. It is equally certain that,
when the distress from which a man can relieve
himself by theft is more terrible than the evil consequences of theft, those consequences will not keep
him from committing theft; yet it by no means
follows that it is irrational to punish him for theft;

for though the fear of punishment is not likely to keep any man from theft when he is actually starving, it is very likely to keep him from being in a starving state. It is of no effect to counteract the irresistible motive which immediately prompts to theft ; but it is of great effect to counteract the motives to that idleness and that profusion which end in bringing a man into a condition in which no law will keep him from committing theft. We can hardly conceive a law more injurious to society than one which should provide that as soon as a man who had neglected his work, or who had squandered his wages in stimulating d.ugs, or gambled them away, had been thirty-six hours without food, and felt the sharp impulse of hunger, he might, with impunity, steal food from his neighbours.

We should therefore think it in the highest degree pernicious to enact that no act done under the fear even of instant death should be an offence. It would *à fortiori* be absurd to enact that no act under the fear of any other evil should be an offence.

There are, as we have said, cases in which it would be useless cruelty to punish acts done under the fear of death, or even of evils less than death. But it appears to us impossible precisely to define these cases. We have, therefore, left them to the Government, which, in the exercise of its clemency, will doubtless be guided in a great measure by the advice of the Courts.

We considered whether it would be desirable to make any distinction between offences committed against freemen and offences committed against slaves. We certainly entered on the consideration of this important question with a strong leaning to the opinion that no such distinction ought to be made. We thought it our duty, however, not to come to a decision without obtaining information and advice from those who were best qualified to give it. We have collected information on the subject from every part of India, and we have now in our office a large collection of documents containing much that is curious, and that in future stages of the work in which we are engaged will be useful. At present we have only to consider the subject with reference to the penal code.

These documents have satisfied us that there is at present no law whatever defining the extent of the power of a master over his slaves; that every thing depends on the disposition of the particular functionary who happens to be in charge of a district, and that functionaries who are in charge of contiguous districts, or who have at different times been in charge of the same district, hold diametrically opposite opinions as to what their official duty requires. Nor is this discrepancy found only in the proceedings of subordinate Courts. The Court of Nizamut Adawlut at Fort William lay down the law thus: "A master would not be punished, the Court opine, for inflicting a slight correction on his legal slave, such as a tutor would be justified in inflicting on a scholar, or a father on a child." The Court of Nizamut Adawlut at Allahabad take a quite different view of the law: "Although," they say, "the Mahomedan law permits the master to correct his slave with moderation, the code by which the magistrates and other criminal authorities are bound to regulate their proceedings does not recognise any such power, and as the regulations of the Government draw no distinction between the slave and the freeman in criminal matters, but place them both on a level, it is the practice of the Courts, following the principles of equal justice, to treat them both alike." The Court of Foujdarry Adawlut at Madras state, that it is not the practice of the Courts to make any distinction whatever in cases which come before them; that a circular order of the Foujdarry Adawlut recognizes the right of a master to inflict corrections in certain cases, but that in practice no such distinction is made. We own that we entertain some doubts whether the practice be universally such as is supposed by the Foujdarry Adawlut. We perceive that two magistrates in the western division of the Madras Presidency differ from each other in opinion on this subject. The magistrate of Canara says, that "the right of the master to inflict punishment has been allowed, but only to a very small extent." The magistrate of Malabar states, that "the relation of a master and slave has never been recognized as justifying acts which would otherwise be punishable, or as constituting a ground for mitigation of punishment." The Court of Foujdarry Adawlut at Bombay has given no opinion on the point, and there is a great difference of opinion among the subordinate authorities in the Bombay Presidency. One gentleman conceives that the imposing of personal restraint is the only act otherwise punishable which the Courts would allow a master to commit when a slave might be concerned. Another conceives that a master has a power of correction similar to that of a father. A third goes further, and is of opinion, that "all but cases of very aggravated nature would be considered as entitled to exemption from or mitigation of punishment on this account." On the other hand, several gentlemen are of opinion that the relation of master and slave would not be considered by the Courts as a plea for any act which would be an offence if committed against a freeman.

It is clear, therefore, that we find the law in a state of utter uncertainty. It is equally clear that we cannot leave it in that state. We must either withdraw from a large class of slaves a protection to which the Courts under the jurisdiction of which they live now think them entitled, or we must extend to a large class a protection greater than what they actually enjoy.

We have not the smallest hesitation in recommending to his Lordship in Council that the law throughout all British India should be conformable to what, in the opinion of the Court of Nizamut Adawlut at Allahabad, is now actually the law in the Presidency of Fort William, and to what, in the opinion of the Court of Foujdarry Adawlut at Fort St. George, is now actually the practice in the Madras Presidency. That is to say, we recommend that no act falling under the definition of an offence should be exempted from punishment because it is committed by a master against his slave.

The distinction which, in the opinion of many respectable functionaries, the law now makes between acts committed against a freeman and acts committed against a slave is in itself an evil, and an evil so great, that nothing but the strongest necessity, proved by the strongest evidence, could justify any Government in maintaining it. We conceive that the circumstances which we have already stated are sufficient to show that no such necessity exists. By removing all doubt on the subject, we shall not deprive the master of a power the right to which has never been questioned, but of a power which is and has for some time been, to say the least, of disputable legality, and which has been held by a very precarious tenure.

To leave the question undecided is impossible. To decide the question by putting any class of slaves in a worse situation than that in which they now are is a course which we cannot think of recommending, and which we are certain that the Government will not adopt. The inference seems to be, that the question ought to be decided by declaring that whatever is an offence when committed against a freeman shall be also an offence when committed against a slave.

It may perhaps be thought that, by framing the law in this manner, we do, in fact, virtually abolish slavery in British India; and undoubtedly, if the law as we have framed it should be really carried into full effect, it will at once deprive slavery of those evils which are its essence, and will insure the speedy and natural extinction of the whole system. The essence of slavery, the circumstance which makes slavery the worst of all social evils, is not in our opinion this, that the master has a legal right to certain services from the slave, but this, that the master has a legal right to enforce the performance of those services without having recourse to the tribunals. He is a judge in his own cause. He is armed with the powers of a magistrate for the protection of his own private interest against the person who owes him service. Every other judge quits the bench as soon as his own cause is called on. The judicial authority of the master begins and ends with cases in which he has a direct stake. The moment that a master is really deprived of this authority, the moment that his right to service really becomes, like his right to money which he has lent, a mere civil right, which he can enforce only by a civil action, the peculiarly odious and malignant evils of slavery disappear at once. The name of slavery may be retained, but the thing is no longer the same. It is evidently impossible that any master can really obtain efficient service from unwilling labourers by means of prosecution before the civil tribunals. Nor is there any instance of any country in which the relation of master and servant is maintained by means of such actions. In some states of society the labourer works because the master inflicts instant correction whenever there is any disobedience or slackness. In a different state of society, the people labour for a master because the master makes it worth their while. Prac-

tically, we believe it will be found that there is no
third way. A labourer who has neither the motive
of the freeman nor that of the slave, who is actuated
neither by the hope of wages nor by the dread of
stripes, will not work at all. The master may indeed, if he chooses, go before the tribunals and
obtain a decree. But scarcely any master would
think it worth while to do so, and scarcely any
labourer would be spurred to constant and vigorous
exertion by the dread of such a legal proceeding.
In fact, we are not even able to form to ourselves
the idea of a society in which the working classes
should have no other motives to industry than the
dread of prosecution. We understand how the
planter of Mauritius formerly induced his negroes to
work. He applied the lash if they loitered. We
understand how our grooms and bearers are induced
to work at Calcutta. They are gainers by working,
and by obtaining a good character; they are losers
by being turned away. But in what other way servants can be induced to work we do not understand.

It appears to us, therefore, that if we can really
prevent the master from exacting service by the use
of any violence or restraint, or by the infliction of
any bodily hurt, one of two effects will inevitably
follow: either the master will obtain no service at
all, or he will find himself under the necessity of
obtaining it by making it a source of advantage to
the labourer as well as to himself. A labourer who
knows that if he idles, his master will not dare to
strike him; that if he absconds, his master will not
dare to confine him; that his master can enforce a
claim to service only by taking more trouble, losing
more time and spending more money than the
service is worth, will not work for fear. It follows
that if the master wishes the labourer to work at all,
the master must have recourse to different motives,
to the motives of a freeman, to the hope of reward,

to the sense of reciprocal benefit. Names are of no consequence. It matters nothing whether the labourer be or or be not called a slave. All that is of real moment is that he should work from the motives and feelings of the freeman.

This effect, we are satisfied, would follow if outrages offered to slaves were really punished exactly as outrages offered to freemen are punished. But we are far indeed from thinking that, by merely framing the law as we have framed it, we shall produce this effect. It is quite certain that slaves are at present often oppressed by their masters in districts where the magistrates and judges conceive that the law now is what we propose that it shall henceforth be. It is therefore evident that they may continue to be oppressed by their masters when the law has been made perfectly clear. To an ignorant labourer, accustomed from his birth to obey a superior for daily food, to submit without resistance to the cruelty and tyranny of that superior, perhaps to be transferred, like a horse or a sheep, from one superior to another, neither the law which we now propose, nor any other law, will of itself give freedom. It is of little use to direct the judge to punish unless we can teach the sufferer to complain.

We have thought it right to state this, lest we should mislead his Lordship in Council into an opinion that the law, framed as we propose to frame it, will really remove all the evils of slavery, and that nothing more will remain to be done. So far are we from thinking that the law, as we propose to frame it, will of itself effect a great practical change, that we greatly doubt whether even a law abolishing slavery would of itself effect any great practical change. Our belief is that even if slavery were expressly abolished, it might, and would, in some parts of India, still continue to exist in practice. We trust, therefore, that his Lordship in Council

will not consider the measure which we now recommend as of itself sufficient to accomplish the
benevolent ends of the British Legislature, and to
relieve the Indian Government from its obligation
to watch over the interests of the slave population.

NOTE (C).

ON THE CHAPTER OF OFFENCES AGAINST THE STATE.

HIS Lordship in Council will perceive that, in this
chapter, we have provided only for offences against
the Government of India, and that we have made
no mention of offences against the General Government of the British Empire. We have done so
because it appears to us doubtful to what extent his
Lordship in Council is competent to legislate respecting such offences. The Act of Parliament
which defines the legislative power of the Council of
India especially prohibits that body from making
any law " which shall in any way affect any preroga-
tive of the Crown or the authority of Parliament, or
any part of the unwritten laws, or constitution of
the United Kingdom of Great Britain and Ireland,
whereon may depend, in any degree, the allegiance
of any person to the Crown of the United Kingdom,
or the sovereignty or dominion of the said Crown
over any part of the said territories."
It might be argued that these words relate only
to laws affecting the rights of the Crown and of
Parliament, and not to laws affecting the penal
sanctions of those rights, and that, therefore, though
the Governor-general in Council has no power to
absolve the King's subjects from their allegiance, he
has power to fix the punishment to which they shall
be liable for violating their allegiance. It seems to

us, however, that there is the closest connexion in this case between the right and the penal sanction; that a power to alter the sanction amounts to a power to abolish the right; and that Parliament, which withheld from the Indian Legislature one of those powers, cannot be supposed to have intended to grant the other.

If the Governor-general in Council has the legal power to fix the punishment of a subject who should, in the territories of the East India Company, conspire the death of the King, or levy war against the King, then the Governor-general in Council has the legal power to fix that punishment at a fine of one anna; and it is plain that a law which should fix such a fine as the only punishment of regicide and rebellion would be a law virtually absolving all subjects within the territories of the East India Company from their allegiance.

This part of the penal law, therefore, we have not ventured to touch. We leave it to the Imperial Legislature. But we trust that we may be permitted to suggest to his Lordship in Council that the early attention of the Home authorities should be called to this subject.

There is no doubt that the criminal statute law of England is not binding generally on a native of India in the Mofussil. Whether the statute law relating to treason be binding on such a native is a question with respect to which we do not venture to give a decided opinion. It seems to us exceedingly doubtful whether that part of the statute law be binding on such a native. It is quite certain that no Court has ever enforced it against such a native; and that, in the opinion of many respectable and intelligent judicial officers in the service of the Company, it could not legally be enforced against such a native. Nor are the Company's judicial officers, by whom alone such a native can legally be tried, likely to be accurately acquainted with the statute law of England on the subject of treason, or with the mass of constructions and precedents by which that law has been overlaid. If such a native be not punishable under the English statute law of treason, it is difficult to say under what law he could be punished for that crime. The regulations contain nothing on the subject. The Council of India, we conceive, is not competent to legislate respecting it. The Mahomedan law might possibly be so violently strained as to reach it in Bengal and in the Madras Presidency; and in the Bombay Presidency it might possibly be brought within that clause which arms the Courts with an enormous discretion in cases in which they conceive that morality and social order require protection. But there are, in our opinion, strong reasons against retaining either the Mahomedan penal law, or the sweeping clause of the Bombay Regulations, to which we have referred.

It may be added that the provision of the Bombay Regulations, to which we have referred, applies only to persons who profess a religion with which a system of penal law is inseparably connected. Unless, therefore, the English statute law on the subject of treason applies to natives in the Mofussil, a point respecting which we entertain great doubt, a native Christian who should, at Surat, assist the levying of war, not against the Company's Government, but against the British Crown, would be liable to no punishment whatever.

This anomalous state of things may be, in some degree, explained by the singular manner in which the British Empire grew up in India. The East India Company was, during a long course of years, in theory at least, under two masters. It was subject to the King of England; it was subject also to the great Mogul. It derived its corporate existence from the British Parliament. It held its territorial possessions by a grant from the Durbar of Delhi. The situation of the native subjects of the Company bore some analogy to that of the inhabitants of Mindelheim, while that fief of the empire was held by the Duke of Marlborough. The inhabitants of Mindelheim were subjects of the Duke of Marlborough, but they owed no allegiance to the English Crown, though their sovereign was subject to that Crown. It was in this way that the British Empire in India originated. It was long considered as a wise policy to disguise the real power of the English under the forms of vassalage, and to leave to the Mogul and his Viceroys the empty honours of a sovereignty which was really held by the Company. This policy was abandoned slowly and by imperceptible degrees. The recognition of the supremacy of the King of Delhi appeared on the seal of the British Government down to a late period, and on its coin down to a still later period. A great change has indeed taken place since the grant of the Dewannee of the lower provinces to the Company, but it has taken place so gradually, that, though it would be absurd to deny that the natives of British India are now subjects of his Majesty, it would be impossible to point out the particular time when they became so.

To these circumstances we attribute most of the anomalies which are to be found in the legal relation subsisting between the natives of British India and the General Government of the empire. It seems highly desirable that the Imperial Legislature should do what cannot be done by the Local Legislature, and should pass a law of high treason for the territories of the East India Company. As far, indeed, as respects the royal person, the present state of the law, though in theory unseemly, is not likely to cause any practical evil. It is highly improbable that any English King will visit his Indian dominions, or that any plot, having for its object the death of an English King, will ever extend its ramifications to India. But it is by no means improbable that persons residing in the territories of the East India Company may be parties to the levying of war against the British Crown, without violating any local regulation. If any insurrection were to take place in any of the British dominions in the Eastern Seas, in Ceylon, for example, or in Mauritius, it is by no means improbable that persons residing within the Company's territories might furnish information and stores to the rebels. And if this were done by a person not subject to the jurisdiction of the Courts established by Royal Charter, we are satisfied that there would be the most serious difficulty in bringing the criminal to legal punishment.

We have, his Lordship in Council will perceive, made the abetting of hostilities against the Government, in certain cases, a separate offence, instead of leaving it to the operation of the general law laid down in the chapter on abetment. We have done so for two reasons. In the first place, war may be waged against the Government by persons in whom it is no offence to wage such war, by foreign princes and their subjects. Our general rules on the subject of abetment would apply to the case of a person residing in the British territories, who should abet a subject of the British Government in waging war against that Government; but they would not reach the case of a person who, while residing in the British territories, should abet the waging of war by any foreign prince against the British Government. In the second place, we agree with the great body of legislators in thinking, that though in general a person who has been a party to a criminal design which has not been carried into effect, ought not to be punished so severely as if that design had been carried into effect, yet an exception to this rule must

be made with respect to high offences against the
state; for state-crimes, and especially the most
heinous and formidable state-crimes, have this
peculiarity, that if they are successfully committed,
the criminal is almost always secure from punishment.
The murderer is in greater danger after his victim
is despatched than before. The thief is in greater
danger after the purse is taken than before. But
the rebel is out of danger as soon as he has subverted the Government. As the penal law is
impotent against a successful rebel, it is consequently
necessary that it should be made strong and sharp
against the first beginnings of rebellion, against
treasonable designs which have been carried no
further than plots and preparations. We have therefore not thought it expedient to leave such plots and
preparations to the ordinary law of abetment. That
law is framed on principles which, though they
appear to us to be quite sound, as respects the great
majority of offences, would be inapplicable here.
Under that general law, a conspiracy for the subversion of the Government would not be punished
at all if the conspirators were detected before they
had done more than discuss plans, adopt resolutions
and interchange promises of fidelity. A conspiracy
for the subversion of the Government, which should
be carried as far as the gunpowder treason or the
assassination plot against William the Third, would
be punished very much less severely than the counterfeiting of a rupee, or the presenting of a forged
checque. We have, therefore, thought it absolutely
necessary to make separate provision for the previous
abetting of great state offences. The subsequent
abetting of such offences may, we think, without
inconvenience, be left to be dealt with according to
the general law.

NOTE (D).

ON THE CHAPTER OF OFFENCES RELATING TO THE ARMY AND NAVY.

A FEW words will explain the necessity of having some provisions of the nature of those which are contained in this chapter.

It is obvious that a person who, not being himself subject to military law, exhorts or assists those who are subject to military law to commit gross breaches of discipline, is a proper subject of punishment. But the general law respecting the abetting of offences will not reach such a person; nor, framed as it is, would it be desirable that it should reach him. It would not reach him, because the military delinquency which he has abetted is not punishable by this code, and therefore is not, in our legal nomenclature, an offence. Nor is it desirable that the punishment of a person not military, who has abetted a breach of military discipline, should be fixed according to the principles on which we have proceeded in framing the law of abetment. We have provided that the punishment of the abettor of an offence shall be equal or proportional to the punishment of the person who commits that offence; and this seems to us a sound principle when applied only to the punishments provided by this code. But the military penal law is, and must necessarily be, far more severe than that under which the body of the people live. The severity of the military penal law can be justified only by reasons drawn from the peculiar habits and duties of soldiers, and from the peculiar relation in which they stand to the Government. The extension of such severity to persons not members of the military profession appears to us altogether unwarrantable. If a person, not military, who abets a breach of military discipline, should be made liable to a punishment regulated, according to our general rules, by the punishment to which such a breach of discipline renders a soldier liable, the whole symmetry of the penal law would be destroyed. He who should induce a soldier to disobey any order of a commanding officer would be liable to be punished more severely than a dacoit, a professional thug, an incendiary, a ravisher, or a kidnapper. We have attempted in this chapter to provide, in a manner more consistent with the general character of the code, for the punishment of persons who, not being military, abet military crimes.

NOTE (E).

ON THE CHAPTER OF THE ABUSE OF THE POWERS OF PUBLIC SERVANTS.

THIS chapter is intended to reach offences which are committed by public servants, and which are of such a description that they can be committed by public servants alone.

We have found considerable difficulty in drawing the line between public 'servants and the great mass of the community. We hope that the description which we have given in clause 14 will be found to comprehend all those whom it is desirable to bring under this part of the law, and we trust that, when the code of procedure is completed, this description may be made both more accurate and more concise.

Those offences which are common between public servants and other members of the community, we leave to the general provisions of the code. If a public servant embezzles public money, we leave him to the ordinary law of criminal breach of trust. If he falsely pretends to have disbursed money for the public, and by this deception induces the Government to allow it in his accounts, we leave him to the ordinary law of cheating. If he produces forged vouchers to back his statement, we leave him to the ordinary law of forgery. We see no reason for punishing these offences more severely when the Government suffers by them than when private people suffer. A Government, indeed, which does not consider the sufferings of private individuals as its own, is not only selfish but shortsighted in its selfishness. The revenue is drawn from the wealth of individuals, and every act of dishonest spoliation which tends to render individuals insecure in the enjoyment of their wealth is really an injury to the revenue. On every account, therefore, we think it desirable that the property of the state should, in general, be protected by exactly the same laws which are considered as sufficient for the protection of the property of the subject.

We are not without apprehension that we may be thought to have treated the transgressions of public servants too favourably, to have passed by without notice some malpractices which deserve punishment, and where we have provided punishments, to have seldom made those punishments sufficiently severe.

It is true that we have altogether omitted to provide any punishment for some kinds of misconduct on the part of public servants. It is true also, that the punishments which we propose in this chapter are not generally proportioned either to the evil which the abuse of power produces, or to the depravity of a man who, having been entrusted with power for the public benefit, employs that power to gratify his own cupidity or revenge.

But it is to be remembered that there is a marked distinction between the penal clauses contained in

this chapter and the other penal clauses of the code.
In general a penal clause sets forth the whole punishment which can be inflicted on an offender by any
public authority. The penalty of theft, of breach of
trust, of cheating, of extortion, of assault, of defamation, has been fixed on the supposition that it is the
whole penalty which the criminal is to suffer, and
that no power in the state can make any addition to
it. But the penalty of an offence committed by a
public functionary in the exercise of his public functions has been fixed on the supposition that it will
often be only a part, and a small part, of the penalty
which he will suffer. It is in the power of the
Government to punish him for many acts which the
law has not made punishable. It is in the power of
the Government to add to any sentence pronounced
by the Courts another sentence which will often be
even more terrible. To a man whose subsistence is
derived from official emoluments, whose habits are
formed to official business, and whose whole ambition
is fixed on official promotion, degradation to a lower
post is a punishment ; dismissal from the public service is a punishment sufficient even for a serious
offence. The mere knowledge that his character has
suffered in the opinion of those superiors on whom
his advancement depends probably gives him as much
pain as a heavy fine.

This is to a great degree the case in every
country, and assuredly not less in India than in any
other country. Indeed, those servants of the Company
by whom all the higher offices in the Indian Government are filled, entertain a feeling about their situations very different from that which is found among
political men in England. It is natural that they
should entertain such a feeling. They are set apart
at an early age as persons destined to hold offices in
India. Their education is conducted at home with
that view. They are transferred when just entering

on manhood to the country which they are to govern.
They pass the best years of their lives in acquiring
knowledge which is most important to men who are
to fill high situations in India, but which in any other
walk of life would bring little profit and little distinction, in mastering languages which, when they
quit this country, are useless to them, in studying a
vast and complicated system of revenue which is
altogether peculiar to the East, in becoming intimately acquainted with the interests, the resources
and the projects of potentates whose very existence is
unknown even to educated men in Europe.   To such
a man, dismissal from the service of the Indian
Government is generally a very great calamity.   His
life has been thrown away.   It has been passed in
acquiring information and experience which, in any
pursuit to which he may now betake himself, will
be of little or no service to him.   There are therefore few convenanted servants of the Company who,
even if they were men destitute of all honourable
feeling, would not look on dismissal from the service
as a most severe punishment.   But the covenanted
servants of the Company are English gentlemen, that
is to say, they are persons to whom the ruin of their
fortunes is less terrible than the ruin of their characters.   There are few of them, we believe, to whom
an intimation that their integrity was suspected by
the Government would not give more pain than
a sentence of six months' imprisonment for an offence
not of a disgraceful kind, and to many of them death
itself would appear less dreadful than ignominious
expulsion from the body of which they are members.

Thus dismissal from the public service is a punishment exceedingly dreaded by public functionaries,
and most dreaded in this country by the highest
class of public functionaries.   Nor is this all.   It is
not merely a severe punishment, but it is also a
punishment which is far more likely to be inflicted

than many punishments which are less severe. Those who are legally competent to inflict it are bound by no rules, except those which their own discretion may impose on them. For what kind and degree of delinquency they shall inflict it, by what evidence that delinquency shall be established, by what tribunals the inquiry shall be conducted; nay, whether there shall be any delinquency, any evidence, any tribunal, is absolutely in their breasts. They may inflict this punishment, and may be justified in inflicting it for transgressions which are not susceptible of precise definition, and which have not been substantiated by decisive proof. They may be justified in inflicting it, because many petty circumstances, each of which separately would be too trivial for notice, have, when taken together, satisfied them that a functionary is unfit for any public employment. They may be justified in inflicting it, because they strongly suspect him of guilt which they cannot bring home to him by evidence to which a Zillah judge would pay any attention. Most of what we have said of the punishment of dismissal from office applies, though not in the same degree, to the slighter punishments of censure, suspension and removal from a higher to a lower post.

We have shown that public functionaries are liable not only to the punishments provided by this code, but also to other peculiar punishments of great severity. It seems therefore to follow, that if those who possess the power of inflicting these peculiar punishments can be trusted, some malpractices of public functionaries may be safely left unnoticed in this code, and that other malpractices need not be visited with legal punishment so rigorous as their enormity might seem to merit. The Executive Government, in our opinion, deserves to be trusted. At all events it must be trusted; for it is quite certain that no laws will prevent corruption

and oppression on the part of the servants of the
Indian Government, if that Government is inclined
to screen the offenders. The Government, to say
nothing of the vast influence which it can indirectly
exert, appoints, promotes and removes judges at its
discretion. It can remit any sentence pronounced
by the Courts. It can, therefore, if it be not honestly
disposed to correct official abuses, render any penal
clauses directed against such abuses almost wholly
inoperative. And if it be honestly disposed, as we
firmly believe that it is, to correct official abuses, it
will use for that purpose its power of rewarding and
punishing its servants.

It will be seen that we propose, under clause 138,
to punish with imprisonment for a term not exceeding three years, or with fine, or both, the corruption
of public functionaries. The punishment of fine
will, we think, be found very efficacious in cases of
this description, if the judges exercise the power
given them as they ought to do, and compel the
delinquent to deliver up the whole of his ill-gotten
wealth.

The mere taking of presents by a public functionary, when it cannot be proved that such presents
were corruptly taken, we have made penal only in one
particular case, to which we shall hereafter call the
attention of his Lordship in Council. We have not
made the taking of presents by public functionaries
generally penal; because, though we think that it is
a practice which ought to be carefully watched and
often severely punished, we are not satisfied that it
is possible to frame any law on the subject which
would not be rendered inoperative either by its extreme severity or by its extreme laxity. Absolutely
to prohibit all public functionaries from taking presents would be to prohibit a son from contributing
to the support of a father, a father from giving a
portion with a daughter, a brother from extricating

a brother from pecuniary difficulties. No government would wish to prevent persons intimately connected by blood, by marriage or by friendship, from rendering services to each other; and no tribunals would enforce a law which should make the rendering of such services a crime. Where no such close connexion exists, the receiving of large presents by a public functionary is generally a very suspicious proceeding. But a lime, a wreath of flowers, a slice of betel nut, a drop of atar of roses poured on his handkerchief, are presents which it would in this country be held churlish to refuse, and which cannot possibly corrupt the most mercenary of mankind. Other presents of more value than these may, on account of their peculiar nature, be accepted, without affording any ground for suspicion. Luxuries socially consumed according to the usages of hospitality are presents of this description. It would be unreasonable to treat a man in office as a criminal for drinking many rupees-worth of champagne in a year at the table of an acquaintance; though if he were to suffer one of his subordinates to accept even a single rupee in specie, he might deserve exemplary punishment.

It appears to us, therefore, that the taking of presents where a corrupt motive cannot be proved, ought not in general to be a crime cognizable by the Courts. Whether in any particular case it ought to be punished or not will depend on innumerable circumstances, which it is impossible accurately to define, on the amount of the present, on the nature of the present, on the relation in which the giver and receiver stand to each other. Suppose that a wealthy English agent, who is interested in a young civil servant of the Company, were to pay the debts of that civil servant; or, suppose that a resident were to furnish money to enable his invalid assistant to proceed to the Cape. In these transactions there might be nothing which the most scrupulous could disapprove; but the case would be widely different if a wealthy native Zemindar were to pay the debts of a Collector of his district, or if any of the officers at the residency were to receive money from the minister of a foreign power. In such a case, though it might be impossible to prove a corrupt motive, we think that the Government would be inexcusable if it suffered the delinquent to remain in the public service.

We have hitherto put only extreme cases, cases in which it is clear that the taking of presents ought not to be punished, or cases in which it is clear that the taking of presents ought to be severely punished. But between the extremes lie an immense variety of cases, some of which call for severe punishment, some for milder punishment, some for censure, some for gentle admonition, while some ought to be tolerated. We have said that if a Collector were to accept a large present of money from a wealthy native Zemindar, he would deserve to be turned out of the service. But if the Collector were to accept such a present from an English indigo planter, the case would be different. The indigo planter might be his uncle, his brother, his father-in-law, his brother-in-law. In that case there might be no impropriety in the transaction. Again, if a native in the public service were to accept a present from a Zemindar who was connected with him by blood, marriage or friendship, there might be no impropriety in the transaction.

By the Act of Parliament to which the mal-practices of the first British conquerors of India gave occasion, the servants of the Company were forbidden to receive presents from Asiatics, but were left at liberty to receive presents from Europeans. The legislators of that time appear to have proceeded on the supposition that the servants of the Company would all be Englishmen, and that no Englishman would ever have any such connexion with any native as would render the receiving of presents from that native unobjectionable.

Natives are now declared by law to be competent to hold any post in the Company's service. It would evidently be improper to interdict an Asiatic in the service of the Company from receiving pecuniary assistance from his Asiatic father, or from receiving a portion with an Asiatic bride. It seems to us therefore that the rule laid down by Parliament, though it will still be in many cases an excellent rule of evidence, ought not, under the altered circumstances of India, to continue to be a rule of law.

Again, it ought to be remembered that the European and native races are not at present divided from each other by so strong a line of separation as at the time when the British Parliament laid down the rule which we are considering. The interval is still wide, but it by no means appears to us as it appeared to the legislators of the last generation, to be impassable. It is evident, therefore, that the rule formerly laid down by Parliament is constantly becoming less and less applicable to the state of India. On these grounds we have thought it advisable to leave this matter to the Executive Government, which will doubtless promulgate from time to time such rules as it may deem proper, and will enforce submission to those rules by visiting its disobedient servants with censure, with degradation, or with dismissal from the public service, according to the circumstances of every case.

We have thought it desirable to make one exception. We propose that a judge who accepts any valuable thing by way of gift from one whom he knows to be a plaintiff or a defendant in any cause pending in his Court shall be severely punished. This rule is not to extend to the taking of food in the interchange of ordinary civilities. It appears to us that the objections which we have made to a general law prohibiting the receipt of presents by public functionaries do not apply to this clause. The rule is clear and definite. The practice against which it is directed is not a practice which ought sometimes to be encouraged, and sometimes to be tolerated. It ought always, and under all circumstances, to be discouraged. It therefore appears to unite all the characteristics which mark out a practice as a fit object of penal legislation.

The only other penal provision of this chapter to which we think it necessary to call the attention of his Lordship in Council is that which is contained in clause 149.

We are of opinion that the preceding clauses, and the power which the Government possesses of suspending, degrading and dismissing public functionaries, will be found sufficient to prevent gross abuses. But there will remain a crowd of petty offences with which it is very difficult to deal, offences which separately are too slight to be brought before the criminal tribunals, which will sometimes be committed by good public servants, and which therefore it would be inexpedient to punish by removal from office, yet which will be very often committed if they can be committed with impunity, and which, if often committed, would impair the efficiency of all departments of the administration, and would produce infinite vexation to the body of the people.

By the existing laws of all the presidencies, a summary judicial power is given in certain cases to certain official superiors for the purpose of restraining their subordinates. We are inclined to believe that this is a wholesome power, and that it has, in the great majority of cases, been honestly employed for the protection of the public. We propose therefore to adopt the principle, and to make the system uniform through all the provinces of the empire, and through all the departments of the public service. We propose that a public functionary who is guilty of neglect of duty, who treats his superiors with disrespect, or who disobeys the lawful orders given by them for his guidance, shall be liable to a fine not exceeding the official pay which he receives in three months. In default of payment he will be liable (see clause 54) to seven days' imprisonment.

In the code of procedure we think that it will be proper to provide that the power of awarding this penalty shall be given, not to the ordinary tribunals, but to the official superiors of the offender. Thus, if a subordinate officer employed in the collection of revenue should incur this penalty, it will be imposed by the collector, and the appeal will probably be to the Board of Revenue. If an officer employed to execute the process of a Zillah Court should neglect his duty, the fine will be imposed by the Zillah judge, and the appeal will probably be to the Sudder Court. If the offence should be committed by a Tide-waiter, the Collector of Customs for the port will probably impose the penalty, and the appeal will be to the Board of Customs. These instances we give merely as illustrations of what, at present, appears to us desirable. The details of this part of the law of procedure cannot be arranged without much consideration and inquiry.

One important question still remains to be considered. We are of opinion that we have provided sufficient punishment for the public servant who receives a bribe. But it may be doubted whether we have provided sufficient punishment for the person who offers it. The person who, without any demand express or implied on the part of a public servant, volunteers an offer of a bribe, and induces that public servant to accept it, will be punishable under the general rule contained in clause 88 as an instigator. But the person who complies with a demand, however signified, on the part of a public servant, cannot be considered as guilty of instigating that public servant to receive a bribe. We do not propose that such a person shall be liable to any punishment, and, as this omission may possibly appear censurable to many persons, we are desirous to explain our reasons.

In all states of society the receiving of a bribe is a bad action, and may properly be made punishable. But whether the giving of a bribe ought or ought not to be punished, is a question which does not admit of a short and general answer. There are countries in which the giver of a bribe ought to be more severely punished than the receiver. There are countries, on the other hand, in which the giving of a bribe may be what it is not desirable to visit with any punishment. In a country situated like England, the giver of a bribe is generally far more deserving of punishment than the receiver. The giver is generally the tempter, the receiver is the tempted. The giver is generally rich, powerful, well educated; the receiver, needy and ignorant. The giver is under no apprehension of suffering any injury if he refuses to give. It is not by fear, but by ambition, that he is generally induced to part with his money. Such a person is a proper subject of punishment. But there are countries where the case is widely different; where men give bribes to magistrates from exactly the same feeling which leads them to give their purses to robbers or to pay ransom to pirates; where men give bribes because no man can, without a bribe, obtain common justice. In such countries we think that the giving of bribes is not a proper subject of punishment. It would be as absurd, in such a state of society, to reproach the giver of a bribe with corrupting the virtue of public servants, as it would be to say that the traveller who delivers his money when a pistol is held to his breast corrupts the virtue of the highwayman.

We would by no means be understood to say that India, under the British Government, is in a state answering to this last description. Still we fear it is undeniable that corruption does prevail to a great extent among the lower class of public functionaries; that the power which those functionaries possess renders them formidable to the body of the people; that in the great majority of cases the receiver of the bribe is really the tempter, and that the giver of the bribe is really acting in self-defence.

Under these circumstances, we are strongly of opinion that it would be unjust and cruel to punish the giving of a bribe in any case in which it could not be proved that the giver had really by his instigations corrupted the virtue of a public servant, who, unless temptation had been put in his way, would have acted uprightly.

NOTE (F).

ON THE CHAPTER OF CONTEMPTS OF THE LAWFUL AUTHORITY OF PUBLIC SERVANTS.

WE were at first disposed to have one chapter for contempts of the lawful authority of Courts of Justice, another for contempts of the lawful authority of Officers of Revenue, and a third for contempts of the lawful authority of Officers of Police. But we soon found that these three chapters would be almost the same, word for word. It appeared to us also that, in the existing state of the civil administration of India, the separation which we were at first inclined to make would produce nothing but perplexity. The functions of Magistrate and Collector are very frequently united in the same person; and that person is perpetually called upon, both as Magistrate and Collector, to perform acts which are judicial in their nature, to try offenders, and to decide litigated questions of civil right. While the division of labour between the different departments of the public service is so imperfect, it would be idle to make nice distinctions between those departments in the penal code.

In order to frame this chapter, we went carefully through the existing regulations of the three presidencies, and extracted the numerous penal provisions which are intended to enforce obedience to the lawful authority of different classes of public servants. Having collected these provisions, and discarded a very few which we thought obviously unreasonable or superfluous, we proceeded to analyse the rest.

It is possible that our analysis may be imperfect; and it is highly probable that the punishments which we propose may require some modification. It will be seen that we propose the same punishment for all the offences which fall, in our analysis, under the same head. For example; one head is the omitting to obey the lawful summons of a public servant. For this offence we have only one punishment; and this punishment will be applicable alike to the witness who omits to obey the lawful summons of the Court of Sudder Dewanny Adawlut, to the witness who omits to obey the lawful summons of a moonsiff, to the putwarree who in Bengal omits to obey the lawful summons of the Collector, to the ryot who in the Madras Presidency omits to obey the lawful summons of the Collector, to the trader who in the same presidency omits to attend a meeting lawfully convened for the distribution of the Vizabuddy. In the same manner we propose one punishment for the captain of a ship in the Hooghly who illegally refuses to admit a custom-house officer on board, for a land-

holder who refuses to admit a surveyor lawfully com-
missioned by the Collector to measure land, for a
distiller who refuses to admit the proper officer to
examine his distillery. Again, we propose the same
punishment for the person who resists the taking of
goods in execution under a decree of a Court of
Justice, for the person who resists the taking of
property by way of distress for arrears of revenue,
for the person who resists the seizure of salt by lawful
authority, for the person who resists the seizure of a
boat in default of toll by lawful authority, for the
person who resists the seizure of smuggled goods by
lawful authority.

We are sensible that there may be reasons which
have escaped us for making distinctions in punishment between offences which in our classification fall
under the same head. But it is impossible to find
in any single person, or in any small body of persons, so extensive and minute a knowledge of every
province of India, and of every department of the
public service, as would be a security against errors
of this description. We have no doubt that if his
Lordship in Council directs the code to be published
for general information, valuable suggestions will be
received from servants of the Company in different
parts of India, and that those suggestions will enable
the Government to modify the provisions which we
propose, by introducing proper aggravations and
mitigations.

The only provision which appears to us to require
any further explanation is that which is contained
in clause 182.

We have, to the best of our ability, framed laws
against acts which ought to be repressed at all times
and places, or at times and places which it is in our
power to define. But there are acts which at one
time and place are perfectly innocent, and which at
another time or place are proper subjects of punish-

ment; nor is it always possible for the legislator to say at what time or at what place such acts ought to be punishable.

Thus it may happen that a religious procession which is in itself perfectly legal, and which, while it passes through many quarters of a town, is perfectly harmless, cannot without great risk of tumult and outrage be suffered to turn down a particular street inhabited by persons who hold the ceremony in abhorrence, and whose passions are excited by being forced to witness it. Again, there are many Hindoo rites which in Hindoo temples and religious assemblies the law tolerates, but which could not with propriety be exhibited in a place which English gentlemen and ladies were in the habit of frequenting for purposes of exercise. Again, at a particular season hydrophobia may be common among the dogs at a particular place, and it may be highly advisable that all people at that place should keep their dogs strictly confined. Again, there may be a particular place in a town which the people are in the habit of using as a receptacle for filth. In general this practice may do no harm, but an unhealthy season may arrive when it may be dangerous to the health of the population, and under such circumstances it is evidently desirable that no person should be allowed to add to the nuisance. It is evident that it is utterly impossible for the legislature to mark out the route of all the religious processions in India, to specify all the public walks frequented by English ladies and gentlemen, to foresee in what months and in what places hydrophobia will be common among dogs, or when a particular dunghill may become dangerous to the health of a town. It is equally evident that it would be unjust to punish a person who cannot be proved to have acted with bad intentions for doing to-day what yesterday was a perfectly innocent act, or for doing in one street what it would be perfectly innocent to do in another street, without giving him some notice.

What we propose, therefore, is to empower the local authorities to forbid acts which these authorities consider as dangerous to the public tranquillity, health, safety or convenience, and to make it an offence in a person to do anything which that person knows to be so forbidden, and which may endanger the public tranquillity, health, safety or convenience. It will be observed that we do not give to the local authorities the power of arbitrarily making anything an offence; for unless the Court before which the person who disobeys the order is tried shall be of opinion that he has done something tending to endanger the public tranquillity, health, safety or convenience, he will be liable to no punishment. The effect of the order of the local authority will be merely to deprive the person who knowingly disobeys the order of the plea that he had no bad intentions. He will not be permitted to allege that if he has caused harm, or risk of harm, it was without his knowledge.

Thus, if in a town where no order for the chaining up of dogs has been made, A. suffers his dog to run about loose, A. will be liable to no punishment for any mischief which the animal may do, unless it can be shown that A. knew the animal to be dangerous. But if an order for confining dogs has been issued, and if A. knew of that order, it will be no defence for him to allege, and even to prove, that he believed his dog to be perfectly harmless. If the Court think that A.'s disobedience has caused harm, or risk of harm, A. will be liable to punishment. On the other hand, if the Court think that there was no danger, and that the local order was a foolish one, A. will not be liable to punishment.

We see some objections to the way in which we have framed this part of the law; but we are unable to frame it better. On the one hand, it is, as we have shown, absolutely necessary to have some local rules which shall not require the sanction of the legislature. On the other hand, we are sensible that there is the greatest reason to apprehend much petty tyranny and vexation from such rules; and this although the framers of those rules may be very excellent and able men. There is scarcely any disposition in a ruler more prejudicial to the happiness of the people than a meddling disposition. Yet, experience shows us that it is a disposition which is often found in company with the best intentions, with great activity and energy, and with a sincere regard for the interest of the community. A public servant of more than ordinary zeal and industry, unless he have very much more than ordinary judgment, is the very man who is likely to harass the people under his care with needless restrictions. We have, therefore, thought it necessary to provide that no person should be punished merely for disobeying a local order, unless it be made to appear that the disobedience has been attended with evil, or risk of evil. Thus no person will be punished for disobeying an idle and vexatious order.

The mode of promulgating these orders belongs to the code of procedure, which will of course contain such provisions as may be required for the purpose of enabling the Government to exercise a constant and efficient control over its local officers.

NOTE (G).

ON THE CHAPTER OF OFFENCES RELATING TO PUBLIC JUSTICE.

MANY offences which interfere with the administration of justice are sufficiently provided for in other

chapters, particularly in the chapter relating to contempts of the lawful authority of public servants.
There still remain, however, some offences of that
description for which the present chapter is intended
to provide.

The rules which we propose touching the offence
of attempting to impose on a Court of Justice by
false evidence differ from those of the English law,
and of the codes which we have had an opportunity
of consulting.

It appears to us, in the first place, that the
offence which we have designated as the fabricating
of false evidence is not punished with adequate
severity under any of the systems to which we refer.
This may perhaps be because the offence, in its
aggravated forms, is not one of very frequent occurrence in western countries. It is notorious, however,
that in this country the practice is exceedingly common, and for obvious reasons. The mere assertion
of a witness commands far less respect in India than
in Europe, or in the United States of America. In
countries in which the standard of morality is high,
direct evidence is generally considered as the best
evidence. In England assuredly it is so considered,
and its value, as compared with the value of circumstantial evidence, is perhaps overrated by the great
majority of the population. But in India we have
reason to believe that the case is different. A judge,
after he has heard a transaction related in the same
manner by several persons who declare themselves
to be eye-witnesses of it, and of whom he knows no
harm, often feels a considerable doubt whether the
whole, from beginning to end, be not a fiction, and
is glad to meet with some circumstance, however
slight, which supports the story, and which is not
likely to have been devised for the purpose of sup-
porting the story.

Hence, in England, a person who wishes to impose on a Court of Justice knows that he is likely to succeed best by perjury, or subornation of perjury. But in India, where a judge is generally on his guard against direct false evidence, a more artful mode of imposition is frequently employed. A lie is often conveyed to a Court, not by means of witnesses, but by means of circumstances, precisely because circumstances are less likely to lie than witnesses. These two modes of imposing on the tribunals appear to us to be equally wicked, and equally mischievous. It will indeed be harder to bring home to an offender the fabricating of false evidence than the giving of false evidence. But wherever the former offence is brought home, we would punish it as severely as the latter. If A. puts a purse in Z.'s bag, with the intention of causing Z. to be convicted as a thief, we would deal with A. as if he had sworn that he saw Z. take a purse. If A. conceals in Z.'s house a paper written in imitation of Z.'s hand, and purporting to be a plan of a treasonable conspiracy, we would deal with A. as if he had sworn that he was present at a meeting of conspirators at which Z. presided.

The exception in clause 190 is in strict conformity with this principle. We propose to treat the giving of false evidence and the fabricating of false evidence in exactly the same way. We have no punishment for false evidence given by a person when on his trial for an offence, though we conceive that such a person ought to be interrogated. The grounds on which this part of the law is founded will shortly be submitted to Government in our report on the law of evidence. As we do not propose to punish a prisoner for lying at the bar in order to escape punishment, so we do not propose to punish him for fabricating evidence with the view of escaping punishment, unless he also contemplated some injury to others as likely to be produced by the evidence so fabricated.

If A. stabs Z., and afterwards on his trial denies that he stabbed Z., we do not propose to punish A. as a giver of false evidence. And on the same principle, if A., after having stabbed Z., in order to escape detection, disposes Z.'s body in such a manner as is likely to lead a jury to think the death accidental, we do not propose to punish A. as the fabricator of false evidence.

It appears to us that the offence of attempting to impose on a Court of Justice by false evidence is an offence of which there are numerous grades, some of which may be easily defined. The authors of the French code have not overlooked these circumstances, though they have not, in our opinion, marked the gradations very successfully. The English law makes no distinction whatever between the man who has attempted to take away his neighbour's life by false swearing, and the man who has strained his conscience to give an undeserved good character to a boy accused of a petty theft. The former is punished far too leniently; the latter perhaps too severely.

The giving of false evidence must always be a grave offence. But few points in penal legislation seem to us clearer than that the law ought to make a distinction between that kind of false evidence which produces great evils, and that kind of false evidence which produces comparatively slight evils.

As the ordinary punishment of false evidence, we propose imprisonment for a term of not more than seven years, nor less than one year. If the false evidence is given or fabricated with intent to cause a person to be convicted of a grave offence not capital, we propose that the person who gives or fabricates such evidence may be punished with the punishment of the offence which he has attempted to fix on another. If the false evidence be given or fabricated with the intention of causing death, we propose to punish it in the same manner in which we propose

to punish the worst attempts to murder. If such
false evidence actually causes death, the person who
has given or fabricated it falls under the definition
of murder, and is liable to capital punishment. In
this last point, the law, as we have framed it, agrees
with the old law of England, which, though in our
opinion just and reasonable, has become obsolete.

We think this the proper place to notice an
offence which bears a close affinity to that of giving
false evidence, and which we leave for the present
unpunished, only on account of the defective state
of the existing law of procedure,—we mean the
crime of deliberately and knowingly asserting falsehoods in pleading. Our opinions on this subject
may startle persons accustomed to that boundless
license which the English law allows to mendacity
in suitors. On what principle that license is allowed
we must confess ourselves unable to discover. A.
lends Z. money; Z. repays it. A. brings an action
against Z. for the money, and affirms in his declaration that he lent the money, and has never been re-
paid. On the trial A.'s receipt is produced. It is
not doubted. A. himself cannot deny that he asserted
a falsehood in his declaration. Ought A. to enjoy
impunity? Again: Z. brings an action against A.
for a debt which is really due. A.'s plea is a positive
averment that he owes Z. nothing. The case comes
to trial; and it is proved by overwhelming evidence
that the debt is a just debt. A. does not even attempt
a defence. Ought A. in this case to enjoy impunity?
If, in either of the cases which we have stated, A.
were to suborn witnesses to support the lie which he
has put on the pleadings, every one of these witnesses,
as well as A. himself, would be liable to severe
punishment. But false evidence in the vast majority
of cases springs out of false pleading, and would be
almost entirely banished from the Courts if false
pleading could be prevented.

It appears to us that all the marks which indicate that an act is a proper subject for legal punishment meet in the act of false pleading. That false pleading always does some harm is plain. Even when it is not followed up by false evidence it always delays justice. That false pleading produces any compensating good to atone for this harm has never, as far as we know, been even alleged. That false pleading will be more common if it is unpunished than if it is punished appears as certain as that rape, theft, embezzlement, would, if unpunished, be more common than they now are. It is evident also that there will be no more difficulty in trying a charge of false pleading than in trying a charge of false evidence. The fact that a statement has been made in pleading will generally be more clearly proved than the fact that a statement has been made in evidence. The falsehood of a statement made in pleading will be proved in exactly the same manner in which the falsehood of a statement made in evidence is proved. Whether the accused person knew that he was pleading falsely, the Courts will determine on the same evidence on which they now determine whether a witness knew that he was giving false testimony.

We have as yet spoken only of the direct injury produced to honest litigants by false pleading. But this injury appears to us to be only a part, and perhaps not the greatest part, of the evil engendered by the practice. If there be any place where truth ought to be held in peculiar honour, from which falsehood ought to be driven with peculiar severity, in which exaggerations, which elsewhere would be applauded as the innocent sport of the fancy, or pardoned as the natural effect of excited passion, ought to be discouraged, that place is a Court of Justice. We object, therefore, to the use of legal fictions, even when the meaning of those fictions is generally understood, and we have done our best to

exclude them from this code. But that a person
should come before a Court, should tell that Court
premeditated and circumstantial lies for the purpose
of preventing or postponing the settlement of a just
demand, and that by so doing he should incur no
punishment whatever, seems to us to be a state of
things to which nothing but habit could reconcile
wise and honest men. Public opinion is vitiated by
the vicious state of the law. Men who, in any other
circumstances, would shrink from falsehood, have no
scruple about setting up false pleas against just
demands. There is one place, and only one, where
deliberate untruths, told with the intent to injure,
are not considered as discreditable, and that place is
a Court of Justice. Thus the authority of the tribunals operates to lower the standard of morality,
and to diminish the esteem in which veracity is held;
and the very place which ought to be kept sacred
from misrepresentations, such as would elsewhere be
venial, becomes the only place where it is considered as
idle scrupulosity to shrink from deliberate falsehood.

We consider a law for punishing false pleading
as indispensably necessary to the expeditious and
satisfactory administration of justice, and we trust
that the passing of such a law will speedily follow the
appearance of the code of procedure. We do not, as
we have stated, at present propose such a law, because, while the system of pleading remains unaltered in the Courts of this country, and particularly
in the Courts established by Royal Charter, it will be
difficult, or to speak more properly, impossible to
enforce such a law. We have, therefore, gone no
further than to provide a punishment for the frivolous
and vexatious instituting of civil suits, a practice
which, even while the existing systems of procedure
remain unaltered, may, without any inconvenience,
be made an offence. The law on the subject of false
evidence will, as it appears to us, render unnecessary

any law for punishing the frivolous and vexatious preferring of criminal charges.

No other part of this chapter appears to require comment.

NOTE (H).

ON OFFENCES RELATING TO THE REVENUE.

IN order to frame this chapter, we took a course similar to that which we took with the chapter relating to contempts of the lawful authority of public servants. We went carefully through the revenue laws of the three presidencies, extracted the penal clauses, analysed them, and reduced them to a small number of general heads.

His Lordship in Council will perceive that we have not thought it proper to insert in the code any provision for the confiscation of property on the ground of a breach of the revenue laws, and that we leave the existing rules on that subject untouched. We have done so, because it does not appear to us that such confiscation is in strictness a punishment. It has indeed much in common with punishment; but it appears to us that there is a marked distinction, and that confiscation of the sort which is authorised in many parts of the regulations of the three presidencies would, considered in the light of a punishment, be anomalous and indefensible. It is a proceeding directed, not against the person who has broken the law, but against the thing with respect to which the law has been broken. It is not necessary that any misconduct should be proved, that any accusation should be brought, that any particular individual should be in the contemplation of the authority which directs the confiscation. Nay, the revenue laws authorise confiscation, not only in cases where misconduct is

not proved, but in cases where it is proved that there
has been no misconduct in any quarter; and, where
there has been misconduct, those laws authorise the
confiscation of the property of a person who is proved
to have had no share in the misconduct.

To give a single example: if tobacco be found
in the island of Bombay after the time at which it
ought to be exported thence, it is confiscated, together with the receptacles which contain it, the
substances in which it is packed, and the carriages
and animals which are employed to convey it. This,
which is a fair specimen of revenue laws respecting
confiscation, is evidently objectionable, considered
as a penal law. The carriages, the animals, the
vessels, the tobacco itself, may all be the property
of persons who are not in the least to blame. Indeed,
we know that under this law the boxes of gentlemen
have repeatedly been seized, because the servants
who packed them had concealed tobacco in the
baggage. Such a law, put into the form of a penal
provision, would be too grotesque to be a subject of
serious argument. It would, in the phraseology of
our code, run thus: " If any person places contraband tobacco in the baggage of any other person, the
person in whose baggage such contraband tobacco is
placed shall be punished with the confiscation of such
baggage." And the following illustration would
make the law, if possible, still more ridiculous :
" Contraband tobacco is hidden in A.'s baggage, by
A.'s servant, without A.'s knowledge, and contrary
to A.'s express command. A. has committed the
offence defined in this clause."

It is evident, therefore, that this law, and many
other laws of the same kind, must be defended on
principles quite different from those on which penal
legislation ought to be conducted. They must be
defended, not as being penal laws directed against
the guilty, but rather as being sharp and stringent

laws of civil procedure which are intended to enable the Government to obtain its due with speed and certainty, at the cost whether of the guilty or of the innocent. Viewing them in this light, and knowing as we know that they are greatly mitigated in practice by the lenity of the Executive Government, we consider them as justifiable; but we are decidedly of opinion that they would be out of place in a penal code.

NOTE (I).

ON THE CHAPTER OF OFFENCES RELATING TO COIN.

MOST of the provisions in this chapter appear sufficiently intelligible without any explanation.

We have proposed that the Government of India should follow the general practice of Governments in punishing more severely the counterfeiting of its own coin than the counterfeiting of foreign coin. It appears to us peculiarly advisable, under the present circumstances of India, to make this distinction. It is much to be wished that the Company's currency may supersede the numerous coinages which are issued from a crowd of mints in the dominions of the petty princes of India. It has appeared to us that this object may be in some degree promoted by the law as we have framed it. That coinage, the purity of which is guarded by the most rigorous penalties, is likely to be the most pure; and that coinage which is likely to be the most pure will be the most readily taken in the course of business.

It is not very probable that any person in this country will employ himself in making counterfeit sovereigns or shillings; but should so improbable an event occur, we think that the King's coin should have the same protection which is given to the coin of the local Government. It may perhaps be thought that

in proposing laws for the protection of the King's
coin, we have departed from the principle which we
laid down in our note on the law of offences against
the State, and that we should have acted more con-
sistently in leaving the British currency to the care
of the British Legislature.   It appears to us, however, that the offence of coining, though, in an arbitrary classification, it may be called by the technical
name of treason, is in substance an offence against
property and trade, that it is an offence of very
nearly the same kind with the forging of a bank note,
and that it would be an offence of exactly the same
kind if the bank note, like the notes of the Bank of
England formerly, were in all cases legal tender, or
if the coin, like the Company's gold mohur at present,
were not legal tender.   We do not therefore conceive
that in proposing a law for punishing the counterfeiting of the King's coin, we are proposing a law
which can reasonably be said to affect any of the
royal prerogatives.

The distinction which we propose to make (see
clauses 241 and 242) between two different classes of
utterers is marked in the French code ; and it is so
obviously agreeable to reason and justice that we are
surprised that, having been marked in that code, it
should not have been adopted by Mr. Livingston.
We are glad to perceive that the code of Bombay
makes this distinction.

An utterer by profession, an utterer who is the
agent employed by the coiner to bring counterfeit
coin into circulation, is guilty of a very high offence.
Such an utterer stands to the coiner in a relation not
very different from that in which a habitual receiver
of stolen goods stands to a thief.   He makes coining
a far less perilous and a far more lucrative pursuit
than it would otherwise be.   He passes his life in
the systematic violation of the law, and in the systematic practice of fraud in one of its most pernicious

forms. He is one of the most mischievous, and is
likely to be one of the most depraved of criminals.
But a casual utterer, an utterer who is not an agent
for bringing counterfeit coin into circulation, but who,
having heedlessly received a bad rupee in the course
of his business, takes advantage of the heedlessness of
the next person with whom he deals to pay that bad
rupee away, is an offender of a very different class.
He is undoubtedly guilty of a dishonest act, but of
one of the most venial of dishonest acts. It is an act
which proceeds not from greediness for unlawful
gain, but from a wish to avoid, by unlawful means
it is true, what to a poor man may be a severe loss.
It is an act which has no tendency to facilitate or
encourage the operations of the coiner. It is an
occasional act, an act which does not imply that the
person who commits it is a person of lawless habits.
We think, therefore, that the offence of a casual
utterer is perhaps the least heinous of all the offences
into which fraud enters.

We considered whether it would be advisable to
make it an offence in a person to have in his possession at one time a certain number of counterfeit
coins, without being able to explain satisfactorily
how he came by them. It did not, after much discussion, appear to us advisable to recommend this or
any similar provision. We entertain strong objections to the practice of making circumstances which
are in truth only evidence of an offence part of the
definition of an offence; nor do we see any reason
for departing in this case from our general rule.

Whether a person who is possessed of bad money
knows the money to be bad, and whether, knowing
it to be bad, he intends to put it in circulation, are
questions to be decided by the tribunals according to
the circumstances of the case, circumstances of which
the mere number of the pieces is only one and may
be one of the least important. A few bad rupees

which should evidently be fresh from the stamp would be stronger evidence than a greater number of bad rupees which appeared to have been in circulation for years. A few bad rupees, all obviously coined with the same die, would be stronger evidence than a greater number obviously coined with different dies. A few bad rupees placed by themselves, and unmixed with good ones, would be far stronger evidence than a much larger number which might be detected in a large mass of treasure.

Note (J).

ON THE CHAPTER OF OFFENCES RELATING TO RELIGION AND CASTE.

THE principle on which this chapter has been framed is a principle on which it would be desirable that all Governments should act, but from which the British Government in India cannot depart without risking the dissolution of society; it is this, that every man should be suffered to profess his own religion, and that no man should be suffered to insult the religion of another.

The question whether insults offered to a religion ought to be visited with punishment does not appear to us at all to depend on the question whether that religion be true or false. The religion may be false, but the pain which such insults give to the professors of that religion is real. It is often, as the most superficial observation may convince us, as real a pain and as acute a pain as is caused by almost any offence against the person, against property or against character. Nor is there any compensating good whatsoever to be set off against this pain. Discussion, indeed, tends to elicit truth. But insults have no such tendency. They can be employed just as easily against the purest faith as against the most monstrous superstition. It is easier to argue against falsehood than against truth. But it is as easy to pull down or defile the temples of truth as those of falsehood. It is as easy to molest with ribaldry and clamour men assembled for purposes of pious and rational worship, as men engaged in the most absurd ceremonies. Such insults, when directed against erroneous opinions, seldom have any other effect than to fix those opinions deeper, and to give a character of peculiar ferocity to theological dissension. Instead of eliciting truth they only inflame fanaticism.

All these considerations apply with peculiar force to India. There is perhaps no country in which the Government has so much to apprehend from religious excitement among the people. The Christians are numerically a very small minority of the population, and in possession of all the highest posts in the Government, in the tribunals, and in the army. Under their rule are placed millions of Mahomedans, of differing sects, but all strongly attached to the fundamental articles of the Mahomedan creed, and tens of millions of Hindoos, strongly attached to doctrines and rites which Christians and Mahomedans join in reprobating. Such a state of things is pregnant with dangers which can only be averted by a firm adherence to the true principles of toleration. On those principles the British Government has hitherto acted with eminent judgment, and with no less eminent success; and on those principles we propose to frame this part of the penal code.

We have provided a punishment of great severity for the intentional destroying or defiling of places of worship, or of objects held sacred by any class of persons. No offence in the whole code is so likely to lead to tumult, to sanguinary outrage, and even to armed insurrection. The slaughter of a cow in a sacred place at Benares in 1809 caused violent tumult, attended with considerable loss of life. The pollution of a mosque at Bangalore was attended with consequences still more lamentable and alarming. We have therefore empowered the Courts, in cases of this description, to pass a very severe sentence on the offender.

The provisions which we have made for the purpose of protecting assemblies held for religious worship, and of guarding from intentional insult the rites of sepulture and the remains of the dead, do not appear to require any explanation or defence.

The intentional depriving a Hindoo of his caste by assault or by deception is not at present an offence in any part of India, though it may be a ground for a civil action. It appears to us, however, that an injury so wanton, an injury which indicates so bad a feeling in the person who causes it, and which gives so much pain and excites so much resentment in the sufferer, is as proper a subject for penal legislation as most of the acts which are made punishable by this code. We have, therefore, made it an offence. The rendering the food of a Hindoo useless to him by causing it to be in what he considers as a polluted state is an injury of the same kind, though comparatively venial. We propose to make it an offence, but not to deal with it severely, unless it should be repeatedly committed by the same person.

In framing clause 282, we had two objects in view. We wish to allow all fair latitude to religious discussion, and at the same time to prevent the professors of any religion from offering, under the pretext of such discussion, intentional insults to what is held sacred by others. We do not conceive that any person can be justified in wounding with deliberate intention the religious feelings of his neighbours by words, gesture, or exhibitions. A warm expression dropped in the heat of controversy, or an argument urged by a person, not for the purpose of insulting and annoying the professors of a different creed, but in good faith for the purpose of vindicating his own, will not fall under the definition contained in this clause.

Clause 283 is intended to prevent such practices as those known among the natives by the names of Dhurna and Traga. Such acts are now punishable by law, and it is unnecessary to adduce any argument for the purpose of showing that they ought to be so.

Note (K).

ON THE CHAPTER OF ILLICIT ENTRANCE INTO AND ILLICIT RESIDENCE IN THE TERRITORIES OF THE EAST INDIA COMPANY.

THE Indian Legislature is required by the Act of Parliament 3 and 4 Wm. IV. cap. 85, section 84, "as soon as conveniently may be, to make laws or regulations providing for the prevention or punishment of the illicit entrance into or residence in the said territories of persons not authorised to enter or reside therein."

We have, therefore, thought it our duty to insert in the penal code provisions for the purpose of carrying the intentions of Parliament into effect.

Note (L).

ON OFFENCES RELATING TO THE PRESS.

THE penal provisions contained in this chapter are taken from the Act of the Governor-General of India in Council, No. 11, of 1835.

Sufficient provision appears to us to have been made in other parts of the code, particularly by clause 195, for the punishment of the offence mentioned in the last section of the Act to which we have referred.

NOTE (M).

ON OFFENCES AGAINST THE BODY.

THE first class of offences against the body consists of those offences which affect human life ; and highest in this first class stand those offences which fall under the definition of voluntary culpable homicide.

This important part of the law appears to us to require fuller explanation than almost any other.

The first point to which we wish to call the attention of his Lordship in Council is the expression " omits what he is legally bound to do " in the definition of voluntary culpable homicide. These words, or other words tantamount in effect, frequently recur in the code. We think this the most convenient place for explaining the reason which has led us so often to employ them ; for if that reason shall appear to be sufficient in cases in which human life is concerned, it will *à fortiori* be sufficient in other cases.

Early in the progress of the code it became necessary for us to consider the following question : When acts are made punishable on the ground that those acts produce, or are intended to produce, or are known to be likely to produce, certain evil effects, to what extent ought omissions which produce, which are intended to produce, or which are known to be likely to produce, the same evil effects to be made punishable?

Two things we take to be evident ; first, that some of these omissions ought to be punished in exactly the same manner in which acts are punished ;

secondly, that all these omissions ought not to be punished. It will hardly be disputed that a gaoler who voluntarily causes the death of a prisoner by omitting to supply that prisoner with food, or a nurse who voluntarily causes the death of an infant entrusted to her care by omitting to take it out of a tub of water into which it has fallen, ought to be treated as guilty of murder. On the other hand, it will hardly be maintained that a man should be punished as a murderer because he omitted to relieve a beggar, even though there might be the clearest proof that the death of the beggar was the effect of this omission, and that the man who omitted to give the alms knew that the death of the beggar was likely to be the effect of the omission. It will hardly be maintained that a surgeon ought to be treated as a murderer for refusing to go from Calcutta to Meerut to perform an operation, although it should be absolutely certain that this surgeon was the only person in India who could perform it, and that if it were not performed, the person who required it would die. It is difficult to say whether a penal code which should put no omissions on the same footing with acts, or a penal code which should put all omissions on the same footing with acts, would produce consequences more absurd and revolting. There is no country in which either of these principles is adopted. Indeed, it is hard to conceive how, if either were adopted, society could be held together.

It is plain, therefore, that a middle course must be taken; but it is not easy to determine what that middle course ought to be. The absurdity of the two extremes is obvious. But there are innumerable intermediate points; and wherever the line of demarcation may be drawn, it will, we fear, include some cases which we might wish to exempt, and will exempt some which we might wish to include.

Mr. Livingston's code provides, that a person

shall be considered as guilty of homicide who omits to save life, which he could save "without personal danger or pecuniary loss." This rule appears to us to be open to serious objection. There may be extreme inconvenience without the smallest personal danger, or the smallest risk of pecuniary loss, as in the case which we lately put of a surgeon summoned from Calcutta to Meerut to perform an operation. He may be offered such a fee that he would be a gainer by going. He may have no ground to apprehend that he should run any greater personal risk by journeying to the Upper Provinces than by continuing to reside in Bengal. But he is about to proceed to Europe immediately, or he expects some members of his family by the next ship, and wishes to be at the presidency to receive them. He, therefore, refuses to go. Surely, he ought not, for so refusing, to be treated as a murderer. It would be somewhat inconsistent to punish one man for not staying three months in India to save the life of another, and to leave wholly unpunished a man who, enjoying ample wealth, should refuse to disburse an anna to save the life of another. Again, it appears to us that it may be fit to punish a person as a murderer for causing death by omitting an act which cannot be performed without personal danger or pecuniary loss. A parent may be unable to procure food for an infant without money. Yet the parent, if he has the means, is bound to furnish the infant with food, and if, by omitting to do so, he voluntarily causes its death, he may with propriety be treated as a murderer. A nurse hired to attend a person suffering from an infectious disease cannot perform her duty without running some risk of infection. Yet if she deserts the sick person, and thus voluntarily cause his death, we should be disposed to treat her as a murderer.

We pronounce with confidence, therefore, that

the line ought not to be drawn where Mr. Livingston
has drawn it. But it is with great diffidence that we
bring forward our own proposition. It is open to objections: cases may be put in which it will operate
too severely, and cases in which it will operate too
leniently; but we are unable to devise a better.

What we propose is this, that where acts are
made punishable on the ground that they have
caused, or have been intended to cause, or have been
known to be likely to cause, a certain evil effect,
omissions which have caused, which have been intended to cause, or which have been known to be
likely to cause the same effect, shall be punishable
in the same manner, provided that such omissions
were, on other grounds, illegal. An omission is
illegal (see clause 28) if it be an offence, if it be a
breach of some direction of law, or if it be such a
wrong as would be a good ground for a civil action.

We cannot defend this rule better than by giving
a few illustrations of the way in which it will operate.
A. omits to give Z. food, and by that omission voluntarily causes Z.'s death. Is this murder? Under
our rule it is murder if A. was Z.'s gaoler, directed
by the law to furnish Z. with food. It is murder if
Z. was the infant child of A., and had therefore a
legal right to sustenance, which right a Civil Court
would enforce against A. It is murder if Z. was a
bedridden invalid, and A. a nurse hired to feed Z.
It is murder if A. was detaining Z. in unlawful confinement, and had thus contracted (see clause 338) a
legal obligation to furnish Z., during the continuance
of the confinement, with necessaries. It is not
murder if Z. is a beggar, who has no other claim on
A. than that of humanity.

A. omits to tell Z. that a river is swollen so high
that Z. cannot safely attempt to ford it, and by this
omission voluntarily causes Z.'s death. This is
murder, if A. is a peon stationed by authority to

warn travellers from attempting to ford the river. It is murder if A. is a guide who had contracted to conduct Z. It is not murder if A. is a person on whom Z. has no other claim than that of humanity.

A savage dog fastens on Z. A. omits to call off the dog, knowing that if the dog be not called off, it is likely that Z. will be killed. Z. is killed. This is murder in A., if the dog belonged to A., inasmuch as his omission to take proper order with the dog is illegal. (Clause 273.) But if A. be a mere passer-by, it is not murder.

We are sensible that in some of the cases which we have put, our rule may appear too lenient; but we do not think that it can be made more severe without disturbing the whole order of society. It is true that the man who, having abundance of wealth, suffers a fellow creature to die of hunger at his feet is a bad man, a worse man, probably, than many of those for whom we have provided very severe punishment. But we are unable to see where, if we make such a man legally punishable, we can draw the line. If the rich man who refuses to save a beggar's life at the cost of a little copper is a murderer, is the poor man just one degree above beggary also to be a murderer if he omits to invite the beggar to partake his hard-earned rice? Again, if the rich man is a murderer for refusing to save the beggar's life at the cost of a little copper, is he also to be a murderer if he refuses to save the beggar's life at the cost of a thousand rupees? Suppose A. to be fully convinced that nothing can save Z.'s life unless Z. leave Bengal and reside a year at the Cape: is A., however wealthy he may be, to be punished as a murderer because he will not, at his own expense, send Z. to the Cape? Surely not. Yet it will be difficult to say on what principle we can punish A. for not spending an anna to save Z.'s life, and leave him unpunished for not spending a thousand rupees to save Z.'s life. The distinction between a legal and an illegal omission is perfectly plain and intelligible ; but the distinction between a large and a small sum of money is very far from being so, not to say that a sum which is small to one man is large to another.

The same argument holds good in the case of the ford. It is true that none but a very depraved man would suffer another to be drowned when he might prevent it by a word. But if we punish such a man, where are we to stop ? How much exertion are we to require ? Is a person to be a murderer if he does not go fifty yards through the sun of Bengal at noon in May in order to caution a traveller against a swollen river ? Is he to be a murderer if he does not go a hundred yards ?—if he does not go a mile ?— if he does not go ten ? What is the precise amount of trouble and inconvenience which he is to endure ? The distinction between the guide who is bound to conduct the traveller as safely as he can, and a mere stranger, is a clear distinction. But the distinction between a stranger who will not give a halloo to save a man's life, and a stranger who will not run a mile to save a man's life, is very far from being equally clear.

It is, indeed, most highly desirable that men should not merely abstain from doing harm to their neighbours, but should render active services to their neighbours. In general, however, the penal law must content itself with keeping men from doing positive harm, and must leave to public opinion, and to the teachers of morality and religion, the office of furnishing men with motives for doing positive good. It is evident that to attempt to punish men by law for not rendering to others all the service which it is their duty to render to others would be preposterous. We must grant impunity to the vast majority of those omissions which a benevolent morality would pronounce reprehensible, and must content ourselves with punishing such omissions only when they are distinguished from the rest by some circumstance which marks them out as peculiarly fit objects of penal legislation. Now, no circumstance appears to us so well fitted to be the mark as the circumstance which we have selected. It will generally be found in the most atrocious cases of omission; it will scarcely ever be found in a venial case of omission; and it is more clear and certain than any other mark that has occurred to us. That there are objections to the line which we propose to draw, we have admitted. But there are objections to every line which can be drawn, and some line must be drawn.

The next point to which we wish to call the attention of his Lordship in Council is the unqualified use of the words "to cause death" in the definition of voluntary culpable homicide.

We long considered whether it would be advisable to except from this definition any description of acts or illegal omissions, on the ground that such acts or illegal omissions do not ordinarily cause death, or that they cause death very remotely. We have determined, however, to leave the clause in its present simple and comprehensive form.

There is undoubtedly a great difference between acts which cause death immediately, and acts which cause death remotely; between acts which are almost certain to cause death, and acts which cause death only under very extraordinary circumstances. But that difference, we conceive, is a matter to be considered by the tribunals when estimating the effect of the evidence in a particular case, not by the legislature in framing the general law. It will require strong evidence to prove that an act of a kind which very seldom causes death, or an act which has caused death very remotely, has actually caused death in a particular case. It will require still stronger evidence to prove that such an act was contemplated by the person who did it as likely to cause death. But if it be proved by satisfactory evidence that death has been so caused, and has been caused voluntarily, we see no reason for exempting the person who caused it from the punishment of voluntary culpable homicide.

Mr. Livingston, we observe, excepts from the definition of homicide cases in which death is produced by the effect of words on the imagination or the passions. The reasoning of that distinguished jurist has by no means convinced us that the distinction which he makes is well founded. Indeed, there are few parts of his code which appear to us to have been less happily executed than this. His words are these: " The destruction must be by the act of another; therefore self-destruction is excluded from the definition. It must be operated by some act; therefore death, although produced by the operation of words on the imagination or the passions, is not homicide. But if words are used which are calculated to produce and do produce some act which is the immediate cause of death, it is homicide. A blind man or a stranger in the dark, directed by words only to a precipice, where he falls and is killed; a direction verbally given to take a drug that it is known will prove fatal, and which has that effect, are instances of this modification of the rule."

This appears to us altogether incoherent. A. verbally directs Z. to swallow a poisonous drug; Z. swallows it, and dies; and this, says Mr. Livingston, is homicide in A. It certainly ought to be so considered. But how, on Mr. Livingston's principles, it can be so considered we do not understand. " Homicide," he says, " must be operated by an act." Where then is the act in this case? Is it the speaking of A.? Clearly not, for Mr. Livingston lays down the doctrine that speaking is not an act. Is it the swallowing by Z.? Clearly not, for the destruction of life, according to Mr. Livingston, is not homicide unless it be by the act of another, and this swallowing is an act performed by Z. himself.

The reasonable course, in our opinion, is to consider speaking as an act, and to treat A. as guilty of voluntary culpable homicide, if by speaking he has voluntarily caused Z.'s death, whether his words operated circuitously by inducing Z. to swallow poison or directly by throwing Z. into convulsions.

There will indeed be few homicides of this latter sort. It appears to us that a conviction, or even a trial, in such a case would be an event of extremely rare occurrence. There would probably not be one such trial in a century. It would be most difficult to prove to the conviction of any Court that death had really been the effect of excitement produced by words. It would be still more difficult to prove that the person who spoke the words anticipated from them an effect which, except under very peculiar circumstances, and on very peculiar constitutions, no words would produce. Still it seems to us that both these points might be made out by overwhelming evidence ; and, supposing them to be so made out, we are unable to perceive any distinction between the case of him who voluntarily causes death in this manner, and the case of him who voluntarily causes death by means of a pistol or a sword. Suppose it to be proved to the entire conviction of a Criminal Court that Z., the deceased, was in a very critical state of health ; that A., the heir to Z.'s property, had been informed by Z.'s physicians that Z.'s recovery absolutely depended on his being kept quiet in mind, and that the smallest mental excitement would endanger his life ; that A. immediately broke into Z.'s sick room, and told him a dreadful piece of intelligence, which was a pure invention ; that Z. went into fits and died on the spot ; that A. had afterwards boasted of having cleared the way for himself to a good property by this artifice. These things being fully proved, no judge could doubt that A. had voluntarily caused the death of Z. ; nor do we perceive any reason for not punishing A. in the same manner in which he would have been punished if he had mixed arsenic in Z.'s medicine.

Again, Mr. Livingston excepts from the definition of homicide the case of a person who dies of a slight wound, which, from neglect or from the application of improper remedies, has proved mortal. We see no reason for excepting such cases from the simple general rule which we propose. It will, indeed, be in general more difficult to prove that death has been caused by a scratch than by a stab which has reached the heart; and it will, in a still greater degree, be more difficult to prove that a scratch was intended to cause death than that a stab was intended to cause death; yet both these points might be fully established. Suppose such a case as the following :—It is proved that A. inflicted a slight wound on Z., a child who stood between him and a large property. It is proved that the ignorant and superstitious servants about Z. applied the most absurd remedies to the wound. It is proved that under their treatment the wound mortified, and the child died. Letters from A. to a confidant are produced. In those letters, A. congratulates himself on his skill, remarks that he could not have inflicted a more severe wound without exposing himself to be punished as a murderer, relates with exultation the mode of treatment followed by the people who have charge of Z., and boasts that he always foresaw that they would turn the slightest incision into a mortal wound. It appears to us, that if such evidence were produced, A. ought to be punished as a murderer.

Again, suppose that A. makes a deliberate attempt to commit assassination. In the presence of numbers he aims a knife at the heart of Z. But the knife glances aside, and inflicts only a slight wound. This happened in the case of Jean Chatel, of Damien, of Guiscard, and of many other assassins of the most desperate character. In such cases there is no doubt whatever as to the intention. Suppose that the person who received the wound is under the necessity of exposing himself to a moist atmosphere immediately afterwards, and that, in consequence, he is attacked with tetanus and dies. Here again, however slight the wound may have been, we are unable to perceive any good reason for not punishing A. as a murderer.

We will only add that this provision of the Code of Louisiana appears to us peculiarly ill-suited to a country in which, we have reason to fear, neglect and bad treatment are far more common than good medical treatment.

The general rule, therefore, which we propose is, that the question whether a person has by an act or illegal omission voluntarily caused death shall be left a question of evidence to be decided by the Courts, according to the circumstances of every case.

We propose that all voluntary culpable homicide shall be designated as murder, unless it fall under one of three heads. We are desirous to call the particular attention of his Lordship in Council to the law respecting the three mitigated forms of voluntary culpable homicide ; and first to the law of manslaughter.

We agree with the great mass of mankind, and with the majority of jurists, ancient and modern, in thinking that homicide committed in the sudden heat of passion, on great provocation, ought to be punished ; but that in general it ought not to be punished so severely as murder. It ought to be punished in order to teach men to entertain a peculiar respect for human life ; it ought to be punished in order to give men a motive for accustoming themselves to govern their passions ; and in some few cases for which we have made provision, we conceive that it ought to be punished with the utmost rigour.

In general, however, we would not visit homicide committed in violent passion, which had been suddenly provoked, with the highest penalties of the law. We think that to treat a person guilty of such homicide as we should treat a murderer would be a highly inexpedient course,—a course which would shock the universal feeling of mankind, and would engage the public sympathy on the side of the delinquent against the law.

His Lordship in Council will remark one important distinction between the law as we have framed it and some other systems. Neither the English law nor the French code extends any indulgence to homicide which is the effect of anger excited by words alone. Mr. Livingston goes still further. "No words whatever," says the code of Louisiana, "are an adequate cause, no gestures merely showing derision or contempt, no assault or battery so slight as to show that the intent was not to inflict great bodily harm."

We greatly doubt whether any good reason can be assigned for this distinction. It is an indisputable fact that gross insults by word or gesture have as great a tendency to move many persons to violent passion as dangerous or painful bodily injuries. Nor does it appear to us that passion excited by insult is entitled to less indulgence than passion excited by pain. On the contrary, the circumstance that a man resents an insult more than a wound is anything but a proof that he is a man of a peculiarly bad heart. It would be a fortunate thing for mankind if every person felt an outrage which left a stain upon his honour more acutely than an outrage which had fractured one of his limbs. If so, why should we treat an offence produced by the blamable excess of a feeling which all wise legislators desire to encourage, more severely than we treat the blamable excess of feelings certainly not more respectable?

One outrage which wounds only the honour and

the affections is admitted by Mr. Livingston to be an adequate provocation. "A discovery of the wife of the accused in the act of adultery with the person killed is an adequate cause." The law of France, the law of England and the Mahomedan law are also indulgent to homicide committed under such circumstances. We must own that we can see no reason for making a distinction between this provocation and many other provocations of the same kind. We cannot consent to lay it down as an universal rule that in all cases this provocation shall be considered as an adequate provocation. Circumstances may easily be conceived which would satisfy a Court that a husband had in such a case acted from no feeling of wounded honour or affection, but from mere brutality of nature, or from disappointed cupidity. On the other hand, we conceive that there are many cases in which as much indulgence is due to the excited feelings of a father or a brother as to those of a husband. That a worthless, unfaithful and tyrannical husband should be guilty only of manslaughter for killing the paramour of his wife, and that an affectionate and high-spirited brother should be guilty of murder for killing, in a paroxysm of rage, the seducer of his sister, appears to us inconsistent and unreasonable.

There is another class of provocations which Mr. Livingston does not allow to be adequate in law, but which have been, and while human nature remains unaltered, will be, adequate in fact to produce the most tremendous effects. Suppose a person to take indecent liberties with a modest female, in the presence of her father, her brother, her husband or her lover. Such an assault might have no tendency to cause pain or danger; yet history tells us what effects have followed from such assaults. Such an assault produced the Sicilian Vespers. Such an assault called forth the memorable blow of Wat Tyler.

It is difficult to conceive any class of cases in which the intemperance of anger ought to be treated with greater lenity. So far, indeed, should we be from ranking a man who acted like Tyler with murderers, that we conceive that a judge would exercise a sound discretion in sentencing such a man to the lowest punishment fixed by the law for manslaughter.

We think it right to add that, though in our remarks on this part of the law we have used illustrations drawn from the history and manners of Europe, the arguments which we have employed apply as strongly to the state of society in India as to the state of society in any part of the globe. There is perhaps no country in which more cruel suffering is inflicted, and more deadly resentment called forth, by injuries which affect only the mental feelings.

A person who should offer a gross insult to the Mahomedan religion in the presence of a zealous professor of that religion; who should deprive some high-born Rajpoot of his caste; who should rudely thrust his head into the covered palanquin of a woman of rank, would probably move those whom he insulted to more violent anger than if he had caused them some severe bodily hurt. That on these subjects our notions and usages differ from theirs is nothing to the purpose. We are legislating for them, and though we may wish that their opinions and feelings may undergo a considerable change, it is our duty, while their opinions and feelings remain unchanged, to pay as much respect to those opinions and feelings as if we partook of them. We are legislating for a country where many men, and those by no means the worst men, prefer death to the loss of caste; where many women, and those by no means the worst women, would consider themselves as dishonoured by exposure to the gaze of strangers: and to legislate for such a country, as if the loss of caste or the exposure of a female face were not provocations of the highest order, would, in our opinion, be unjust and unreasonable.

The second mitigated form of voluntary culpable homicide is that to which we have given the name of voluntary culpable homicide by consent. It appears to us that this description of homicide ought to be punished, but that it ought not to be punished so severely as murder. We have elsewhere given our reasons for thinking that this description of homicide ought to be punished.[1]

Our reasons for not punishing it so severely as murder are these. In the first place, the motives which prompt men to the commission of this offence are generally far more respectable than those which prompt men to the commission of murder. Sometimes it is the effect of a strong sense of religious duty, sometimes of a strong sense of honour, not unfrequently of humanity. The soldier, who, at the entreaty of a wounded comrade, puts that comrade out of pain, the friend who supplies laudanum to a person suffering the torment of a lingering disease, the freedman who in ancient times held out the sword that his master might fall on it, the high-born native of India who stabs the females of his family at their own entreaty in order to save them from the licentiousness of a band of marauders, would, except in Christian societies, scarcely be thought culpable, and even in Christian societies would not be regarded by the public, and ought not to be treated by the law, as assassins.

Again, this crime is by no means productive of so much evil to the community as murder. One evil ingredient of the utmost importance is altogether wanting to the offence of voluntary culpable homicide by consent. It does not produce general insecurity. It does not spread terror through society. When we punish murder with such signal severity, we have

[1] See Note (B).

two ends in view. One end is, that people may not be murdered. Another end is, that people may not live in constant dread of being murdered. This second end is perhaps the more important of the two. For if assassination were left unpunished, the number of persons assassinated would probably bear a very small proportion to the whole population; but the life of every human being would be passed in constant anxiety and alarm. This property of the offence of murder is not found in the offence of voluntary culpable homicide by consent. Every man who has not given his consent to be put to death is perfectly certain that this latter offence cannot at present be committed on him, and that it never will be committed unless he shall first be convinced that it is his interest to consent to it. We know that two or three midnight assassinations are sufficient to keep a city of a million of inhabitants in a state of con-sternation during several weeks, and to cause every private family to lay in arms and watchmen's rattles. No number of suicides, or of homicides committed with the unextorted consent of the person killed, could possibly produce such alarm among the sur-vivors.

The distinction between murder and voluntary culpable homicide by consent has never, as far as we are aware, been recognised by any code in the dis-tinct manner in which we propose to recognise it; but it may be traced in the laws of many countries, and often, when neglected by those who have framed the laws, it has had a great effect on the decisions of the tribunals, and particularly on the decisions of tribunals popularly composed. It may be proper to observe that the burning of a Hindoo widow by her own consent, though it is now, as it ought to be, an offence by the regulations of every Presidency, is in no Presidency punished as murder.

The third mitigated form of voluntary culpable

homicide is that which we have designated as voluntary culpable homicide in defence.

We have been forced to leave the law on the
subject of private defence, as we have elsewhere
said, in an unsatisfactory state; and, though we
hope and believe that it may be greatly improved,
we fear that it must always continue to be one of
the least precise parts of every system of jurisprudence. That portion of the law of homicide which
we are now considering is closely connected with
the law of private defence, and must necessarily partake of the imperfections of the law of private
defence. But wherever the limits of the right of
private defence may be placed, and with whatever
degree of accuracy they may be marked, we are
inclined to think that it will always be expedient to
make a separation between murder and what we have
designated as voluntary culpable homicide in defence.

The chief reason for making this separation is that
the law itself invites men to the very verge of the
crime which we have designated as voluntary culpable homicide in defence. It prohibits such homicide, indeed, but it authorises acts which lie very
near to such homicide; and this circumstance, we
think, greatly mitigates the guilt of such homicide.

That a man who deliberately kills another in
order to prevent that other from pulling his nose
should be allowed to go absolutely unpunished,
would be most dangerous. The law punishes and
ought to punish such killing. But we cannot think
that the law ought to punish such killing as murder.
For the law itself has encouraged the slayer to inflict on the assailant any harm short of death which
may be necessary for the purpose of repelling the outrage,—to give the assailant a cut with a knife across
the fingers which may render his right hand useless to
him for life, or to hurl him down stairs with such force
as to break his leg; and it seems difficult to conceive

that circumstances which would be a full justification of any violence short of homicide should not be a mitigation of the guilt of homicide. That a man should be merely exercising a right by fracturing the skull and knocking out the eye of an assailant, and should be guilty of the highest crime in the code if he kills the same assailant; that there should be only a single step between perfect innocence and murder, between perfect impunity and liability to capital punishment, seems unreasonable. In a case in which the law itself empowers an individual to inflict any harm short of death, it ought hardly, we think, to visit him with the highest punishment if he inflicts death.

It is to be considered also that the line between those aggressions which it is lawful to repel by killing, and those which it is not lawful so to repel, is in our code, and must be in every code, to a great extent an arbitrary line, and that many individual cases will fall on one side of that line which, if we had framed the law with a view to those cases alone, we should place on the other. Thus we allow a man to kill if he has no other means of preventing an incendiary from burning a house; and we do not allow him to kill for the purpose of preventing the commission of a simple theft. But a house may be a wretched heap of mats and thatch, propped by a few bamboos, and not worth altogether twenty rupees. A simple theft may deprive a man of a pocket-book which contains bills to a great amount, the savings of a long and laborious life, the sole dependence of a large family. That in these cases the man who kills the incendiary should be pronounced guiltless of any offence, and that the man who kills the thief should be sentenced to the gallows, or, if he is treated with the utmost lenity which the Courts can show, to perpetual transportation or imprisonment, would be generally condemned as a shocking injustice. We are, therefore, clearly of opinion that the offence which we have designated as voluntary culpable homicide in defence ought to be distinguished from murder in such a manner that the Courts may have it in their power to inflict a slight or a merely nominal punishment on acts which, though not within the letter of the law which authorises killing in self defence, are yet within the reason of that law.

We have hitherto been considering the law of voluntary culpable homicide. But homicide may be culpable, yet not voluntary. There will probably be little difference of opinion as to the expediency of providing a punishment for the rash and negligent causing of death. But it may be thought that we have dealt too leniently by the offender who, while committing a crime, causes death which he did not intend to cause or know himself to be likely to cause.

The law, as we have framed it, differs widely from the English law. " If," says Sir William Blackstone, " one intends to do another felony, and undesignedly kills a man, this is murder;" and he gives the following illustration of the rule : " If one gives a woman with child a medicine to produce abortion, and it operates so violently as to kill the woman, this is murder in the person who gave it."

Under the provisions of our code, this case would be very differently dealt with according to circumstances. If A. kills Z. by administering abortives to her, with the knowledge that those abortives are likely to cause her death, he is guilty of voluntary culpable homicide, which will be voluntary culpable homicide by consent, if Z. agreed to run the risk, and murder if Z. did not so agree. If A. causes miscarriage to Z., not intending to cause Z.'s death, nor thinking it likely that he shall cause Z.'s death, but so rashly or negligently as to cause her death, A. is guilty of culpable homicide not voluntary, and will be liable to the punishment provided for the causing of miscarriage, increased by imprisonment for a term not exceeding two years. Lastly, if A. took such precautions that there was no reasonable probability that Z.'s death would be caused, and if the medicine were rendered deadly by some accident which no human sagacity could have foreseen, or by some peculiarity in Z.'s constitution such as there was no ground whatever to expect, A. will be liable to no punishment whatever on account of her death, but will of course be liable to the punishment provided for causing miscarriage.

It may be proper for us to offer some arguments in defence of this part of the code.

It will be admitted that when an act is in itself innocent, to punish the person who does it because bad consequences, which no human wisdom could have foreseen, have followed from it, would be in the highest degree barbarous and absurd.

A pilot is navigating the Hooghly with the utmost care and skill: he directs the vessel against a sand-bank which has been recently formed, and of which the existence was altogether unknown till this disaster. Several of his passengers are consequently drowned. To hang the pilot as a murderer on account of this misfortune would be universally allowed to be an act of atrocious injustice. But if the voyage of the pilot be itself a high offence, ought that circumstance alone to turn his misfortune into a murder? Suppose that he is engaged in conveying an offender beyond the reach of justice; that he has kidnapped some natives, and is carrying them to a ship which is to convey them to some foreign slave-colony; that he is violating the laws of quarantine at a time when it is of the highest importance that those laws should be strictly observed; that he is carrying supplies, deserters and intelligence to the enemies of the state. The offence of such a pilot ought, undoubtedly, to be severely punished. But to pronounce him guilty of one offence because a misfortune befel him while he was committing another offence,—to pronounce him the murderer of people whose lives he never meant to endanger, whom he was doing his best to carry safe to their destination, and whose death has been purely accidental,—is surely to confound all the boundaries of crime.

Again, A. heaps fuel on a fire, not in an imprudent manner, but in such a manner that the chance of harm is not worth considering. Unhappily the flame bursts out more violently than there was reason to expect. At the same moment a sudden puff of wind blows Z.'s light dress towards the hearth. The dress catches fire, and Z. is burned to death. To punish A. as a murderer on account of such an unhappy event would be senseless cruelty. But suppose that the fuel which caused the flame to burst forth was a will which A. was fraudulently destroying: ought this circumstance to make A. the murderer of Z. ? We think not. For the fraudulent destroying of wills we have provided, in other parts of the code, punishments which we think sufficient. If not sufficient, they ought to be made so. But we cannot admit that Z.'s death has, in the smallest degree, aggravated A.'s offence, or ought to be considered in apportioning A.'s punishment.

To punish as a murderer every man who, while committing a heinous offence, causes death by pure misadventure, is a course which evidently adds nothing to the security of human life. No man can so conduct himself as to make it absolutely certain that he shall not be so unfortunate as to cause the death of a fellow-creature. The utmost that he can do is to abstain from every thing which is at all likely to cause death. No fear of punishment can make him do more than this; and, therefore, to punish a man who has done this can add nothing to the security

of human life. The only good effect which such
punishment can produce will be to deter people from
committing any of those offences which turn into
murders what are in themselves mere accidents. It
is in fact an addition to the punishment of those
offences, and it is an addition made in the very worst
way. For example, hundreds of persons in some
great cities are in the habit of picking pockets.
They know that they are guilty of a great offence;
but it has never occurred to one of them, nor would
it occur to any rational man, that they are guilty of
an offence which endangers life. Unhappily one of
these hundreds attempts to take the purse of a gentleman who has a loaded pistol in his pocket. The
thief touches the trigger, the pistol goes off, the
gentleman is shot dead. To treat the case of this
pickpocket differently from that of the numerous
pickpockets who steal under exactly the same circumstances, with exactly the same intentions, with
no less risk of causing death, with no greater care to
avoid causing death ; to send them to the house of
correction as thieves, and him to the gallows as a
murderer, appears to us an unreasonable course. If
the punishment for stealing from the person be too
light, let it be increased, and let the increase fall
alike on all the offenders. Surely the worst mode of
increasing the punishment of an offence is to provide that, besides the ordinary punishment, every
offender shall run an exceedingly small risk of being
hanged. The more nearly the amount of punishment can be reduced to a certainty the better ; but
if chance is to be admitted, there are better ways of
admitting it. It would be a less capricious, and
therefore a more salutary course, to provide that
every fiftieth or every hundredth thief selected by
lot should be hanged, than to provide that every thief
should be hanged who, while engaged in stealing,
should meet with an unforeseen misfortune, such as

might have befallen the most virtuous man while performing the most virtuous action.

We trust that his Lordship in Council will think that we have judged correctly in proposing that when a person engaged in the commission of an offence causes death by pure accident, he shall suffer only the punishment of his offence, without any addition on account of such accidental death.

When a person engaged in the commission of an offence causes death by rashness or negligence, but without either intending to cause death, or thinking it likely that he shall cause death, we propose that he shall be liable to the punishment of the offence which he was engaged in committing, superadded to the ordinary punishment of involuntary culpable homicide.

The arguments and illustrations which we have employed for the purpose of showing that the involuntary causing of death, without either rashness or negligence, ought, under no circumstances, to be punished at all, will, with some modifications, which will readily suggest themselves, serve to show that the involuntary causing of death by rashness or negligence, though always punishable, ought under no circumstances to be punished as murder.

It gives us great pleasure to observe, that Mr. Livingston's provisions on this subject, though in details they differ widely from ours, are framed on the principles which we have here defended.

We wish next to call the attention of his Lordship in Council to clauses 308 and 309.

These clauses appear to us absolutely necessary to the completeness of the code. We have provided, under the head of bodily hurt, for cases in which hurt is inflicted in an attempt to murder; under the head of assault, for assaults committed in attempting to murder; under the head of criminal trespass, for some criminal trespasses committed in order to murder. But there will still remain many atrocious and deliberate attempts to murder which are not trespasses, which are not assaults, and which cause no hurt.   A., for example, digs a pit in his garden, and conceals the mouth of it, intending that Z. may fall in and perish there.   Here A. has committed no trespass, for the ground is his own ; and no assault, for he has applied no force to Z.   He may not have caused bodily hurt, for Z. may have received a timely caution, or may not have gone near the pit.   But A.'s crime is evidently one which ought to be punished as severely as if he had laid hands on Z. with the intention of cutting his throat.

Again, A. sets poisoned food before Z.   Here A. may have committed no trespass, for the food may be his own ; and if so, he violates no right of property by mixing arsenic with it.   He commits no assault, for he means the taking of the food to be Z.'s voluntary act.   If Z. does not swallow enough of the poisoned food to disorder him, A. causes no bodily hurt.   Yet it is plain that A. has been guilty of a crime of a most atrocious description.

Similar attempts may be made to commit voluntary culpable homicide in any of the three mitigated forms.   A., for example, is excited to violent passion by Z., and fires a pistol intending to kill Z.   If the shot proves fatal, A. will be guilty of manslaughter ; and he surely ought not to be exempted from all punishment if the ball only grazes the intended victim.

It is to meet cases of this description that clauses 308 and 309 are intended.

With respect to the law on the subject of abortion, we think it necessary to say only that we entertain strong apprehensions that this or any other law on that subject may, in this country, be abused to the vilest purposes.   The charge of abortion is one which, even where it is not substantiated, often leaves a stain on the honour of families.   The power of bringing a false accusation of this description is therefore a formidable engine in the hands of unprincipled men. This part of the law will, unless great care be taken, produce few convictions, but much misery and terror to respectable families, and a large harvest of profit to the vilest pests of society. We trust that it may be in our power in the code of procedure to lay down rules which may prevent such an abuse. Should we not be able to do so, we are inclined to think that it would be our duty to advise his Lordship in Council rather to suffer abortion, where the mother is a party to the offence, to remain wholly unpunished, than to repress it by provisions which would occasion more suffering to the innocent than to the guilty.

Every one of those offences against the human body which remain to be considered falls under some one or more of the following heads : Hurt, Restraint, Assault, Kidnapping, Rape, Unnatural crimes.

Many of the offences which fall under the head of Hurt will also fall under the head of assault. A stab, a blow which fractures a limb, the flinging of boiling water over a person, are assaults, and are also acts which cause bodily hurt. But bodily hurt may be caused by many acts which are not assaults. A person, for example, who mixes a deleterious potion, and places it on the table of another ; a person who conceals a scythe in the grass on which another is in the habit of walking ; a person who digs a pit in a public path, intending that another may fall into it, may cause serious hurt, and may be justly punished for causing such hurt ; but they cannot, without extreme violence to language, be said to have committed assaults.

We propose to designate all pain, disease and infirmity by the name of hurt.

We have found it very difficult to draw a line between those bodily hurts which are serious and those which are slight. To draw such a line with perfect accuracy is, indeed, absolutely impossible; but it is far better that such a line should be drawn, though rudely, than that offences some of which approach in enormity to murder, while others are little more than frolics which a good-natured man would hardly resent, should be classed together.

We have, therefore, designated certain kinds of hurt as *grievous*.

We have given this name to emasculation,—to the loss of the sight of either eye,—to the loss of the hearing of either ear,—to the loss of any member or joint,—to the permanent loss of the perfect use of any member or joint,—to the permanent disfiguration of the head or face,—to the fracture and to the dislocation of bones. Thus far we proceed on sure ground. But a more difficult task remains. Some hurts which are not, like those kinds of hurt which we have just mentioned, distinguished by a broad and obvious line from slight hurts, may nevertheless be most serious. A wound, for example, which neither emasculates the sufferer, nor blinds him, nor destroys his hearing, nor deprives him of a member or a joint, nor permanently deprives him of the use of a member or a joint, nor disfigures his countenance, nor breaks his bones, nor dislocates them, may yet cause intense pain, prolonged disease, lasting injury to the constitution. It is evidently desirable that the law should make a distinction between such a wound, and a scratch which is healed with a little sticking plaster. A beating, again, which does not maim the sufferer or break his bones, may be so cruel as to bring him to the point of death. Such a beating, it is clear, ought not to be confounded with a bruise, which requires only to be bathed with vinegar, and of which the traces disappear in a day.

After a long consideration we have determined

to give the name of grievous bodily hurt to all hurt which causes the sufferer to be in pain, diseased or unable to pursue his ordinary avocations, during the space of twenty days.

This provision was suggested to us by article 309 of the French Penal Code. That article runs thus: "Sera puni de la peine de la réclusion, tout individu qui aura fait des blessures ou porté des coups, s'il est resulté de ces actes de violence une maladie ou incapacité de travail personnel pendant plus de vingt jours." *Réclusion*, it is to be observed, signifies imprisonment and hard labour for a term of not less than five nor more than ten years.

This law appears, from the *procès verbal* of Napoleon's council of state, to have been adopted without calling forth a single [1] observation; but it has since been severely criticised by French jurists, and has been mitigated by the French legislature. Indeed, it ought to have been completely recast, for it is undoubtedly one of the most exceptionable laws in the code.

A man who means only to inflict a slight hurt may, without intending or expecting to do so, cause a hurt which is exceedingly serious. A push which to a man in health is a trifle may, if it happens to be directed against a diseased part of an infirm person, occasion consequences which the offender never contemplated as possible. A blow designed to inflict only the pain of a moment may cause the person struck to lose his footing, to fall from a considerable height, and to break a limb. In such cases, to punish the assailant with five years of strict imprisonment would be in the highest degree unjust and cruel. It is said, and we can easily believe it,[2] that, in such cases, the French juries have frequently

---

[1] Locré, Législation de France. Vol. xxx., p. 362.

[2] Paillet, Manuel de Droit Français. Note on clause 309 of the Penal Code.

refused, in spite of the clearest evidence, to pronounce a decision which would have subjected the
accused to a punishment so obviously disproportioned
to his offence.

We have attempted to preserve and to extend
what is good in this article of the French code, and
to avoid the evils which we have noticed. It appears
to us that the length of time during which a sufferer
is in pain, diseased or incapacitated from pursuing
his ordinary avocations, though a defective criterion
of the severity of a hurt, is still the best criterion
that has ever been devised. It is a criterion which
may, we think, with propriety be employed not
merely in cases where violence has been used, but in
cases where hurt has been caused without any
assault, as by the administration of drugs, the setting of traps, the digging of pit-falls, the placing of
ropes across a road. But though we have borrowed
from the French code this test of the severity of
bodily injuries, we have framed our penal provisions
on a principle quite different from that by which the
authors of the French code appear to have been
guided. In apportioning the punishment, we take
into consideration both the extent of the hurt and
the intention of the offender.

What we propose is, that the voluntary infliction
of simple bodily hurt shall be punished with imprisonment of either description, which may extend
to one year, or fine, or both; the voluntary infliction
of grievous bodily hurt with imprisonment of either
description for a term which may extend to ten years
and must not be less than six months, to which fine
may be added.

These are the ordinary punishments; but there
are certain aggravating and mitigating circumstances
which make a considerable difference.

Where bodily hurt is voluntarily inflicted in an
attempt to murder the person hurt, we propose to

punish the offender with transportation for life, or
with imprisonment for a term which may extend
to life, and cannot be less than seven years. It does
not appear to us that, where the murderous intention
is made out, the severity of the hurt inflicted is a
circumstance which ought to be considered in apportioning the punishment. It is undoubtedly a
circumstance which will be important as evidence.
A Court will generally be more easily satisfied of the
murderous intention of an assailant who has fractured
a man's skull, than of one who has only caused a
slight contusion.   But the proof might be complete.
To take examples which are universally known :—
Harley was laid up more than twenty days by the
wound which he received from Guiscard ; the scratch
which Damien gave to Louis the Fifteenth was so
slight that it was followed by no feverish symptoms.
Yet it will be allowed that it would be absurd to
make a distinction between the two assassins on this
ground.

We propose that when bodily hurt is inflicted by
way of torture, the punishment shall be very severe.
In England, happily, such a provision would be unnecessary.   But the execrable cruelties which are
committed by robbers in this country for the purpose
of extorting property, or information relating to
property, render it absolutely necessary here.   We
propose that in such cases, if the hurt inflicted be
what we have designated as *grievous*, the offender
shall be punished with transportation for life, or
with imprisonment for a term which may extend to
life, and which shall not be less than seven years.
Where the hurt is not grievous, we propose that the
imprisonment shall be for a term of not more than
fourteen years, nor less than one year.

Bodily hurt may be inflicted by means the use
of which generally indicates great malignity. A
blow with the fist may cause as much pain, and

produce as lasting injury, as laceration with a knife, or branding with a hot iron. But it will scarcely be disputed that, in the vast majority of cases, the offender who has used a knife or a hot iron for the purpose of wreaking his hatred is a far worse and more dangerous member of society than he who has only used his fist. It appears to us that many hurts which would not, according to our classification, be designated as grievous, ought yet, on account of the mode in which they are inflicted, to be punished more severely than many grievous hurts. We propose, therefore, that where bodily hurt is voluntarily caused by means of any sharp instrument, of fire, of any heated substance, of any corrosive substance, of any explosive substance, of any poison internal or external, or of any animal, the maximum of imprisonment may be increased, in cases of grievous bodily hurt, to fourteen years, in other cases to three years.

In cases where bodily hurt is voluntarily caused on grave and sudden provocation, we propose to mitigate the punishment. This mitigation is common to cases of hurt and of grievous hurt. But the voluntary causing of grievous hurt on great and sudden provocation will still be punishable more severely than the voluntary causing of hurt not grievous on grave and sudden provocation. The provisions which we propose on this subject are framed on the same principles on which we have framed the law of manslaughter, and may be defended by the same arguments by which the law of manslaughter is defended.

Hitherto we have been considering cases in which hurt has been caused voluntarily. But hurt may be caused involuntarily, yet culpably. There may have been no design to cause hurt, no expectation that hurt would be caused. Yet there may have been a want of due care not to cause hurt. For these cases of the involuntary yet culpable infliction of bodily hurt, we have provided rules which bear a close analogy to those which we have provided for cases of involuntary culpable homicide.

The provision contained in clause 329 bears, it will be seen, a close analogy to those contained in clauses 308 and 309. We have provided, under the head of assault, for cases in which an assault is committed in an attempt to cause grievous bodily hurt. But there may be most malignant and atrocious attempts to cause grievous bodily hurt without any assault. For example, Z. is directed to use a lotion for his eyes. A. substitutes for that lotion a corrosive substance, intending that it may destroy Z.'s eyesight. Again; A. makes up a letter addressed to Z., and sends it to the post-office, having placed a strongly explosive substance under the seal, intending that the explosion may seriously injure Z. These are not assaults; yet they are evidently acts which deserve severe punishment, and that punishment is provided by clause 329.

By wrongful restraint, we mean the keeping a man out of a place where he wishes to be, and has a right to be. Wrongful confinement, which is a form of wrongful restraint, is the keeping a man within limits out of which he wishes to go, and has a right to go.

The offence of wrongful restraint, when it does not amount to wrongful confinement, and when it is not accompanied with violence, or with the causing of bodily hurt, is seldom a serious offence, and we propose, therefore, to visit it with a light punishment.

The offence of wrongful confinement may be also a slight offence; but, when attended by aggravating circumstances, it may be one of the most serious that can be committed.

One aggravating circumstance is the duration of the confinement. Confinement for a quarter of an hour may sometimes be a mere frolic, which would deserve only a nominal punishment, which, indeed, might be so harmless as not to amount to an offence. (See clause 73.) But wrongful confinement continued during many days will always be a most serious offence. We have attempted to frame the law on this subject in such a manner as to give the offender a strong motive for abridging the detention of his prisoner. Another aggravating circumstance is the circumstance that the offender persists in wrongfully confining a person notwithstanding an order issued by a competent authority for the liberation or production of that person. The mode in which these orders are to be issued will be set forth in the code of procedure. A third aggravating circumstance is the circumstance that the offender uses criminal confinement for purposes of extortion. For all these aggravated forms of wrongful confinement we have provided severe punishments.

We have also provided a separate punishment for a person who, while detaining another in wrongful confinement, omits to supply his prisoner with every thing necessary to health, ease and comfort. The effect of this provision is, that a person who wrongfully confines another will be answerable for any bodily hurt which he may cause by wrongfully omitting so to supply his prisoner.

We have found great difficulty in giving a definition of assault, and are by no means satisfied with that which we now offer. As, however, it at present appears to us to include all that we mean to include, and to exclude all that we mean to exclude, we have adopted it in spite of the objections which we feel to its harsh and quaint phraseology. We have adopted it with the less scruple, because we trust that the illustrations will render every part of it intelligible to an attentive reader.

A large proportion of the acts which we have designated as assaults will be offences falling under the heads of hurt and restraint. Thus, a stab with a knife is an offence falling under the head of hurt, and it is also an assault. The seizing a man by the collar, and thus preventing him from proceeding on his way, is unlawful restraint, and is also an assault. But there will be many assaults which it is absolutely necessary to punish, yet which cause neither bodily hurt nor unlawful restraint. A man who impertinently puts his arm round a lady's waist, who aims a severe stroke at a person with a horsewhip, who maliciously throws a stone at a person, squirts dirty water over a person, or sets a dog at a person, may cause no hurt and no restraint, yet it is evident that such acts ought to be prevented.

The ordinary punishment which we propose for assault is slight. But we propose to punish assaults which are committed in attempting murder with transportation for life, or with imprisonment for a term which may extend to life, and which cannot be less than seven years. We have also provided severe punishments for assault, when it is committed in an attempt to commit any grave offence against the person, when it is committed with the intention of dishonouring the sufferer, or when it is an outrage offered to female modesty.

The offence of kidnapping is sometimes committed by means of assault, and is sometimes attended with restraint. But this will not always be the case. A child, for example, who is decoyed from its guardians, who soon forgets its home, and who consents to remain with the kidnapper, cannot be said to have been assaulted or restrained. A labourer who has been induced to embark on board of a ship by false assurances that he shall be taken to a country where he shall have good wages, but whom the captain of the ship intends to sell for a slave, has not, as yet, been either assaulted or restrained.

The crime of kidnapping consists, according to our definition of it, in conveying a person without his consent, or the consent of some person legally authorized to consent on his behalf, or with such consent obtained by deception, out of the protection of the law, or of those whom the law has appointed his guardians.

This offence may be committed on a child by removing that child out of the keeping of its lawful guardian or guardians. On a grown man it can only be committed by conveying him beyond the limits of the Company's territories, or by receiving him on board of a ship for that purpose.

The carrying of a grown-up person by force from one place within the Company's territories to another, and the enslaving him within the Company's territories, are offences sufficiently provided for under the heads of restraint and confinement.

The enticing a grown-up person by false promises to go from one place in the Company's territories to another place also within those territories, may be a subject for a civil action, and, under certain circumstances, for a criminal prosecution; but it does not appear to us to come properly under the head of kidnapping.

We propose to make the punishment of kidnapping peculiarly severe when it is committed with murderous intentions, as in the case of those subjects of the Company who were lately carried into the Jyntenh country for purposes of human sacrifice.

We also propose to enhance the punishment of kidnapping in cases in which it is committed with the intention of inflicting grievous bodily harm on the person kidnapped, or of reducing that person to slavery, and when it is committed for purposes of rape or of unnatural lust.

We have placed under this head a provision for punishing persons who export labourers by sea from the Company's territories, in contravention of the Act recently passed by Government on that subject.

The provisions which we propose on the subject of rape do not appear to require any remark.

Clauses 361 and 362 relate to an odious class of offences respecting which it is desirable that as little as possible should be said. We leave, without comment, to the judgment of his Lordship in Council the two clauses which we have provided for these offences. We are unwilling to insert, either in the text or in the notes, any thing which could give rise to public discussion on this revolting subject; as we are decidedly of opinion that the injury which would be done to the morals of the community by such discussion would far more than compensate for any benefits which might be derived from legislative measures framed with the greatest precision.

NOTE (N).

ON THE CHAPTER OF OFFENCES AGAINST PROPERTY.

THERE is such a mutual relation between the different parts of the law that those parts must all attain per fection together. That portion, be it what it may, which is selected to be first put into the form of a code, with whatever clearness and precision it may be expressed and arranged, must necessarily partake to a considerable extent of the uncertainty and obscurity in which other portions are still left.

This observation applies with peculiar force to that important portion of the penal code which we now propose to consider. The offences defined in this chapter are made punishable on the ground that they are violations of the right of property; but the right of property is itself the creature of the law. It is evident, therefore, that if the substantive civil law touching this right be imperfect or obscure, the penal law which is auxiliary to that substantive law, and of which the object is to add a sanction to that substantive law, must partake of the imperfection or obscurity. It is impossible for us to be certain that we have made proper penal provisions for violations of civil rights till we have a complete knowledge of all civil rights; and this we cannot have while the law respecting those rights is either obscure or unsettled. As the present state of the civil law causes perplexity to the legislator in framing the penal code, so it will occasionally cause perplexity to the judges in administering that code. If it be matter of doubt what things are the subjects of a certain right, in whom that right resides, and to what that right extends, it must also be matter of doubt whether that right has or has not been violated.

For example, A., without Z.'s permission, shoots snipes on Z.'s ground, and carries them away: here, if the law of civil rights grants the property in such birds to any person who can catch them, A. has not, by killing them and carrying them away, invaded Z.'s right of property. If, on the other hand, the law of civil right declares such birds the property of the person on whose lands they are, A. has invaded Z's right of property. If it be matter of doubt what the state of the civil law on the subject actually is, it must also be matter of doubt whether A. has wronged Z. or not.

By the English law,[1] pigeons, while they frequent a dove-cote, are the property of the owner of the dove-cote. By the Roman law[2] they were not so. By the French law[3] they are his property at one time of the year, and not his property at another. Here it is evident that the taking of such a pigeon, which would in England be a violation of the right

[1] Blackstone, Book II. Chap. 25.

[2] Columbarum fera natura est, nec ad rem pertinet, quod ex consuetudine evolare et revolare solent.—Inst. Lib. II. Tit. I.

[3] Paillet, Manuel de Droit Français.

of property, would be none in a country governed by the Roman law, and that, in France, it would depend on the time of the year whether it were so, or not.

A. lends a horse to B. B. sells the horse to Z., who buys it, believing in good faith that B. has a right to sell it. A. sees the horse feeding. He mounts it and rides away with it. Here, if the law of civil rights provides that a thing sold by one who has no right to sell it shall nevertheless be the property of a *bonâ fide* purchaser, A. has invaded Z.'s right of property. If, on the other hand, A.'s right is not affected by what has passed between B. and Z., A. does not commit an infraction of Z.'s right of property. If it be doubtful whether the right to the horse be in A. or in Z., it must also be doubtful whether A. has or has not committed an infraction of Z.'s right.

A path running across a field which belongs to Z. has, during three years, been used as a public way. A., in spite of a prohibition from Z., uses it as such. Here, if by the civil law, an usage of three years is sufficient to create a right of way, A. has committed no infraction of Z.'s right. But if a prescription of more than three years, or an express grant, be necessary to create a right of way, A. has committed an infraction of Z.'s right of property.

A. discovers a mine on land occupied by him. Here, if the civil law assigns all minerals to the occupier of the land, A. violates no right of property by appropriating the minerals. But if the civil law assigns all minerals to the Government, A. violates the right of property by such appropriation.

The sea recedes, and leaves dry land in the immediate neighbourhood of Z.'s property. Z. cultivates the land. A. turns cattle on the land, and destroys Z.'s crops. Here, if the civil law assigns alluvial additions to the occupier of the nearest land, A. is a wrong-doer. If it declares alluvial additions common, A. is not a wrong-doer. If it assigns alluvial addi-

tions to the Government, both A. and Z. are wrong-
doers. If it be uncertain to whom the law assigns alluvial additions, it must be also uncertain who is the
wrong-doer, and whether there be any wrong-doer.

The substantive civil law, in the instances which
we have given, is different in different countries,
and in the same country at different times. As the
substantive civil law varies, the penal law, which is
added as a guard to the substantive civil law, must
vary also. And while many important questions of
substantive civil right are undetermined, the Courts
must occasionally feel doubtful whether the provisions of the penal code do or do not apply to a
particular case.

It would evidently be impossible for us to determine in the penal code all the momentous questions
of civil right which, in the unsettled state of Indian
jurisprudence, will admit of dispute. We have, indeed, ventured to take for granted in our illustrations
many things which properly belong to the domain
of the civil law, because, without doing so, it would
have been impossible for us to explain our meaning ;
but we have, to the best of our judgment, avoided
questions respecting which, even in the present state
of Indian jurisprudence, much doubt could exist.
And in the text of the law we have, as closely as was
possible, confined ourselves to what is in strictness
the duty of persons engaged in framing a penal
code. We have provided punishments for the infraction of rights, without determining in whom
those rights vest, or to what those rights extend.
We are inclined to hope that, even if the penal code
should come into operation before the code of civil
rights has been framed, the number of cases in
which the want of a code of civil rights would occasion perplexity to the criminal tribunals will bear
but a very small proportion to those in which no
such perplexity will exist.

All the violations of the rights of property which we propose to make punishable by this chapter fall under one or more of the following heads :

1. Theft.
2. Extortion.
3. Robbery.
4. The criminal misappropriation of property not in possession.
5. Criminal breach of trust.
6. The receiving of stolen property.
7. Cheating.
8. Fraudulent bankruptcy.
9. Mischief.
10. Criminal trespass.

All these offences resemble each other in this, that they cause, or have some tendency, directly or indirectly, to cause some party not to have such a dominion over property as that party is entitled by law to have.

The first great line which divides these offences may be easily traced. Some of them merely prevent or disturb the enjoyment of property by one who has a right to it. Others transfer property to one who has no right to it. Some merely cause injury to the sufferer. Others, by means of wrongful loss to the sufferer, cause wrongful gain to some other party. The latter class of offences are designated in this code as fraudulent. (See clause 16.)

Every offence against property may be fraudulently committed; but theft, extortion, robbery, the criminal misappropriation of property not in possession, criminal breach of trust, the receiving of stolen property, fraudulent bankruptcy and cheating, must be in all cases fraudulently committed. Fraud enters into the definition of every one of these offences ; but fraud does not enter into the definition of mischief or of criminal trespass.

Theft, the criminal misappropriation of property

not in possession, and criminal breach of trust, are in the great majority of cases easily distinguishable. But the distinction becomes fainter and fainter as we approach the line of demarcation, and at length the offences fade imperceptibly into each other. This indistinctness may be greatly increased by unskilful legislation; but it has its origin in the nature of things, and in the imperfection of language, and must still remain in spite of all that legislation can effect.

We believe it to be impossible to mark with precision, by any words, the circumstances which constitute possession. It is easy to put cases about which no doubt whatever exists, and about which the language of lawyers and of the multitude would be the same. It will hardly be doubted, for example, that a gentleman's watch lying on a table in his room is in his possession, though it is not in his hand, and though he may not know whether it is on his writing-table or on his dressing-table. As little will it be doubted that a watch which a gentleman lost a year ago on a journey, and which he has never heard of since, is not in his possession. It will not be doubted that when a person gives a dinner, his silver forks, while in the hands of his guests, are still in his possession; and it will be as little doubted that his silver forks are not in his possession when he has deposited them with a pawnbroker as a pledge. But between these extreme cases lie many cases in which it is difficult to pronounce, with confidence, either that property is or that it is not in a person's possession.

This difficulty, sufficiently great in itself, would, we conceive, be increased by laws which should pronounce that in a set of cases arbitrarily selected from the mass, property is in the possession of some party in whose possession, according to the understanding of all mankind, it is not. The rule of

English law respecting what is called breaking bulk
is an instance of what we mean. A person who has
entrusted a hamper of wine to another to carry to a
great distance is not in possession of that hamper of
wine. But if the person in trust opens the hamper
and takes out a bottle, the possession, according to
the English law books, forthwith flies back to the
distant owner. Mr. Livingston has laid down a rule
of a similar kind, the effect of which, if we understand it rightly, is to annul the whole law of theft
as he has framed it, and indeed to render it impossible that theft can be committed in Louisiana.
Theft is defined by him to be "the fraudulently
taking of corporal personal property having some
assignable value, and belonging to another, from his
possession and without his assent." But in a subsequent clause he says that "neither the ownership
nor the legal possession of property is changed by
theft alone, without the circumstances required in
such case by the civil code, in order to produce a
change of property; therefore, stolen goods, if fraudulently taken from the thief, are stolen from the
original proprietor." But if stolen by the second
thief from the original proprietor, they must, according to Mr. Livingston's definition of theft, be
taken by the second thief out of the possession of
the original proprietor; therefore, the first thief has
left them in the possession of the original proprietor;
that is to say, the first thief has not committed theft.

It will not be imagined that we refer to this
inconsistency in the code of Louisiana, for the purpose of throwing any censure on the distinguished
author of that code. To do so would be unjust, and
in us especially most ungrateful, and also most imprudent; for we are by no means confident that
inconsistencies quite as remarkable will not be detected in the code which we now submit to Government. We note this error of Mr. Livingston for the

purpose of showing how dangerous it is for a legislator to attempt to escape from a difficulty by giving a technical sense to an expression which he nevertheless continues to use in a popular sense.

For the purpose of preventing any difference of opinion from arising in cases likely to occur very often, we have laid down a few rules (see clauses 17, 18, 19,) which we believe to be in accordance with the general sense of mankind as to what shall be held to constitute possession. But, in general, we leave it to the tribunals, without any direction, to determine whether particular property is at a particular time in the possession of a particular person or not.

Much uncertainty will still remain. This we cannot prevent. But we can, as it appears to us, prevent the uncertainty from producing any practical evil. The provision contained in clause 61 will, we think, obviate all the inconveniences which might arise from doubts as to the exact limits which separate theft from misappropriation and from breach of trust.

The effect of that clause will be to prevent the judges from wasting their time and ingenuity in devising nice distinctions. If a case which is plainly theft comes before them, the offender will be punished as a thief. If a case which is plainly breach of trust comes before them, the offender will be punished as guilty of breach of trust. If they have to try a case which lies on the frontier, one of those thefts which are hardly distinguishable from breaches of trust, or one of those breaches of trust which are hardly distinguishable from theft, they will not trouble themselves with subtle distinctions, but, leaving it undetermined by which name the offence should be called, will proceed to determine what is infinitely of greater importance, what shall be the punishment.

In theft, as we have defined it, the object of the offender always is to take property which is in the possession of a person out of that person's possession; nor have we admitted a single exception to this rule. In the great majority of cases, our classification will coincide with the popular classification. But there are a few aggravated cases of what we designate as misappropriation and breach of trust, which bear such an affinity to theft that it may seem idle to distinguish them from thefts; and it certainly would be idle to distinguish such cases from thefts if the distinction were made with a view to those cases alone. But, as we have a line of distinction which we think it desirable to maintain in the great majority of cases, we think it desirable also to maintain that line in a few cases in which it may separate things which are of a very similar description.

One offence which it may be thought that we ought to have placed among thefts is the pillaging of property during the interval which elapses between the time when the possessor of the property dies, and the time when it comes into the possession of some person authorised to take charge of it. This crime, in our classification, falls under the head, not of theft, but of misappropriation of property not in possession.

The ancient Roman jurists viewed it in the same light. The property taken under such circumstances, they argued, being in no person's possession, could not be taken out of any person's possession. The taking, therefore, was not *furtum*, but belonged to a separate head, called the *crimen expilatæ hæreditatis.*[1] The French lawyers, however, long ago found out a legal fiction by means of which this offence was treated as theft in those parts of France where the Roman law was in force.[2] Mr. Livingston's definition of theft appears to us to exclude this species of

[1] Justinian, Dig. Lib. XLVII. Tit. 19.   [2] Domat. Sup. III.

offence, nor indeed do we think that it could be reached by any provision of his code. That it ought to be punished with severity under some name or other is indisputable. By what name it should be designated may admit of some dispute. If we call it theft, we speak the popular language. If we call it misappropriation of property not in possession, we avoid an anomaly, and maintain a line which, in the great majority of cases, is reasonable and convenient. On the whole, we are inclined to maintain this line.

Again, a carrier who opens a letter entrusted to his charge, and takes thence a bank note, would be commonly called a thief. It is certain that his offence is not morally distinguishable from theft. Here, however, as before, we think it expedient to maintain our general rule ; and we therefore designate the offence of the carrier not as theft, but as criminal breach of trust.

The illustrations which we have appended to the provisions respecting theft, the misappropriation of property not in possession, and breach of trust, will, we hope, sufficiently explain to his Lordship in Council the reasons for most of those provisions.

It may possibly be remarked, that we have not, like Mr. Livingston, made it part of our definition of theft, that the property should be of some assignable value. We would, therefore, observe that we have not done so only because we conceive that the law, as framed by us, obtains the same end by a different road. By one of the general exceptions which we have proposed (clause 73), it is provided, that nothing shall be an offence by reason of any harm which it may cause, or be intended to cause, or be known to be likely to cause, if the whole of that harm is so slight that no person of ordinary sense and temper would complain of such harm. This provision will prevent the law of theft from being abused for the purpose of punishing those venial violations of the

right of property which the common sense of mankind readily distinguishes from crimes, such as the
act of a traveller who tears a twig from a hedge, of a
boy who takes stones from another person's ground
to throw at birds, of a servant who dips his pen in
his master's ink.   It does not appear to us that any
further rule on this subject is necessary.

The offence of extortion is distinguished from the
three offences which we have been considering by
this obvious circumstance, that it is committed by the
wrongful obtaining of a consent.   In one single class
of cases, theft and extortion are in practice confounded together so inextricably, that no judge, however sagacious, could discriminate between them.
This class of cases therefore has, in all systems of
jurisprudence with which we are acquainted, been
treated as a perfectly distinct class; and we think
that this arrangement, though somewhat anomalous,
is strongly recommended by convenience.   We have
therefore made robbery a separate crime.

There can be no case of robbery which does not
fall within the definition either of theft or of extortion;
but in practice it will perpetually be matter of doubt
whether a particular act of robbery was a theft or an
extortion.   A large proportion of robberies will be
half theft, half extortion.   A. seizes Z., threatens to
murder him, unless he delivers all his property, and
begins to pull off Z.'s ornaments.   Z. in terror begs
that A. will take all he has, and spare his life, assists
in taking off his ornaments, and delivers them to A.
Here, such ornaments as A. took without Z.'s consent are taken by theft.   Those which Z. delivered
up from fear of death are acquired by extortion.   It
is by no means improbable that Z.'s right-arm bracelet may have been obtained by theft, and left-arm
bracelet by extortion; that the rupees in Z.'s girdle
may have been obtained by theft, and those in his
turban by extortion.   Probably in nine-tenths of the

robberies which are committed, something like this
actually takes place, and it is probable that a few
minutes later neither the robber nor the person
robbed would be able to recollect in what proportions
theft and extortion were mixed in the crime; nor is
it at all necessary for the ends of justice that this
should be ascertained. For though, in general, the
consent of a sufferer is a circumstance which very
materially modifies the character of the offence, and
which ought, therefore, to be made known to the
Courts, yet the consent which a person gives to the
taking of his property by a ruffian who holds a pistol to
his breast is a circumstance altogether immaterial.

His Lordship in Council will perceive that we
have provided punishment of exemplary severity for
that atrocious crime which is designated in the Regulations of Bengal and Madras by the name of Dacoity.
This name we have thought it convenient to retain,
for the purpose of denoting, not only actual gang-
robbery, but the attempting to rob when such an
attempt is made or aided by a gang.

The law relating to the offence of receiving stolen
goods appears to require no comment.

The offence of cheating must, like that of extortion, be committed by the wrongful obtaining of a
consent. The difference is, that the extortioner obtains the consent by intimidation, and a cheat by
deception. There is no offence in the code with
which we have found it so difficult to deal as that of
cheating. It is evident that the practising of intentional deceit for purposes of gain ought sometimes to be punished. It is equally evident that it
ought not always to be punished. It will hardly be
disputed that a person who defrauds a banker by
presenting a forged cheque, or who sells ornaments of
paste as diamonds, may with propriety be made liable
to severe penalties. On the other hand, to punish
every defendant who obtains pecuniary favours by

false professions of attachment to a patron; every
legacy hunter who obtains a bequest by cajoling a
rich testator; every debtor who moves the compassion of his creditors by overcharged pictures of his
misery; every petitioner who, in his appeals to the
charitable, represents his distresses as wholly un-
merited, when he knows that he has brought them
on himself by intemperance and profusion, would be
highly inexpedient. In fact, if all the misrepresentations and exaggerations in which men indulge for
the purpose of gaining at the expense of others were
made crimes, not a day would pass in which many
thousands of buyers and sellers would not incur the
penalties of the law. It happens hourly that an
article which is worth ten rupees is affirmed by the
seller to be cheap at twelve rupees and by the buyer
to be dear at eight rupees. The seller comes down
to eleven rupees, and declares that to be his last
word; the buyer rises to nine, and says that he will
go no higher; the seller falsely pretends that the
article is unusually good of its kind, the buyer that
it is unusually bad of its kind; the seller that the
price is likely soon to rise, the buyer that it is likely
soon to fall. Here we have deceptions practised for
the sake of gain, yet no judicious legislator would
punish these deceptions. A very large part of the
ordinary business of life is conducted all over the
world, and nowhere more than in India, by means of
a conflict of skill, in the course of which deception
to a certain extent perpetually takes place. The
moralist may regret this; but the legislator sees
that the result of the attempts of the buyer and
seller to gain an unfair advantage over each other is
that, in the vast majority of cases, articles are sold
for the prices which it is desirable that they should
fetch; and therefore he does not think it necessary
to interfere. It is enough for him to know that all
this great mass of falsehood practically produces the

same effect which would be produced by truth; and that any law directed against such falsehood would in all probability be a dead letter, and would, if carried into rigorous execution, do more mischief in a month than all the lies which are told in the making of bargains throughout all the bazaars of India produce in a century.

If, then, it be admitted that many deceptions committed for the sake of gain ought to be punished, and that many such deceptions ought not to be punished, where ought the line to run?

It appears to us that the line which we have drawn is correct in theory; that it is not more inconvenient in practice than any other line must be which can be drawn while the civil law of India remains in its present state, and that it will be unexceptionable whenever the civil law of India shall be ascertained, digested and corrected.

We propose to make it cheating to obtain property by deception in all cases where the property is fraudulently obtained; that is to say. in all cases where the intention of the person who has by deceit obtained the property was to cause a distribution of property which the law pronounces to be a wrongful distribution, and in no other case whatever. However immoral a deception may be, we do not consider it as an offence against the rights of property if its object is only to cause a distribution of property which the law recognises as rightful. A few examples will show the way in which this principle will operate.

A. intentionally deceives Z. into a belief that he is strongly attached to Z. A. thus induces Z. to make a will, by which a large legacy is left to A. Here A.'s conduct is immoral and scandalous. But still A. has a legal right on Z.'s death to receive the legacy. Even if the clearest proofs of A.'s insincerity are laid before a tribunal, even if A. in open court avows his insincerity, the will cannot, on that account, be set aside. The gain, therefore, which A. obtains under Z.'s will is not, in the legal sense of the expression, wrongful gain. He has practised deception. He has thus caused gain to himself and loss to others. But that gain is a gain to which the civil law declares him entitled, and which the civil law will assist him to recover if it be withheld from him. That loss is a loss with which the civil law declares that the losers must put up. A. therefore has not committed the offence of cheating under our definition.

But suppose that the civil law should contain, as we think that it ought to contain, a provision declaring null a will made in favour of strangers by a testator who erroneously believed his children to be dead; and suppose that A. intentionally deceives Z. into a belief that Z.'s only son has been lost at sea, and by this deception induces Z. to make a will by which everything is left to A. Here the case will be different. The will being null, any property which A. could obtain under that will would be property which he had no legal right so to obtain, and to which another person had a legal right. The object of A. has therefore been wrongful gain to himself, attended with wrongful loss to another party. A. has, therefore, under our definition, been guilty of cheating.

Again, take the case which we before put, of a buyer and a seller. They have told each other many untruths, but none of those untruths was such as, after the article had been delivered and the price paid, would be held by a civil court to be a ground for pronouncing that either of them possessed what he had no right to possess. Though the buyer has falsely depreciated the article, yet when he takes it and pays for it, the legal right to it is transferred to him, as well as the possession. Though the seller has falsely extolled the article, yet when he receives the price and delivers the article, the legal right to the price passes with the possession. However censurable, in a moral point of view, the deceptions practised by both may have been, yet those deceptions were intended to produce a distribution of property strictly legal. Neither the buyer nor the seller, therefore, has been guilty of cheating. But if the seller has produced a sample of the article, and has falsely assured the buyer that the article corresponds to that sample, the case is different. If the article does not correspond to the sample, the buyer is entitled to have the purchase-money back. The seller has taken and kept the purchase-money without having a legal right to take or keep it, and it may be recovered from him by a legal proceeding. His gain is therefore wrongful, and is attended with wrongful loss to the buyer. He is therefore guilty of cheating under the definition.

So if the seller passes off ornaments of paste on the buyer for diamonds, the price which the seller receives is a price to which he has no right, and which the buyer may recover from him by an action. Here, therefore, the object of the seller has been wrongful gain attended with wrongful loss to the buyer. The seller is therefore guilty of cheating.

So if the buyer, intending to acquire possession of the goods without paying for them, induces the seller by deception to take a note which the buyer knows will be dishonoured, the buyer is guilty of cheating. His object is to retain in his own possession money which he is legally bound to pay to the seller. The gain which he makes by retaining the money is wrongful gain, and is attended with wrongful loss to the seller. He is, therefore, within the definition.

Whether the principle on which this part of the law is framed be a sound principle, is a question which will be best determined by examining, first, whether our definition excludes anything that ought to be included, and, secondly, whether it includes anything that ought to be excluded.

It can scarcely, we think, be contended that our definition excludes anything that ought to be included. For surely it would be unreasonable to punish, as an offence against the right of property, an act which has caused, and was intended to cause, a distribution of property which the law declares to be right, and refuses to disturb. If such an act be an offence, it must be an offence on some ground distinct from the effect which it produces on the state of property. Thus, if a person to whom a debt is due, thinking that he shall obtain payment more easily if he assumes the appearance of being in the public service, wears a badge of office which he has no right to wear when he goes to make his demand, he is guilty of the offence defined in clause 150; but if he gains only what he has a legal right to possess, if he deprives the debtor only of that which the debtor has no legal right to retain, he is not a wrong-doer as respects property, inasmuch as he has only rectified a wrong distribution of property.

Indeed, it appears to us that there is the strongest objection to punishing a man for a deception, and yet allowing him to retain what he has gained by that deception. What the civil law ought to say may be doubtful. But there can be no doubt that the civil and criminal law ought to say the same thing; that the one ought not to invite while the other repels; that the code ought not to be divided against itself. To send a person to prison for obtaining a sum of money, and yet to suffer him to keep that sum of money, is to hold out at once motives to deter and motives to incite. Humanity requires that punishment should be the last resource, a resource only employed when no other means can be found of producing the desired effect. Penal laws clearly ought not to be made for the preventing of deception, if deception could be prevented by means of the civil code. To tempt men, therefore, to deceive by means of the civil code, and then to punish them for deceiving, is contrary to every sound principle.

We are, therefore, not apprehensive that we shall be thought to have granted impunity to any deception which ought to be punished as cheating.

But it is possible that our definition may be thought to include much that ought to be excluded. It certainly includes many acts which are not punishable by the law of England or of France. We propose to punish as guilty of cheating a man who, by false representations, obtains a loan of money, not meaning to repay it; a man who, by false representations, obtains an advance of money, not meaning to perform the service or to deliver the article for which the advance is given; a man who, by falsely pretending to have performed work for which he was hired, obtains pay to which he is not entitled.

In all these cases there is deception. In all, the deceiver's object is fraudulent. He intends in all these cases to acquire or retain wrongful possession of that to which some other person has a better claim, and which that other person is entitled to recover by law. In all these cases, therefore, the object has been wrongful gain, attended with wrongful loss. In all, therefore, there has, according to our definition, been cheating. We cannot see why such acts as these should be treated as mere civil injuries,— why they should be classed with the mere non-payment of a debt, and the mere non-performance of a contract. They are infractions of a legal right effected by deliberate dishonesty. They are more pernicious than most of the acts which will be punishable under our code. They indicate more depravity, more want of principle, more want of shame than most of the acts which will be punishable under

our code. We punish the man who gives another
an angry push.   We punish the man who locks
another up for a morning.   We punish the man who
makes a sarcastic epigram on another.   We punish the
man who merely threatens another with outrage.   And
surely the man who, by premeditated deceit, enriches
himself to the wrongful loss, perhaps to the utter
ruin, of another is not less deserving of punishment.

That some deceptions of this sort ought to be
punished is admitted.   But almost every argument
which can be urged for punishing any is an argument for punishing all.   The line between wilful
fraudulent deception and good faith is a plain line.
If there is any difficulty in applying it, that difficulty
will arise, not from any defect in the line, but from
the want of evidence in particular cases.   But we
are unable to find any reason for distinguishing one
sort of fraudulent deception from another sort.   The
French courts apply a test which appears to us to be
very objectionable.   They have decided that it is
not *escroquerie* to cheat by false promises, or by
exciting chimerical hopes, unless the sufferer had
reasons of weight for believing that the promises
were sincere, and the hopes well grounded.[1]   This
rule seems to us to be a license for deception granted
to cunning against simplicity.   A weak and credulous person is more easily imposed on than a judicious
and discerning person.   And just so an infant is
poisoned with a dose of laudanum which would hardly
put a grown person to sleep ; yet the poisoner is a
murderer : a pregnant woman is grievously hurt by
a blow which would make no impression on a boxer;
yet the person who gives such a blow is punished
with exemplary severity.   The law in such cases
inquires only whether the harm has been voluntarily
caused or no.   And why should the violation by deceit of the right of property be treated differently ?

[1] Paillet, Manuel de Droit Français.   Note on Clause 408 of the
Penal Code.

The deceiver proportions his artifices to the mental strength of those whom he has to deal with, just as the poisoner proportions his drugs to their bodily strength; and we see no more reason for exempting the deceiver from punishment, because he has effected his purpose by a gross fiction which could have duped only a weak person, than for exempting the poisoner from punishment because he has effected his purpose with a few drops of laudanum, which could have been fatal only to a young child.

Some persons may be startled at our proposing to punish as a cheat every man who obtains a loan by making promises of payment which he does not mean to keep. But let it be considered that a debtor, though he may have contracted his debts honestly, though it may be from absolute inability that he does not pay them, though his misfortunes may be the effect of no want of industry or caution on his part, is now actually liable to imprisonment. Surely it is unreasonable to detain in prison the man who, by mere misfortune, has involuntarily violated the rights of property, and to leave unpunished the man who has voluntarily, and by wilful deceit, attacked those rights, if only he is lucky enough to have money to satisfy the demands on him.

For example: A. and B. both borrow money from Z. A. obtains it by boasting falsely of his great means, of the large remittances which he looks for from England, of his expectations from rich relations, of the promises of preferment which he has received from the Government. Having obtained it, he secretly embarks on board of a ship, intending to abscond without repaying what he has borrowed. B., on the other hand, has obtained a loan without the smallest misrepresentation, and fully purposes to repay it. The failure of an agency house in which all his funds were placed renders it impossible for him to meet his engagements. Can it be doubt d

which of these two debtors ought rather to be sent to
prison ? Can it be doubted that A. is a proper subject
of punishment, and that B. is not so ? Yet at present
A., if he is arrested before the ship sails, and lays
down the money, enjoys entire impunity, while B.
may pass years in a gaol. It would be improper for
us here to discuss at length the question of imprisonment for debt. But it seems clear that whether it
be or be not proper that a debtor, as such, should be
imprisoned, a distinction ought to be made between
the honest and dishonest debtor. We are inclined
to believe that the indiscriminate imprisonment of
all debtors would be found to be unnecessary if this
distinction were made. But while they are all put
on the same footing, the law must be formed upon a
rough calculation of the chances of dishonesty. All
must be treated worse than honest debtors ought to
be treated, because none are treated so severely as
dishonest debtors ought to be treated. A respectable
man must be imprisoned for a storm, a bad season,
or a fire, because his dishonest neighbour is not
liable to criminal proceedings for cheating. We are
satisfied that the only way to get rid of imprisonment
for debt, as debt, is to extend the penal law on the
subject of cheating in a manner similar to that in
which we propose to extend it.

The provisions which we have framed on the subject of fraudulent bankruptcy are necessarily imperfect, and must remain so, until the whole of that
important part of the law has undergone an entire
revision.

The provisions which we propose on the subject
of mischief do not appear to us to require any
explanation.

We have given the name of trespass to every
usurpation, however slight, of dominion over property.
We do not propose to make trespass, as such, an
offence, except when it is committed in order to the

commission of some offence injurious to some person interested in the property on which the trespass is committed, or for the purpose of causing annoyance to such a person. Even then we propose to visit it with a light punishment, unless it be attended with aggravating circumstances.

These aggravating circumstances are of two sorts. Criminal trespass may be aggravated by the way in which it is committed. It may also be aggravated by the end for which it is committed.

There is no sort of property which it is so desirable to guard against unlawful intrusion as the habitations in which men reside, and the buildings in which they keep their goods. The offence of trespassing on these places we designate as house-trespass, and we treat it as an aggravated form of criminal trespass.

House-trespass, again, may be aggravated by being committed in a surreptitious or in a violent manner. The former aggravated form of house-trespass we designate as lurking house-trespass; the latter we designate as house-breaking. Again, house-trespass, in every form, may be aggravated by the time at which it is committed. Trespass of this sort has, for obvious reasons, always been considered as a more serious offence when committed by night than when committed by day. Thus we have four aggravated forms of that sort of criminal trespass which we designate as house-trespass, lurking house-trespass, house-breaking, lurking house-trespass by night, and house-breaking by night.

These are aggravations arising from the way in which the criminal trespass is committed. But criminal trespass may also be aggravated by the end for which it is committed. It may be committed for a frolic. It may be committed in order to a murder. It may also often happen that a criminal trespass which is venial, as respects the mode, may be of the greatest enormity as respects the end ; and that a criminal trespass committed in the most reprehensible mode, may be committed for an end of no great atrocity. Thus A. may commit house-breaking by night for the purpose of playing some idle trick on the inmates of a dwelling. B. may commit simple criminal trespass by merely entering another's field for the purpose of murder or gang-robbery. Here A. commits trespass in the worst way. B. commits trespass with the worst object. In our provisions we have endeavoured to combine the aggravating circumstances in such a way that each may have its due effect in settling the punishment.

NOTE (O).

ON THE CHAPTER OF THE ILLEGAL PURSUIT OF LEGAL RIGHTS.

This chapter is intended to prevent the enforcing of just claims by means which are so liable to be abused that, even when used for an honest end, they ought not to be tolerated. A creditor, for example, who has repeatedly in vain urged his debtor to pay him, finds that he has no chance of recovering his money without a troublesome and expensive lawsuit. He accordingly seizes on property belonging to the debtor, sells it, keeps only just as much as will satisfy the debt, and sends back the surplus to the debtor. This act is distinguished from theft by one of the broadest lines of demarcation which can be found in the code. It is not a fraudulent act. It is intended to correct a wrongful distribution of property, to do what the courts of law, if recourse were had to them, would order to be done. Public feeling would be shocked if such a creditor were called by the ignominious name of a thief.

At the same time, it cannot be doubted that it would be most dangerous to allow men to pronounce judgment, however honestly, in their own favour, and to proceed to take property in execution for the purpose of satisfying that judgment. A specific thing, indeed, which a man has a right to possess, it is no offence in him to take wherever he finds it. He may commit other offences in order to take it. But the mere taking is no crime at all. If Z. has borrowed A.'s horse, and illegally refuses to return it, it is no offence at all in A. to take the horse if he sees it feeding by the roadside. If A. enters Z.'s stable in order to take it, he may commit house-trespass, but he commits no theft. If A. knocks Z. down in order to take it, he may be guilty of assault, or of voluntarily causing bodily hurt, but he commits no robbery. This license, as it appears to us, must be confined to cases in which specific things are taken. In such cases the chance of abuse is very small. But where one thing is due, and another is taken, where a man seizes on another's furniture in satisfaction of a promissory note, or drives away another's cattle by way of paying himself for a suit of clothes, the case is very different. Honest men so often think themselves entitled to more than a court of justice would award to them, that it will be difficult to say, in cases in which the taker really has a plausible claim, and in which the value of what has been taken is not out of all proportion to the value of what is claimed, that the taker has acted dishonestly. In such cases, therefore, we think it absolutely necessary to provide a punishment for the illegal pursuit of legal rights. We observe that the French courts have decided that the taking of property by a creditor in good faith, for the purpose of paying himself, is not theft ; and this decision seems to us, as we have said, to be well grounded. But it does not appear to us that such an act is

punishable under any clause of the French code
and this we consider as a serious omission.

NOTE (P).

ON THE CHAPTER OF THE CRIMINAL BREACH OF CONTRACTS OF SERVICE.

WE agree with the great body of jurists in thinking
that in general a mere breach of contract ought not
to be an offence, but only to be the subject of a civil
action.

To this general rule there are, however, some
exceptions. Some breaches of contract are very
likely to cause evil such as no damages or only very
high damages can repair, and are also very likely to
be committed by persons from whom it is exceedingly improbable that any damages can be obtained.
Such breaches of contract are, we conceive, proper
subjects for penal legislation.

In England it would be unnecessary to provide a
punishment for a stage-coachman who should, however
maliciously or dishonestly, drive on, leaving behind
a passenger whom he is bound to carry. The evil inflicted is seldom very serious. The country is everywhere well inhabited. The roads are secure. The
means of conveyance can easily be obtained, and damages sufficient to compensate for any inconvenience or
expense which may have been suffered can easily be
recovered from the coach proprietors. But the mode
of performing journeys and the state of society in
this country are widely different. It is often necessary for travellers of the upper classes, even for
English ladies, ignorant perhaps of the native languages, and with young children at their breasts, to
perform journeys of many miles over uninhabited

wastes, and through jungles in which it is dangerous to linger for a moment, in palanquins borne by persons of the lowest class. If, as sometimes happens, these persons should, in a solitary place, set down the palanquin and run away, it is difficult to conceive a more distressing situation than that in which their employer would be left. None but very high damages would be any reparation for such a wrong. But the class of people by whom alone such a wrong is at all likely to be committed can pay no damages. The whole property of all the delinquents would probably not cover the expense of prosecuting them civilly. It therefore appears to us that breaches of contract of this description may, with strict propriety, be treated as crimes.

The law which we have framed on this subject applies, it will be perceived, only to cases in which the contract with the bearers is lawful. The traveller, therefore, who resorts to the highly culpable, though we fear too common, practice of unlawfully compelling persons against their will to carry his palanquin or his baggage will not be protected by it. If they quit him, it is what they have a legal right to do, nor will they be punishable, whatever may be the consequence of their desertion.

Another species of contract which ought, we conceive, to be guarded by a penal sanction is that by which seamen are bound to their employers. The insubordination of seamen during a voyage often produces fatal consequences. Their desertion in port may cause evils such as very large damages only could repair.' But they are utterly unable to pay any damages for which it would be worth while to sue. If a ship in the Hooghly, at a critical time of the year, is compelled by the desertion of some of the crew to put off its voyage for a fortnight, it would be mere mockery to tell the owners that they may sue the runaways for damages in the Supreme Court.

We also think that persons who contract to take care of infants of the sick and of the helpless lay themselves under an obligation of a very peculiar kind, and may with propriety be punished if they omit to discharge their duty. The misery and distress which their neglect may cause is such as the largest pecuniary payment would not repair. They generally come from the lower ranks of life, and would be unable to pay any thing. We therefore propose to add to this class of contracts the sanction of the penal law.

Here we are inclined to stop. We have indeed been urged to go further, and to punish as a criminal every menial servant who, before the expiration of the term for which he is hired, quits his employer. But it does not appear to us that in the existing state of the market for that description of labour in India, good masters are in much danger of being voluntarily deserted by their menial servants, or that the loss or inconvenience occasioned by the sudden departure of a cook, a groom, a hurkaru or a khidmutgar, would often be of a very serious description. We are greatly apprehensive that by making these petty breaches of contracts offences, we should give no protection to good masters, but means of oppression to bad ones.

NOTE (Q).

ON THE CHAPTER OF OFFENCES RELATING TO MARRIAGE.

As this is a part of the law in which the English inhabitants of India are peculiarly interested, and which we have framed on principles widely different from those in which the English law on the same subject is framed, we think it necessary to offer some explanations.

The act which in the English law is designated as bigamy is always an immoral act. But it may be one of the most serious crimes that can be committed. It may be attended with circumstances which may excuse though they cannot justify it.

The married man who, by passing himself off as unmarried, induces a modest woman to become, as she thinks, his wife, but in reality his concubine, and the mother of an illegitimate issue, is guilty of one of the most cruel frauds that can be conceived. Such a man we would punish with exemplary severity.

But suppose that a person arrives from England, and pays attentions to one of his countrywomen at Calcutta. She refuses to listen to him on any other terms than those of marriage. He candidly owns that he is already married. She still presses him to go through the ceremony with her. She represents to him that if they live together without being married she shall be an outcast from society, that nobody in India knows that he has a wife, that he may very likely never fall in with his wife again, and that she is ready to take the risk. The lover accordingly agrees to go through the forms of marriage.

It cannot be disputed that there is an immense difference between these two cases. Indeed, in the second case the man can hardly be said to have injured any individual in such a manner as calls for legal punishment. For what individual has he injured? His second wife? He has acted by her consent, and at her solicitation. His first wife? He has certainly been unfaithful to his first wife. But we have no punishment for mere conjugal infidelity. He will often have injured his first wife no more than he would have done by keeping a mistress, calling that mistress by his own name, introducing her into every society as his wife, and procuring for her the consideration of a wife from all his acquaintance. The legal rights of the first wife and of her children remain unaltered. She is the wife; the second is the concubine. But suppose that the first wife has herself left her husband, and is living in adultery with another man. No individual can then be said to be injured by this second invalid marriage. The only party injured is society, which has undoubtedly a deep interest in the sacredness of the matrimonial contract, and which may therefore be justified in punishing those who go through the forms of that contract for the purpose of imposing on the public.

The law of England on the subject of bigamy appears to us to be in some cases too severe, and in others too lenient. It seems to bear a close analogy to the law of perjury. The English law on these two subjects has been framed less for the purpose of preventing people from injuring each other, than for the purpose of preventing the profanation of a religious ceremony. It therefore makes no distinction between perjury which is intended to destroy the life of the innocent, and perjury which is intended to save the innocent; between bigamy which produces the most frightful suffering to individuals, and bigamy which produces no suffering to individuals at all. We have proceeded on a different principle. While we admit that the profanation of a ceremony so important to society as that of marriage is a great evil, we cannot but think that evil immensely aggravated when the profanation is made the means of tricking an innocent woman into the most miserable of all situations. We have therefore proposed that a man who deceives a woman into believing herself his lawful wife when he knows that she is not so, and induces her, under that persuasion, to cohabit with him, should be punished with great severity.

There are reasons similar, but not exactly the same, for punishing a woman who deceives a man into contracting with her a marriage which she knows to be invalid. For this offence we propose a punishment which, for reasons too obvious to require explanation, is much less severe than that which we have provided for a similar deception practised by a man on a woman.

We also propose to punish every person who, with what we have defined as a fraudulent intention, goes through the forms of a marriage which he knows to be invalid.

We do not at present propose any law for punishing a person who, without practising any deception, or intending any fraud, goes through the forms of a marriage which he knows to be invalid. The difficulty of framing such a law in this country is great. To make all classes subject to one law would, evidently, be impossible. If the law be made dependent on the race, birthplace or religion of the offender, endless perplexity would arise. Races are mixed; religion may be changed or dissembled. An East Indian, half English, half Asiatic by blood, may call himself a Mahomedan or a Hindoo; and there exists no test by which he can be convicted of deception. We by no means intend to express an opinion that these difficulties may not be got over. But we are satisfied that this part of the penal law cannot be brought to perfection till the law of marriage and divorce has been thoroughly revised.

We leave it to his Lordship in Council to consider whether, during the interval which must elapse before the necessary inquiry can be made, it might not be, on the whole, better to retain the existing law applicable to Christians in India, objectionable as that law is, than to allow absolute impunity to bigamy.

We considered whether it would be advisable to provide a punishment for adultery, and in order to enable ourselves to come to a right conclusion on the subject, we collected facts and opinions from all the three presidencies. The opinions differ widely. But as to the facts, there is a remarkable agreement.

The following positions we consider as fully established; first, that the existing laws for the punishment of adultery are altogether inefficacious for the purpose of preventing injured husbands of the higher classes from taking the law into their own hands; secondly, that scarcely any native of the higher classes ever has recourse to the courts of law in a case of adultery for redress against either his wife or her gallant; thirdly, that the husbands who have recourse in cases of adultery to the courts of law, are generally poor men whose wives have run away : that these husbands seldom have any delicate feelings about the intrigue, but think themselves injured by the elopement; that they consider their wives as useful members of their small households; that they generally complain, not of the wound given to their affections, not of the stain on their honour, but of the loss of a menial whom they cannot easily replace, and that generally, their principal object is that the woman may be sent back. The fiction by which seduction is made the subject of an action in the English Courts is, it seems, the real gist of most proceedings for adultery in the Mofussil. The essence of the injury is considered by the sufferer as lying in the " per quod servitium amisit." Where the complainant does not ask to have his wife again, he generally demands to be reimbursed for the expenses of his marriage.

These things being established, it seems to us that no advantage is to be expected from providing a punishment for adultery. The population seems to be divided into two classes—those whom neither the existing punishment, nor any punishment which we should feel ourselves justified in proposing, will satisfy, and those who consider the injury produced by adultery as one for which a pecuniary compensation will sufficiently atone. Those whose feelings of honour are painfully affected by the infidelity of their wives will not apply to the tribunals at all. Those whose feelings are less delicate will be satisfied by a payment of money. Under such circumstances, we think it best to treat adultery merely as a civil injury.

Some who admit that the penal law now existing on this subject is in practice of little or no use, yet think that the code ought to contain a provision against adultery. They think that such a provision, though inefficacious for the repressing of vice, would be creditable to the Indian Government, and that, by omitting such a provision, we should give a sanction to immorality. They say, and we believe with truth, that the higher class of natives consider the existing penal law on the subject as far too lenient. and are unable to understand on what principle adultery is treated with more tenderness than forgery or perjury.

These arguments have not satisfied us that adultery ought to be made punishable by law. We cannot admit that a penal code is by any means to be considered as a body of ethics, that the legislature ought to punish acts merely because those acts are immoral, or that, because an act is not punished at all, it follows ,that the legislature considers that act as innocent. Many things which are not punishable are morally worse than many things which are punishable. The man who treats a generous benefactor with gross ingratitude and insolence deserves more severe reprehension than the man who aims a blow in a passion, or breaks a window in a frolic. Yet we have punishments for assault and mischief,

and none for ingratitude.   The rich man who refuses
a mouthful of rice to save a fellow-creature from
death may be a far worse man than the starving
wretch who snatches and devours the rice.   Yet we
punish the latter for theft, and we do not punish the
former for hard-heartedness.

That some classes of the natives of India disapprove of the lenity with which adultery is now
punished we fully believe, but this, in our opinion,
is a strong argument against punishing adultery
at all.   There are only two courses which, in our
opinion, can properly be followed with respect to
this and other great immoralities.   They ought to
be punished very severely, or they ought not to be
punished at all.   The circumstance that they are
left altogether unpunished does not prove that the
legislature does not regard them with disapprobation.   But when they are made punishable, the
degree of severity of the punishment will always be
considered as indicating the degree of disapprobation
with which the legislature regards them.   We have
no doubt that the natives would be far less shocked
by the total silence of the penal law touching adultery than by seeing an adulterer sent to prison for a
few months while a coiner is imprisoned for fourteen
years.

An example will illustrate our meaning.   We
have determined not to make it penal in a wealthy
man to let a fellow-creature, whose life he could
save by disbursing a few pice, die at his feet of
hunger.   No rational person, we are convinced, will
suppose, because we have framed the law thus, that
we do not hold such inhumanity in detestation.
But if we had proposed to punish such inhumanity
with a fine not exceeding fifty rupees, we should
have offered a gross outrage to the feelings of mankind.   That we do not think a certain act a proper
subject for penal legislation, does not prove that we

do not think that act a great crime. But that, thinking it a proper subject for penal legislation, we propose to visit it with a slight penalty, does seem to indicate that we do not think it a great crime.

Nobody proposes that adultery should be punished with a severity at all proportioned to the misery which it produces in cases where there is strong affection and a quick sensibility to family honour. We apprehend that among the higher classes in this country nothing short of death would be considered as an expiation for such a wrong. In such a state of society we think it far better that the law should inflict no punishment than that it should inflict a punishment which would be regarded as absurdly and immorally lenient.

There is yet another consideration which we cannot wholly leave out of sight. Though we well know that the dearest interests of the human race are closely connected with the chastity of women and the sacredness of the nuptial contract, we cannot but feel that there are some peculiarities in the state of society in this country which may well lead a humane man to pause before he determines to punish the infidelity of wives. The condition of the women of this country is, unhappily, very different from that of the women of England and France. They are married while still children. They are often neglected for other wives while still young. They share the attentions of a husband with several rivals. To make laws for punishing the inconstancy of the wife, while the law admits the privilege of the husband to fill his zenana with women, is a course we are most reluctant to adopt. We are not so visionary as to think of attacking, by law, an evil so deeply rooted in the manners of the people of this country as polygamy. We leave it to the slow, but we trust the certain, operation of education and of

time. But while it exists, while it continues to pro
duce its never-failing effects on the happiness and
respectability of women, we are not inclined to
throw into a scale, already too much depressed, the
additional weight of the penal law. We have given
the reasons which lead us to believe that any enact-
ment on this subject would be nugatory. And we
are inclined to think that if not nugatory it would
be oppressive. It would strengthen hands already
too strong. It would weaken a class already too
weak. It will be time enough to guard the matrimonial contract by penal sanctions when that contract
becomes just, reasonable and mutually beneficial.

NOTE (R).

ON THE CHAPTER OF DEFAMATION.

THE essence of the offence of defamation consists in
its tendency to cause that description of pain which
is felt by a person who knows himself to be the
object of the unfavourable sentiments of his fellow-
creatures, and those inconveniences to which a person
who is the object of such unfavourable sentiments is
exposed.

According to the theory of the criminal law of
England, the essence of the crime of private libel
consists in its tendency to provoke breach of the
peace; and, though this doctrine has not, in practice, been followed out to all the startling consequences to which it would legitimately lead, it has
not failed to produce considerable inconvenience.

It appears to us evident that between the offence
of defaming and the offence of provoking to a breach
of the peace, there is a distinction as broad as that
which separates theft and murder. Defamatory im-

putations of the worst kind may have no tendency to cause acts of violence. Words which convey no discreditable imputation whatever may have that tendency in the highest degree. Even in cases where defamation has a tendency to cause acts of violence, the heinousness of the defamation, considered as defamation, is by no means proportioned to its tendency to cause such acts; nay, circumstances which are great aggravations of the offence, considered as defamation, may be great mitigations of the same offence, considered as a provocation to a breach of the peace. A scurrilous satire against a friendless woman, published by a person who carefully conceals his name, would be defamation in one of its most odious forms. But it would be only by a legal fiction that the satirist could be said to provoke a breach of the peace. On the other hand, an imputation on the courage of an officer contained in a private letter, meant to be seen only by that officer and two or three other persons, might, considered as defamation, be a very venial offence. But such an imputation would have an obvious tendency to cause a serious breach of the peace.

On these grounds we have determined to propose that defamation shall be made an offence, without any reference to its tendency to cause acts of illegal violence.

We considered whether it would be advisable to make a distinction between the different modes in which defamatory imputations may be conveyed; and we came to the conclusion that it would not be advisable to make any such distinction.

By the English law, defamation is a crime only when it is committed by writing, printing, engraving or some similar process. Spoken words reflecting on private character, however atrocious may be the imputations which those words convey, however numerous may be the assembly before which such words

are uttered, furnish ground only for a civil action.
Herein the English law is scarcely consistent with
itself. For if defamation be punished on account of
its tendency to cause breach of the peace, spoken
defamation ought to be punished even more severely
than written defamation, as having that tendency in
a higher degree. A person who reads in a pamphlet
a calumnious reflection on himself, or on some one
for whom he is interested, is less likely to take a
violent revenge than a person who hears the same
calumnious reflection uttered. Public men who
have, by long habit, become callous to slander and
abuse in a printed form, often show acute sensibility
to imputations thrown on them to their faces. Indeed, defamatory words, spoken in the presence of
the person who is the object of them, necessarily
have more of the character of a personal affront, and
are, therefore, more likely to cause breach of the
peace than any printed libel.

The distinction which the English criminal law
makes between written and spoken defamation is
generally defended on the ground that written defamation is likely to be more widely spread and to
be more permanent than spoken defamation. These
considerations do not appear to us to be entitled to
much weight. In the first place, it is by no means
necessarily the fact that written defamation is more
extensively circulated than spoken defamation. Written defamation may be contained in a letter intended
for a single eye. Spoken defamation may be heard by
an assembly of many thousands. It seems to us most
unreasonable that it should be penal to say, in a
private letter, that a man is dissipated, and not penal
to stand up at the town-hall, and there, before the
whole society of Calcutta, falsely to accuse him of
poisoning his father.

In the second place, it is not necessarily the fact
that the harm caused by defamation is proportioned

to the extent to which the defamation is circulated. Some slanders—and those slanders of a most malignant kind—can produce harm only while confined to a very small circle, and would be at once refuted if they were published. A malignant whisper addressed to a single hearer, and meant to go no further, may indicate greater depravity, may cause more intense misery, and may deserve more severe punishment than a satire which has run through twenty editions. A person, for example, who, in private conversation, should infuse into the mind of a husband suspicions of the fidelity of a virtuous wife, might be a defamer of a far worse description than one who should insert the lady's name in a printed lampoon.

It must be allowed that, in general, a printed story is likely to live longer than a story which is only circulated in conversation. But, on the other hand, it is far easier for a calumniated person to clear his character, either by argument or by legal proceedings, from a charge fixed in a printed form, than from a shifting rumour, which nobody repeats exactly as he heard it. In general, we believe, a man would rather see in a newspaper a story discreditable to him which he had the means of refuting, than know that such a story, though not published, was current in society.

On the whole, we are so far from being able to discover any reason for exempting any mode of defamation from all punishment, that we have not even thought it right to provide different degrees of punishment for different modes of defamation. We do not conceive that on this subject any general rule can, with propriety, be laid down. We have, therefore, thought it best to leave to the courts the business of apportioning punishment, with due regard to the circumstances of every case.

We have thought it necessary, under the peculiar circumstances of this country, to lay down for the guidance of the courts a rule which, if we were legislating for a population among whom there was an uniform standard of morality and honour, might appear superfluous. India is inhabited by races which differ widely from each other in manners, tastes, and religious opinions. Practices which are regarded as innocent by one large portion of society, excite the horror of another large portion. A Hindoo would be driven to despair if he knew that he was believed by persons of his own race to have done something which a Christian or a Mussulman would consider as indifferent or as laudable. Where such diversities of opinion exist, that part of the law which is intended to prevent pain arising from opinion ought to be sufficiently flexible to suit those diversities. We have, therefore, directed the judge not to decide the question whether an imputation be or be not defamatory, by reference to any particular standard, however correct, of honour, of morality, or of taste; but to extend an impartial protection to opinions which he regards as erroneous, and to feelings with which he has no sympathy.

There are nine excepted cases (see clauses from 470 to 478 inclusive) in which we propose to tolerate imputations prejudicial to character.

The exception which stands first in order will probably be thought by many persons objectionable. It is opposed to the rules of the English criminal law. It goes, we fear, beyond what even the boldest reformers of English law have proposed. It is at variance with the provisions of the French code, and with the sentiments of the most distinguished French jurists. It is at variance also with the provisions of the code of Louisiana. It is, therefore, with some diffidence that we venture to lay before the Governor-General in Council the results of a long and anxious consideration of this question.

The question is, whether the truth of an imputation prejudicial to character should, in all cases, exempt the author of that imputation from punishment as a defamer. We conceive that it ought to exempt him.

It will hardly be disputed, even by those who dissent from us on this point, that there is a marked distinction between true and false imputations, as respects both the degree of malignity which they indicate, and the degree of mischief which they produce. The accusing a man of what he has not done implies, in a vast majority of cases, greater depravity than the accusing him of what he has done. The pain which a false imputation gives to the person who is the object of it is clear, uncompensated evil. There is no set-off whatever. The pain which a true imputation gives to the person who is the object of it is in itself an evil, and, therefore, ought not to be wantonly inflicted. But there is often some counterbalancing good. A true imputation may produce a wholesome effect on the person who has, by his misconduct, exposed himself to it. It may deter others from imitating his example. It may set them on their guard against his bad designs.

Not only do true imputations generally produce some good to counterbalance the evil caused by them, but in many cases this counterbalancing good appears to us greatly to preponderate. However skilfully penal laws may be framed, however vigorously they may be carried into execution, many bad practices will always be out of reach of the tribunals. The state of society would be deplorable if public opinion did not repress much that legislators are compelled to tolerate. The wisest legislators have felt this, and have assigned it as a reason for not visiting certain acts with legal punishment, that those acts will be sufficiently punished by general disapprobation. It seems inconsistent and unwise to rely on the public opinion in certain cases as a valuable auxiliary to the law, and at the same time to treat the expression of that opinion in those very cases as a crime.

It is easy to put cases about which there could scarcely be any difference of opinion. A person who has been guilty of gross acts of swindling at the Cape comes to Calcutta, and proposes to set up a house of agency. A person who has been forced to fly from England on account of his infamous vices repairs to India, opens a school, and exerts himself to obtain pupils. A captain of a ship induces natives to emigrate, by promising to convey them to a country where they will have large wages and little work. He takes them to a foreign colony, where they are treated like slaves, and returns to India to hold out similar temptations to others. A man introduces a common prostitute as his wife into the society of all the most respectable ladies of the presidency. A person in a high station is in the habit of encouraging ruinous play among young servants of the Company. In all these cases, and in many others which might be named, we conceive that a writer who publishes the truth renders a great service to the public, and cannot, without a violation of every sound principle, be treated as a criminal.

There are undoubtedly many cases in which the spreading of true reports, prejudicial to the character of an individual, would hurt the feelings of that individual, without producing compensating advantage in any other quarter. The proclaiming to the world that a man keeps a mistress, that he is too much addicted to wine, that he is penurious in his housekeeping, that he is slovenly in his person; the raking up of ridiculous and degrading stories about the youthful indiscretions of a man who has long lived irreproachably as a husband and a father, and who has attained some post which requires gravity and even sanctity of character, can seldom or never produce any good to the public sufficient to compensate for the pain given to the person attacked, and to those who are connected with him. Yet we greatly doubt whether, where the imputations are true, it be advisable to inflict on the propagators of such miserable scandal any legal punishment, in addition to that general aversion and contempt with which their calling and their persons are everywhere regarded. Even in such cases, the question whether the imputation be true or false is not an unimportant question. Those who would not allow truth to be in such cases a justification, would admit that it ought generally to be a mitigating circumstance. Indeed, we find it impossible to imagine any case in which we should punish a man who told no more than the truth respecting another, as severely as if what he told had been a lie invented to blast the reputation of that other.

These two propositions, then, we consider as established ;—first, that in some cases of prosecution for defamation, the truth of the imputations alleged to be defamatory ought to be a justification ; secondly, —that in the vast majority of such cases, if not in all, truth, if it be not a justification, ought to be a mitigation.

From these two propositions a third proposition necessarily follows :—that in all cases of prosecution for defamation, if the defendant avers that the imputations complained of as defamatory are true, the court ought to go into the question of the truth of those imputations.

This ought to be done, not only in justice to the public and to the defendant, but in justice to the innocent complainant. It must not be forgotten, that one of the most important ends which a person proposes to himself in prosecuting a slanderer is the refuting of the slander. He generally considers the punishment of the offender as a secondary object;

and, when there is no circumstance of peculiar aggravation in the case, is often willing to stay proceedings after obtaining a retractation and apology. To clear his fame is his first object. It is, we conceive, an object for the attaining of which he is entitled to the assistance of the law. But it is an object which cannot be attained unless the courts go into the question of truth.

The effect of a rule excluding evidence of the truth is to put on a par descriptions of persons between whom it is desirable to make the widest distinction. The public-spirited man who warns the mercantile community against a notorious cheat, or advises families not to admit into their intimacy a practised seducer of innocence, is placed on the same footing with the slanderer who invents the most infamous falsehoods against persons of the purest character. On the other hand, a man who has, without the slightest reason, been held up to the world as a seducer or a swindler, is placed in exactly the same situation with one who well deserves those disgraceful names. So defective is the investigation that it leaves a suspicion lying on the most innocent, and no more than a suspicion lying on the most guilty.

We therefore think that in all cases of prosecution for defamation, the courts ought to allow the question of truth to be gone into. But if in all cases the courts allow the question of truth to be gone into, we are satisfied that no respectable person will venture to institute a prosecution for defamation in a case in which he knows that the truth of the defamatory matter is likely to be proved. He will feel that, by prosecuting, he should injure his own character far more deeply than any libeller can do. However disagreeable it may be to his feelings that a discreditable story concerning him should be repeated in society, and should furnish paragraphs for the newspapers, it must be much more disagreeable that such a story should be proved in open court by legal evidence. By prosecuting, he turns what was at most a strong suspicion into an absolute certainty. While he forbears to prosecute, many people will probably disbelieve the scandalous report; many will doubt about its truth. The mere circumstance that he abstains from prosecuting is no proof of guilt. It is notorious that slanders are often passed by with silent contempt by those who are the objects of them. Indeed, in a country where the press is free, a man whose station exposes him to remark would have nothing to do but to prosecute, if he should institute legal proceedings every time that he might be calumniated.

It seems to us, therefore, certain, that a man on whose character imputations have been thrown, which can be proved to be true, will, if he possess ordinary prudence and ordinary sensibility, abstain from having recourse to a court of law, which will fully investigate the truth of those imputations. By having recourse to a court of law, he would show that he belonged to a class of persons who are the last that a legislator would wish to favour, to that class of persons in whom the sense of shame is weak, and the malicious passions strong, and who are content to incur dishonour for the chance of obtaining revenge.

Being, therefore, of opinion, that in all cases of prosecution for defamation, evidence of the truth of the imputations alleged to be defamatory ought to be received, and being of opinion that practically there is no difference between receiving evidence of truth and allowing truth to be a justification, we have thought it advisable to provide, expressly, that truth shall always be a justification. By framing the law thus, we have not in the smallest degree diminished the real security of private character, or the real risk of detraction. We have merely made the language of the code correspond with its virtual operation.

As we are satisfied that no practical mischief will be produced by the rule which we have proposed, we think that its perfect simplicity and certainty are strong reasons for adopting it.

If it be not adopted, it will be necessary to take one of two courses; either to provide that truth shall in no case be a justification, or to provide that truth shall be a justification in some cases and not in others. To the former course we feel, for reasons which we have already assigned, insurmountable objections. The effect of such a state of the law would be, that eminent public services would often be treated as crimes. If the latter course be taken, we are convinced that it would be found impossible to draw any line approaching to accuracy. We are convinced that it would be necessary to leave to the judges an almost boundless discretion, a discretion which no two judges would exercise in the same manner.

It has been suggested to us, from quarters entitled to great respect, that it would be a preferable course to admit in every case the truth of matter alleged to be defamatory to be given in evidence, for the purpose of proving that the accused person had not acted maliciously; but not to allow the proof of the truth to be a justification if it should appear that reputation had been maliciously assailed.

If a provision of this kind were adopted, it would, for the reasons which we have already given, be in practice nugatory. For no respectable person would prosecute the author of an imputation which could be proved to be true. And we take it for granted that the law of procedure will not be framed in so cruel and unreasonable a manner as to permit a prosecution for defamation to be instituted in opposition to the wishes of the person defamed. Such a power of prosecution would scarcely ever be used by a friend of the person defamed ; it would never be used by a judicious friend ; and it would be a most formidable weapon in the hands of a malignant enemy.

But if the provision which we are considering were not certain to be in practice nugatory, we should think it a highly objectionable provision. When an act is of such a description that it would be better that it should not be done, it is quite proper to look at the motives and intentions of the doer, for the purpose of deciding whether he shall be punished or not. But when an act which is really useful to society, an act of a sort which it is desirable to encourage, has been done, it is absurd to inquire into the motives of the doer, for the purpose of punishing him if it shall appear that his motives were bad.

If A. kills L. it is proper to inquire whether the killing was malicious ; for killing is *primâ facie* a bad act. But if A. saves Z.'s life, no tribunal inquires whether A. did so from good feeling, or from malice to some person who was bound to pay Z. an annuity ; for it is better that human life should be saved from malice than not at all. If A. sets on fire a quantity of cotton belonging to Z., it is proper to inquire whether A. acted maliciously ; for the destruction of valuable property by fire is *primâ facie* a bad act. But if Z.'s cotton is burning, and A. puts it out, no tribunal inquires whether A. did so from good feeling or from malice to some other dealer in cotton, who, if Z.'s stock had been destroyed, would have been a great gainer ; for the saving of valuable property from destruction is an act which it is desirable to encourage, and it is better that such property should be saved from bad motives than that it should be suffered to perish. Since, then, no act ought to be made punishable on account of malicious intention, unless it be in itself an act of a kind which

it is desirable to prevent, it follows that malice is
not a test which can with propriety be used for the
purpose of determining what true imputations on
character ought to be punished, and what true imputations on character ought not to be punished;
for the throwing of true imputations on character is
not *primâ facie* a pernicious act. It may, indeed,
be a very pernicious act. But we are not prepared
to say that in the majority of instances it is so. We
are sure that it is often a great public service; and
we are sure that it may be very pernicious when it
is not done from malice, and that it may be a great
public service when it is done from malice. It is
perfectly conceivable that a person might, from no
malicious feeling, but from an honest though austere
and injudicious zeal for what he might consider as
the interests of religion and morality, drag before
the public frailties which it would be far better to
leave in obscurity. It is also perfectly conceivable
that a person who has been concerned in some odious
league of villany and has quarrelled with his accomplices, may, from vindictive feelings, publish the
history of their proceedings, and may by doing so
render a great service to society. Suppose that a
knot of sharpers lives by seducing young men to the
gaming-table and pillaging them to their last rupee.
Suppose that one of these knaves, thinking himself
ill-used in the division of the plunder, should revenge
himself by printing an account of the transactions in
which he has been concerned. He is prosecuted by
the rest of the gang for defamation. He proves that
every word in his account is true. But it is admitted that his only motives for publishing it were
rancorous hatred and disappointed rapacity. It
would surely be most unreasonable in the court to
say:—" You have told the public a truth which it
greatly concerned the public to know; you have been
the saving of many promising youths; you have been

the means of ridding society of a dreadful pest; you
have done, in short, what it was most desirable that
you should do; but as you have done this, not from
public spirit, but from dislike of your old associates,
we pronounce you guilty of an offence, and condemn
you to fine and imprisonment."

It is evident that society cannot spare any portion
of the services which it receives. Far from scru-
tinizing the motives which lead people to render
such services, and punishing such services when
they proceed from bad motives, all societies are in
the habit of offering motives addressed to the selfish
passions of bad men for the purpose of inducing
those men to do what is beneficial to the mass.
We offer pardons and pecuniary rewards to the
worst members of the community for the purpose of
inducing them to betray their accomplices in guilt.
That the quarrels of rogues are the security of
honest men is an important truth which has passed
into a proverb; and of that security we should to a
certain extent deprive honest men if we were to
make it an offence in one rogue to speak the truth
about another rogue under the influence of passions
excited in the course of a quarrel.

We have hitherto argued this point on the supposition that by malice is meant real malice, and
not a fictitious, a constructive malice. We have the
strongest objections to introducing into the code
such a kind of malice—a malice of which a person
may be acquitted when it is clear that he has acted
from the most deadly personal rancour, and found
guilty when those who find him guilty are satisfied
that he has acted only from the best feelings—a
malice which may be only the technical name for
benevolence.

On these grounds, we recommend to the Governor-
general in Council that the first exception, as we have
drawn it, be suffered to stand part of the code.

The remaining exceptions will not require so long a defence : by clause 471 we allow the public conduct of public functionaries to be discussed, provided that such discussion be conducted in good faith. That the advantages arising from such discussion far more than compensate for the pain which it occasionally gives, will hardly be disputed by any English statesman.

But there are public men who are not public functionaries. Persons who hold no office may yet, in this country, take a very active part in urging or opposing the adoption of measures in which the community is deeply interested. It appears clear to us that every person ought to be allowed to comment, in good faith, on the proceedings of these volunteer servants of the public, with the same freedom with which we allow him to comment on the proceedings of the official servants of the public. We have provided for this by clause 472.

By clause 473 we have allowed all persons freely to discuss in good faith the proceedings of courts of law, and the characters of parties, agents, and witnesses as connected with those proceedings. It is almost universally acknowledged that the courts of law ought to be thrown open to the public. But the advantage of throwing them open to the public will be small indeed, if the few who are able to press their way into a court are forbidden to report what has passed there to the vast numbers who were absent, or if those who are allowed to know what has passed are not allowed to comment on what has passed. The only reason that the whole community is not admitted to hear every trial that takes place is that it is physically impossible that they should find room ; and, by clause 473, we do our best to counteract the effect of this physical impossibility.

Whether public writers ought to be allowed to publish comments on trials while those trials are still pending is a question which, in the present state of India, it is hardly worth while to discuss. We have not thought it necessary to insert any provision on that subject in the chapter of offences against public justice; and such a provision, even if it were necessary, would evidently not belong to the head of defamation, for the harm done by such comments, as respects public justice, is exactly the same when the comments are laudatory as when they are abusive.

By clause 474 we allow every person to criticise, in good faith, published books, works of art which are publicly exhibited, and other similar performances.

By clause 475 we allow a person under whose authority others have been placed, either by their own consent or by the law, to censure, in good faith, those who are so placed under his authority, as far as regards matter to which that authority relates.

By clause 476 we allow a person to prefer an accusation against another, in good faith, to any person who has lawful authority to restrain or punish the accused.

By clause 477 we have excepted from the definition of defamation private communications which a person makes, in good faith, for the protection of his own interests; and by clause 478 we have excepted private communications which a person makes in good faith for the benefit of others.

It will be observed that in the eight last exceptions, we do not require that an imputation should be true. We require only that it should be made in good faith. For to require in these cases that the imputation should be true, would be to render these exceptions mere nullities. Whether a public functionary is or is not fit for his situation; whether a person who has bestirred himself to get up a petition in favour of a public measure ought to be considered as an enlightened and public-spirited citizen, or as a foolish meddler; whether a person

who has been tried for an offence was or was not
guilty; which of two witnesses who contradicted
each other on a trial ought to be believed; whether
a portrait is like; whether a song has been well
sung; whether a book is well written;—these are
questions about which honest and discerning men
may hold opinions diametrically opposite; and to
require a man to prove to the satisfaction of a court
of law that the opinion which he has expressed on
such a question is a right opinion is to prohibit all
discussion on such questions. The same may be
said of those private communications which we propose to allow. It is plainly desirable that a merchant
should disclose to his partners his unfavourable
opinion of the honesty of a person with whom the
firm has dealings. It is desirable that a father should
caution his son against marrying a woman of bad
character. But if the merchant is permitted to say to
his partners, if the father is permitted to say to his
son, only what can be legally proved before a court,
it is evident that the permission is worth nothing.

Whether an imputation be or be not made in
good faith is a question for the courts of law. The
burden of the proof will lie sometimes on the person who has made the imputation, and sometimes on
the person on whom the imputation has been thrown.
No general rule can be laid down. Yet scarcely any
case could arise respecting which a sensible and impartial judge would feel any doubt. If, for example,
a public functionary were to prosecute for defamation
a writer who had described him in general terms as
incapable, the court would probably require the prosecutor to give some proof of bad faith. If the
prosecutor had no such proof to offer, the defendant
would be acquitted. If the prosecutor were to prove
that the defendant had applied to him for money,
had promised to write in his praise if the money
were advanced, and had threatened to abuse him if

the money were withheld, the court would, probably, be of opinion that the defendant had not written in good faith, and would convict him.

On the other hand, if the imputation were an imputation of some particular fact, or an imputation which, though general in form, yet implied the truth of some particular fact which, if true, might be proved, the court would probably hold that the burden of proving good faith lay on the defendant. Thus if a person were to publish that a collector was in the habit of receiving bribes from the zemindars of his district, and were unable to specify a single case, or to give any authority for his assertion, the courts would probably be of opinion that the imputation had not been made in good faith.

Again : if a critic described a writer as a plagiarist, the courts would not consider this as defamation without very strong proof of bad faith. But if it were proved that the critic had, like Lauder, interpolated passages in old books in order to bear out the charge of plagiarism, the court would doubtless be of opinion that he had not criticised in good faith, and would convict him of defamation.

It will be necessary to provide in the code of procedure rules for pleading in cases of defamation, which may give to an innocent man who has been calumniated the means of clearing his character. It will be proper to provide that a defendant who is accused of defamation, and who rests his defence on the truth of the imputation alleged to be defamatory, shall be held strictly to the proof of the substance of the imputation if the imputation be particular, and shall be compelled to descend to particulars in his plea if the imputation be general. It will not be expected that we should here go into any details respecting the law of criminal pleading. It is sufficient here to say, that the importance of framing that part of the law in such a manner as to give full protection to persons whose character has been unjustly aspersed has not escaped our attention.

We may here observe that an imputation which is not defamatory may, under certain circumstances, be punishable on other grounds. Such an imputation may be intended to excite disaffection. If so, though not punishable as defamation, it will be punishable as sedition. An attack made, in good faith, on the public administration of the Governor of a presidency, will in no case be a defamation. But if the author of it designed to inflame the people against the Government, he will be liable to punishment under clause 113.

Again: an imputation which is not defamatory may be intended to excite a mob to violence against an individual. If so, the author of the imputation is punishable under clause 94.

Again: an imputation which is not defamatory may be uttered in the hearing of the person who is the object of it, for the purpose of wantonly and maliciously annoying that person. If so, it is punishable under clause 485. There are many cases in which it is fit that unpleasant truth should be told respecting an individual. But there is no case in which it is desirable that such truth should be told in such a way that the telling of it is a gross personal outrage. A person who has detected, or thinks that he has detected, a dishonest misrepresentation in a book has a right to expose it publicly. But he cannot be allowed to intrude into the presence of the author of the book, and to tell him to his face that he is a liar. A person who knows the mistress of a female school to be a woman of infamous character deserves well of society if he states what he knows. But he cannot be allowed to follow her through the streets calling her by opprobrious names, though he may be able to prove that all those names were merited. A person who brings to notice the malversation of a public functionary deserves applause. But a person who hangs a public functionary in effigy at that functionary's door, with an opprobrious label, does what cannot be permitted, even though every word on the label, and every imputation which the exhibition was meant to convey, may be perfectly true.

We do not apprehend that the clauses relating to the printers and publishers of defamatory matter require any explanation or defence.

LAYS OF ANCIENT ROME.

PREFACE.

THAT what is called the history of the Kings and early Consuls of Rome is to a great extent fabulous, few scholars have, since the time of Beaufort, ventured to deny. It is certain that, more than three hundred and sixty years after the date ordinarily assigned for the foundation of the city, the public records were, with scarcely an exception, destroyed by the Gauls. It is certain that the oldest annals of the commonwealth were compiled more than a century and a half after this destruction of the records. It is certain, therefore, that the great Latin writers of the Augustan age did not possess those materials, without which a trustworthy account of the infancy of the republic could not possibly be framed. Those writers own, indeed, that the chronicles to which they had access were filled with battles that were never fought, and Consuls that were never inaugurated; and we have abundant proof that, in these chronicles, events of the greatest importance, such as the issue of the war with Porsena, and the issue of the war with Brennus, were grossly misrepresented. Under these circumstances a wise man will look with great suspicion on the legend which has come down to us. He will perhaps be

inclined to regard the princes who are said to have
founded the civil and religious institutions of Rome,
the son of Mars, and the husband of Egeria, as mere
mythological personages, of the same class with
Perseus and Ixion. As he draws nearer and nearer
to the confines of authentic history, he will become
less and less hard of belief. He will admit that the
most important parts of the narrative have some
foundation in truth. But he will distrust almost
all the details, not only because they seldom rest on
any solid evidence, but also because he will constantly detect in them, even when they are within
the limits of physical possibility, that peculiar character, more easily understood than defined, which
distinguishes the creations of the imagination from
the realities of the world in which we live.

The early history of Rome is indeed far more
poetical than any thing else in Latin literature.
The loves of the Vestal and the God of War, the
cradle laid among the reeds of Tiber, the fig-
tree, the she-wolf, the shepherd's cabin, the recognition, the fratricide, the rape of the Sabines, the
death of Tarpeia, the fall of Hostus Hostilius, the
struggle of Mettus Curtius through the marsh, the
women rushing with torn raiment and dishevelled
hair between their fathers and their husbands, the
nightly meetings of Numa and the Nymph by the
well in the sacred grove, the fight of the three
Romans and the three Albans, the purchase of the
Sibylline books, the crime of Tullia, the simulated
madness of Brutus, the ambiguous reply of the
Delphian oracle to the Tarquins, the wrongs of
Lucretia, the heroic actions of Horatius Cocles, of

Scævola, and of Clœlia, the battle of Regillus won
by the aid of Castor and Pollux, the defence of
Cremera, the touching story of Coriolanus, the still
more touching story of Virginia, the wild legend
about the draining of the Alban lake, the combat
between Valerius Corvus and the gigantic Gaul, are
among the many instances which will at once suggest
themselves to every reader.

In the narrative of Livy, who was a man of fine
imagination, these stories retain much of their
genuine character. Nor could even the tasteless
Dionysius distort and mutilate them into mere
prose. The poetry shines, in spite of him, through
the dreary pedantry of his eleven books. It is discernible in the most tedious and in the most superficial modern works on the early times of Rome. It
enlivens the dulness of the Universal History, and
gives a charm to the most meagre abridgements of
Goldsmith.

Even in the age of Plutarch there were discerning men who rejected the popular account of the
foundation of Rome, because that account appeared
to them to have the air, not of a history, but of a
romance or a drama. Plutarch, who was displeased
at their incredulity, had nothing better to say in
reply to their arguments than that chance sometimes
turns poet, and produces trains of events not to be
distinguished from the most elaborate plots which
are constructed by art.[1] But though the existence

[1] Ὕποπτον μὲν ἐνίοις ἐστὶ τὸ
δραματικὸν καὶ πλασματῶδες· οὐ
δεῖ δὲ ἀπιστεῖν,,τὴν τύχην ὁρῶντας,
οἵων ποιημάτων δημιουργός ἐστι.
—Plut. Rom. viii. This remarkable passage has been more
grossly misinterpreted than any
other in the Greek language,
where the senso was so obvious.
The Latin version of Cruserius,

of a poetical element in the early history of the Great City was detected so many ages ago, the first critic who distinctly saw from what source that poetical element had been derived was James Perizonius, one of the most acute and learned antiquaries of the seventeenth century. His theory, which, in his own days, attracted little or no notice, was revived in the present generation by Niebuhr, a man who would have been the first writer of his time, if his talent for communicating truths had borne any proportion to his talent for investigating them. That theory has been adopted by several eminent scholars of our own country, particularly by the Bishop of St. David's, by Professor Malden, and by the lamented Arnold. It appears to be now generally received by men conversant with classical antiquity; and indeed it rests on such strong proofs, both internal and external, that it will not be easily subverted. A popular exposition of this theory, and of the evidence by which it is supported, may not be without interest even for readers who are unacquainted with the ancient languages.

The Latin literature which has come down to us is of later date than the commencement of the second Punic war, and consists almost exclusively of works fashioned on Greek models. The Latin metres, heroic, elegiac, lyric, and dramatic, are of Greek origin. The best Latin epic poetry is the feeble echo of the Iliad and Odyssey. The best Latin eclogues are imitations of Theocritus. The

the French version of Amyot, the old English version by several hands, and the later English version by Langhorne, are all equally destitute of every trace of the meaning of the original. None of the translators saw even that ποίημα is a poem. They all render it an event.

plan of the most finished didactic poem in the Latin tongue was taken from Hesiod. The Latin tragedies are bad copies of the masterpieces of Sophocles and Euripides. The Latin comedies are free translations from Demophilus, Menander, and Apollodorus. The Latin philosophy was borrowed, without alteration, from the Portico and the Academy; and the great Latin orators constantly proposed to themselves as patterns the speeches of Demosthenes and Lysias.

But there was an earlier Latin literature, a literature truly Latin, which has wholly perished, which had, indeed, almost wholly perished long before those whom we are in the habit of regarding as the greatest Latin writers were born. That literature abounded with metrical romances, such as are found in every country where there is much curiosity and intelligence, but little reading and writing. All human beings, not utterly savage, long for some information about past times, and are delighted by narratives which present pictures to the eye of the mind. But it is only in very enlightened communities that books are readily accessible. Metrical composition, therefore, which, in a highly civilised nation, is a mere luxury, is, in nations imperfectly civilised, almost a necessary of life, and is valued less on account of the pleasure which it gives to the ear, than on account of the help which it gives to the memory. A man who can invent or embellish an interesting story, and put it into a form which others may easily retain in their recollection, will always be highly esteemed by a people eager for amusement and information, but destitute of libraries. Such is the origin of ballad poetry, a species of composition which scarcely ever

fails to spring up and flourish in every society, at a
certain point in the progress towards refinement.
Tacitus informs us that songs were the only me-
morials of the past which the ancient Germans possessed. We learn from Lucan and from Ammianus
Marcellinus that the brave actions of the ancient
Gauls were commemorated in the verses of Bards.
During many ages, and through many revolutions,
minstrelsy retained its influence over both the
Teutonic and the Celtic race. The vengeance
exacted by the spouse of Attila for the murder of
Siegfried was celebrated in rhymes, of which Germany is still justly proud. The exploits of Athel-
stane were commemorated by the Anglo-Saxons, and
those of Canute by the Danes, in rude poems, of
which a few fragments have come down to us. The
chants of the Welsh harpers preserved, through ages
of darkness, a faint and doubtful memory of Arthur.
In the Highlands of Scotland may still be gleaned
some relics of the old songs about Cuthullin and
Fingal. The long struggle of the Servians against
the Ottoman power was recorded in lays full of
martial spirit. We learn from Herrera that, when a
Peruvian Inca died, men of skill were appointed to
celebrate him in verses, which all the people learned
by heart, and sang in public on days of festival.
The feats of Kurroglou, the great freebooter of
Turkistan, recounted in ballads composed by him-
self, are known in every village of Northern Persia.
Captain Beechey heard the bards of the Sandwich
Islands recite the heroic achievements of Tame-
hameha, the most illustrious of their kings. Mungo
Park found in the heart of Africa a class of singing

men, the only annalists of their rude tribes, and heard them tell the story of the victory which Damel, the negro prince of the Jaloffs, won over Abdulkader, the Mussulman tyrant of Foota Torra. This species of poetry attained a high degree of excellence among the Castilians, before they began to copy Tuscan patterns. It attained a still higher degree of excellence among the English and the Lowland Scotch, during the fourteenth, fifteenth, and sixteenth centuries. But it reached its full perfection in ancient Greece : for there can be no doubt that the great Homeric poems are generically ballads, though widely distinguished from all other ballads, and indeed from almost all other human compositions, by transcendent sublimity and beauty.

As it is agreeable to general experience that, at a certain stage in the progress of society, ballad-poetry should flourish, so is it also agreeable to general experience that, at a subsequent stage in the progress of society, ballad-poetry should be undervalued and neglected. Knowledge advances : manners change : great foreign models of composition are studied and imitated. The phraseology of the old minstrels becomes obsolete. Their versification, which, having received its laws only from the ear, abounds in irregularities, seems licentious and uncouth. Their simplicity appears beggarly when compared with the quaint forms and gaudy colouring of such artists as Cowley and Gongora. The ancient lays, unjustly despised by the learned and polite, linger for a time in the memory of the vulgar, and are at length too often irretrievably lost. We cannot wonder that the ballads of Rome should have altogether disappeared, when we remember how very narrowly, in spite of the invention of printing, those of our own country and those of Spain escaped the same fate. There is indeed little doubt that oblivion covers many English songs equal to any that were published by Bishop Percy, and many Spanish songs as good as the best of those which have been so happily translated by Mr. Lockhart. Eighty years ago England possessed only one tattered copy of Childe Waters and Sir Cauline, and Spain only one tattered copy of the noble poem of the Cid. The snuff of a candle, or a mischievous dog, might in a moment have deprived the world for ever of any of those fine compositions. Sir Walter Scott, who united to the fire of a great poet the minute curiosity and patient diligence of a great antiquary, was but just in time to save the precious relics of the Minstrelsy of the Border. In Germany, the lay of the Nibelungs had been long utterly forgotten, when, in the eighteenth century, it was, for the first time, printed from a manuscript in the old library of a noble family. In truth, the only people who, through their whole passage from simplicity to the highest civilisation, never for a moment ceased to love and admire their old ballads, were the Greeks.

That the early Romans should have had ballad-poetry, and that this poetry should have perished, is therefore not strange. It would, on the contrary, have been strange if these things had not come to pass; and we should be justified in pronouncing them highly probable, even if we had no direct evidence on the subject. But we have direct evidence of unquestionable authority.

Ennius, who flourished in the time of the Second Punic War, was regarded in the Augustan age as the father of Latin poetry. He was, in truth, the father of the second school of Latin poetry, the only school of which the works have descended to us. But from Ennius himself we learn that there were poets who stood to him in the same relation in which the author of the romance of Count Alarcos stood to Garcilaso, or the author of the "Lytell Geste of Robyn Hode" to Lord Surrey. Ennius speaks of verses which the Fauns and the Bards were wont to chant in the old time, when none had yet studied the graces of speech, when none had yet climbed the peaks sacred to the Goddesses of Grecian song. "Where," Cicero mournfully asks, "are those old verses now?"[1]

Contemporary with Ennius was Quintus Fabius Pictor, the earliest of the Roman annalists. His account of the infancy and youth of Romulus and Remus has been preserved by Dionysius, and contains a very remarkable reference to the ancient

[1] "Quid? Nostri versus ubi sunt?
. . . . . 'Quos olim Fauni vatesque canebant,
Cum neque Musarum scopulos quisquam superârat,
Nec dicti studiosus erat.'"
                              Brutus, xxii.

The Muses, it should be observed, are Greek divinities. The Italian Goddesses of verse were the Camœnæ. At a later period, the appellations were used indiscriminately; but in the age of Ennius there was probably a distinction. In the epitaph of Nævius, who was the representative of the old Italian school of poetry, the Camœnæ, not the Muses, are represented as grieving for the loss of their votary. The "Musarum scopuli" are evidently the peaks of Parnassus.

Scaliger, in a note on Varro (*De Lingua Latina*, lib. vi.), suggests, with great ingenuity, that the Fauns, who were represented by the superstition of later ages as a race of monsters, half gods and half brutes, may really have been a class of men who exercised in Latium, at a very remote period, the same functions which belonged to the Magians in Persia and to the Bards in Gaul.

Latin poetry. Fabius says that, in his time, his countrymen were still in the habit of singing ballads about the Twins. "Even in the hut of Faustulus,"—so these old lays appear to have run,—"the children of Rhea and Mars were, in port and in spirit, not like unto swineherds or cowherds, but such that men might well guess them to be of the blood of Kings and Gods." [1]

[1] Οἱ δὲ ἀνδρωθέντες γίνονται, κατά τε ἀξίωσιν μορφῆς καὶ φρονήματος ὄγκον οὐ συοφορβοῖς καὶ βουκόλοις ἐοικότες, ἀλλ᾽ οἵους ἄν τις ἀξιώσειε τοὺς ἐκ βασιλείου τε φύντας γένους, καὶ ἀπὸ δαιμόνων σπορᾶς γενέσθαι νομιζομένους, ὡς ἐν τοῖς πατρίοις ὕμνοις ὑπὸ Ῥωμαίων ἔτι καὶ νῦν ᾄδεται.—Dion. Hal. i. 79. This passage has sometimes been cited as if Dionysius had been speaking in his own person, and had, Greek as he was, been so industrious or so fortunate as to discover some valuable remains of that early Latin poetry which the greatest Latin writers of his age regretted as hopelessly lost. Such a supposition is highly improbable; and indeed it seems clear from the context that Dionysius, as Reiske and other editors evidently thought, was merely quoting from Fabius Pictor. The whole passage has the air of an extract from an ancient chronicle, and is introduced by the words, Κόϊντος μὲν Φάβιος, ὁ Πίκτωρ λεγόμενος, τῇδε γράφει.

Another argument may be urged which seems to deserve consideration. The author of the passage in question mentions a thatched hut which, in his time, stood between the summit of Mount Palatine and the Circus.

This hut, he says, was built by Romulus, and was constantly kept in repair at the public charge, but never in any respect embellished. Now, in the age of Dionysius there certainly was at Rome a thatched hut, said to have been that of Romulus. But this hut, as we learn from Vitruvius, stood, not near the Circus, but in the Capitol. (Vit. ii. 1.) If, therefore, we understand Dionysius to speak in his own person, we can reconcile his statement with that of Vitruvius only by supposing that there were at Rome, in the Augustan age, two thatched huts, both believed to have been built by Romulus, and both carefully repaired and held in high honour. The objections to such a supposition seem to be strong. Neither Dionysius nor Vitruvius speaks of more than one such hut. Dio Cassius informs us that twice, during the long administration of Augustus, the hut of Romulus caught fire. (xlviii. 43, liv. 29.) Had there been two such huts, would he not have told us of which he spoke? An English historian would hardly give an account of a fire at Queen's College without saying whether it was at Queen's College, Oxford, or at Queen's College, Cambridge.

Cato the Censor, who also lived in the days of the Second Punic War, mentioned this lost literature in his lost work on the antiquities of his country. Many ages, he said, before his time, there were ballads in praise of illustrious men; and these ballads it was the fashion for the guests at banquets to sing in turn while the piper played. " Would," exclaims Cicero, " that we still had the old ballads of which Cato speaks!"[1]

Marcus Seneca, Macrobius, and Conon, a Greek writer from whom Photius has made large extracts, mention only one hut of Romulus, that in the Capitol. (*M. Seneca, Contr.* i. 6.; *Macrobius, Sat.* i. 15.; *Photius, Bibl.* 186.) Ovid, Livy, Petronius, Valerius Maximus, Lucius Seneca, and St. Jerome, mention only one hut of Romulus, without specifying the site. (*Ovid. Fasti,* iii. 183.; *Liv.* v. 53.; *Petronius Fragm.; Val. Max.* iv. 4.; *L. Seneca, Consolatio ad Helviam; D. Hieron. ad Paulinianum de Didymo.*)

The whole difficulty is removed, if we suppose that Dionysius was merely quoting Fabius Pictor. Nothing is more probable than that the cabin, which in the time of Fabius stood near the Circus, might, long before the age of Augustus, have been transported to the Capitol, as the place fittest, by reason both of its safety and of its sanctity, to contain so precious a relic.

The language of Plutarch confirms this hypothesis. He describes, with great precision, the spot where Romulus dwelt, on the slope of Mount Palatine,

leading to the Circus; but he says not a word implying that the dwelling was still to be seen there. Indeed, his expressions imply that it was no longer there. The evidence of Solinus is still more to the point. He, like Plutarch, describes the spot where Romulus had resided, and says expressly that the hut had been there, but that in his time it was there no longer. The site, it is certain, was well remembered; and probably retained its old name, as Charing Cross and the Haymarket have done. This is probably the explanation of the words, " casa Romuli," in Victor's description of the Tenth Region of Rome, under Valentinian.

[1] Cicero refers twice to this important passage in Cato's Antiquities:—" Gravissimus auctor in Originibus dixit Cato, morem apud majores hunc epularum fuisse, ut deinceps, qui accubarent, canerent ad tibiam clarorum virorum laudes atque virtutes. Ex quo perspicuum est, et cantus tum fuisse rescriptos vocum sonis, et carmina."—*Tusc. Quæst.* iv. 2. Again: " Utinam exstarent illa carmina, quæ, multis sæculis ante

Valerius Maximus gives us exactly similar information, without mentioning his authority, and observes that the ancient Roman ballads were probably of more benefit to the young than all the lectures of the Athenian schools, and that to the influence of the national poetry were to be ascribed the virtues of such men as Camillus and Fabricius.[1]

Varro, whose authority on all questions connected with the antiquities of his country is entitled to the greatest respect, tells us that at banquets it was once the fashion for boys to sing, sometimes with and sometimes without instrumental music, ancient ballads in praise of men of former times. These young performers, he observes, were of unblemished character, a circumstance which he probably mentioned because, among the Greeks, and indeed in his time among the Romans also, the morals of singing boys were in no high repute.[2]

The testimony of Horace, though given incidentally, confirms the statements of Cato, Valerius Maximus, and Varro. The poet predicts that, under the peaceful administration of Augustus, the Romans will, over their full goblets, sing to the pipe, after the fashion of their fathers, the deeds of brave cap-

suam ætatem, in epulis esse cantitata a singulis convivis de clarorum virorum laudibus, in Originibus scriptum reliquit Cato." —*Brutus*, xix.

[1] "Majores natu in conviviis ad tibias egregia superiorum opera carmine comprehensa pangebant, quo ad ea imitanda juventutem alacriorem redderent. . . . Quas Athenas, quam scholam, quæ alienigena studia huic domesticæ disciplinæ prætulerim? Inde oriebantur Camilli, Scipiones, Fabricii, Marcelli, Fabii."—*Val. Max.* ii. 1.

[2] "In conviviis pueri modesti ut cantarent carmina antiqua, in quibus laudes erant majorum, et assa voce, et cum tibicine." Nonius, *Assa voce pro sola.*

tains, and the ancient legends touching the origin of the city.[1]

The proposition, then, that Rome had ballad-poetry is not merely in itself highly probable, but is fully proved by direct evidence of the greatest weight.

This proposition being established, it becomes easy to understand why the early history of the city is unlike almost every thing else in Latin literature, native where almost every thing else is borrowed, imaginative where almost every thing else is prosaic. We can scarcely hesitate to pronounce that the magnificent, pathetic, and truly national legends, which present so striking a contrast to all that surrounds them, are broken and defaced fragments of that early poetry which, even in the age of Cato the Censor, had become antiquated, and of which Tully had never heard a line.

That this poetry should have been suffered to perish will not appear strange when we consider how complete was the triumph of the Greek genius over the public mind of Italy. It is probable that, at an early period, Homer and Herodotus furnished some hints to the Latin Minstrels;[2] but it was not till after the war with Pyrrhus that the poetry of Rome began to put off its old Ausonian character. The transformation was soon consummated. The conquered, says Horace, led captive the conquerors. It was precisely at the time at which the Roman people

<hr/>

[1] "Nosque et profestis luci' us et sacris,
Inter jocosi munera Liberi,
Cum prole matronisque nostris,
Rite Deos prius apprecati,
Virtute functos, more patrum, duces,
Lydis remixto carmine tibiis,

Trojamque, et Anchisen, et almæ
Progeniem Veneris canemus."
Carm. iv. 15.

[2] See the Preface to the Lay of the Battle of Regillus.

rose to unrivalled political ascendency that they stooped to pass under the intellectual yoke. It was precisely at the time at which the sceptre departed from Greece that the empire of her language and of her arts became universal and despotic. The revolution indeed was not effected without a struggle. Nævius seems to have been the last of the ancient line of poets. Ennius was the founder of a new dynasty. Nævius celebrated the First Punic War in Saturnian verse, the old national verse of Italy.[1]

[1] Cicero speaks highly in more than one place of this poem of Nævius; Ennius sneered at it, and stole from it.

As to the Saturnian measure, see Hermann's *Elementa Doctrinæ Metricæ*, iii. 9.

The Saturnian line, according to the grammarians, consisted of two parts. The first was a catalectic dimeter iambic: the second was composed of three trochees. But the licence taken by the early Latin poets seems to have been almost boundless. The most perfect Saturnian line which has been preserved was the work, not of a professional artist, but of an amateur:

" Dabunt malum Metelli Nævio poetæ."

There has been much difference of opinion among learned men respecting the history of this measure. That it is the same with a Greek measure used by Archilochus is indisputable. (*Bentley, Phalaris*, xi.) But in spite of the authority of Terentianus Maurus, and of the still higher authority of Bentley, we may venture to doubt whether the coincidence was not fortuitous. We constantly find the same rude and simple numbers in different countries, under circumstances which make it impossible to suspect that there has been imitation on either side. Bishop Heber heard the children of a village in Bengal singing " Radha, Radha," to the tune of "My boy Billy." Neither the Castilian nor the German minstrels of the middle ages owed anything to Paros or to ancient Rome. Yet both the poem of the Cid and the poem of the Nibelungs contain many Saturnian verses; as,—

" Estas nuevas a mio Cid eran venidas."
"A mi lo dicen; a ti dan las orejadas."
" Man möhte michel wunder von Sifride sagen."
" Wa ich den Künic vinde daz sol man mir sagen."

Indeed, there cannot be a more perfect Saturnian line than one which is sung in every English nursery—

"The queen was in her parlour eating bread and honey; "

yet the author of this line, we may be assured, borrowed nothing from either Nævius or Archilochus.

On the other hand, it is by

Ennius sang the Second Punic War in numbers borrowed from the Iliad. The elder poet, in the epitaph

no means improbable that, two or three hundred years before the time of Ennius, some Latin minstrel may have visited Sybaris or Crotona, may have heard some verses of Archilochus sung, may have been pleased with the metre, and may have introduced it at Rome. Thus much is certain, that the Saturnian measure, if not a native of Italy, was at least so early and so completely naturalised there that its foreign origin was forgotten.

Bentley says indeed that the Saturnian measure was first brought from Greece into Italy by Nævius. But this is merely *obiter dictum*, to use a phrase common in our courts of law, and would not have been deliberately maintained by that incomparable critic, whose memory is held in reverence by all lovers of learning. The arguments which might be brought against Bentley's assertion—for it is mere assertion, supported by no evidence— are innumerable. A few will suffice.

1. Bentley's assertion is opposed to the testimony of Ennius. Ennius sneered at Nævius for writing on the First Punic War in verses such as the old Italian bards used before Greek literature had been studied. Now the poem of Nævius was in Saturnian verse. Is it possible that Ennius could have used such expressions, if the Saturnian verse had been just imported from Greece for the first time?

2. Bentley's assertion is opposed to the testimony of Horace. "When Greece," says Horace, "introduced her arts into our uncivilised country, those rugged Saturnian numbers passed away." Would Horace have said this, if the Saturnian numbers had been imported from Greece just before the hexameter?

3. Bentley's assertion is opposed to the testimony of Festus and of Aurelius Victor, both of whom positively say that the most ancient prophecies attributed to the Fauns were in Saturnian verse.

4. Bentley's assertion is opposed to the testimony of Terentianus Maurus, to whom he has himself appealed. Terentianus Maurus does indeed say that the Saturnian measure, though believed by the Romans from a very early period ("credidit vetustas") to be of Italian invention, was really borrowed from the Greeks. But Terentianus Maurus does not say that it was first borrowed by Nævius. Nay, the expressions used by Terentianus Maurus clearly imply the contrary: for how could the Romans have believed, from a very early period, that this measure was the indigenous production of Latium, if it was really brought over from Greece in an age of intelligence and liberal curiosity, in the age which gave birth to Ennius, Plautus, Cato the Censor, and other distinguished writers? If Bentley's assertion were correct, there could have been no more doubt at Rome about the Greek origin of the Saturnian measure than about the Greek origin of hexameters, or Sapphics.

which he wrote for himself, and which is a fine specimen of the early Roman diction and versification, plaintively boasted that the Latin language had died with him.[1] Thus what to Horace appeared to be the first faint dawn of Roman literature appeared to Nævius to be its hopeless setting. In truth, one literature was setting, and another dawning.

The victory of the foreign taste was decisive: and indeed we can hardly blame the Romans for turning away with contempt from the rude lays which had delighted their fathers, and giving their whole admiration to the immortal productions of Greece. The national romances, neglected by the great and the refined whose education had been finished at Rhodes or Athens, continued, it may be supposed, during some generations to delight the vulgar. While Virgil, in hexameters of exquisite modulation, described the sports of rustics, those rustics were still singing their wild Saturnian ballads.[2] It is not improbable that, at the time when Cicero lamented the irreparable loss of the poems mentioned by Cato, a search among the nooks of the Apennines, as active as the search which Sir Walter Scott made among the descendants of the mosstroopers of Liddesdale, might have brought to light many fine remains of ancient minstrelsy. No such search was made. The Latin ballads perished for ever. Yet discerning critics have thought that they could still perceive in the early history of Rome numerous fragments of this lost poetry, as the traveller on classic ground sometimes finds, built into the heavy wall of a fort or convent, a pillar rich

[1] Aulus Gellius, Noctes Atticæ, i. 24.　　　　[2] See Servius, in Georg. ii. 385.

with acanthus leaves, or a frieze where the Amazons
and Bacchanals seem to live. The theatres and
temples of the Greek and the Roman were degraded
into the quarries of the Turk and the Goth. Even so
did the ancient Saturnian poetry become the quarry
in which a crowd of orators and annalists found the
materials for their prose.

It is not difficult to trace the process by which
the old songs were transmuted into the form which
they now wear. Funeral panegyric and chronicle
appear to have been the intermediate links which
connected the lost ballads with the histories now extant. From a very early period it was the usage that
an oration should be pronounced over the remains of
a noble Roman. The orator, as we learn from Polybius, was expected, on such an occasion, to recapitulate all the services which the ancestors of the deceased had, from the earliest time, rendered to the
commonwealth. There can be little doubt that the
speaker on whom this duty was imposed would make
use of all the stories suited to his purpose which
were to be found in the popular lays. There can be
as little doubt that the family of an eminent man
would preserve a copy of the speech which had
been pronounced over his corpse. The compilers of
the early chronicles would have recourse to these
speeches; and the great historians of a later period
would have recourse to the chronicles.

It may be worth while to select a particular story,
and to trace its probable progress through these
stages. The description of the migration of the
Fabian house to Cremera is one of the finest of the
many fine passages which lie thick in the earlier books

of Livy. The Consul, clad in his military garb, stands in the vestibule of his house, marshalling his clan, three hundred and six fighting men, all of the same proud patrician blood, all worthy to be attended by the fasces, and to command the legions. A sad and anxious retinue of friends accompanies the adventurers through the streets; but the voice of lamentation is drowned by the shouts of admiring thousands. As the procession passes the Capitol, prayers and vows are poured forth, but in vain. The devoted band, leaving Janus on the right, marches to its doom, through the Gate of Evil Luck. After achieving high deeds of valour against overwhelming numbers, all perish save one child, the stock from which the great Fabian race was destined again to spring, for the safety and glory of the commonwealth. That this fine romance, the details of which are so full of poetical truth, and so utterly destitute of all show of historical truth, came originally from some lay which had often been sung with great applause at banquets, is in the highest degree probable. Nor is it difficult to imagine a mode in which the transmission might have taken place. The celebrated Quintus Fabius Maximus, who died about twenty years before the First Punic War, and more than forty years before Ennius was born, is said to have been interred with extraordinary pomp. In the eulogy pronounced over his body all the great exploits of his ancestors were doubtless recounted and exaggerated. If there were then extant songs which gave a vivid and touching description of an event, the saddest and the most glorious in the long history of the Fabian house, nothing could be more natural than that the panegyrist should borrow from such songs their finest touches, in order to adorn his speech. A few generations later the songs would perhaps be forgotten, or remembered only by shepherds and vine-dressers. But the speech would certainly be preserved in the archives of the Fabian nobles. Fabius Pictor would be well acquainted with a document so interesting to his personal feelings, and would insert large extracts from it in his rude chronicle. That chronicle, as we know, was the oldest to which Livy had access. Livy would at a glance distinguish the bold strokes of the forgotten poet from the dull and feeble narrative by which they were surrounded, would retouch them with a delicate and powerful pencil, and would make them immortal.

That this might happen at Rome can scarcely be doubted ; for something very like this has happened in several countries, and, among others, in our own. Perhaps the theory of Perizonius cannot be better illustrated than by showing that what he supposes to have taken place in ancient times has, beyond all doubt, taken place in modern times.

" History," says Hume with the utmost gravity, " has preserved some instances of Edgar's amours, from which, as from a specimen, we may form a conjecture of the rest." He then tells very agreeably the stories of Elfleda and Elfrida, two stories which have a most suspicious air of romance, and which, indeed, greatly resemble, in their general character, some of the legends of early Rome. He cites, as his authority for these two tales, the chronicle of William of Malmesbury, who lived in the time of King Stephen. The great majority of readers sup-

pose that the device by which Elfleda was substituted
for her young mistress, the artifice by which Athel-
wold obtained the hand of Elfrida, the detection of
that artifice, the hunting party, and the vengeance
of the amorous king, are things about which there is
no more doubt than about the execution of Anne
Boleyn, or the slitting of Sir John Coventry's nose.
But when we turn to William of Malmesbury, we
find that Hume, in his eagerness to relate these
pleasant fables, has overlooked one very important
circumstance. William does indeed tell both the
stories; but he gives us distinct notice that he does
not warrant their truth, and that they rest on no
better authority than that of ballads.[1]

Such is the way in which these two well-known
tales have been handed down. They originally appeared in a poetical form. They found their way
from ballads into an old chronicle. The ballads
perished ; the chronicle remained. A great historian,
some centuries after the ballads had been altogether
forgotten, consulted the chronicle. He was struck
by the lively colouring of these ancient fictions : he
transferred them to his pages ; and thus we find
inserted, as unquestionable facts, in a narrative which
is likely to last as long as the English tongue, the
inventions of some minstrel whose works were probably never committed to writing, whose name is
buried in oblivion, and whose dialect has become
obsolete. It must, then, be admitted to be possible,
or rather highly probable, that the stories of Romulus

[1] "Infamias quas post dicam magis resperserunt cantilenæ." Edgar appears to have been most mercilessly treated in the Anglo-Saxon ballads. He was the favourite of the monks ; and the monks and minstrels were at deadly feud.

and Remus, and of the Horatii and Curiatii, may have had a similar origin.

Castilian literature will furnish us with another parallel case. Mariana, the classical historian of Spain, tells the story of the ill-starred marriage which the King Don Alonso brought about between the heirs of Carrion and the two daughters of the Cid. The Cid bestowed a princely dower on his sons-in-law. But the young men were base and proud, cowardly and cruel. They were tried in danger, and found wanting. They fled before the Moors, and once, when a lion broke out of his den, they ran and crouched in an unseemly hiding-place. They knew that they were despised, and took counsel how they might be avenged. They parted from their father-in-law with many signs of love, and set forth on a journey with Doña Elvira and Doña Sol. In a solitary place the bridegrooms seized their brides, stripped them, scourged them, and departed, leaving them for dead. But one of the house of Bivar, suspecting foul play, had followed the travellers in disguise. The ladies were brought back safe to the house of their father. Complaint was made to the king. It was adjudged by the Cortes that the dower given by the Cid should be returned, and that the heirs of Carrion together with one of their kindred should do battle against three knights of the party of the Cid. The guilty youths would have declined the combat; but all their shifts were vain. They were vanquished in the lists, and for ever disgraced, while their injured wives were sought in marriage by great princes.[1]

[1] Mariana, lib. x. cap. 4.

Some Spanish writers have laboured to show, by an examination of dates and circumstances, that this story is untrue. Such confutation was surely not needed; for the narrative is on the face of it a romance. How it found its way into Mariana's history is quite clear. He acknowledges his obligations to the ancient chronicles; and had doubtless before him the "Cronica del famoso Cavallero Cid Ruy Diez Campeador," which had been printed as early as the year 1552. He little suspected that all the most striking passages in this chronicle were copied from a poem of the twelfth century, a poem of which the language and versification had long been obsolete, but which glowed with no common portion of the fire of the Iliad. Yet such was the fact. More than a century and a half after the death of Mariana, this venerable ballad, of which one imperfect copy on parchment, four hundred years old, had been preserved at Bivar, was for the first time printed. Then it was found that every interesting circumstance of the story of the heirs of Carrion was derived by the eloquent Jesuit from a song of which he had never heard, and which was composed by a minstrel whose very name had long been forgotten.[1]

Such, or nearly such, appears to have been the process by which the lost ballad-poetry of Rome was transformed into history. To reverse that process, to transform some portions of early Roman history

[1] See the account which Sanchez gives of the Bivar manuscript in the first volume of the *Coleccion de Poesias Castellanas anteriores al Siglo XV.* Part of the story of the lords of Carrion, in the poem of the Cid, has been translated by Mr. Frere in a manner above all praise.

back into the poetry out of which they were made, is
the object of this work.

In the following poems the author speaks, not in
his own person, but in the persons of ancient minstrels who know only what a Roman citizen, born
three or four hundred years before the Christian
æra, may be supposed to have known, and who are
in nowise above the passions and prejudices of their
age and nation. To these imaginary poets must be
ascribed some blunders which are so obvious that it
is unnecessary to point them out. The real blunder
would have been to represent these old poets as
deeply versed in general history, and studious of
chronological accuracy. To them must also be attributed the illiberal sneers at the Greeks, the furious
party-spirit, the contempt for the arts of peace, the
love of war for its own sake, the ungenerous exultation over the vanquished, which the reader will
sometimes observe. To portray a Roman of the age
of Camillus or Curius as superior to national anti-
pathies, as mourning over the devastation and
slaughter by which empire and triumphs were to
be won, as looking on human suffering with the sympathy of Howard, or as treating conquered enemies
with the delicacy of the Black Prince, would be to
violate all dramatic propriety. The old Romans had
some great virtues, fortitude, temperance, veracity,
spirit to resist oppression, respect for legitimate
authority, fidelity in the observing of contracts,
disinterestedness, ardent patriotism ; but Christian
charity and chivalrous generosity were alike unknown
to them.

It would have been obviously improper to mimic

the manner of any particular age or country. Something has been borrowed, however, from our own old ballads, and more from Sir Walter Scott, the great restorer of our ballad-poetry. To the Iliad still greater obligations are due; and those obligations have been contracted with the less hesitation, because there is reason to believe that some of the old Latin minstrels really had recourse to that inexhaustible store of poetical images.

It would have been easy to swell this little volume to a very considerable bulk, by appending notes filled with quotations; but to a learned reader such notes are not necessary; for an unlearned reader they would have little interest; and the judgment passed both by the learned and by the unlearned on a work of the imagination will always depend much more on the general character and spirit of such a work than on minute details.

HORATIUS.

THERE can be little doubt that among those parts of early Roman history which had a poetical origin was the legend of Horatius Cocles. We have several versions of the story, and these versions differ from each other in points of no small importance. Polybius, there is reason to believe, heard the tale recited over the remains of some Consul or Prætor descended from the old Horatian patricians; for he introduces it as a specimen of the narratives with which the Romans were in the habit of embellishing their funeral oratory. It is remarkable that, according to him, Horatius defended the bridge alone, and perished in the waters. According to the chronicles which Livy and Dionysius followed, Horatius had two companions, swam safe to shore and was loaded with honours and rewards.

These discrepancies are easily explained. Our own literature, indeed, will furnish an exact parallel to what may have taken place at Rome. It is highly probable that the memory of the war of Porsena was preserved by compositions much resembling the two ballads which stand first in the *Relics of Ancient English Poetry*. In both those ballads the English, commanded by the Percy, fight with the Scots, commanded by the Douglas. In one of the ballads the Douglas is killed by a nameless English archer, and the Percy by a Scottish spearman; in the other, the Percy slays the Douglas in single combat, and is himself made prisoner. In the former, Sir Hugh Montgomery is shot through the heart by a Northumbrian bowman ; in the latter he is taken and exchanged for the Percy. Yet both the ballads relate to the same event, and that an event which probably took place within the memory of persons who were alive when both the ballads were made. One of the minstrels says :

> " Old men that knowen the grounde well yenoughe
> Call it the battell of Otterburn :
> At Otterburn began this spurne
> Upon a monnyn day.
> Ther was the dougghte Doglas slean :
> The Perse never went away."

The other poet sums up the event in the following lines :

> " Thys fraye bygan at Otterborne
> Bytwene the nyghte and the day :
> Ther the Dowglas lost hys lyfe,
> And the Percy was lede away."

It is by no means unlikely that there were two old Roman lays about the defence of the bridge ; and that, while the story which Livy has transmitted to us was preferred by the multitude, the other, which ascribed the whole glory to Horatius alone, may have been the favourite with the Horatian house.

The following ballad is supposed to have been made about a hundred and twenty years after the war which it celebrates, and just before the taking of Rome by the Gauls. The author seems to have been an honest citizen, proud of the military glory of his country, sick of the disputes of factions, and much given to pining after good old times which had never really existed. The allusion, however, to the partial manner in which the public lands were allotted could proceed only from a plebeian ; and the allusion to the fraudulent sale of spoils marks the date of the poem, and shows that the poet shared in the general discontent with which the proceedings of Camillus, after the taking of Veii, were regarded.

The penultimate syllable of the name Porsena has been shortened in spite of the authority of Niebuhr, who pronounces, without assigning any ground for his opinion, that Martial was guilty of a decided blunder in the line,

> " Hanc spectare manum Porsena non potuit."

It is not easy to understand how any modern scholar, whatever his attainments may be,—and those of Niebuhr were undoubtedly immense,—can venture to pronounce that Martial did not know the quantity of a word which he must have uttered and heard uttered a hundred times before he left school. Niebuhr seems also to have forgotten that Martial has fellow-culprits to keep him in countenance. Horace has committed the same decided blunder ; for he gives us, as a pure iambic line,

> " Minacis aut Etrusca Porsenæ manus."

Silius Italicus has repeatedly offended in the same way, as when he says,

> " Cernitur effugiens ardentem Porsena dextram :"

and again,

> " Clusinum vulgus, cum, Porsena magne, jubebas."

A modern writer may be content to err in such company.

Niebuhr's supposition that each of the three defenders of the bridge was the representative of one of the three patrician tribes is both ingenious and probable, and has been adopted in the following poem.

HORATIUS.

A LAY MADE ABOUT THE YEAR OF THE CITY CCCLX.

I.

Lars Porsena of Clusium
  By the Nine Gods he swore
That the great house of Tarquin
  Should suffer wrong no more.
By the Nine Gods he swore it,
  And named a trysting day,
And bade his messengers ride forth,
East and west and south and north,
  To summon his array.

II.

East and west and south and north
  The messengers ride fast,
And town and tower and cottage
  Have heard the trumpet's blast.
Shame on the false Etruscan
  Who lingers in his home,
When Porsena of Clusium
  Is on the march for Rome.

III.

The horsemen and the footmen
　Are pouring in amain
From many a stately market-place;
　From many a fruitful plain;
From many a lonely hamlet,
　Which, hid by beech and pine,
Like an eagle's nest, hangs on the crest
　Of purple Apennine;

IV.

From lordly Volaterræ,
　Where scowls the far-famed hold
Piled by the hands of giants
　For godlike kings of old;
From seagirt Populonia
　Whose sentinels descry
Sardinia's snowy mountain-tops
　Fringing the southern sky;

V.

From the proud mart of Pisæ,
　Queen of the western waves,
Where ride Massilia's triremes
　Heavy with fair-haired slaves;
From where sweet Clanis wanders
　Through corn and vines and flowers;
From where Cortona lifts to heaven
　Her diadem of towers.

VI.

Tall are the oaks whose acorns
　Drop in dark Auser's rill;
Fat are the stags that champ the boughs
　Of the Ciminian hill;

Beyond all streams Clitumnus
  Is to the herdsman dear ;
Best of all pools the fowler loves
  The great Volsinian mere.

VII.

But now no stroke of woodman
  Is heard by Auser's rill ;
No hunter tracks the stag's green path
  Up the Ciminian hill ;
Unwatched along Clitumnus
  Grazes the milk-white steer ;
Unharmed the water fowl may dip
  In the Volsinian mere.

VIII.

The harvests of Arretium,
  This year, old men shall reap ;
This year, young boys in Umbro
  Shall plunge the struggling sheep ;
And in the vats of Luna,
  This year, the must shall foam
Round the white feet of laughing girls
  Whose sires have marched to Rome.

IX.

There be thirty chosen prophets,
  The wisest of the land,
Who alway by Lars Porsena
  Both morn and evening stand :
Evening and morn the Thirty
  Have turned the verses o'er,
Traced from the right on linen white
  By mighty seers of yore.

X.

And with one voice the Thirty
  Have their glad answer given :
" Go forth, go forth, Lars Porsena ;
  Go forth, beloved of Heaven ;
Go, and return in glory
  To Clusium's royal dome ;
And hang round Nurscia's altars
  The golden shields of Rome."

XI.

And now hath every city
  Sent up her tale of men ;
The foot are fourscore thousand,
  The horse are thousands ten.
Before the gates of Sutrium
  Is met the great array.
A proud man was Lars Porsena
  Upon the trysting day.

XII.

For all the Etruscan armies
  Were ranged beneath his eye,
And many a banished Roman,
  And many a stout ally ;
And with a mighty following
  To join the muster came
The Tusculan Mamilius,
  Prince of the Latian name.

XIII.

But by the yellow Tiber
  Was tumult and affright :
From all the spacious champaign
  To Rome men took their flight.

A mile around the city,
The throng stopped up the ways;
A fearful sight it was to see
Through two long nights and days.

XIV.

For aged folks on crutches,
And women great with child,
And mothers sobbing over babes
That clung to them and smiled,
And sick men borne in litters
High on the necks of slaves,
And troops of sun-burned husbandmen
With reaping-hooks and staves,

XV.

And droves of mules and asses
Laden with skins of wine,
And endless flocks of goats and sheep,
And endless herds of kine,
And endless trains of waggons
That creaked beneath the weight
Of corn-sacks and of household goods,
Choked every roaring gate.

XVI.

Now, from the rock Tarpeian,
Could the wan burghers spy
The line of blazing villages
Red in the midnight sky.
The Fathers of the City,
They sat all night and day,
For every hour some horseman came
With tidings of dismay.

XVII.

To eastward and to westward
  Have spread the Tuscan bands:
Nor house, nor fence, nor dovecote
  In Crustumerium stands.
Verbenna down to Ostia
  Hath wasted all the plain;
Astur hath stormed Janiculum,
  And the stout guards are slain.

XVIII.

I wis, in all the Senate,
  There was no heart so bold,
But sore it ached, and fast it beat,
  When that ill news was told.
Forthwith up rose the Consul,
  Up rose the Fathers all;
In haste they girded up their gowns,
  And hied them to the wall.

XIX.

They held a council standing,
  Before the River-Gate;
Short time was there, ye well may guess,
  For musing or debate.
Out spake the Consul roundly:
  "The bridge must straight go down;
For, since Janiculum is lost,
  Nought else can save the town."

XX.

Just then a scout came flying,
  All wild with haste and fear:
"To arms! to arms! Sir Consul:
  Lars Porsena is here."

On the low hills to westward
  The Consul fixed his eye,
Aud saw the swarthy storm of dust
  Rise fast along the sky.

XXI.

And nearer fast and nearer
  Doth the red whirlwind come ;
And louder still and still more loud,
From underneath that rolling cloud,
Is heard the trumpet's war-note proud,
  The trampling, and the hum.
And plaiuly and more plainly
  Now through the gloom appears,
Far to left and far to right,
In broken gleams of dark-blue light,
The long array of helmets bright,
  The long array of spears.

XXII.

And plaiuly and more plainly,
  Above that glimmering line,
Now might ye see the banners
  Of twelve fair cities shine ;
But the banner of proud Clusium
  Was highest of them all,
The terror of the Umbrian,
  The terror of the Gaul.

XXIII.

And plainly and more plainly
  Now might the burghers know,
By port and vest, by horse and crest,
  Each warlike Lucumo.
There Cilnius of Arretium
  On his fleet roan was seen ;

And Astur of the four-fold shield,
Girt with the brand none else may wield,
Tolumnius with the belt of gold,
And dark Verbenna from the hold
　By reedy Thrasymene

XXIV.

Fast by the royal standard,
　O'erlooking all the war,
Lars Porsena of Clusium
　Sat in his ivory car.
By the right wheel rode Mamilius,
　Prince of the Latian name;
And by the left false Sextus,
　That wrought the deed of shame.

XXV.

But when the face of Sextus
　Was seen among the foes,
A yell that rent the firmament
　From all the town arose.
On the house-tops was no woman
　But spat towards him and hissed,
No child but screamed out curses,
　And shook its little fist.

XXVI.

But the Consul's brow was sad,
　And the Consul's speech was low,
And darkly looked he at the wall,
　And darkly at the foe.
" Their van will be upon us
　Before the bridge goes down;
And if they once may win the bridge,
　What hope to save the town ? "

XXVII.

Then out spake brave Horatius
  The Captain of the Gate:
" To every man upon this earth
  Death cometh soon or late.
And how can man die better
  Than facing fearful odds,
For the ashes of his fathers,
  And the temples of his Gods,

XXVIII.

" And for the tender mother
  Who dandled him to rest,
And for the wife who nurses
  His baby at her breast,
And for the holy maidens
  Who feed the eternal flame,
To save them from false Sextus
  That wrought the deed of shame?

XXIX.

" Hew down the bridge, Sir Consul,
  With all the speed ye may;
I, with two more to help me,
  Will hold the foe in play.
In yon strait path a thousand
  May well be stopped by three.
Now who will stand on either hand,
  And keep the bridge with me?"

XXX.

Then out spake Spurius Lartius;
  A Ramnian proud was he:
" Lo, I will stand at thy right hand,
  And keep the bridge with thee."

And out spake strong Herminius;
  Of Titian blood was he:
" I will abide on thy left side,
  And keep the bridge with thee."

XXXI.

" Horatius," quoth the Consul,
  " As thou sayest, so let it be."
And straight against that great array
  Forth went the dauntless Three.
For Romans in Rome's quarrel
  Spared neither land nor gold,
Nor son nor wife, nor limb nor life,
  In the brave days of old.

XXXII.

Then none was for a party;
  Then all were for the state;
Then the great man helped the poor,
  And the poor man loved the great:
Then lands were fairly portioned;
  Then spoils were fairly sold:
The Romans were like brothers
  In the brave days of old.

XXXIII.

Now Roman is to Roman
  More hateful than a foe,
And the Tribunes beard the high,
  And the Fathers grind the low.
As we wax hot in faction,
  In battle we wax cold:
Wherefore men fight not as they fought
  In the brave days of old.

XXXIV.

Now while the Three were tightening
  Their harness on their backs,
The Consul was the foremost man
  To take in hand an axe:
And Fathers mixed with Commons
  Seized hatchet, bar, and crow,
And smote upon the planks above,
  And loosed the props below.

XXXV.

Meanwhile the Tuscan army,
  Right glorious to behold,
Come flashing back the noonday light,
Rank behind rank, like surges bright
  Of a broad sea of gold.
Four hundred trumpets sounded
  A peal of warlike glee,
As that great host, with measured tread,
And spears advanced, and ensigns spread,
Rolled slowly towards the bridge's head,
  Where stood the dauntless Three.

XXXVI.

The Three stood calm and silent,
  And looked upon the foes,
And a great shout of laughter
  From all the vanguard rose:
And forth three chiefs came spurring
  Before that deep array;
To earth they sprang, their swords they drew,
And lifted high their shields, and flew
  To win the narrow way;

XXXVII.

Aunus from green Tifernum,
  Lord of the Hill of Vines;
And Seius, whose eight hundred slaves
  Sicken in Ilva's mines;
And Picus, long to Clusium
  Vassal in peace and war,
Who led to fight his Umbrian powers
From that grey crag where, girt with towers,
The fortress of Nequinum lowers
  O'er the pale waves of Nar.

XXXVIII.

Stout Lartius hurled down Aunus
  Into the stream beneath;
Herminius struck at Seius,
  And clove him to the teeth;
At Picus brave Horatius
  Darted one fiery thrust;
And the proud Umbrian's gilded arms
  Clashed in the bloody dust.

XXXIX.

Then Ocnus of Falerii
  Rushed on the Roman Three;
And Lausulus of Urgo,   .
  The rover of the sea;
And Aruns of Volsinium,
  Who slew the great wild boar,
The great wild boar that had his den
Amidst the reeds of Cosa's fen,
And wasted fields, and slaughtered men,
  Along Albinia's shore.

XL.

Herminius smote down Aruns:
  Lartius laid Ocnus low:
Right to the heart of Lausulus
  Horatius sent a blow.
" Lie there," he cried, " fell pirate!
  No more, aghast and pale,
From Ostia's walls the crowd shall mark
The track of thy destroying bark.
No more Campania's hinds shall fly
To woods and caverns when they spy
  Thy thrice accursed sail."

XLI.

But now no sound of laughter
  Was heard among the foes.
A wild and wrathful clamour
  From all the vanguard rose.
Six spears' lengths from the entrance
  Halted that deep array,
And for a space no man came forth
  To win the narrow way.

XLII.

But hark! the cry is Astur:
  And lo! the ranks divide;
And the great Lord of Luna
  Comes with his stately stride.
Upon his ample shoulders
  Clangs loud the four-fold shield,
And in his hand he shakes the brand
  Which none but he can wield.

XLIII.

He smiled on those bold Romans
　A smile serene and high;
He eyed the flinching Tuscans,
　And scorn was in his eye.
Quoth he, " The she-wolf's litter
　Stand savagely at bay:
But will ye dare to follow,
　If Astur clears the way?"

XLIV.

Then, whirling up his broadsword
　With both hands to the height,
He rushed against Horatius,
　And smote with all his might.
With shield and blade Horatius
　Right deftly turned the blow.
The blow, though turned, came yet too nigh;
It missed his helm, but gashed his thigh:
The Tuscans raised a joyful cry
　To see the red blood flow.

XLV.

He reeled, and on Herminius
　He leaned one breathing-space;
Then, like a wild cat mad with wounds,
　Sprang right at Astur's face.
Through teeth, and skull, and helmet
　So fierce a thrust he sped,
The good sword stood a hand-breadth out
　Behind the Tuscan's head.

XLVI.

And the great Lord of Luna
　Fell at that deadly stroke,
As falls on Mount Alvernus
　A thunder smitten oak.
Far o'er the crashing forest
　The giant arms lie spread;
And the pale augurs, muttering low,
　Gaze on the blasted head.

XLVII.

On Astur's throat Horatius
　Right firmly pressed his heel,
And thrice and four times tugged amain,
　Ere he wrenched out the steel.
"And see," he cried, "the welcome,
　Fair guests, that waits you here!
What noble Lucumo comes next
　To taste our Roman cheer?"

XLVIII.

But at his haughty challenge
　A sullen murmur ran,
Mingled of wrath, and shame, and dread,
　Along that glittering van.
There lacked not men of prowess,
　Nor men of lordly race;
For all Etruria's noblest
　Were round the fatal place.

XLIX.

But all Etruria's noblest
　Felt their hearts sink to see
On the earth the bloody corpses,
　In the path the dauntless Three:

And, from the ghastly entrance
  Where those bold Romans stood,
All shrank, like boys who unaware,
Ranging the woods to start a hare,
Come to the mouth of the dark lair
Where, growling low, a fierce old bear
  Lies amidst bones and blood.

L.

Was none who would be foremost
  To lead such dire attack:
But those behind cried "Forward!"
  And those before cried "Back!"
And backward now and forward
  Wavers the deep array;
And on the tossing sea of steel,
To and fro the standards reel;
And the victorious trumpet-peal
  Dies fitfully away.

LI.

Yet one man for one moment
  Strode out before the crowd;
Well known was he to all the Three,
  And they gave him greeting loud.
"Now welcome, welcome, Sextus!
  Now welcome to thy home!
Why dost thou stay, and turn away?
  Here lies the road to Rome."

LII.

Thrice looked he at the city;
  Thrice looked he at the dead;
And thrice came on in fury,
  And thrice turned back in dread:

And, white with fear and hatred,
    Scowled at the narrow way
Where, wallowing in a pool of blood,
    The bravest Tuscans lay.

LIII.

But meanwhile axe and lever
    Have manfully been plied;
And now the bridge hangs tottering
    Above the boiling tide.
" Come back, come back, Horatius!"
    Loud cried the Fathers all.
" Back, Lartius! back, Herminius!
    Back, ere the ruin fall!"

LIV.

Back darted Spurius Lartius;
    Herminius darted back:
And, as they passed, beneath their feet
    They felt the timbers crack.
But when they turned their faces,
    And on the farther shore
Saw brave Horatius stand alone,
    They would have crossed once more.

LV.

But with a crash like thunder
    Fell every loosened beam,
And, like a dam, the mighty wreck
    Lay right athwart the stream:
And a long shout of triumph
    Rose from the walls of Rome,
As to the highest turret-tops
    Was splashed the yellow foam.

LVI.

And, like a horse unbroken
  When first he feels the rein,
The furious river struggled hard,
  And tossed his tawny mane,
And burst the curb and bounded,
  Rejoicing to be free,
And whirling down, in fierce career,
Battlement, and plank, and pier,
  Rushed headlong to the sea.

LVII.

Alone stood brave Horatius,
  But constant still in mind;
Thrice thirty thousand foes before,
  And the broad flood behind.
" Down with him ! " cried false Sextus,
  With a smile on his pale face.
" Now yield thee," cried Lars Porsena,
  " Now yield thee to our grace."

LVIII.

Round turned he, as not deigning
  Those craven ranks to see ;
Nought spake he to Lars Porsena,
  To Sextus nought spake he ;
But he saw on Palatinus
  The white porch of his home ;
And he spake to the noble river
  That rolls by the towers of Rome.

LIX.

" Oh, Tiber ! father Tiber !
  To whom the Romans pray,
A Roman's life, a Roman's arms,
  Take thou in charge this day ! "

So hé spake, and speaking sheathed
　The good sword by his side,
And with his harness on his back,
　Plunged headlong in the tide.

LX.

No sound of joy or sorrow
　Was heard from either bank;
But friends and foes in dumb surprise,
With parted lips and straining eyes,
　Stood gazing where he sank;
And when above the surges
　They saw his crest appear,
All Rome sent forth a rapturous cry,
And even the ranks of Tuscany
　Could scarce forbear to cheer.

LXI.

But fiercely ran the current,
　Swollen high by months of rain:
And fast his blood was flowing;
　And he was sore in pain,
And heavy with his armour,
　And spent with changing blows:
And oft they thought him sinking,
　But still again he rose.

LXII.

Never, I ween, did swimmer,
　In such an evil case,
Struggle through such a raging flood
　Safe to the landing place:

But his limbs were borne up bravely
   By the brave heart within,
And our good father Tiber
   Bare bravely up his chin.[1]

LXIII.

" Curse on him ! " quoth false Sextus ;
   " Will not the villain drown ?
But for this stay, ere close of day
   We should have sacked the town ! "
" Heaven help him ! " quoth Lars Porsena,
   " And bring him safe to shore ;
For such a gallant feat of arms
   Was never seen before."

LXIV.

And now he feels the bottom ;
   Now on dry earth he stands ;
Now round him throng the Fathers ;
   To press his gory hands ;
And now, with shouts and clapping,
   And noise of weeping loud,
He enters through the River-Gate,
   Borne by the joyous crowd.

LXV.

They gave him of the corn-land,
   That was of public right,
As much as two strong oxen
   Could plough from morn till night ;

---

[1] " Our ladye bare upp her chinne."
                  Ballad of Childe Waters.

   " Never heavier man and horse
   Stemmed a midnight torrent's force ;
    *   *   *   *   *   *

   Yet, through good heart and our Lady's grace,
   At length he gained the landing place."
                  Lay of the Last Minstrel, I.

And they made a molten image,
  And set it up on high,
And there it stands unto this day
  To witness if I lie.

LXVI.

It stands in the Comitium,
  Plain for all folk to see;
Horatius in his harness,
  Halting upon one knee:
And underneath is written,
  In letters all of gold,
How valiantly he kept the bridge
  In the brave days of old.

LXVII.

And still his name sounds stirring
  Unto the men of Rome,
As the trumpet-blast that cries to them
  To charge the Volscian home;
And wives still pray to Juno
  For boys with hearts as bold
As his who kept the bridge so well
  In the brave days of old.

LXVIII.

And in the nights of winter,
  When the cold north winds blow,
And the long howling of the wolves
  Is heard amidst the snow;
When round the lonely cottage
  Roars loud the tempest's din,
And the good logs of Algidus
  Roar louder yet within;

LXIX.

When the oldest cask is opened,
  And the largest lamp is lit;
When the chestnuts glow in the embers,
  And the kid turns on the spit;
When young and old in circle
  Around the firebrands close;
When the girls are weaving baskets,
  And the lads are shaping bows;

LXX.

When the goodman mends his armour,
  And trims his helmet's plume;
When the goodwife's shuttle merrily
  Goes flashing through the loom;
With weeping and with laughter
  Still is the story told,
How well Horatius kept the bridge
  In the brave days of old.

THE BATTLE OF THE LAKE REGILLUS.

The following poem is supposed to have been produced about ninety years after the lay of Horatius. Some persons mentioned in the lay of Horatius make their appearance again, and some appellations and epithets used in the lay of Horatius have been purposely repeated : for, in an age of ballad-poetry, it scarcely ever fails to happen, that certain phrases come to be appropriated to certain men and things, and are regularly applied to those men and things by every minstrel. Thus we find, both in the Homeric poems and in Hesiod, βίη ῾Ηρακληείη, περικλύτος ᾽Αμφιγυήεις, διάκτορος ᾽Αργειφόντης, ἑπτάπυλος Θήβη, ῾Ελένης ἕνεκ᾽ ἠϋκόμοιο. Thus, too, in our own national songs, Douglas is almost always the doughty Douglas : England is merry England : all the gold is red ; and all the ladies are gay.

The principal distinction between the lay of Horatius and the lay of the Lake Regillus is that the former is meant to be purely Roman, while the latter, though national in its general spirit, has a slight tincture of Greek learning and of Greek superstition. The story of the Tarquins, as it has come down to us, appears to have been compiled from the works of several popular poets ; and one, at least, of those poets appears to have visited the Greek colonies in Italy, if not Greece itself, and to have had some acquaintance with the works of Homer and Herodotus. Many of the most striking adventures of the house of Tarquin, before Lucretia makes her appearance, have a Greek character. The Tarquins themselves are represented as Corinthian nobles of the great house of the Bacchiadæ, driven from their country by the tyranny, of that Cypselus, the tale of whose strange escape Herodotus has related with incomparable simplicity and liveliness.[1] Livy and Dionysius tell us that, when Tarquin the Proud was asked what was the best mode of governing a conquered city, he replied only by beating down with his staff all the tallest poppies in his garden.[2] This is exactly what Herodotus, in the passage to which reference has already been made, relates of the counsel given to Periander, the son of Cypselus. The stratagem by which the town of Gabii is brought under the power of the Tarquins is, again, obviously copied from Herodotus.[3] The embassy of the young Tarquins to the oracle at Delphi is just such a story as would be told by a poet whose head was full of the Greek mythology; and the ambiguous answer returned by Apollo is in the exact style of the prophecies which, according to Herodotus, lured Crœsus to destruction. Then the character of the narrative changes. From the first mention of Lucretia to the retreat of Porsena nothing seems to be borrowed from foreign sources. The villany of Sextus, the suicide of his victim, the revolution, the death of the sons of Brutus, the defence of the bridge, Mucius burning his hand,[4] Clœlia swimming through Tiber, seem to be all strictly Roman. But when we have done with the Tuscan war, and enter upon the

[1] Herodotus, v. 92. Livy, i. 34. Dionysius, iii. 46.
[2] Livy, i. 54. Dionysius, iv. 56.
[3] Herodotus, iii. 154. Livy, i. 53.
[4] M. de Pouilly attempted, a hundred and twenty years ago, to prove that the story of Mucius was of Greek origin ; but he was signally confuted by the Abbé Sallier. See the *Mémoires de l'Académie des Inscriptions*, vi. 27, 66.

war with the Latines, we are again struck by the
Greek air of the story. The Battle of the Lake
Regillus is in all respects a Homeric battle, except
that the combatauts ride astride on their horses, instead of driving chariots. The mass of fighting men
is hardly mentioned. The leaders single each other
out, and engage hand to haud. The great object of
the warriors on both sides is, as in the Iliad, to obtain
possession of the spoils and bodies of the slain ; and
several circumstances are related which forcibly
remind us of the great slaughter round the corpses
of Sarpedon and Patroclus.

But there is one circumstance which deserves
especial notice. Both the war of Troy and the war
of Regillus were caused by the licentious passious of
young princes, who were therefore peculiarly bound
not to be sparing of their own persons in the day of
battle. Now the conduct of Sextus at Regillus, as
described by Livy, so exactly resembles that of Paris,
as described at the beginning of the third book of
the Iliad, that it is difficult to believe the resemblance accidental. Paris appears before the Trojan
ranks, defying the bravest Greek to encounter him.

Τρωσὶν μὲν προμάχιζεν ᾿Αλέξανδρος θεοειδὴς,
. . . . ᾿Αργείων προκαλίζετο πάντας ἀρίστους,
ἀντίβιον μαχέσασθαι ἐν αἰνῇ δηϊοτῆτι.

Livy introduces Sextus in a similar manner : " Fero-
cem juvenem Tarquinium, ostentantem se in prima
exsulum acie." Menelaus rushes to meet Paris. A
Roman noble, eager for vengeance, spurs his horse
towards Sextus. Both the guilty princes are in-
stantly terror-stricken :

Τὸν δ' ὡς οὖν ἐνόησεν ᾿Αλέξανδρος θεοειδὴς
ἐν προμάχοισι φανέντα, κατεπλήγη φίλον ἦτορ·
ἂψ δ' ἑτάρων εἰς ἔθνος ἐχάζετο κῆρ' ἀλεείνων.

"Tarquinius," says Livy, " retro in agmen suorum
infenso cessit hosti." If this be a fortuitous coin-

cidence, it is one of the most extraordinary in literature.

In the following poem, therefore, images and incidents have been borrowed, not merely without scruple, but on principle, from the incomparable battle-pieces of Homer.

The popular belief at Rome, from an early period, seems to have been that the event of the great day of Regillus was decided by supernatural agency. Castor and Pollux, it was said, had fought, armed and mounted, at the head of the legions of the commonwealth, and had afterwards carried the news of the victory with incredible speed to the city. The well in the Forum at which they had alighted was pointed out. Near the well rose their ancient temple. A great festival was kept to their honour on the Ides of Quintilis, supposed to be the anniversary of the battle; and on that day sump-tuous sacrifices were offered to them at the public charge. One spot on the margin of Lake Regillus was regarded during many ages with superstitious awe. A mark, resembling in shape a horse's hoof, was discernible in the volcanic rock; and this mark was believed to have been made by one of the celes-tial chargers.

How the legend originated cannot now be ascer-tained: but we may easily imagine several ways in which it might have originated; nor is it at all necessary to suppose, with Julius Frontinus, that two young men were dressed up by the Dictator to per-sonate the sons of Leda. It is probable that Livy is correct when he says that the Roman general, in the hour of peril, vowed a temple to Castor. If so, nothing could be more natural than that the multi-tude should ascribe the victory to the favour of the Twin Gods. When such was the prevailing sentiment, any man who chose to declare that, in the midst of the confusion and slaughter, he had seen two godlike forms on white horses scattering the Latines, would find ready credence. We know, indeed, that, in modern times, a very similar story actually found credence among a people much more civilised than the Romans of the fifth century before Christ. A chaplain of Cortes, writing about thirty years after the conquest of Mexico, in an age of printing presses, libraries, universities, scholars, logicians, jurists, and statesmen, had the face to assert that, in one engagement against the Indians, Saint James had appeared on a grey horse at the head of the Castilian adventurers. Many of those adventurers were living when this lie was printed. One of them, honest Bernal Diaz, wrote an account of the expedition. He had the evidence of his own senses against the legend; but he seems to have distrusted even the evidence of his own senses. He says that he was in the battle, and that he saw a grey horse with a man on his back, but that the man was, to his thinking, Francesco de Morla, and not the ever-blessed apostle Saint James. "Nevertheless," Bernal adds, "it may be that the person on the grey horse was the glorious apostle Saint James, and that I, sinner that I am, was unworthy to see him." The Romans of the age of Cincinnatus were probably quite as credulous as the Spanish subjects of Charles the Fifth. It is therefore conceivable that the appearance of Castor and Pollux may have become an article of faith before the generation which had fought at Regillus had passed away. Nor could anything be more natural than that the poets of the next age should embellish this story, and make the celestial horsemen bear the tidings of victory to Rome.

Many years after the temple of the Twin Gods had been built in the Forum, an important addition was made to the ceremonial by which the state annually testified its gratitude for their protection. Quintus Fabius and Publius Decius were elected

Censors at a momentous crisis. It had become absolutely necessary that the classification of the citizens
should be revised.   On that classification depended
the distribution of political power.   Party-spirit ran
high : and the republic seemed to be in danger of
falling under the dominion either of a narrow oli-
garchy or of an ignorant and head-strong rabble.
Under such circumstances, the most illustrious patrician and the most illustrious plebeian of the age were
entrusted with the office of arbitrating between the
angry factions ; and they performed their arduous
task to the satisfaction of all honest and reasonable
men.

One of their reforms was a remodelling of the
equestrian order ; and, having effected this reform,
they determined to give their work a sanction derived
from religion.   In the chivalrous societies of modern
times, societies which have much more than may at
first sight appear in common with the equestrian
order of Rome, it has been usual to invoke the
special protection of some Saint, and to observe his
day with peculiar solemnity.   Thus the Companions
of the Garter wear the image of St. George depend-
ing from their collars, and meet, on great occasions,
in St. George's Chapel.   Thus, when Lewis the
Fourteenth instituted a new order of chivalry for
the rewarding of military merit, he commended it
to the favour of his own glorified ancestor and patron,
and decreed that all the members of the fraternity
should meet at the royal palace on the feast of Saint
Lewis, should attend the king to chapel, should hear
mass, and should subsequently hold their great
annual assembly.   There is a considerable resemblance between this rule of the order of Saint Lewis
and the rule which Fabius and Decius made respecting the Roman knights.   It was ordained that a
grand muster and inspection of the equestrian body
should be part of the ceremonial performed, on the

anniversary of the battle of Regillus, in honour of
Castor and Pollux, the two equestrian Gods. All the
knights, clad in purple and crowned with olive, were
to meet at a temple of Mars in the suburbs. Thence
they were to ride in state to the Forum, where the
temple of the Twins stood. This pageant was, during
several centuries, considered as one of the most
splendid sights of Rome. In the time of Dionysius
the cavalcade sometimes consisted of five thousand
horsemen, all persons of fair repute and easy fortune.[1]

There can be no doubt that the Censors who instituted this august ceremony acted in concert with
the Pontiffs to whom, by the constitution of Rome,
the superintendence of the public worship belonged;
and it is probable that those high religious functionaries were, as usual, fortunate enough to find in
their books or traditions some warrant for the innovation.

The following poem is supposed to have been
made for this great occasion. Songs, we know, were
chanted at the religious festivals of Rome from an
early period, indeed from so early a period, that
some of the sacred verses were popularly ascribed to
Numa, and were utterly unintelligible in the age of
Augustus. In the Second Punic War a great feast
was held in honour of Juno, and a song was sung
in her praise. This song was extant when Livy
wrote; and, though exceedingly rugged and uncouth, seemed to him not wholly destitute of merit.[2]
A song, as we learn from Horace,[3] was part of the
established ritual at the great Secular Jubilee. It
is therefore likely that the Censors and Pontiffs,
when they had resolved to add a grand procession of

[1] See Livy, ix. 46. Val. Max.
ii. 2. Aurel. Vict. De Viris
Illustribus, 32. Dionysius, vi.
13. Plin. Hist. Nat. xv. 5. See
also the singularly ingenious
chapter in Niebuhr's posthumous
volume, *Die Censur des Q. Fabius
und P. Decius.*

[2] Livy, xxvii. 37.

[3] Hor. Carmen Seculare.

knights to the other solemnities annually performed on the Ides of Quintilis, would call in the aid of a poet. Such a poet would naturally take for his subject the battle of Regillus, the appearance of the Twin Gods, and the institution of their festival. He would find abundant materials in the ballads of his predecessors ; and he would make free use of the scanty stock of Greek learning which he had himself acquired. He would probably introduce some wise and holy Pontiff enjoining the magnificent ceremonial which, after a long interval, had at length been adopted. If the poem succeeded, many persons would commit it to memory. Parts of it would be sung to the pipe at banquets. It would be peculiarly interesting to the great Posthumian House, which numbered among its many images that of the Dictator Aulus, the hero of Regillus. The orator who, in the following generation, pronounced the funeral panegyric over the remains of Lucius Posthumius Megellus, thrice Consul, would borrow largely from the lay ; and thus some passages, much disfigured, would probably find their way into the chronicles which were afterwards in the hands of Dionysius and Livy.

Antiquaries differ widely as to the situation of the field of battle. The opinion of those who suppose that the armies met near Cornufelle, between Frascati and the Monte Porzio, is at least plausible, and has been followed in the poem.

As to the details of the battle, it has not been thought desirable to adhere minutely to the accounts which have come down to us. Those accounts, indeed, differ widely from each other, and, in all probability, differ as widely from the ancient poem from which they were originally derived.

It is unnecessary to point out the obvious imitations of the Iliad, which have been purposely introduced.

THE

BATTLE OF THE LAKE REGILLUS,

A LAY SUNG AT THE FEAST OF CASTOR AND POLLUX
ON THE IDES OF QUINTILIS,

IN THE YEAR OF THE CITY CCCCLI.

I.

Ho, trumpets, sound a war-note!
  Ho, lictors, clear the way!
The Knights will ride, in all their pride,
  Along the streets to-day.
To-day the doors and windows
  Are hung with garlands all,
From Castor in the Forum,
  To Mars without the wall.
Each Knight is robed in purple,
  With olive each is crowned;
A gallant war-horse under each
  Paws haughtily the ground.
While flows the Yellow River,
  While stands the Sacred Hill,
The proud Ides of Quintilis
  Shall have such honour still.
Gay are the Martian Kalends:
  December's Nones are gay:
But the proud Ides, when the squadron rides,
  Shall be Rome's whitest day.

II.

Unto the Great Twin Brethren
   We keep this solemn feast.
Swift, swift, the Great Twin Brethren
   Came spurring from the east.
They came o'er wild Parthenius
   Tossing in waves of pine,
O'er Cirrha's dome, o'er Adria's foam,
   O'er purple Apennine,
From where with flutes and dances
   Their ancient mansion rings,
In lordly Lacedæmon,
   The City of two kings,
To where, by Lake Regillus,
   Under the Porcian height,
All in the lands of Tusculum,
   Was fought the glorious fight.

III.

Now on the place of slaughter
   Are cots and sheepfolds seen,
And rows of vines, and fields of wheat,
   And apple-orchards green:
The swine crush the big acorns
   That fall from Corne's oaks.
Upon the turf by the Fair Fount
   The reaper's pottage smokes.
The fisher baits his angle;
   The hunter twangs his bow;
Little they think on those strong limbs
   That moulder deep below.
Little they think how sternly
   That day the trumpets pealed;
How in the slippery swamp of blood
   Warrior and war-horse reeled;

How wolves came with fierce gallop,
　　And crows on eager wings,
To tear the flesh of captains,
　　And peck the eyes of kings;
How thick the dead lay scattered
　　Under the Porcian height;
How through the gates of Tusculum
　　Raved the wild stream of flight;
And how the Lake Regillus
　　Bubbled with crimson foam,
What time the Thirty Cities
　　Came forth to war with Rome.

IV.

But, Roman, when thou standest
　　Upon that holy ground,
Look thou with heed on the dark rock
　　That girds the dark lake round.
So shalt thou see a hoof-mark
　　Stamped deep into the flint:
It was no hoof of mortal steed
　　That made so strange a dint:
There to the Great Twin Brethren
　　Vow thou thy vows, and pray
That they, in tempest and in fight,
　　Will keep thy head alway.

V.

Since last the Great Twin Brethren
　　Of mortal eyes were seen,
Have years gone by an hundred
　　And fourscore and thirteen.
That summer a Virginius
　　Was Consul first in place;
The second was stout Aulus,
　　Of the Posthumian race.

The Herald of the Latines
    From Gabii came in state :
The Herald of the Latines
    Passed through Rome's Eastern Gate :
The Herald of the Latines
    Did in our Forum stand ;
And there he did his office,
    A sceptre in his hand.

VI.

" Hear, Senators and people
    Of the good town of Rome,
The Thirty Cities charge you
    To bring the Tarquins home :
And if ye still be stubborn,
    To work the Tarquins wrong,
The Thirty Cities warn you,
    Look that your walls be strong."

VII.

Then spake the Consul Aulus,
    He spake a bitter jest :
" Once the jays sent a message
    Unto the eagle's nest :—
Now yield thou up thine eyrie
    Unto the carrion-kite,
Or come forth valiantly, and face
    The jays in deadly fight.—
Forth looked in wrath the eagle ;
    And carrion-kite and jay,
Soon as they saw his beak and claw,
    Fled screaming far away."

s 2

VIII.

The Herald of the Latines
    Hath hied him back in state :
The Fathers of the City
    Are met in high debate.
Then spake the elder Consul,
    An ancient man and wise :
" Now hearken, Conscript Fathers,
    To that which I advise.
In seasons of great peril
    'Tis good that one bear sway ;
Then choose we a Dictator,
    Whom all men shall obey.
Camerium knows how deeply
    The sword of Aulus bites,
And all our city calls him
    The man of seventy fights.
Then let him be Dictator
    For six months and no more,
And have a Master of the Knights,
    And axes twenty-four."

IX.

So Aulus was Dictator,
    The man of seventy fights ;
He made Æbutius Elva
    His Master of the Knights.
On the third morn thereafter,
    At dawning of the day,
Did Aulus and Æbutius
    Set forth with their array.
Sempronius Atratinus
    Was left in charge at home
With boys, and with grey-headed men,
    To keep the walls of Rome.

Hard by the Lake Regillus
  Our camp was pitched at night :
Eastward a mile the Latines lay,
  Under the Porcian height.
Far over hill and valley
  Their mighty host was spread ;
And with their thousand watch-fires
  The midnight sky was red.

x.

Up rose the golden morning
  Over the Porcian height,
The proud Ides of Quintilis
  Marked evermore with white.
Not without secret trouble
  Our bravest saw the foes ;
For girt by threescore thousand spears,
  The thirty standards rose.
From every warlike city
  That boasts the Latian name,
Foredoomed to dogs and vultures,
  That gallant army came ;
From Setia's purple vineyards,
  From Norba's ancient wall,
From the white streets of Tusculum,
  The proudest town of all ;
From where the Witch's Fortress
  O'erhangs the dark-blue seas ;
From the still glassy lake that sleeps
  Beneath Aricia's trees—
Those trees in whose dim shadow
  The ghastly priest doth reign,
The priest who slew the slayer,
  And shall himself be slain ;
From the drear banks of Ufens,
  Where flights of marsh-fowl play,

And buffaloes lie wallowing
  Through the hot summer's day ;
From the gigantic watch-towers,
  No work of earthly men,
Whence Cora's sentinels o'erlook
  The never-ending fen ;
From the Laurentian jungle,
  The wild hog's reedy home ;
From the green steeps whence Anio leaps
  In floods of snow-white foam.

XI.

Aricia, Cora, Norba,
  Velitræ, with the might
Of Setia and of Tusculum,
  Were marshalled on the right :
The leader was Mamilius,
  Prince of the Latian name ;
Upon his head a helmet
  Of red gold shone like flame :
High on a gallant charger
  Of dark-grey hue he rode ;
Over his gilded armour
  A vest of purple flowed,
Woven in the land of sunrise
  By Syria's dark-browed daughters,
And by the sails of Carthage brought
  Far o'er the southern waters.

XII.

Lavinium and Laurentum
  Had on the left their post,
With all the banners of the marsh,
  And banners of the coast.
Their leader was false Sextus,
  That wrought the deed of shame :

With restless pace and haggard face
  To his last field he came.
Men said he saw strange visions
  Which none beside might see;
And that strange sounds were in his ears
  Which none might hear but he.
A woman fair and stately,
  But pale as are the dead,
Oft through the watches of the night
  Sat spinning by his bed.
And as she plied the distaff,
  In a sweet voice and low,
She sang of great old houses,
  And fights fought long ago.
So spun she, and so sang she,
  Until the east was grey,
Then pointed to her bleeding breast,
  And shrieked, and fled away.

XIII.

But in the centre thickest
  Were ranged the shields of foes.
And from the centre loudest
  The cry of battle rose.
There Tibur marched and Pedum
  Beneath proud Tarquin's rule,
And Ferentinum of the rock,
  And Gabii of the pool.
There rode the Volscian succours:
  There, in a dark stern ring,
The Roman exiles gathered close
  Around the ancient king.
Though white as Mount Soracte,
  When winter nights are long,
His beard flowed down o'er mail and belt,
  His heart and hand were strong:

Under his hoary eyebrows
  Still flashed forth quenchless rage :
And, if the lance shook in his gripe,
  'Twas more with hate than age.
Close at his side was Titus
  On an Apulian steed,
Titus, the youngest Tarquin,
  Too good for such a breed.

XIV.

Now on each side the leaders
  Gave signal for the charge ;
And on each side the footmen
  Strode on with lance and targe ;
And on each side the horsemen
  Struck their spurs deep in gore
And front to front the armies
  Met with a mighty roar :
And under that great battle
  The earth with blood was red ;
And, like the Pomptine fog at morn,
  The dust hung overhead ;
And louder still and louder
  Rose from the darkened field
The braying of the war-horns,
  The clang of sword and shield,
The rush of squadrons sweeping
  Like whirlwinds o'er the plain,
The shouting of the slayers,
  And screeching of the slain.

XV.

False Sextus rode out foremost,
  His look was high and bold ;
His corslet was of bison's hide,
  Plated with steel and gold.

As glares the famished eagle
  From the Digentian rock
On a choice lamb that bounds alone
  Before Bandusia's flock,
Herminius glared on Sextus,
  And came with eagle speed,
Herminius on black Auster,
  Brave champion on brave steed ;
In his right hand the broadsword
  That kept the bridge so well,
And on his helm the crown he won
  When proud Fidenæ fell.
Woe to the maid whose lover
  Shall cross his path to-day !
False Sextus saw, and trembled,
  And turned, and fled away.
As turns, as flies, the woodman
  In the Calabrian brake,
When through the reeds gleams the round eye
  Of that fell speckled snake ;
So turned, so fled, false Sextus,
  And hid him in the rear,
Behind the dark Lavinian ranks,
  Bristling with crest and spear.

XVI.

But far to north Æbutius,
  The Master of the Knights,
Gave Tubero of Norba
  To feed the Porcian kites.
Next under those red horse-hoofs
  Flaccus of Setia lay ;
Better had he been pruning
  Among his elms that day.
Mamilius saw the slaughter,
  And tossed his golden crest,

And towards the Master of the Knights
  Through the thick battle pressed.
Æbutius smote Mamilius
  So fiercely on the shield
That the great lord of Tusculum
  Well nigh rolled on the field.
Mamilius smote Æbutius,
  With a good aim and true,
Just where the neck and shoulder join,
  And pierced him through and through;
And brave Æbutius Elva
  Fell swooning to the ground:
But a thick wall of bucklers
  Encompassed him around.
His clients from the battle
  Bare him some little space
And filled a helm from the dark lake,
  And bathed his brow and face;
And when at last he opened
  His swimming eyes to light,
Men say, the earliest words he spake
  Were, " Friends, how goes the fight ?"

XVII.

But meanwhile in the centre
  Great deeds of arms were wrought;
There Aulus the Dictator
  And there Valerius fought.
Aulus with his good broadsword
  A bloody passage cleared
To where, amidst the thickest foes,
  He saw the long white beard.
Flat lighted that good broadsword
  Upon proud Tarquin's head.
He dropped the lance: he dropped the reins:
  He fell as fall the dead.
Down Aulus springs to slay him,
  With eyes like coals of fire;

But faster Titus hath sprung down,
  And hath bestrode his sire.
Latian captains, Roman knights,
  Fast down to earth they spring,
And hand to hand they fight on foot
  Around the ancient king.
First Titus gave tall Cæso
  A death wound in the face ;
Tall Cæso was the bravest man
  Of the brave Fabian race :
Aulus slew Rex of Gabii,
  The priest of Juno's shrine :
Valerius smote down Julius,
  Of Rome's great Julian line ;
Julius, who left his mansion,
  High on the Velian hill,
And through all turns of weal and woe
  Followed proud Tarquin still.
Now right across proud Tarquin
  A corpse was Julius laid :
And Titus groaned with rage and grief,
  And at Valerius made.
Valerius struck at Titus,
  And lopped off half his crest ;
But Titus stabbed Valerius
  A span deep in the breast.
Like a mast snapped by the tempest,
  Valerius reeled and fell.
Ah ! woe is me for the good house
  That loves the people well !
Then shouted loud the Latines :
  And with one rush they bore
The struggling Romans backward
  Three lances' length and more :
And up they took proud Tarquin,
  And laid him on a shield,
And four strong yeomen bare him,
  Still senseless, from the field.

XVIII.

But fiercer grew the fighting
    Around Valerius dead ;
For Titus dragged him by the foot,
    And Aulus by the head.
" On, Latines, on ! " quoth Titus,
    " See how the rebels fly ! "
" Romans, stand firm ! " quoth Aulus,
    " And win this fight or die !
They must not give Valerius
    To raven and to kite ;
For aye Valerius loathed the wrong,
    And aye upheld the right.:
And for your wives and babies
    In the front rank he fell.
Now play the men for the good house
    That loves the people well ! "

XIX.

Then tenfold round the body
    The roar of battle rose,
Like the roar of a burning forest,
    When a strong north wind blows.
Now backward, and now forward,
    Rocked furiously the fray,
Till none could see Valerius,
    And none wist where he lay.
For shivered arms and ensigns
    Were heaped there in a mound,
And corpses stiff, and dying men
    That writhed and gnawed the ground ;
And wounded horses kicking,
    And snorting purple foam :
Right well did such a couch befit
    A Consular of Rome.

XX.

But north looked the Dictator;
    North looked he long and hard,
And spake to Caius Cossus,
    The Captain of his Guard;
" Caius, of all the Romans
    Thou hast the keenest sight,
Say, what through yonder storm of dust
    Comes from the Latian right ? "

XXI.

Then answered Caius Cossus :
    " I see an evil sight ;
The banner of proud Tusculum
    Comes from the Latian right ;
I see the plumed horsemen ;
    And far before the rest
I see the dark-grey charger,
    I see the purple vest ;
I see the golden helmet
    That shines far off like flame
So ever rides Mamilius,
    Prince of the Latian name."

XXII.

" Now hearken, Caius Cossus :
    Spring on thy horse's back ;
Ride as the wolves of Apennine
    Were all upon thy track ;
Haste to our southward battle :
    And never draw thy rein
Until thou find Herminius,
    And bid him come amain."

XXIII.

So Aulus spake, and turned him
　　Again to that fierce strife;
And Caius Cossus mounted,
　　And rode for death and life.
Loud clanged beneath his horse-hoofs
　　The helmets of the dead,
And many a curdling pool of blood
　　Splashed him from heel to head.
So came he far to southward,
　　Where fought the Roman host,
Against the banners of the marsh
　　And banners of the coast.
Like corn before the sickle
　　The stout Lavinians fell,
Beneath the edge of the true sword
　　That kept the bridge so well.

XXIV.

" Herminius! Aulus greets thee;
　　He bids thee come with speed,
To help our central battle;
　　For sore is there our need.
There wars the youngest Tarquin,
　　And there the Crest of Flame,
The Tusculan Mamilius,
　　Prince of the Latian name.
Valerius hath fallen fighting
　　In front of our array;
And Aulus of the seventy fields
　　Alone upholds the day."

XXV.

Herminius beat his bosom:
　　But never a word he spake.
He clapped his hand on Auster's mane:
　　He gave the reins a shake,

Away, away, went Auster,
    Like an arrow from the bow:
Black Auster was the fleetest steed
    From Aufidus to Po.

XXVI.

Right glad were all the Romans
    Who, in that hour of dread,
Against great odds bare up the war
    Around Valerius dead,
When from the south the cheering
    Rose with a mighty swell;
" Herminius comes, Herminius,
    Who kept the bridge so well!"

XXVII.

Mamilius spied Herminius,
    And dashed across the way.
" Herminius! I have sought thee
    Through many a bloody day.
One of us two, Herminius,
    Shall never more go home.
I will lay on for Tusculum,
    And lay thou on for Rome!"

XXVIII.

All round them paused the battle,
    While met in mortal fray
The Roman and the Tusculan,
    The horses black and grey.
Herminius smote Mamilius
    Through breast-plate and through breast
And fast flowed out the purple blood
    Over the purple vest.

Mamilius smote Herminius
  Through head-piece and through head;
And side by side those chiefs of pride
  Together fell down dead.
Down fell they dead together
  In a great lake of gore;
And still stood all who saw them fall
  While men might count a score.

XXIX.

Fast, fast, with heels wild spurning,
  The dark-grey charger fled:
He burst through ranks of fighting men;
  He sprang o'er heaps of dead.
His bridle far out-streaming,
  His flanks all blood and foam,
He sought the southern mountains,
  The mountains of his home.
The pass was steep and rugged,
  The wolves they howled and whined;
But he ran like a whirlwind up the pass,
  And he left the wolves behind.
Through many a startled hamlet
  Thundered his flying feet;
He rushed through the gate of Tusculum,
  He rushed up the long white street;
He rushed by tower and temple,
  And paused not from his race
Till he stood before his master's door
  In the stately market-place.
And straightway round him gathered
  A pale and trembling crowd,
And when they knew him, cries of rage
  Brake forth, and wailing loud:
And women rent their tresses
  For their great prince's fall;
And old men girt on their old swords,
  And went to man the wall.

XXX.

But, like a graven image,
  Black Auster kept his place,
And ever wistfully he looked
  Into his master's face.
The raven-mane that daily,
  With pats and fond caresses,
The young Herminia washed and combed,
  And twined in even tresses,
And decked with coloured ribands
  From her own gay attire,
Hung sadly o'er her father's corpse
  In carnage and in mire.
Forth with a shout sprang Titus,
  And seized black Auster's rein.
Then Aulus sware a fearful oath,
  And ran at him amain.
" The furies of thy brother
  With me and mine abide,
If one of your accursed house
  Upon black Auster ride!"
As on an Alpine watch-tower
  From heaven comes down the flame,
Full on the neck of Titus
  The blade of Aulus came:
And out the red blood spouted,
  In a wide arch and tall,
As spouts a fountain in the court
  Of some rich Capuan's hall.
The knees of all the Latines
  Were loosened with dismay,
When dead, on dead Herminius,
  The bravest Tarquin lay.

XXXI.

And Aulus the Dictator
  Stroked Auster's raven mane,

With heed he looked unto the girths,
 With heed unto the rein.
" Now bear me well, black Auster,
 Into yon thick array ;
And thou and I will have revenge
 For thy good lord this day."

XXXII.

So spake he ; and was buckling
 Tighter black Auster's band,
When he was aware of a princely pair
 That rode at his right hand.
So like they were, no mortal
 Might one from other know :
White as snow their armour was :
 Their steeds were white as snow.
Never on earthly anvil
 Did such rare armour gleam ;
And never did such gallant steeds
 Drink of an earthly stream.

XXXIII.

And all who saw them trembled,
 And pale grew every cheek ;
And Aulus the Dictator
 Scarce gathered voice to speak.
" Say by what name men call you ?
 What city is your home ?
And wherefore ride ye in such guise
 Before the ranks of Rome ? "

XXXIV.

" By many names men call us ;
 In many lands we dwell :
Well Samothracia knows us ;
 Cyrene knows us well.

Our house in gay Tarentum
  Is hung each morn with flowers:
High o'er the masts of Syracuse
  Our marble portal towers;
But by the proud Eurotas
  Is our dear native home;
And for the right we come to fight
  Before the ranks of Rome."

XXXV.

So answered those strange horsemen,
  And each couched low his spear;
And forthwith all the ranks of Rome
  Were bold, and of good cheer:
And on the thirty armies
  Came wonder and affright,
And Ardea wavered on the left,
  And Cora on the right.
" Rome to the charge!" cried Aulus;
  " The foe begins to yield!
Charge for the hearth of Vesta!
  Charge for the Golden Shield!
Let no man stop to plunder,
  But slay, and slay, and slay;
The Gods who live for ever
  Are on our side to-day."

XXXVI.

Then the fierce trumpet-flourish
  From earth to heaven arose,
The kites know well the long stern swell
  That bids the Romans close.
Then the good sword of Aulus
  Was lifted up to slay:
Then, like a crag down Apennine,
  Rushed Auster through the fray.

But under those strange horsemen
  Still thicker lay the slain;
And after those strange horses
  Black Auster toiled in vain.
Behind them Rome's long battle
  Came rolling on the foe,
Ensigns dancing wild above,
  Blades all in line below.
So comes the Po in flood-time
  Upon the Celtic plain:
So comes the squall, blacker than night,
  Upon the Adrian main.
Now, by our Sire Quirinus,
  It was a goodly sight
To see the thirty standards
  Swept down the tide of flight.
So flies the spray of Adria
  When the black squall doth blow;
So corn-sheaves in the flood-time
  Spin down the whirling Po.
False Sextus to the mountains
  Turned first his horse's head;
And fast fled Ferentinum,
  And fast Lanuvium fled.
The horsemen of Nomentum
  Spurred hard out of the fray;
The footmen of Velitræ
  Threw shield and spear away.
And underfoot was trampled,
  Amidst the mud and gore,
The banner of proud Tusculum,
  That never stooped before:
And down went Flavius Faustus,
  Who led his stately ranks
From where the apple blossoms wave
  On Anio's echoing banks,
And Tullus of Arpinum,
  Chief of the Volscian aids,

And Metius with the long fair curls,
　The love of Anxur's maids,
And the white head of Vulso,
　The great Arician seer,
And Nepos of Laurentum,
　The hunter of the deer;
And in the back false Sextus
　Felt the good Roman steel,
And wriggling in the dust he died,
　Like a worm beneath the wheel:
And fliers and pursuers
　Were mingled in a mass;
And far away the battle
　Went roaring through the pass.

XXXVII.

Sempronius Atratinus
　Sate in the Eastern Gate,
Beside him were three Fathers,
　Each in his chair of state;
Fabius, whose nine stout grandsons
　That day were in the field,
And Manlius, eldest of the Twelve
　Who keep the Golden Shield;
And Sergius, the High Pontiff,
　For wisdom far renowned;
In all Etruria's colleges
　Was no such Pontiff found.
And all around the portal,
　And high above the wall,
Stood a great throng of people,
　But sad and silent all;
Young lads and stooping elders
　That might not bear the mail,
Matrons with lips that quivered,
　And maids with faces pale.

Since the first gleam of daylight,
  Sempronius had not ceased
To listen for the rushing
  Of horse-hoofs from the east.
The mist of eve was rising,
  The sun was hastening down,
When he was aware of a princely pair
  Fast pricking towards the town.
So like they were, man never
  Saw twins so like before ;
Red with gore their armour was,
  Their steeds were red with gore.

XXXVIII.

" Hail to the great Asylum !
  Hail to the hill-tops seven !
Hail to the fire that burns for aye,
  And the shield that fell from heaven !
This day, by Lake Regillus,
  Under the Porcian height,
All in the lands of Tusculum
  Was fought a glorious fight.
To-morrow your Dictator
  Shall bring in triumph home
The spoils of thirty cities
  To deck the shrines of Rome ! "

XXXIX.

Then burst from that great concourse
  A shout that shook the towers,
And some ran north, and some ran south,
  Crying, " The day is ours ! "
But on rode these strange horsemen,
  With slow and lordly pace ;
And none who saw their bearing
  Durst ask their name or race.

On rode they to the Forum,
　While laurel-boughs and flowers,
From house-tops and from windows,
　Fell on their crests in showers.
When they drew nigh to Vesta,
　They vaulted down amain,
And washed their horses in the well
　That springs by Vesta's fane.
And straight again they mounted,
　And rode to Vesta's door :
Then, like a blast, away they passed,
　And no man saw them more.

XL.

And all the people trembled,
　And pale grew every cheek ;
And Sergius the High Pontiff
　Alone found voice to speak :
" The gods who live for ever
　Have fought for Rome to-day !
These be the Great Twin Brethren
　To whom the Dorians pray.
Back comes the Chief in triumph,
　Who, in the hour of fight,
Hath seen the Great Twin Brethren
　In harness on his right.
Safe comes the ship to haven,
　Through billows and through gales,
If once the Great Twin Brethren
　Sit shining on the sails.
Wherefore they washed their horses
　In Vesta's holy well,
Wherefore they rode to Vesta's door,
　I know, but may not tell.
Here, hard by Vesta's temple,
　Build we a stately dome
Unto the Great Twin Brethren
　Who fought so well for Rome.

And when the months returning
   Bring back this day of fight,
The proud Ides of Quintilis,
   Marked evermore with white,
Unto the Great Twin Brethren
   Let all the people throng,
With chaplets and with offerings,
   With music and with song ;
And let the doors and windows
   Be hung with garlands all,
And let the knights be summoned
   To Mars without the wall :
Thence let them ride in purple
   With joyous trumpet-sound,
Each mounted on his war-horse,
   And each with olive crowned ;
And pass in solemn order
   Before the sacred dome,
Where dwell the Great Twin Brethren
   Who fought so well for Rome."

VIRGINIA.

A COLLECTION consisting exclusively of war-songs would give an imperfect, or rather an erroneous, notion of the spirit of the old Latin ballads. The Patricians, during more than a century after the expulsion of the Kings, held all the high military commands. A Plebeian, even though, like Lucius Siccius, he were distinguished by his valour and knowledge of war, could serve only in subordinate posts. A minstrel, therefore, who wished to celebrate the early triumphs of his country, could hardly take any but Patricians for his heroes. The warriors who are mentioned in the two preceding lays, Horatius, Lartius, Herminius, Aulus Posthumius, Æbutius Elva, Sempronius Atratinus, Valerius Poplicola, were all members of the dominant order; and a poet who was singing their praises, whatever his own political opinions might be, would naturally abstain from insulting the class to which they belonged, and from reflecting on the system which had placed such men at the head of the legions of the Commonwealth.

But there was a class of compositions in which the great families were by no means so courteously treated. No parts of early Roman history are richer with poetical colouring than those which relate to the long contest between the privileged houses and the commonalty. The population of Rome was, from a very early period, divided into hereditary castes, which, indeed, readily united to repel foreign enemies, but which regarded each other, during many years, with bitter animosity. Between those castes there was a barrier hardly less strong than that which, at Venice, parted the members of the Great Council from their countrymen. In some respects, indeed, the line which separated an Icilius or a Duilius from a Posthumius or a Fabius was even more deeply marked than that which separated the rower of a gondola from a Contarini or a Morosini. At Venice the distinction was merely civil. At Rome it was both civil and religious. Among the grievances under which the Plebeians suffered, three were felt as peculiarly severe. They were excluded from the highest magistracies; they were excluded from all share in the public lands; and they were ground down to the dust by partial and barbarous legislation touching pecuniary contracts. The ruling class in Rome was a moneyed class; and it made and administered the laws with a view solely to its own interest. Thus the relation between lender and borrower was mixed up with the relation between sovereign and subject. The great men held a large portion of the community in dependence by means of advances at enormous usury. The law of debt, framed by creditors, and for the protection of creditors, was the most horrible that has ever been known among men. The liberty, and even the life of the insolvent were at the mercy of the Patrician money-lenders. Children often became slaves in consequence of the misfortunes of their parents. The debtor was imprisoned, not in a public gaol under the care of impartial public functionaries, but in a private workhouse belonging to the creditor. Frightful stories were told respecting these dungeons. It was said that torture and brutal violation were common; that tight stocks, heavy chains, scanty measures of food, were used to punish wretches guilty of nothing but poverty; and that brave soldiers, whose breasts were covered with honourable scars, were often marked still more deeply on the back by the scourges of high-born usurers.

The Plebeians were, however, not wholly without constitutional rights. From an early period they had been admitted to some share of political power. They were enrolled each in his century, and were allowed a share, considerable though not proportioned to their numerical strength, in the disposal of those high dignities from which they were themselves excluded. Thus their position bore some resemblance to that of the Irish Catholics during the interval between the year 1792 and the year 1829. The Plebeians had also the privilege of annually appointing officers, named Tribunes, who had no active share in the government of the Commonwealth, but who, by degrees, acquired a power formidable even to the ablest and most resolute Consuls and Dictators. The person of the Tribune was inviolable ; and, though he could directly effect little, he could obstruct every thing.

During more than a century after the institution of the Tribuneship, the Commons struggled manfully for the removal of the grievances under which they laboured ; and, in spite of many checks and reverses, succeeded in wringing concession after concession from the stubborn aristocracy. At length in the year of the city 378, both parties mustered their whole strength for their last and most desperate conflict. The popular and active Tribune, Caius Licinius, proposed the three memorable laws which are called by his name, and which were intended to redress the three great evils of which the Plebeians complained. He was supported, with eminent ability and firmness, by his colleague, Lucius Sextius. The struggle appears to have been the fiercest that ever in any community terminated without an appeal to arms. If such a contest had raged in any Greek city, the streets would have run with blood. But, even in the paroxysms of faction, the Roman retained his gravity, his respect for law, and his tenderness for the lives of his fellow-citizens. Year after year Licinius and Sextius were re-elected Tribunes. Year after year, if the narrative which has come down to us is to be trusted, they continued to exert, to the full extent, their power of stopping the whole machine of government. No curule magistrates could be chosen; no military muster could be held. We know too little of the state of Rome in those days to be able to conjecture how, during that long anarchy, the peace was kept, and ordinary justice administered between man and man. The animosity of both parties rose to the greatest height. The excitement, we may well suppose, would have been peculiarly intense at the annual election of Tribunes. On such occasions there can be little doubt that the great families did all that could be done, by threats and caresses, to break the union of the Plebeians. That union, however, proved indissoluble. At length the good cause triumphed. The Licinian laws were carried. Lucius Sextius was the first Plebeian Consul, Caius Licinius the third.

The results of this great change were singularly happy and glorious. Two centuries of prosperity, harmony, and victory followed the reconciliation of the orders. Men who remembered Rome engaged in waging petty wars almost within sight of the Capitol lived to see her the mistress of Italy. While the disabilities of the Plebeians continued, she was scarcely able to maintain her ground against the Volscians and Hernicans. When those disabilities were removed, she rapidly became more than a match for Carthage and Macedon.

During the great Licinian contest the Plebeian poets were, doubtless, not silent. Even in modern times songs have been by no means without influence on public affairs; and we may therefore infer that,

in a society where printing was unknown, and where
books were rare, a pathetic or humorous party-ballad
must have produced effects such as we can but faintly
conceive. It is certain that satirical poems were common at Rome from a very early period. The rustics,
who lived at a distance from the seat of government,
and took little part in the strife of factions, gave vent
to their petty local animosities in coarse Fescennine
verse. The lampoons of the city were doubtless of a
higher order; and their sting was early felt by the
nobility. For in the Twelve Tables, long before the
time of the Licinian laws, a severe punishment was
denounced against the citizen who should compose or
recite verses reflecting on another.[1] Satire is, indeed,
the only sort of composition in which the Latin poets,
whose works have come down to us, were not mere
imitators of foreign models; and it is therefore the
only sort of composition in which they have never
been rivalled. It was not, like their tragedy, their
comedy, their epic and lyric poetry, a hothouse plant
which, in return for assiduous and skilful culture,
gave only scanty and sickly fruits. It was hardy and
full of sap: and in all the various juices which it
yielded might be distinguished the flavour of the
Ausonian soil. "Satire," said Quinctilian, with just
pride, "is all our own." Satire sprang, in truth,
naturally from the constitution of the Roman government and from the spirit of the Roman people; and,
though at length subjected to metrical rules derived
from Greece, retained to the last an essentially Roman
character. Lucilius was the earliest satirist whose
works were held in esteem under the Cæsars. But
many years before Lucilius was born, Nævius had

---

[1] Cicero justly infers from this
law that there had been early
Latin poets whose works had
been lost before his time. "Quam-
quam id quidem etiam xii tabulæ
declarant, condi jam tum solitum
esse carmen, quod ne licere fieri
ad alterius injuriam lege sanxe-
runt."—*Tusc.* iv. 2.

been flung into a dungeon, and guarded there with circumstances of unusual rigour, on account of the bitter lines in which he had attacked the great Cæcilian family.[1] The genius and spirit of the Roman satirists survived the liberty of their country, and were not extinguished by the cruel despotism of the Julian and Flavian Emperors. The great poet who told the story of Domitian's turbot, was the legitimate successor of those forgotten minstrels whose songs animated the factions of the infant Republic.

Those minstrels, as Niebuhr has remarked, appear to have generally taken the popular side. We can hardly be mistaken in supposing that, at the great crisis of the civil conflict, they employed themselves in versifying all the most powerful and virulent speeches of the Tribunes, and in heaping abuse on the leaders of the aristocracy. Every personal defect, every domestic scandal, every tradition dishonourable to a noble house, would be sought out, brought into notice, and exaggerated. The illustrious head of the aristocratical party, Marcus Furius Camillus, might perhaps be, in some measure, protected by his venerable age and by the memory of his great services to the State. But Appius Claudius Crassus enjoyed no such immunity. He was descended from a long line of ancestors distinguished by their haughty demeanour, and by the inflexibility with which they had withstood all the demands of the Plebeian order. While the political conduct and the deportment of the Claudian nobles drew upon them the fiercest public hatred, they were accused of wanting, if any credit is due to the early history of Rome, a class of qualities which, in a military Commonwealth, is sufficient to cover a multitude of offences. The chiefs of the family appear to have

---

[1] Plautus, Miles Gloriosus. Aulus Gellius, iii. 3.

been eloquent, versed in civil business, and learned
after the fashion of their age; but in war they were
not distinguished by skill or valour. Some of them,
as if conscious where their weakness lay, had,
when filling the highest magistracies, taken internal administration as their department of public
business, and left the military command to their
colleagues.[1] One of them had been entrusted with
an army, and had failed ignominiously.[2] None of
them had been honoured with a triumph. None of
them had achieved any martial exploit, such as those
by which Lucius Quinctius Cincinnatus, Titus Quinctius Capitolinus, Aulus Cornelius Cossus, and, above
all, the great Camillus, had extorted the reluctant
esteem of the multitude. During the Licinian conflict, Appius Claudius Crassus signalised himself by
the ability and severity with which he harangued
against the two great agitators. He would naturally,
therefore, be the favourite mark of the Plebeian
satirists; nor would they have been at a loss to find
a point on which he was open to attack.

His grandfather, called, like himself, Appius
Claudius, had left a name as much detested as that
of Sextus Tarquinius. This elder Appius had been
Consul more than seventy years before the introduc-
tion of the Licinian laws. By availing himself of a
singular crisis in public feeling, he had obtained the
consent of the Commons to the abolition of the
Tribuneship, and had been the chief of that Council
of Ten to which the whole direction of the State had
been committed. In a few months his administration had become universally odious. It had been
swept away by an irresistible outbreak of popular
fury; and its memory was still held in abhorrence by
the whole city. The immediate cause of the down-
fall of this execrable government was said to have

[1] In the years of the city 260, 304, and 330.
[2] In the year of the city 282.

been an attempt made by Appius Claudius upon the chastity of a beautiful young girl of humble birth. The story ran that the Decemvir, unable to succeed by bribes and solicitations, resorted to an outrageous act of tyranny. A vile dependent of the Claudian house laid claim to the damsel as his slave. The cause was brought before the tribunal of Appius. The wicked magistrate, in defiance of the clearest proofs, gave judgment for the claimant. But the girl's father, a brave soldier, saved her from servitude and dishonour by stabbing her to the heart in the sight of the whole Forum. That blow was the signal for a general explosion. Camp and city rose at once; the Ten were pulled down; the Tribuneship was re-established; and Appius escaped the hands of the executioner only by a voluntary death.

It can hardly be doubted that a story so admirably adapted to the purposes both of the poet and of the demagogue would be eagerly seized upon by minstrels burning with hatred against the Patrician order, against the Claudian house, and especially against the grandson and namesake of the infamous Decemvir.

In order that the reader may judge fairly of these fragments of the lay of Virginia, he must imagine himself a Plebeian who has just voted for the re-election of Sextius and Licinius. All the power of the Patricians has been exerted to throw out the two great champions of the Commons. Every Posthumius, Æmilius, and Cornelius has used his influence to the utmost. Debtors have been let out of the workhouses on condition of voting against the men of the people; clients have been posted to hiss and interrupt the favourite candidates: Appius Claudius Crassus has spoken with more than his usual eloquence and asperity: all has been in vain; Licinius and Sextius have a fifth time carried all the tribes: work is suspended: the booths are closed:

the Plebeians bear on their shoulders the two champions of liberty through the Forum. Just at this
moment it is announced that a popular poet, a
zealous adherent of the Tribunes, has made a new
song which will cut the Claudian nobles to the
heart. The crowd gathers round him, and calls on
him to recite it. He takes his stand on the spot
where, according to tradition, Virginia, more than
seventy years ago, was seized by the pandar of
Appius, and he begins his story.

VIRGINIA.

FRAGMENTS OF A LAY SUNG IN THE FORUM ON THE DAY
WHEREON LUCIUS SEXTIUS SEXTINUS LATERANUS AND
CAIUS LICINIUS CALVUS STOLO WERE ELECTED TRI-
BUNES OF THE COMMONS THE FIFTH TIME, IN THE
YEAR OF THE CITY CCCLXXXII.

YE good men of the Commons, with loving hearts
    and true,
Who stand by the bold Tribunes that still have stood
    by you,
Come, make a circle round me, and mark my tale
    with care,
A tale of what Rome once hath borne, of what Rome
    yet may bear.
This is no Grecian fable, of fountains running wine,
Of maids with snaky tresses, or sailors turned to
    swine.
Here, in this very Forum, under the noonday sun,
In sight of all the people, the bloody deed was done.
Old men still creep among us who saw that fearful
    day,
Just seventy years and seven ago, when the wicked
    Ten bare sway.

  Of all the wicked Ten still the names are held
    accursed,
And of all the wicked Ten Appius Claudius was the
    worst.
He stalked along the Forum like King Tarquin in
    his pride :
Twelve axes waited on him, six marching on a side :

The townsmen shrank to right and left, and eyed
    askance with fear
His lowering brow, his curling mouth which always
    seemed to sneer ;
That brow of hate, that mouth of scorn, marks all the
    kindred still ;
For never was there Claudius yet but wished the
    Commons ill :
Nor lacks he fit attendance ; for close behind his
    heels,
With outstretched chin and crouching pace, the client
    Marcus steals,
His loins girt up to run with speed, be the errand
    what it may,
And the smile flickering on his cheek, for aught his
    lord may say.
Such varlets pimp and jest for hire among the lying
    Greeks :
Such varlets still are paid to hoot when brave Lici-
    nius speaks.
Where'er ye shed the honey, the buzzing flies will
    crowd ;
Where'er ye fling the carrion, the raven's croak is
    loud ;
Where'er down Tiber garbage floats, the greedy pike
    ye see ;
And wheresoe'er such lord is found, such client still
    will be.

    Just then, as through one cloudless chink in a
    black stormy sky
Shines out the dewy morning-star, a fair young girl
    came by.
With her small tablets in her hand, and her satchel
    on her arm,
Home she went bounding from the school, nor
    dreamed of shame or harm ;

And past those dreaded axes she innocently ran,
With bright, frank brow that had not learned to
    blush at gaze of man ;
And up the Sacred Street she turned, and, as she
    danced along,
She warbled gaily to herself lines of the good old
    song,
How for a sport the princes came spurring from the
    camp,
And found Lucrece, combing the fleece, under the
    midnight lamp.
The maiden sang as sings the lark, when up he darts
    his flight,
From his nest in the green April corn, to meet the
    morning light ;
And Appius heard her sweet young voice, and saw
    her sweet young face,
And loved her with the accursed love of his accursed
    race,
And all along the Forum, and up the Sacred Street,
His vulture eye pursued the trip of those small
    glancing feet.

   *   *   *   *   *   *

    Over the Alban mountains the light of morning
    broke ;
From all the roofs of the Seven Hills curled the thin
    wreaths of smoke :
The city-gates were opened; the Forum, all alive,
With buyers and with sellers was humming like a
    hive:
Blithely on brass and timber the craftsman's stroke
    was ringing,
And blithely o'er her panniers the market-girl was
    singing,
And blithely young Virginia came smiling from her
    home :
Ah! woe for young Virginia, the sweetest maid in
    Rome !

With her small tablets in her hand, and her satchel
  on her arm,
Forth she went bounding to the school, nor dreamed
  of shame or harm.
She crossed the Forum shining with stalls in alleys
  gay,
And just had reached the very spot whereon I stand
  this day,
When up the varlet Marcus came ; not such as when
  erewhile
He crouched behind his patron's heels with the true
  client smile :
He came with lowering forehead, swollen features,
  and clenched fist,
And strode across Virginia's path, and caught her by
  the wrist.
Hard strove the frighted maiden, and screamed with
  look aghast ;
And at her scream from right and left the folk came
  running fast ;
The money-changer Crispus, with his thin silver hairs,
And Hanno from the stately booth glittering with
  Punic wares,
And the strong smith Muræna, grasping a half-forged
  brand,
And Volero the flesher, his cleaver in his hand.
All came in wrath and wonder ; for all knew that
  fair child ;
And, as she passed them twice a day, all kissed their
  hands and smiled ;
And the strong smith Muræna gave Marcus such a
  blow,
The caitiff reeled three paces back, and let the maiden
  go.
Yet glared he fiercely round him, and growled in
  harsh, fell tone,
" She's mine, and I will have her : I seek but for
  mine own :

She is my slave, born in my house, and stolen away
    and sold,
The year of the sore sickness, ere she was twelve
    hours old.
'Twas in the sad September, the month of wail and
    fright,
Two augurs were borne forth that morn ; the Consul
    died ere night.
I wait on Appius Claudius, I waited on his sire :
Let him who works the client wrong beware the ·
    patron's ire ! "

  So spake the varlet Marcus ; and dread and silence
    came
On all the people at the sound of the great Claudian
    name.
For then there was no Tribune to speak the word of
    might,
Which makes the rich man tremble, and guards the
    poor man's right.
There was no brave Licinius, no honest Sextius then ;
But all the city, in great fear, obeyed the wicked Ten.
Yet ere the varlet Marcus again might seize the
    maid,
Who clung tight to Muræna's skirt, and sobbed, and
    shrieked for aid,
Forth through the throng of gazers the young Icilius
    pressed,
And stamped his foot, and rent his gown, and smote
    upon his breast,
And sprang upon that column, by many a minstrel
    sung,
Whereon three mouldering helmets, three rusting
    swords, are hung,
And beckoned to the people, and in bold voice and
    clear
Poured thick and fast the burning words which
    tyrants quake to hear.

" Now, by your children's cradles, now by your
    fathers' graves,
Be men to-day, Quirites, or be for ever slaves!
For this did Servius give us laws? For this did
    Lucrece bleed?
For this was the great vengeance wrought on Tar-
    quin's evil seed?
For this did those false sons make red the axes of
    their sire?
For this did Scævola's right hand hiss in the Tuscan
    fire?
Shall the vile fox-earth awe the race that stormed
    the lion's den?
Shall we, who could not brook one lord, crouch to
    the wicked Ten?
Oh for that ancient spirit which curbed the Senate's
    will!
Oh for the tents which in old time whitened the
    Sacred Hill!
In those brave days our fathers stood firmly side by
    side;
They faced the Marcian fury; they tamed the Fabian
    pride:
They drove the fiercest Quinctius an outcast forth
    from Rome;
They sent the haughtiest Claudius with shivered fasces
    home.
But what their care bequeathed us our madness
    flung away;
All the ripe fruit of threescore years was blighted in
    a day.
Exult, ye proud Patricians! The hard-fought fight
    is o'er.
We strove for honours—'twas in vain: for freedom—
    'tis no more.
No crier to the polling summons the eager throng;
No tribune breathes the word of might that guards
    the weak from wrong.

Our very hearts, that were so high, sink down be-
neath your will.
Riches, and lands, and power, and state—ye have
them :—keep them still.
Still keep the holy fillets ; still keep the purple gown,
The axes, and the curule chair, the car, and laurel
crown :
Still press us for your cohorts, and, when the fight is
done,
Still fill your garners from the soil which our good
swords have won.
Still, like a spreading ulcer, which leech-craft may
not cure,
Let your foul usance eat away the substance of the
poor.
Still let your haggard debtors bear all their fathers
bore ;
Still let your dens of torment be noisome as of yore ;
No fire when Tiber freezes ; no air in dog-star heat ;
And store of rods for free-born backs, and holes for
free-born feet.
Heap heavier still the fetters; bar closer still the
grate ;
Patient as sheep we yield us up unto your cruel hate.
But, by the Shades beneath us, and by the Gods above,
Add not unto your cruel hate your yet more cruel love!
Have ye not graceful ladies, whose spotless lineage
springs
From Consuls, and High Pontiffs, and ancient Alban
kings ?
Ladies, who deign not on our paths to set their ten-
der feet,
Who from their cars look down with scorn upon the
wondering street,
Who in Corinthian mirrors their own proud smiles
behold,
And breathe of Capuan odours, and shine with Spanish
gold ?

Then leave the poor Plebeian his single tie to
life—
The sweet, sweet love of daughter, of sister, and of
wife,
The gentle speech, the balm for all that his vexed
soul endures,
The kiss, in which he half forgets even such a yoke
as yours.
Still let the maiden's beauty swell the father's breast
with pride ;
Still let the bridegroom's arms infold an unpolluted
bride.
Spare us the inexpiable wrong, the unutterable shame,
That turns the coward's heart to steel, the sluggard's
blood to flame,
Lest, when our latest hope is fled, ye taste of our
despair,
And learn by proof, in some wild hour, how much the
wretched dare."

* * * * * *
* * * * * *

Straightway Virginius led the maid a little space
aside,
To where the reeking shambles stood, piled up with
horn and hide,
Close to yon low dark archway, where, in a crimson
flood,
Leaps down to the great sewer the gurgling stream
of blood.
Hard by, a flesher on a block had laid his whittle
down :
Virginius caught the whittle up, and hid it in his
gown.
And then his eyes grew very dim, and his throat
began to swell,
And in a hoarse, changed voice he spake, "Farewell,
sweet child! Farewell!

Oh, how I loved my darling! Though stern I some-
    times be,
To thee, thou know'st, I was not so.   Who could be
    so to thee?
And how my darling loved me!   How glad she was
    to hear
My footstep on the threshold when I came back last
    year!
And how she danced with pleasure to see my civic
    crown,
And took my sword, and hung it up, and brought
    me forth my gown!
Now, all those things are over—yes, all thy pretty
    ways,
Thy needlework, thy prattle, thy snatches of old lays;
And none will grieve when I go forth, or smile when
    I return,
Or watch beside the old man's bed, or weep upon
    his urn.
The house that was the happiest within the Roman
    walls,
The house that envied not the wealth of Capua's
    marble halls,
Now, for the brightness of thy smile, must have
    eternal gloom,
And for the music of thy voice, the silence of the
    tomb.
The time is come. See how he points his eager
    hand this way!
See how his eyes gloat on thy grief, like a kite's
    upon the prey!
With all his wit, he little deems, that, spurned, be-
    trayed, bereft,
Thy father hath in his despair one fearful refuge left.
He little deems that in this hand I clutch what still
    can save
Thy gentle youth from taunts and blows, the portion
    of the slave;

Yea, and from nameless evil, that passeth taunt and
    blow—
Foul outrage which thou knowest not, which thou
    shalt never know.
Then clasp me round the neck once more, and give
    me one more kiss ;
And now mine own dear little girl, there is no way
    but this."
With that he lifted high the steel, and smote her in
    the side,
And in her blood she sank to earth, and with one sob
    she died.

    Then, for a little moment, all people held their
    breath ;
And through the crowded Forum was stillness as of
    death ;
And in another moment brake forth from one and all
A cry as if the Volscians were coming o'er the wall.
Some with averted faces shrieking fled home amain ;
Some ran to call a leech ; and some ran to lift the
    slain :
Some felt her lips and little wrist, if life might there
    be found ;
And some tore up their garments fast, and strove to
    stanch the wound.
In vain they ran, and felt, and stanched ; for never
    truer blow
That good right arm had dealt in fight against a
    Volscian foe.

    When Appius Claudius saw that deed, he shud-
    dered and sank down,
And hid his face some little space with the corner
    of his gown,
Till, with white lips and bloodshot eyes, Virginius
    tottered nigh,
And stood before the judgment-seat, and held the
    knife on high.

" Oh ! dwellers in the nether gloom, avengers of the
    slain,
By this dear blood I cry to you, do right between us
    twain ;
And even as Appius Claudius hath dealt by me and
    mine,
Deal you by Appius Claudius and all the Claudian
    line !' "
So spake the slayer of his child, and turned, and
    went his way ;
But first he cast one haggard glance to where the
    body lay,
And writhed, and groaned a fearful groan, and then,
    with steadfast feet,
Strode right across the market-place unto the Sacred
    Street.

   Then up sprang Appius Claudius: " Stop him ;
    alive or dead !
Ten thousand pounds of copper to the man who
    brings his head."
He looked upon his clients ; but none would work his
    will.
He looked upon his lictors ; but they trembled and
    stood still.
And, as Virginius through the press his way in silence
    cleft,
Ever the mighty multitude fell back to right and
    left.
And he hath passed in safety unto his woeful
    home,
And there ta'en horse to tell the camp what deeds
    are done in Rome.

   By this the flood of people was swollen from
    every side,
And streets and porches round were filled with that
    o'erflowing tide ;

And close around the body gathered a little train
Of them that were the nearest and dearest to the slain.
They brought a bier, and hung it with many a cypress
    crown,
And gently they uplifted her, and gently laid her
    down.
The face of Appius Claudius wore the Claudian scowl
    and sneer,
And in the Claudian note he cried, " What doth this
    rabble here ?
Have they no crafts to mind at home, that hither-
    ward they stray ?
Ho ! lictors, clear the market-place, and fetch the
    corpse away ! "
The voice of grief and fury till then had not been
    loud ;
But a deep sullen murmur wandered among the
    crowd,
Like the moaning noise that goes before the whirl-
    wind on the deep,
Or the growl of a fierce watch-dog but half-aroused
    from sleep.
But when the lictors at that word, tall yeomen all
    and strong,
Each with his axe and sheaf of twigs, went down
    into the throng,
Those old men say, who saw that day of sorrow and
    of sin,
That in the Roman Forum was never such a din.
The wailing, hooting, cursing, the howls of grief and
    hate,
Were heard beyond the Pincian Hill, beyond the
    Latin Gate.
But close around the body, where stood the little train
Of them that were the nearest and dearest to the slain,
No cries were there, but teeth set fast, low whispers
    and black frowns,
And breaking up of benches, and girding up of gowns.

'Twas well the lictors might not pierce to where the
    maiden lay,
Else surely had they been all twelve torn limb from
    limb that day.
Right glad they were to struggle back, blood stream-
    ing from their heads,
With axes all in splinters, and raiment all in shreds.
Then Appius Claudius gnawed his lip, and the blood
    left his cheek;
And thrice he beckoned with his hand, and thrice
    he strove to speak;
And thrice the tossing Forum set up a frightful
    yell;
" See, see, thou dog! what thou hast done; and hide
    thy shame in hell!
Thou that wouldst make our maidens slaves must
    first make slaves of men.
Tribunes! Hurrah for Tribunes! Down with the
    wicked Ten!"
And straightway, thick as hailstones, came whizzing
    through the air,
Pebbles, and bricks, and potsherds, all round the
    curule chair:
And upon Appius Claudius great fear and trembling
    came,
For never was a Claudius yet brave against aught
    but shame.
Though the great houses love us not, we own, to do
    them right,
That the great houses, all save one, have borne them
    well in fight.
Still Caius of Corioli, his triumphs and his wrongs,
His vengeance and his mercy, live in our camp-fire
    songs.
Beneath the yoke of Furius oft have Gaul and Tus-
    can bowed;
And Rome may bear the pride of him of whom her-
    self is proud.

But evermore a Claudius shrinks from a stricken field,
And changes colour like a maid at sight of sword
    and shield.
The Claudian triumphs all were won within the city
    towers;
The Claudian yoke was never pressed on any necks
    but ours.
A Cossus, like a wild cat, springs ever at the face;
A Fabius rushes like a boar against the shouting chase;
But the vile Claudian litter, raging with currish spite,
Still yelps and snaps at those who run, still runs from
    those who smite.
So now 'twas seen of Appius. When stones began
    to fly,
He shook, and crouched, and wrung his hands, and
    smote upon his thigh.
" Kind clients, honest lictors, stand by me in this fray!
Must I be torn in pieces? Home, home, the nearest
    way!"
While yet he spake, and looked around with a be-
    wildered stare,
Four sturdy lictors put their necks beneath the
    curule chair;
And fourscore clients on the left, and fourscore on
    the right,
Arrayed themselves with swords and staves, and loins
    girt up for fight.
But, though without or staff or sword, so furious was
    the throng,
That scarce the train with might and main could
    bring their lord along.
Twelve times the crowd made at him; five times
    they seized his gown;
Small chance was his to rise again, if once they got
    him down:
And sharper came the pelting; and evermore the
    yell—
" Tribunes! we will have Tribunes!"—rose with a
    louder swell:

And the chair tossed as tosses a bark with tattered sail
When raves the Adriatic beneath an eastern gale,
When the Calabrian sea-marks are lost in clouds of
    spume,
And the great Thunder-Cape has donned his veil of
    inky gloom.
One stone hit Appius in the mouth, and one beneath
    the ear;
And ere he reached Mount Palatine, he swooned with
    pain and fear.
His cursed head, that he was wont to hold so high
    with pride,
Now, like a drunken man's, hung down, and swayed
    from side to side;
And when his stout retainers had brought him to
    his door,
His face and neck were all one cake of filth and
    clotted gore.
As Appius Claudius was that day, so may his grand-
    son be!
God send Rome one such other sight, and send me
    there to see!

      *   *   *   *   *

THE PROPHECY OF CAPYS.

It can hardly be necessary to remind any reader that according to the popular tradition, Romulus, after he had slain his grand-uncle Amulius, and restored his grandfather Numitor, determined to quit Alba, the hereditary domain of the Sylvian princes, and to found a new city. The Gods, it was added, vouchsafed the clearest signs of the favour with which they regarded the enterprise, and of the high destinies reserved for the young colony.

This event was likely to be a favourite theme of the old Latin minstrels. They would naturally attribute the project of Romulus to some divine intimation of the power and prosperity which it was decreed that his city should attain. They would probably introduce seers foretelling the victories of unborn Consuls and Dictators, and the last great victory would generally occupy the most conspicuous place in the prediction. There is nothing strange in the supposition that the poet who was employed to celebrate the first great triumph of the Romans over the Greeks might throw his song of exultation into this form.

The occasion was one likely to excite the strongest feelings of national pride. A great outrage had been followed by a great retribution. Seven years before this time, Lucius Posthumius Megellus, who sprang from one of the noblest houses of Rome, and had been thrice Consul, was sent ambassador to Tarentum, with charge to demand reparation for grievous injuries. The Tarentines gave him audience in their theatre, where he addressed them in such Greek as he could command, which, we may well believe, was not exactly such as Cineas would have spoken. An exquisite sense of the ridiculous belonged to the Greek character; and closely connected with this faculty was a strong propensity to flippancy and impertinence. When Posthumius placed an accent wrong, his hearers burst into a laugh. When he remonstrated, they hooted him, and called him barbarian; and at length hissed him off the stage as if he had been a bad actor. As the grave Roman retired, a buffoon who, from his constant drunkenness, was nicknamed the Pint-pot, came up with gestures of the grossest indecency, and bespattered the senatorial gown with filth. Posthumius turned round to the multitude, and held up the gown, as if appealing to the universal law of nations. The sight only increased the insolence of the Tarentines. They clapped their hands, and set up a shout of laughter which shook the theatre. " Men of Tarentum," said Posthumius, " it will take not a little blood to wash this gown." [1]

Rome, in consequence of this insult, declared war against the Tarentines. The Tarentines sought for allies beyond the Ionian Sea. Pyrrhus, king of Epirus, came to their help with a large army; and, for the first time, the two great nations of antiquity were fairly matched against each other.

The fame of Greece in arms, as well as in arts, was then at the height. Half a century earlier, the career of Alexander had excited the admiration and terror of all nations from the Ganges to the Pillars of Hercules. Royal houses, founded by Macedonian captains, still reigned at Antioch and Alexandria. That barbarian warriors, led by barbarian chiefs,

---

[1] Dion. Hal. De Legationibus.

should win a pitched battle against Greek valour guided by Greek science, seemed as incredible as it would now seem that the Burmese or the Siamese should, in the open plain, put to flight an equal number of the best English troops. The Tarentines were convinced that their countrymen were irresistible in war; and this conviction had emboldened them to treat with the grossest indignity one whom they regarded as the representative of an inferior race. Of the Greek generals then living Pyrrhus was indisputably the first. Among the troops who were trained in the Greek discipline his Epirotes ranked high. His expedition to Italy was a turning-point in the history of the world. He found there a people who, far inferior to the Athenians and Corinthians in the fine arts, in the speculative sciences, and in all the refinements of life, were the best soldiers on the face of the earth. Their arms, their gradations of rank, their order of battle, their method of intrenchment, were all of Latin origin, and had all been gradually brought near to perfection, not by the study of foreign models, but by the genius and experience of many generations of great native commanders. The first words which broke from the king, when his practised eye had surveyed the Roman encampment, were full of meaning:—" These barbarians," he said, " have nothing barbarous in their military arrangements." He was at first victorious; for his own talents were superior to those of the captains who were opposed to him; and the Romans were not prepared for the onset of the elephants of the East, which were then for the first time seen in Italy —moving mountains, with long snakes for hands.[1] But the victories of the Epirotes were fiercely disputed, dearly purchased, and altogether unprofitable. At length, Manius Curius Dentatus, who had in his

---

[1] *Anguimanus* is the old Latin epithet for an elephant. Lucretius, ii. 538, v. 1302.

first Consulship won two triumphs, was again placed
at the head of the Roman Commonwealth, and sent
to encounter the invaders.   A great battle was fought
near Beneventum.   Pyrrhus was completely defeated
He repassed the sea; and the world learned, with
amazement, that a people had been discovered, who,
in fair fighting, were superior to the best troops that
had been drilled on the system of Parmenio and An-
tigonus.

The conquerors had a good right to exult in
their success; for their glory was all their own.
They had not learned from their enemy how to conquer him.   It was with their own national arms, and
in their own national battle-array, that they had
overcome weapons and tactics long believed to be
invincible.   The pilum and the broadsword had
vanquished the Macedonian spear.   The legion had
broken the Macedonian phalanx.   Even the elephants,
when the surprise produced by their first appearance
was over, could cause no disorder in the steady yet
flexible battalions of Rome.

It is said by Florus, and may easily be believed,
that the triumph far surpassed in magnificence any
that Rome had previously seen.   The only spoils
which Papirius Cursor and Fabius Maximus could
exhibit were flocks and herds, waggons of rude struc-
ture, and heaps of spears and helmets.   But now,
for the first time, the riches of Asia and the arts of
Greece adorned a Roman pageant.   Plate, fine stuffs,
costly furniture, rare animals, exquisite paintings
and sculptures, formed part of the procession.   At
the banquet would be assembled a crowd of warriors and statesmen, among whom Manius Curius
Dentatus would take the highest room.   Caius
Fabricius Luscinus, then, after two Consulships and
two triumphs, Censor of the Commonwealth, would
doubtless occupy a place of honour at the board.   In
situations less conspicuous probably lay some of

those who were, a few years later, the terror of
Carthage; Caius Duilius, the founder of the maritime
greatness of his country; Marcus Atilius Regulus,
who owed to defeat a renown far higher than that
which he had derived from his victories; and Caius
Lutatius Catulus, who, while suffering from a grievous
wound, fought the great battle of the Ægates, and
brought the first Punic war to a triumphant close.
It is impossible to recount the names of these eminent citizens, without reflecting that they were all,
without exception, Plebeians, and would, but for the
ever-memorable struggle maintained by Caius Licinius and Lucius Sextius, have been doomed to hide
in obscurity, or to waste in civil broils, the capacity
and energy which prevailed against Pyrrhus and
Hamilcar.

On such a day we may suppose that the patriotic
enthusiasm of a Latin poet would vent itself in re-
iterated shouts of *Io triumphe*, such as were uttered
by Horace on a far less exciting occasion, and in
boasts resembling those which Virgil put into the
mouth of Anchises. The superiority of some foreign
nations, and especially of the Greeks, in the lazy arts
of peace, would be admitted with disdainful candour;
but pre-eminence in all the qualities which fit a
people to subdue and govern mankind would be
claimed for the Romans.

The following lay belongs to the latest age of
Latin ballad-poetry. Nævius and Livius Andronicus
were probably among the children whose mothers
held them up to see the chariot of Curius go by.
The minstrel who sang on that day might possibly
have lived to read the first hexameters of Ennius,
and to see the first comedies of Plautus. His poem,
as might be expected, shows a much wider acquaintance with the geography, manners, and productions
of remote nations, than would have been found in
compositions of the age of Camillus. But he troubles

himself little about dates, and having heard travellers talk with admiration of the Colossus of Rhodes, and of the structures and gardens with which the Macedonian kings of Syria had embellished their residence on the banks of the Orontes, he has never thought of inquiring whether these things existed in the age of Romulus.

THE PROPHECY OF CAPYS.

A LAY SUNG AT THE BANQUET IN THE CAPITOL, ON THE DAY WHEREON MANIUS CURIUS DENTATUS, A SECOND TIME CONSUL, TRIUMPHED OVER KING PYRRHUS AND THE TARENTINES, IN THE YEAR OF THE CITY CCCCLXXIX.

I.

Now slain is King Amulius,
  Of the great Sylvian line,
Who reigned in Alba Longa,
  On the throne of Aventine.
Slain is the Pontiff Camers,
  Who spake the words of doom:
"The children to the Tiber,
  The mother to the tomb."

II.

In Alba's lake no fisher
  His net to-day is flinging:
On the dark rind of Alba's oaks
  To-day no axe is ringing:
The yoke hangs o'er the manger:
  The scythe lies in the hay:
Through all the Alban villages
  No work is done to-day.

III.

And every Alban burgher
   Hath donned his whitest gown ;
And every head in Alba
   Weareth a poplar crown ;
An l every Alban door-post
   With boughs and flowers is gay,
For to-day the dead are living ;
   The lost are found to-day.

IV.

They were doomed by a bloody king :
   They were doomed by a lying priest :
They were cast on the raging flood :
   They were tracked by the raging beast.
Raging beast and raging flood
   Alike have spared the prey ;
And to-day the dead are living :
   The lost are found to-day.

V.

The troubled river knew them,
   And smoothed his yellow foam
And gently rocked the cradle
   That bore the fate of Rome.
The ravening she-wolf knew them,
   And licked them o'er and o'er,
And gave them of her own fierce milk,
   Rich with raw flesh and gore.
Twenty winters, twenty springs,
   Since then have rolled away ;
And to-day the dead are living :
   The lost are found to-day.

VI.

Blithe it was to see the twins,
    Right goodly youths and tall,
Marching from Alba Longa
    To their old grandsire's hall.
Along their path fresh garlands
    Are hung from tree to tree :
Before them stride the pipers,
    Piping a note of glee.

VII.

On the right goes Romulus,
    With arms to the elbows red,
And in his hand a broadsword,
    And on the blade a head—
A head in an iron helmet,
    With horse-hair hanging down,
A shaggy head, a swarthy head,
    Fixed in a ghastly frown—
The head of King Amulius
    Of the great Sylvian line,
Who reigned in Alba Longa,
    On the throne of Aventine.

VIII.

On the left side goes Remus,
    With wrists and fingers red,
And in his hand a boar-spear,
    And on the point a head—
A wrinkled head and aged,
    With silver beard and hair,
And holy fillets round it,
    Such as the pontiffs wear—

The head of ancient Camers,
　　Who spake the words of doom:
" The children to the Tiber;
　　The mother to the tomb."

IX.

Two and two behind the twins
　　Their trusty comrades go,
Four and forty valiant men,
　　With club, and axe, and bow.
On each side every hamlet
　　Pours forth its joyous crowd,
Shouting lads and baying dogs,
　　And children laughing loud,
And old men weeping fondly
　　As Rhea's boys go by,
And maids who shriek to see the heads,
　　Yet, shrieking, press more nigh.

X.

So they marched along the lake;
　　They marched by fold and stall,
By cornfield and by vineyard,
　　Unto the old man's hall.

XI.

In the hall-gate sat Capys,
　　Capys, the sightless seer;
From head to foot he trembled
　　As Romulus drew near.
And up stood stiff his thin white hair,
　　And his blind eyes flashed fire:
" Hail! foster child of the wonderous nurse!
　.Hail! son of the wonderous sire!

XII.

" But thou—what dost thou here
 In the old man's peaceful hall ?
What doth the eagle in the coop,
 The bison in the stall ?
Our corn fills many a garner ;
 Our vines clasp many a tree ;
Our flocks are white on many a hill
 But these are not for thee.

XIII.

" For thee no treasure ripens
 In the Tartessian mine :
For thee no ship brings precious bales
 Across the Libyan brine ;
Thou shalt not drink from amber ;
 Thou shalt not rest on down ;
Arabia shall not steep thy locks,
 Nor Sidon tinge thy gown.

XIV.

" Leave gold and myrrh and jewels,
 Rich table and soft bed,
To them who of man's seed are born,
 Whom woman's milk have fed.
Thou wast not made for lucre,
 For pleasure, nor for rest ;
Thou, that art sprung from the War-god's loins,
 And hast tugged at the she-wolf's breast.

XV.

" From sunrise unto sunset
 All earth shall hear thy fame :
A glorious city thou shalt build,
 And name it by thy name :

And there, unquenched through ages,
Like Vesta's sacred fire,
Shall live the spirit of thy nurse,
The spirit of thy sire.

XVI.

" The ox toils through the furrow,
Obedient to the goad ;
The patient ass, up flinty paths,
Plods with his weary load :
With whine and bound the spaniel
His master's whistle hears ;
And the sheep yields her patiently
To the loud clashing shears.

XVII.

" But thy nurse will hear no master,
Thy nurse will bear no load ;
And woe to them that shear her,
And woe to them that goad !
When all the pack, loud baying,
Her bloody lair surrounds,
She dies in silence, biting hard,
Amidst the dying hounds.

XVIII.

" Pomona loves the orchard ;
And Liber loves the vine ;
And Pales loves the straw-built shed
Warm with the breath of kine ;
And Venus loves the whispers
Of plighted youth and maid,
In April's ivory moonlight
Beneath the chestnut shade.

XIX.

" But thy father loves the clashing
 Of broadsword and of shield :
He loves to drink the steam that reeks
 From the fresh battle-field :
He smiles a smile more dreadful
 Than his own dreadful frown,
When he sees the thick black cloud of **smoke**
 Go up from the conquered town.

XX.

" And such as is the War-god,
 The author of thy line,
And such as she who suckled thee,
 Even such be thou and thine.
Leave to the soft Campanian
 His baths and his perfumes ;
Leave to the sordid race of Tyre
 Their dyeing-vats and looms :
Leave to the sons of Carthage
 The rudder and the oar :
Leave to the Greek his marble Nymphs
 And scrolls of wordy lore.

XXI.

" Thine, Roman, is the pilum :
 Roman, the sword is thine,
The even trench, the bristling mound,
 The legion's ordered line ;
And thine the wheels of triumph,
 Which with their laurelled train
Move slowly up the shouting streets
 To Jove's eternal fane.

XXII.

" Beneath thy yoke the Volscian
    Shall vail his lofty brow:
Soft Capua's curled revellers
    Before thy chairs shall bow:
The Lucumoes of Arnus
    Shall quake thy rods to see;
And the proud Samnite's heart of steel
    Shall yield to only thee.

XXIII.

" The Gaul shall come against thee
    From the land of snow and night:
Thou shalt give his fair-haired armies
    To the raven and the kite.

XXIV.

" The Greek shall come against thee,
    The conqueror of the East.
Beside him stalks to battle
    The huge earth-shaking beast,
The beast on whom the castle
    With all its guards doth stand,
The beast who hath between his eyes
    The serpent for a hand.
First march the bold Epirotes,
    Wedged close with shield and spear,
And the ranks of false Tarentum
    Are glittering in the rear.

XXV.

" The ranks of false Tarentum
    Like hunted sheep shall fly:
In vain the bold Epirotes
    Shall round their standards die:

And Apennine's grey vultures
  Shall have a noble feast
On the fat and the eyes
  Of the huge earth-shaking beast.

XXVI.

" Hurrah ! for the good weapons
  That keep the War-god's land.
Hurrah ! for Rome's stout pilum
  In a stout Roman hand.
Hurrah ! for Rome's short broadsword
  That through the thick array
Of level spears and serried shields
  Hews deep its gory way.

XXVII.

" Hurrah ! for the great triumph
  That stretches many a mile.
Hurrah ! for the wan captives
  That pass in endless file.
Ho ! bold Epirotes, whither
  Hath the Red King ta'en flight?
Ho ! dogs of false Tarentum,
  Is not the gown washed white ?

XXVIII.

" Hurrah ! for the great triumph
  That stretches many a mile.
Hurrah ! for the rich dye of Tyre,
  And the fine web of Nile,
The helmets gay with plumage
  Torn from the pheasant's wings,
The belts set thick with starry gems
  That shone on Indian kings.

The urns of massy silver,
    The goblets rough with gold,
The many-coloured tablets bright
    With loves and wars of old,
The stone that breathes and struggles,
    The brass that seems to speak ;—
Such cunning they who dwell on high
    Have given unto the Greek.

XXIX.

" Hurrah ! for Manius Curius,
    The bravest son of Rome,
Thrice in utmost need sent forth,
    Thrice drawn in triumph home.
Weave, weave, for Manius Curius
    The third embroidered gown :
Make ready the third lofty car,
    And twine the third green crown ;
And yoke the steeds of Rosea
    With necks like a bended bow,
And deck the bull, Mevania's bull,
    The bull as white as snow.

XXX.

" Blest and thrice blest the Roman
    Who sees Rome's brightest day
Who sees that long victorious pomp
    Wind down the Sacred Way,
And through the bellowing Forum,
    And round the Suppliant's Grove,
Up to the everlasting gates
    Of Capitolian Jove.

XXXI.

" Then where, o'er two bright havens,
    The towers of Corinth frown ;
Where the gigantic King of Day
    On his own Rhodes looks down ;
Where soft Orontes murmurs
    Beneath the laurel shades ;
Where Nile reflects the endless length
    Of dark red colonnades ;
Where in the still deep water,
    Sheltered from waves and blasts,
Bristles the dusky forest
    Of Byrsa's thousand masts ;
Where fur-clad hunters wander
    Amidst the northern ice ;
Where through the sand of morning-land
    The camel bears the spice ;
Where Atlas flings his shadow
    Far o'er the western foam,
Shall be great fear on all who hear
    The mighty name of Rome."

MISCELLANEOUS POEMS,

INSCRIPTIONS, ETC.

r 2

EPITAPH ON HENRY MARTYN. (1812.)

HERE Martyn lies. In Manhood's early bloom
The Christian Hero finds a Pagan tomb.
Religion, sorrowing o'er her favourite son,
Points to the glorious trophies that he won.
Eternal trophies! not with carnage red,
Not stained with tears by hapless captives shed,
But trophies of the Cross! for that dear name,
Through every form of danger, death, and shame,
Onward he journeyed to a happier shore,
Where danger, death, and shame assault no more.

LINES TO THE MEMORY OF PITT. (1813.)

Oh Britain! dear Isle, when the annals of story
  Shall tell of the deeds that thy children have
    done,
When the strains of each poet shall sing of their
  glory,
  And the triumphs their skill and their valour have
    won ;

When the olive and palm in thy chaplet are blended,
  When thy arts, and thy fame, and thy commerce
    increase,
When thy arms through the uttermost coasts are
  extended,
  And thy war is triumphant, and happy thy peace ;

When the ocean, whose waves like a rampart flow
  round thee,
  Conveying thy mandates to every shore,
And the empire of nature no longer can bound thee,
  And the world be the scene of thy conquests no
    more :

Remember the man who in sorrow and danger,
  When thy glory was set, and thy spirit was low,
When thy hopes were o'erturned by the arms of the
  stranger,
  And thy banners displayed in the halls of the foe,

Stood forth in the tempest of doubt and disaster,
  Unaided, and single, the danger to brave,
Asserted thy claims, and the rights of his master,
  Preserved thee to conquer, and saved thee to save.

A RADICAL WAR SONG. (1820.)

AWAKE, arise, the hour is come,
  For rows and revolutions;
There's no receipt like pike and drum
  For crazy constitutions.
Close, close the shop! Break, break the loom,
  Desert your hearths and furrows,
And throng in arms to seal the doom
  Of England's rotten boroughs.

We'll stretch that tort'ring Castlereagh
  On his own Dublin rack, sir;
We'll drown the King in Eau de vie,
  The Laureate in his sack, sir.
Old Eldon and his sordid hag
  In molten gold we'll smother,
And stifle in his own green bag
  The Doctor and his brother.

In chains we'll hang in fair Guildhall
  The City's famed Recorder,
And next on proud St. Stephen's fall,
  Though Wynne should squeak to order.
In vain our tyrants then shall try
  To 'scape our martial law, sir;
In vain the trembling Speaker cry
  That " Strangers must withdraw," sir.

Copley to hang offends no text;
    A rat is not a man, sir:
With schedules and with tax bills next
    We'll bury pious Van, sir.
The slaves who loved the Income Tax,
    We'll crush by scores, like mites, sir,
And him, the wretch who freed the blacks,
    And more enslaved the whites, sir.

The peer shall dangle from his gate,
    The bishop from his steeple,
Till all recanting, own, the State
    Means nothing but the People.
We'll fix the church's revenues
    On Apostolic basis,
One coat, one scrip, one pair of shoes
    Shall pay their strange grimaces.

We'll strap the bar's deluding train
    In their own darling halter,
And with his big church bible brain
    The parson at the altar.
Hail glorious hour, when fair Reform
    Shall bless our longing nation,
And Hunt receive commands to form
    A new administration.

Carlile shall sit enthroned, where sat
    Our Cranmer and our Secker;
And Watson show his snow-white hat
    In England's rich Exchequer.
The breast of Thistlewood shall wear
    Our Wellesley's star and sash, man;
And many a mausoleum fair
    Shall rise to honest Cashman.

Then, then beneath the nine-tailed cat
    Shall they who used it writhe, sir :
And curates lean, and rectors fat,
    Shall dig the ground they tithe, sir.
Down with your Bayleys, and your Bests,
    Your Giffords, and your Gurneys :
We'll clear the island of the pests,
    Which mortals name attorneys.

Down with your sheriffs, and your mayors,
    Your registrars, and proctors,
We'll live without the lawyer's cares,
    And die without the doctor's.
No discontented fair shall pout
    To see her spouse so stupid ;
We'll tread the torch of Hymen out,
    And live content with Cupid.

Then, when the high-born and the great
    Are humbled to our level,
On all the wealth of Church and State,
    Like aldermen, we'll revel.
We'll live, when hushed the battle's din,
    In smoking and in cards, sir,
In drinking unexcised gin,
    And wooing fair Poissardes, sir.

IVRY. (1824.)

A SONG OF THE HUGUENOTS.

Now glory to the Lord of Hosts, from whom all
   glories are!
And glory to our Sovereign Liege, King Henry of
   Navarre!
Now let there be the merry sound of music and of
   dance,
Through thy corn-fields green, and sunny vines, oh
   pleasant land of France!
And thou, Rochelle, our own Rochelle, proud city of
   the waters,
Again let rapture light the eyes of all thy mourning
   daughters.
As thou wert constant in our ills, be joyous in
   our joy,
For cold, and stiff, and still are they who wrought
   thy walls annoy.
Hurrah! hurrah! a single field hath turned the
   chance of war,
Hurrah! hurrah! for Ivry, and Henry of Navarre.

Oh! how our hearts were beating, when, at the dawn
   of day,
We saw the army of the League drawn out in long
   array;

With all its priest-led citizens, and all its rebel
   peers,
And Appenzel's stout infantry, and Egmont's Flemish
   spears.
There rode the brood of false Lorraine, the curses of
   our land ;
And dark Mayenne was in the midst, a truncheon in
   his hand :
And as we looked on them, we thought of Seine's
   empurpled flood,
And good Coligni's hoary hair all dabbled with his
   blood ;
And we cried unto the living God, who rules the
   fate of war,
To fight for his own holy name, and Henry of
   Navarre.

The King is come to marshal us, in all his armour
   drest,
And he has bound a snow-white plume upon his
   gallant crest.
He looked upon his people, and a tear was in his
   eye ;
He looked upon the traitors, and his glance was
   stern and high.
Right graciously he smiled on us, as rolled from
   wing to wing,
Down all our line, a deafening shout, "God save
   our Lord the King."
" An if my standard-bearer fall, as fall full well he
   may,
For never saw I promise yet of such a bloody
   fray,
Press where ye see my white plume shine, amidst
   the ranks of war,
And be your oriflamme to-day the helmet of
   Navarre."

Hurrah! the foes are moving. Hark to the mingled
  din,
Of fife, and steed, and trump, and drum, and roaring
  culverin.
The fiery Duke is pricking fast across Saint André's
  plain,
With all the hireling chivalry of Guelders and
  Almayne.
Now by the lips of those ye love, fair gentlemen of
  France,
Charge for the golden lilies,—upon them with the
  lance.
A thousand spurs are striking deep, a thousand
  spears in rest,
A thousand knights are pressing close behind the
  snow-white crest;
And in they burst, and on they rushed, while, like a
  guiding star,
Amidst the thickest carnage blazed the helmet of
  Navarre.

Now, God be praised, the day is ours. Mayenne
  hath turned his rein.
D'Aumale hath cried for quarter. The Flemish
  count is slain.
Their ranks are breaking like thin clouds before a
  Biscay gale;
The field is heaped with bleeding steeds, and flags,
  and cloven mail.
And then we thought on vengeance, and, all along
  our van,
"Remember Saint Bartholomew," was passed from
  man to man.
But out spake gentle Henry, "No Frenchman is
  my foe:
Down, down with every foreigner, but let your
  brethren go."

Oh ! was there ever such a knight, in friendship or
    in war,
As our Sovereign Lord, King Henry, the soldier of
    Navarre ?

Right well fought all the Frenchmen who fought
    for France to-day ;
And many a lordly banner God gave them for a
    prey.
But we of the religion have borne us best in fight ;
And the good Lord of Rosny hath ta'en the cornet
    white.
Our own true Maximilian the cornet white hath
    ta'en,
The cornet white, with crosses black, the flag of
    false Lorraine.
Up with it high ; unfurl it wide ; that all the host
    may know
How God hath humbled the proud house which
    wrought his church such woe.
Then on the ground, while trumpets sound their
    loudest point of war,
Fling the red shreds, a footcloth meet for Henry of
    Navarre.

Ho ! maidens of Vienna ; ho ! matrons of Lucerne ;
Weep, weep, and rend your hair for those who never
    shall return.
Ho ! Philip, send, for charity, thy Mexican pistoles,
That Antwerp monks may sing a mass for thy poor
    spearmen's souls.
Ho ! gallant nobles of the League, look that your
    arms be bright ;
Ho ! burghers of Saint Genevieve, keep watch and
    ward to-night.

For our God hath crushed the tyrant, our God hath
    raised the slave,
And mocked the counsel of the wise, and the valour
    of the brave,
Then glory to his holy name, from whom all glories
    are ;
And glory to our Sovereign Lord, King Henry of
    Navarre.

THE BATTLE OF MONCONTOUR. (1824).

Oh, weep for Moncontour! oh! weep for the hour
When the children of darkness and evil had power,
When the horsemen of Valois triumphantly trod
On the bosoms that bled for their rights and their
    God.

Oh, weep for Moncontour! oh! weep for the slain,
Who for faith and for freedom lay slaughtered in vain;
Oh, weep for the living, who linger to bear
The renegade's shame, or the exile's despair.

One look, one last look, to our cots and our towers,
To the rows of our vines, and the beds of our
    flowers,
To the church where the bones of our fathers
    decayed,
Where we fondly had dreamed that our own would
    be laid.

Alas! we must leave thee, dear desolate home,
To the spearmen of Uri, the shavelings of Rome,
To the serpent of Florence, the vulture of Spain,
To the pride of Anjou, and the guile of Lorraine.

Farewell to thy fountains, farewell to thy shades,
To the song of thy youths, and the dance of thy
    maids,
To the breath of thy gardens, the hum of thy bees,
And the long waving line of the blue Pyrenees.

Farewell, and for ever. The priest and the slave
May rule in the halls of the free and the brave.
Our hearths we abandon; our lands we resign;
But, Father, we kneel to no altar but thine.

SONGS OF THE CIVIL WAR.

I.   THE BATTLE OF NASEBY, BY OBADIAH BIND-THEIR-KINGS-
     IN - CHAINS - AND - THEIR - NOBLES - WITH-LINKS-OF-IRON,
     SERJEANT IN IRETON'S REGIMENT.   (1824.)

Oh! wherefore come ye forth, in triumph from the
        North,
    With your hands, and your feet, and your raiment
        all red?
And wherefore doth your rout send forth a joyous
        shout?
    And whence be the grapes of the wine-press which
        ye tread?

Oh evil was the root, and bitter was the fruit,
    And crimson was the juice of the vintage that we
        trod;
For we trampled on the throng of the haughty and
        the strong,
    Who sate in the high places, and slew the saints
        of God.

It was about the noon of a glorious day of June,
    That we saw their banners dance, and their cuir-
        asses shine,
And the Man of blood was there, with his long
        essenced hair,
    And Astley, and Sir Marmaduke, and Rupert of
        the Rhine.

Like a servant of the Lord, with his Bible and his
    sword,
The General rode along us to form us to the fight,
When a murmuring sound broke out, and swell'd into
    a shout,
    Among the godless horsemen upon the tyrant's
    right.

And hark! like the roar of the billows on the shore,
    The cry of battle rises along their charging line!
For God! for the Cause! for the Church, for the
    Laws!
    For Charles King of England, and Rupert of the
    Rhine!

The furious German comes, with his clarions and
    his drums,
His bravoes of Alsatia, and pages of Whitehall;
They are bursting on our flanks. Grasp your pikes,
    close your ranks;
    For Rupert never comes but to conquer or to fall.

They are here! They rush on! We are broken! We
    are gone!
    Our left is borne before them like stubble on the
    blast.
O Lord, put forth thy might! O Lord, defend the
    right!
    Stand back to back, in God's name, and fight it
    to the last.

Stout Skippon hath a wound; the centre hath given
    ground:
    Hark! hark!—What means the trampling of
    horsemen on our rear?
Whose banner do I see, boys? 'Tis he, thank God,
    'tis he, boys.
    Bear up another minute: brave Oliver is here.

Their heads all stooping low, their points all in a row,
    Like a whirlwind on the trees, like a deluge on
      the dykes,
Our cuirassiers have burst on the ranks of the Accurst,
    And at a shock have scattered the forest of his
      pikes.

Fast, fast, the gallants ride, in some safe nook to hide
    Their coward heads, predestined to rot on Temple
      Bar :
And he—he turns, he flies:—shame on those cruel
    eyes
    That bore to look on torture, and dare not look
    on war.

Ho ! comrades, scour the plain ; and, ere ye strip
    the slain,
    First give another stab to make your search secure,
Then shake from sleeves and pockets their broad-
    pieces and lockets,
    The tokens of the wanton, the plunder of the poor.

Fools ! your doublets shone with gold, and your
    hearts were gay and bold,
    When you kissed your lily hands to your lemans
    to-day ;
And to-morrow shall the fox, from her chambers in
    the rocks,
    Lead forth her tawny cubs to howl above the prey.

Where be your tongues that late mocked at heaven
    and hell and fate,
    And the fingers that once were so busy with your
    blades,
Your perfum'd satin clothes, your catches and your
    oaths,
    Your stage-plays and your sonnets, your diamonds
    and your spades ?

Down, down, for ever down with the mitre and the
    crown,
  With the Belial of the Court, and the Mammon of
    the Pope;
There is woe in Oxford Halls; there is wail in Dur-
    ham's Stalls:
  The Jesuit smites his bosom: the Bishop rends
    his cope.

And She of the seven hills shall mourn her children's
    ills,
  And tremble when she thinks on the edge of Eng-
    land's sword;
And the Kings of earth in fear shall shudder when
    they hear
  What the hand of God hath wrought for the
    Houses and the Word.

HERE warlike cobblers railed from tops of casks
At lords and love-locks, monarchy and masques.
There many a graceless page blaspheming reel'd,
From his dear cards and bumpers, to the field:
The famished rooks, impatient of delay,
Gnaw their cogg'd dice and curse the lingering prey:
His sad Andromache, with fruitless care,
Paints her wan lips and braids her borrowed hair:
For Church and King he quits his favourite arts,
Forsakes his Knaves, forsakes his Queen of Hearts:
For Church and King he burns to stain with gore
His doublet, stained with nought but sack before.

From a MS. Poem.

II.   THE CAVALIER'S MARCH TO LONDON.   (1824.)

To horse! to horse! brave Cavaliers!
    To horse for Church and Crown!
Strike, strike your tents! snatch up your spears!
    And ho for London town!
The imperial harlot, doom'd a prey
    To our avenging fires,
Sends up the voice of her dismay
    From all her hundred spires.

The Strand resounds with maiden's shrieks,
    The 'Change with merchants' sighs,
And blushes stand on brazen cheeks,
    And tears in iron eyes;
And, pale with fasting and with fright,
    Each Puritan Committee
Hath summon'd forth to prayer and fight
    The Roundheads of the City.

And soon shall London's sentries hear
    The thunder of our drum,
And London's dames, in wilder fear,
    Shall cry, Alack! They come!

Fling the fascines;—tear up the spikes;
  And forward, one and all.
Down, down with all their train-band pikes,
  Down with their mud-built wall.

Quarter?—Foul fall your whining noise,
  Ye recreant spawn of fraud!
No quarter! Think on Strafford, boys.
  No quarter! Think on Laud.
What ho! The craven slaves retire.
  On! Trample them to mud,
No quarter!—Charge.—No quarter!—Fire.
  No quarter!—Blood!—Blood!—Blood!—

Where next? In sooth there lacks no witch,
  Brave lads, to tell us where,
Sure London's sons be passing rich,
  Her daughters wondrous fair:
And let that dastard be the theme
  Of many a board's derision,
Who quails for sermon, cuff, or scream
  Of any sweet Precisian.

Their lean divines, of solemn brow,
  Sworn foes to throne and steeple,
From an unwonted pulpit now
  Shall edify the people:
Till the tir'd hangman, in despair,
  Shall curse his blunted shears,
And vainly pinch, and scrape, and tear,
  Around their leathern ears.

We'll hang, above his own Guildhall,
  The city's grave Recorder,
And on the den of thieves we'll fall,
  Though Pym should speak to order,
In vain the lank-haired gang shall try
  To cheat our martial law;
In vain shall Lenthall trembling cry
  That strangers must withdraw.

Of bench and woolsack, tub and chair,
　　We'll build a glorious pyre,
And tons of rebel parchment there
　　Shall crackle in the fire.
With them shall perish, cheek by jowl,
　　Petition, psalm, and libel,
The Colonel's canting muster-roll,
　　The Chaplain's dog-ear'd bible.

We'll tread a measure round the blaze
　　Where England's pest expires,
And lead along the dance's maze
　　The beauties of the Friars:
Then smiles in every face shall shine,
　　And joy in every soul.
Bring forth, bring forth the oldest wine,
　　And crown the largest bowl.

And as with nod and laugh ye sip
　　The goblet's rich carnation,
Whose bursting bubbles seem to tip
　　The wink of invitation;
Drink to those names,—those glorious names,—
　　Those names no time shall sever,—
Drink, in a draught as deep as Thames,
　　Our Church and King for ever!

SERMON IN A CHURCHYARD. (1825.)

LET pious Damon take his seat,
  With mincing step, and languid smile,
And scatter from his 'kerchief sweet,
  Sabæan odours o'er the aisle ;
And spread his little jewelled hand,
  And smile round all the parish beauties,
And pat his curls, and smooth his band,
  Meet prelude to his saintly duties.

Let the thronged audience press and stare,
  Let stifled maidens ply the fan,
Admire his doctrines and his hair,
  And whisper " What a good young man ! "
While he explains what seems most clear
  So clearly that it seems perplexed,
I'll stay, and read my sermon here ;
  And skulls, and bones, shall be the text.

Art thou the jilted dupe of fame ?
  Dost thou with jealous anger pine
Whene'er she sounds some other name,
  With fonder emphasis than thine ?
To thee I preach ; draw near ; attend !
  Look on these bones, thou fool, and see
Where all her scorns and favours end,
  What Byron is, and thou must be.

Dost thou revere, or praise, or trust
   Some clod like those that here we spurn;
Some thing that sprang like thee from dust,
   And shall like thee to dust return?
Dost thou rate statesmen, heroes, wits,
   At one sear leaf or wandering feather?
Behold the black, damp, narrow pits,
   Where they and thou must lie together.

Dost thou beneath the smile or frown
   Of some vain woman bend thy knee?
Here take thy stand, and trample down
   Things that were once as fair as she.
Here rave of her ten thousand graces,
   Bosom, and lip, and eye, and chin,
While, as in scorn, the fleshless faces
   Of Hamiltons and Waldegraves grin.

Whate'er thy losses or thy gains,
   Whate'er thy projects or thy fears,
Whate'er the joys, whate'er the pains,
   That prompt thy baby smiles and tears,
Come to my school, and thou shalt learn,
   In one short hour of placid thought,
A stoicism, more deep, more stern,
   Than ever Zeno's porch hath taught.

The plots and feats of those that press
   To seize on titles, wealth, or power,
Shall seem to thee a game of chess,
   Devised to pass a tedious hour.
What matters it to him who fights
   For shows of unsubstantial good,
Whether his Kings, and Queens, and Knights,
   Be things of flesh, or things of wood?

We check and take; exult and fret;
   Our plans extend, our passions rise,
Till in our ardour we forget
   How worthless is the victor's prize.

Soon fades the spell, soon comes the night :
  Say will it not be then the same,
Whether we played the black or white,
  Whether we lost or won the game ?

Dost thou among these hillocks stray,
  O'er some dear idol's tomb to moan ?
Know that thy foot is on the clay
  Of hearts once wretched as thy own.
How many a father's anxious schemes,
  How many rapturous thoughts of lovers,
How many a mother's cherished dreams,
  The swelling turf before thee covers !

Here for the living, and the dead,
  The weepers and the friends they weep,
Hath been ordained the same cold bed,
  The same dark night, the same long sleep.
Why shouldst thou writhe, and sob, and rave
  O'er those, with whom thou soon must be ?
Death his own sting shall cure—the grave
  Shall vanquish its own victory.

Here learn that all the griefs and joys,
  Which now torment, which now beguile,
Are children's hurts and children's toys,
  Scarce worthy of one bitter smile.
Here learn that pulpit, throne, and press,
  Sword, sceptre, lyre, alike are frail,
That science is a blind man's guess,
  And History a nurse's tale.

Here learn that glory and disgrace,
  Wisdom and folly, pass away,
That mirth hath its appointed space,
  That sorrow is but for a day ;
That all we love, and all we hate,
  That all we hope, and all we fear,
Each mood of mind, each turn of fate,
  Must end in dust and silence here.

TRANSLATION FROM A. V. ARNAULT.

Fables: livre v., fable 16. (1826.)

THOU poor leaf, so sear and frail,
Sport of every wanton gale,
Whence, and whither, dost thou fly,
Through this bleak autumnal sky?
On a noble oak I grew,
Green, and broad, and fair to view;
But the monarch of the shade
By the tempest low was laid.
From that time, I wander o'er
Wood and valley, hill and moor,
Wheresoe'er the wind is blowing,
Nothing caring, nothing knowing:
Thither go I whither goes
Glory's laurel, Beauty's rose.

——De ta tige détachée,
Pauvre feuille desséchée,
Où vas-tu ?—Je n'en sais rien.
L'orage a frappé le chêne
Qui seul était mon soutien.
De son inconstante haleine,
Le zéphyr ou l'aquilon
Depuis ce jour me promène
De la forêt à la plaine,
De la montagne au vallon.
Je vais où le vent me mène,
Sans me plaindre ou m'effrayer,
Je vais où va toute chose,
Où va la feuille de rose
Et la feuille de laurier.

DIES IRÆ.   (1826.)

ON that great, that awful day,
This vain world shall pass away
Thus the sibyl sang of old,
Thus hath Holy David told.
There shall be a deadly fear
When the Avenger shall appear,
And unveiled before his eye
All the works of man shall lie.
Hark! to the great trumpet's tones
Pealing o'er the place of bones:
Hark! it waketh from their bed
All the nations of the dead,—
In a countless throng to meet,
At the eternal judgment seat.
Nature sickens with dismay,
Death may not retain his prey;
And before the Maker stand
All the creatures of his hand.
The great book shall be unfurled,
Whereby God shall judge the world:
What was distant shall be near,
What was hidden shall be clear.
To what shelter shall I fly?
To what guardian shall I cry?
Oh, in that destroying hour,
Source of goodness, Source of power,
Show thou, of thine own free grace,
Help unto a helpless race.

Though I plead not at thy throne
Aught that I for thee have done,
Do not thou unmindful be,
Of what thou hast borne for me:
Of the wandering, of the scorn,
Of the scourge, and of the thorn.
Jesus, hast *thou* borne the pain,
And hath all been borne in vain?
Shall thy vengeance smite the head
For whose ransom thou hast bled?
Thou, whose dying blessing gave
Glory to a guilty slave:
Thou, who from the crew unclean
Didst release the Magdalene:
Shall not mercy vast and free,
Evermore be found in thee?
Father, turn on me thine eyes,
See my blushes, hear my cries;
Faint though be the cries I make,
Save me, for thy mercy's sake,
From the worm, and from the fire,
From the torments of thine ire.
Fold me with the sheep that stand
Pure and safe at thy right hand.
Hear thy guilty child implore thee,
Rolling in the dust before thee.
Oh the horrors of that day!
When this frame of sinful clay,
Starting from its burial place,
Must behold thee face to face.
Hear and pity, hear and aid,
Spare the creatures thou hast made.
Mercy, mercy, save, forgive,
Oh, who shall look on thee and live?

THE MARRIAGE OF TIRZAH AND AHIRAD.
(1827.)

GENESIS VI. 3.

———

It is the dead of night :
Yet more than noonday light
Beams far and wide from many a gorgeous hall.
  Unnumbered harps are tinkling,
  Unnumbered lamps are twinkling,
In the great city of the fourfold wall.
  By the brazen castle's moat,
  The sentry hums a livelier note.
  The ship-boy chaunts a shriller lay
  From the galleys in the bay.
  Shout, and laugh, and hurrying feet
  Sound from mart and square and street,
  From the breezy laurel shades,
  From the granite colonnades,
  From the golden statue's base,
  From the stately market-place,
  Where, upreared by captive hands,
  The great Tower of Triumph stands,
  All its pillars in a blaze
  With the many-coloured rays,
  Which lanthorns of ten thousand dyes
  Shed on ten thousand panoplies.
    But closest is the throng,
    And loudest is the song,

In that sweet garden by the river's side,
  The abyss of myrtle bowers,
  The wilderness of flowers,
Where Cain hath built the palace of his pride.
  Such palace ne'er shall be again
  Among the dwindling race of men.
From all its threescore gates the light
  Of gold and steel afar was thrown;
Two hundred cubits rose in height
  The outer wall of polished stone.
  On the top was ample space
  For a gallant chariot race.
  Near either parapet a bed
  Of the richest mould was spread,
Where amidst flowers of every scent and hue
Rich orange trees, and palms, and giant cedars
    grew.

  In the mansion's public court
  All is revel, song, and sport;
For there, till morn shall tint the east,
Menials and guards prolong the feast.
The boards with painted vessels shine;
The marble cisterns foam with wine.
A hundred dancing girls are there
With zoneless waists and streaming hair;
And countless eyes with ardour gaze,
  And countless hands the measure beat,
As mix and part in amorous maze
  Those floating arms and bounding feet.
But none of all the race of Cain,
  Save those whom he hath deigned to grace
With yellow robe and sapphire chain,
  May pass beyond that outer space.
  For now within the painted hall
  The Firstborn keeps high festival.

Before the glittering valves all night
  Their post the chosen captains hold,
Above the portal's stately height
  The legend flames in lamps of gold:
" In life united and in death
  May Tirzah and Ahirad be,
The bravest he of all the sons of Seth,
  Of all the house of Cain the loveliest she."

Through all the climates of the earth
This night is given to festal mirth.
The long continued war is ended.
The long divided lines are blended.
Ahirad's bow shall now no more
Make fat the wolves with kindred gore.
The vultures shall expect in vain
Their banquet from the sword of Cain.
Without a guard the herds and flocks
Along the frontier moors and rocks
  From eve to morn may roam;
Nor shriek, nor shout, nor reddened sky,
Shall warn the startled hind to fly
  From his beloved home.
Nor to the pier shall burghers crowd
  With straining necks and faces pale,
And think that in each flitting cloud
  They see a hostile sail.
The peasant without fear shall guide
Down smooth canal or river wide
  His painted bark of cane,
Fraught, for some proud bazaar's arcades,
With chestnuts from his native shades,
  And wine, and milk, and grain.
Search round the peopled globe to-night,
  Explore each continent and isle,
There is no door without a light,
  No face without a smile.

The noblest chiefs of either race,
　　From north and south, from west and east,
Crowd to the painted hall to grace
　　The pomp of that atoning feast.
With widening eyes and labouring breath
Stand the fair-haired sons of Seth,
As bursts upon their dazzled sight
The endless avenue of light,
The bowers of tulip, rose, and palm,
The thousand cressets fed with balm,
The silken vests, the boards piled high
With amber, gold, and ivory,
The crystal founts whence sparkling flow
The richest wines o'er beds of snow,
The walls where blaze in living dyes
The king's three hundred victories.
The heralds point the fitting seat
To every guest in order meet,
And place the highest in degree
Nearest th' imperial canopy.
Beneath its broad and gorgeous fold,
With naked swords and shields of gold,
Stood the seven princes of the tribes of Nod.
　　Upon an ermine carpet lay
　　Two tiger cubs in furious play,
Beneath the emerald throne where sat the signed of
　　　　God.

　　Over that ample forehead white
　　　　The thousandth year returneth.
　　Still, on its commanding height,
　　With a fierce and blood-red light,
　　　　The fiery token burneth.
　　Wheresoe'er that mystic star
　　Blazeth in the van of war,
　　　　Back recoil before its ray
　　Shield and banner, bow and spear,
　　　　Maddened horses break away

From the trembling charioteer.
The fear of that stern king doth lie
On all that live beneath the sky;
All shrink before the mark of his despair,
The seal of that great curse which he alone can bear.

Blazing in pearls and diamonds' sheen,
   Tirzah, the young Ahirad's bride,
Of humankind the destined queen,
   Sits by her great forefather's side.
The jetty curls, the forehead high,
   The swanlike neck, the eagle face,
The glowing cheek, the rich dark eye,
   Proclaim her of the elder race.
With flowing locks of auburn hue,
And features smooth and eye of blue,
   Timid in love as brave in arms,
The gentle heir of Seth askance
Snatches a bashful, ardent glance
   At her majestic charms;
Blest when across that brow high musing flashes
   A deeper tint of rose,
Thrice blest when from beneath the silken lashes
   Of her proud eye she throws
The smile of blended fondness and disdain
Which marks the daughters of the house of Cain

All hearts are light around the hall
Save his who is the lord of all.
The painted roofs, the attendant train,
The lights, the banquet, all are vain.
He sees them not.   His fancy strays
To other scenes and other days.
A cot by a lone forest's edge,
   A fountain murmuring through the trees,
A garden with a wild flower hedge,
   Whence sounds the music of the bees,
   A little flock of sheep at rest

Upon a mountain's swarthy breast.
On his rude spade he seems to lean
 Beside the well-remembered stone,
Rejoicing o'er the promise green
 Of the first harvest man hath sown.
He sees his mother's tears;
His father's voice he hears,
Kind as when first it praised his youthful skill.
 And soon a seraph-child,
 In boyish rapture wild,
With a light crook comes bounding from the hill,
 Kisses his hands, and strokes his face,
 And nestles close in his embrace.
 In his adamantine eye
 None might discern his agony;
But they who had grown hoary next his side,
 And read his stern dark face with deepest skill,
Could trace strange meanings in that lip of pride,
 Which for one moment quivered and was still.
No time for them to mark or him to feel
 Those inward stings; for clarion, flute, and lyre
 And the rich voices of a countless quire,
Burst on the ear in one triumphant peal.
In breathless transport sits the admiring throng,
As sink and swell the notes of Jubal's lofty song.

" Sound the timbrel, strike the lyre,
 Wake the trumpet's blast of fire,
  Till the gilded arches ring.
 Empire, victory, and fame,
 Be ascribed unto the name
  Of our father and our king.
 Of the deeds which he hath done,
 Of the spoils which he hath won,
  Let his grateful children sing.

" When the deadly fight was fought,
 When the great revenge was wrought,

A A 2

When on the slaughtered victims lay
The minion stiff and cold as they,
Doomed to exile, sealed with flame,
From the west the wanderer came.
Six score years and six he strayed
A hunter through the forest shade.
The lion's shaggy jaws he tore,
To earth he smote the foaming boar,
He crushed the dragon's fiery crest,
And scaled the condor's dizzy nest;
Till hardy sons and daughters fair
Increased around his woodland lair.
Then his victorious bow unstrung
On the great bison's horn he hung.
Giraffe and elk he left to hold
   The wilderness of boughs in peace,
And trained his youth to pen the fold,
   To press the cream and weave the fleece.
As shrunk the streamlet in its bed,
   As black and scant the herbage grew,
O'er endless plains his flocks he led
   Still to new brooks and pastures new.
So strayed he till the white pavilions
Of his camp were told by millions,
Till his children's households seven
Were numerous as the stars of heaven.
Then he bade us rove no more;
   And in the place that pleased him best,
On the great river's fertile shore,
   He fixed the city of his rest.
He taught us then to bind the sheaves,
   To strain the palm's delicious milk,
And from the dark green mulberry leaves
   To cull the filmy silk.
Then first from straw-built mansions roamed
   O'er flower-beds trim the skilful bees;
Then first the purple wine vats foamed
   Around the laughing peasant's knees;

And olive-yards, and orchards green,
O'er all the hills of Nod were seen.

" Of our father and our king
Let his grateful children sing.
From him our race its being draws,
His are our arts, and his our laws.
Like himself he bade us be,
Proud, and brave, and fierce, and free.
True, through every turn of fate,
In our friendship and our hate.
Calm to watch, yet prompt to dare;
Quick to feel, yet firm to bear;
Only timid, only weak,
Before sweet woman's eye and cheek.
We will not serve, we will not know,
The God who is our father's foe.
In our proud cities to his name
No temples rise, no altars flame.
Our flocks of sheep, our groves of spice
To him afford no sacrifice.
Enough that once the House of Cain
Hath courted with oblation vain
    The sullen power above.
Henceforth we bear the yoke no more;
The only gods whom we adore
    Are glory, vengeance, love.

" Of our father and our king
Let his grateful children sing.
What eye of living thing may brook
On his blazing brow to look?
What might of living thing may stand
Against the strength of his right hand?
First he led his armies forth
Against the Mammoths of the north,
What time they wasted in their pride
Pasture and vineyard far and wide.

Then the White River's icy flood
Was thawed with fire and dyed with blood,
And heard from many a league the sound
Of the pine forests blazing round,
And the death-howl and trampling din
Of the gigantic herd within.
From the surging sea of flame
Forth the tortured monsters came;
As of breakers on the shore
Was their onset and their roar;
As the cedar-trees of God
Stood the stately ranks of Nod.
One long night and one short day
The sword was lifted up to slay.
 Then marched the firstborn and his sons
O'er the white ashes of the wood,
And counted of that savage brood
 Nine times nine thousand skeletons.

" On the snow with carnage red
The wood is piled, the skins are spread.
A thousand fires illume the sky;
Round each a hundred warriors lie.
But, long ere half the night was spent,
Forth thundered from the golden tent
 The rousing voice of Cain.
A thousand trumps in answer rang,
And fast to arms the warriors sprang
 O'er all the frozen plain.
A herald from the wealthy bay
Hath come with tidings of dismay.
From the western ocean's coast
Seth hath led a countless host,
And vows to slay with fire and sword
All who call not on the Lord.
His archers hold the mountain forts;
His light armed ships blockade the ports;

His horsemen tread the harvest down.
On twelve proud bridges he hath passed
The river dark with many a mast,
And pitched his mighty camp at last
  Before the imperial town.

" On the south and on the west,
  Closely was the city prest.
  Before us lay the hostile powers.
  The breach was wide between the towers.
  Pulse and meal within were sold
  For a double weight of gold.
  Our mighty father hath gone forth
  Two hundred marches to the north.
  Yet in that extreme of ill
  We stoutly kept his city still;
  And swore beneath his royal wall,
  Like his true sons, to fight and fall.

" Hark, hark, to gong and horn,
  Clarion, and fife, and drum,
  The morn, the fortieth morn,
  Fixed for the great assault is come.
  Between the camp and city spreads
  A waving sea of helmed heads.
  From the royal car of Seth
  Was hung the blood-red flag of death :
  At sight of that thrice-hallowed sign
  Wide flew at once each banner's fold ;
  The captains clashed their arms of gold ;
  The war cry of Elohim rolled
  Far down their endless line.
  On the northern hills afar
  Pealed an answering note of war.
  Soon the dust in whirlwinds driven,
  Rushed across the northern heaven.
  Beneath its shroud came thick and loud
  The tramp as of a countless crowd ;

And at intervals were seen
Lance and hauberk glancing sheen;
And at intervals were heard
Charger's neigh and battle word.

"Oh what a rapturous cry
From all the city's thousand spires arose,
    With what a look the hollow eye
Of the lean watchman glared upon the foes,
With what a yell of joy the mother pressed
The moaning baby to her withered breast,
When through the swarthy cloud that veiled the plain
Burst on his children's sight the flaming brow of
        Cain!"

There paused perforce that noble song;
For from all the joyous throng,
Burst forth a rapturous shout which drowned
Singer's voice and trumpet's sound.
Thrice that stormy clamour fell,
Thrice rose again with mightier swell.
The last and loudest roar of all
Had died along the painted wall.
The crowd was hushed; the minstrel train
Prepared to strike the chords again;
When on each ear distinctly smote
A low and wild and wailing note.
It moans again. In mute amaze
Menials, and guests, and harpers gaze.
They look above, beneath, around,
No shape doth own that mournful sound.
It comes not from the tuneful quire;
    It comes not from the feasting peers;
There is no tone of earthly lyre
    So soft, so sad, so full of tears.
Then a strange horror came on all
Who sate at that high festival.

The far famed harp, the harp of gold,
Dropped from Jubal's trembling hold.
Frantic with dismay the bride
Clung to her Ahirad's side.
And the corpse-like hue of dread
Ahirad's haughty face o'erspread.
Yet not even in that agony of awe
Did the young leader of the fair-haired race
From Tirzah's shuddering grasp his hand withdraw
Or turn his eyes from Tirzah's livid face.
The tigers to their lord retreat,
And crouch and whine beneath his feet.
Prone sink to earth the golden shielded seven.
All hearts are cowed save his alone
Who sits upon the emerald throne;
For he hath heard Elohim speak from heaven.
Still thunders in his ear the peal;
Still blazes on his front the seal:
And on the soul of the proud king
No terror of created thing
From sky, or earth, or hell, hath power
Since that unutterable hour.

He rose to speak, but paused, and listening stood,
Not daunted, but in sad and curious mood,
With knitted brow, and searching eye of fire.
A deathlike silence sank on all around,
And through the boundless space was heard no sound,
Save the soft tones of that mysterious lyre.
Broken, faint, and low,
At first the numbers flow.
Louder, deeper, quicker, still
Into one fierce peal they swell,
And the echoing palace fill
With a strange funereal yell.
A voice comes forth. But what, or where?
On the earth, or in the air?

Like the midnight winds that blow
Round a lone cottage in the snow,
With howling swell and sighing fall,
It wails along the trophied hall.
In such a wild and dreary moan
    The watches of the Seraphim
    Poured out all night their plaintive hymn
Before the eternal throne.
Then, when from many a heavenly eye
    Drops as of earthly pity fell
For her who had aspired too high,
    For him who loved too well.
When, stunned by grief, the gentle pair
From the nuptial garden fair,
Linked in a sorrowful caress,
Strayed through the untrodden wilderness;
And close behind their footsteps came
The desolating sword of flame,
And drooped the cedared alley's pride,
And fountains shrank, and roses died.

" Rejoice, oh Son of God, rejoice,"
    Sang that melancholy voice,
" Rejoice, the maid is fair to see;
    The bower is decked for her and thee;
The ivory lamps around it throw
A soft and pure and mellow glow.
Where'er the chastened lustre falls
On roof or cornice, floor or walls,
Woven of pink and rose appear
Such words as love delights to hear.
The breath of myrrh, the lute's soft sound,
Float through the moonlight galleries round.
O'er beds of violet and through groves of spice,
    Lead thy proud bride into the nuptial bower;
For thou hast bought her with a fearful price,
    And she hath dowered thee with a fearful
        dower.

The price is life.   The dower is death.
Accursed loss !   Accursed gain !
For her thou givest the blessedness of Seth,
And to thine arms she brings the curse of
Cain.
Round the dark curtains of the fiery throne
Pauses awhile the voice of sacred song :
From all the angelic ranks goes forth a groan,
' How long, O Lord, how long ? '
The still small voice makes answer, ' Wait and
see,
Oh sons of glory, what the end shall be.'

" But in the outer darkness of the place
Where God hath shown his power without his
grace,
Is laughter and the sound of glad acclaim,
Loud as when, on wings of fire,
Fulfilled of his malign desire,
From Paradise the conquering serpent came.
The giant ruler of the morning star
From off his fiery bed
Lifts high his stately head,
Which Michael's sword hath marked with many a
scar.
At his voice the pit of hell
Answers with a joyous yell,
And flings her dusky portals wide
For the bridegroom and the bride.

" But louder still shall be the din
In the halls of Death and Sin,
When the full measure runneth o'er,
When mercy can endure no more,
When he who vainly proffers grace,
Comes in his fury to deface

The fair creation of his hand
When from the heaven streams down amain
For forty days the sheeted rain;
And from his ancient barriers free,
With a deafening roar the sea
   Comes foaming up the land.
Mother, cast thy babe aside:
Bridegroom, quit thy virgin bride:
Brother, pass thy brother by:
'Tis for life, for life, ye fly.
Along the drear horizon raves
The swift advancing line of waves.
On, on: their frothy crests appear
Each moment nearer and more near.
Urge the dromedary's speed;
Spur to death the reeling steed;
If perchance ye yet may gain
The mountains that o'erhang the plain.

" Oh thou haughty land of Nod,
  Hear the sentence of thy God.
  Thou hast said ' Of all the hills
  Whence, after autumn rains, the rills
    In silver trickle down,
  The fairest is that mountain white
  Which intercepts the morning light
    From Cain's imperial town.
  On its first and gentlest swell
  Are pleasant halls where nobles dwell;
  And marble porticoes are seen
  Peeping through terraced gardens green.
  Above are olives, palms, and vines;
  And higher yet the dark-blue pines;
  And highest on the summit shines
    The crest of everlasting ice.
  Here let the God of Abel own
  That human art hath wonders shown
    Beyond his boasted paradise.'

" Therefore on that proud mountain's crown
    Thy few surviving sons and daughters
Shall see their latest sun go down
    Upon a boundless, waste of waters.
None salutes and none replies;
    None heaves a groan or breathes a prayer;
They crouch on earth with tearless eyes,
    And clenched hands, and bristling hair.
The rain pours on: no star illumes
    The blackness of the roaring sky.
And each successive billow booms
    Nigher still and still more nigh.
And now upon the howling blast
The wreaths of spray come thick and fast;
And a great billow by the tempest curled
    Falls with a thundering crash; and all is o'er.
And what is left of all this glorious world?
    A sky without a beam, a sea without a shore.

" Oh thou fair land, where from their starry home
Cherub and seraph oft delight to roam,
Thou city of the thousand towers,
    Thou palace of the golden stairs,
Ye gardens of perennial flowers,
    Ye moated gates, ye breezy squares;
Ye parks amidst whose branches high
Oft peers the squirrel's sparkling eye ;
Ye vineyards, in whose trellised shade
Pipes many a youth to many a maid;
Ye ports where rides the gallant ship;
    Ye marts where wealthy burghers meet;
Ye dark green lanes which know the trip
    Of woman's conscious feet ;
Ye grassy meads where, when the day is done,
    The shepherd pens his fold ;
Ye purple moors on which the setting sun
    Leaves a rich fringe of gold ;

Ye wintry deserts where the larches grow ;
Ye mountains on whose everlasting snow
　　No human foot hath trod ;
　　Many a fathom shall ye sleep
　　Beneath the grey and endless deep,
In the great day of the revenge of God."

THE COUNTRY CLERGYMAN'S TRIP TO CAMBRIDGE.

An Election Ballad. (1827.)

As I sate down to breakfast in state,
   At my living of Tithing-cum-Boring,
With Betty beside me to wait,
   Came a rap that almost beat the door in.
I laid down my basin of tea,
   And Betty ceased spreading the toast,
" As sure as a gun, sir," said she,
   " That must be the knock of the post."

A letter—and free—bring it here—
   I have no correspondent who franks.
No! yes! Can it be ? Why, my dear,
   'Tis our glorious, our Protestant Bankes.
" Dear sir, as I know you desire
   That the Church should receive due protection,
I humbly presume to require
   Your aid at the Cambridge election.

" It has lately been brought to my knowledge,
   That the Ministers fully design
To suppress each cathedral and college,
   And eject every learned divine.

To assist this detestable scheme
    Three nuncios from Rome are come over;
They left Calais on Monday by steam,
    And landed to dinner at Dover.

" An army of grim Cordeliers,
    Well furnished with relics and vermin,
Will follow, Lord Westmoreland fears,
    To effect what their chiefs may determine.
Lollard's tower good authorities say,
    Is again fitting up for a prison;
And a wood-merchant told me to-day
    'Tis a wonder how faggots have risen.

" The finance scheme of Canning contains
    A new Easter-offering tax;
And he means to devote all the gains
    To a bounty on thumb-screws and racks.
Your living, so neat and compact—
    Pray, don't let the news give you pain!—
Is promised, I know for a fact,
    To an olive-faced Padre from Spain."

I read, and I felt my heart bleed,
    Sore wounded with horror and pity;
So I flew, with all possible speed,
    To our Protestant champion's committee.
True gentlemen, kind and well-bred!
    No fleering! no distance! no scorn!
They asked after my wife who is dead,
    And my children who never were born.

They then, like high-principled Tories,
    Called our sovereign unjust and unsteady,
And assailed him with scandalous stories,
    Till the coach for the voters was ready.
That coach might be well called a casket
    Of learning and brotherly love:
There were parsons in boot and in basket;
    There were parsons below and above.

There were Sneaker and Griper, a pair
  Who stick to Lord Mulesby like leeches;
A smug chaplain of plausible air,
  Who writes my Lord Goslingham's speeches.
Dr. Buzz, who alone is a host,
  Who, with arguments weighty as lead,
Proves six times a week in the Post
  That flesh somehow differs from bread.

Dr. Nimrod, whose orthodox toes
  Are seldom withdrawn from the stirrup;
Dr. Humdrum, whose eloquence flows,
  Like droppings of sweet poppy syrup;
Dr. Rosygill puffing and fanning,
  And wiping away perspiration;
Dr. Humbug, who proved Mr. Canning
  The beast in St. John's Revelation.

A layman can scarce form a notion
  Of our wonderful talk on the road;
Of the learning, the wit, and devotion,
  Which almost each syllable showed:
Why divided allegiance agrees
  So ill with our free constitution;
How Catholics swear as they please,
  In hope of the priest's absolution

How the Bishop of Norwich had bartered
  His faith for a legate's commission;
How Lyndhurst, afraid to be martyr'd,
  Had stooped to a base coalition;
How Papists are eased from compassion
  By bigotry, stronger than steel;
How burning would soon come in fashion,
  And how very bad it must feel.

We were all so much touched and excited
  By a subject so direly sublime,
That the rules of politeness were slighted,
  And we all of us talked at a time;

And in tones, which each moment grew louder,
　　Told how we should dress for the show,
And where we should fasten the powder,
　　And if we should bellow or no.

Thus from subject to subject we ran,
　　And the journey passed pleasantly o'er,
Till at last Dr. Humdrum began ;
　　From that time I remember no more.
At Ware he commenced his prelection,
　　In the dullest of clerical drones ;
And when next I regained recollection
　　We were rumbling o'er Trumpington stones.

SONG. (1827.)

O STAY, Madonna! stay;
  'Tis not the dawn of day
That marks the skies with yonder opal streak:
  The stars in silence shine;
  Then press thy lips to mine,
And rest upon my neck thy fervid cheek.

  O sleep, Madonna! sleep;
  Leave me to watch and weep
O'er the sad memory of departed joys,
  O'er hope's extinguished beam,
  O'er fancy's vanished dream,
O'er all that nature gives and man destroys.

  O wake, Madonna! wake;
  Even now the purple lake
Is dappled o'er with amber flakes of light;
  A glow is on the hill;
  And every trickling rill
In golden threads leaps down from yonder height.

  O fly, Madonna! fly,
  Lest day and envy spy
What only love and night may safely know:
  Fly, and tread softly, dear!
  Lest those who hate us hear
The sounds of thy light footsteps as they go.

B B 2

THE DELIVERANCE OF VIENNA.

TRANSLATED FROM VINCENZIO DA FILICAIA.

(Published in the " Winter's Wreath,"
Liverpool, 1828.)

———

" Le corde d'oro elette," &c.

THE chords, the sacred chords of gold,
 Strike, oh Muse, in measure bold ;
And frame a sparking wreath of joyous songs
For that great God to whom revenge belongs.
 Who shall resist his might,
 Who marshals for the fight
Earthquake and thunder, hurricane and flame ?
 He smote the haughty race
 Of unbelieving Thrace,
And turned their rage to fear, their pride to shame.
 He looked in wrath from high,
  Upon their vast array ;
 And, in the twinkling of an eye,
 Tambour, and trump, and battle-cry,
 And steeds, and turbaned infantry,
  Passed like a dream away.
Such power defends the mansions of the just :
 But, like a city without walls,
 The grandeur of the mortal falls
Who glories in his strength, and makes not God his
  trust.

The proud blasphemers thought all earth their own ;
  They deemed that soon the whirlwind of their ire
  Would sweep down tower and palace, dome and
    spire,
The Christian altars and the Augustan throne.
    And soon, they cried, shall Austria bow
    To the dust her lofty brow.
      The princedoms of Almayne
      Shall wear the Phrygian chain ;
In humbler waves shall vassal Tiber roll ;
    And Rome, a slave forlorn,
    Her laurelled tresses shorn,
Shall feel our iron in her inmost soul.
      Who shall bid the torrent stay ?
      Who shall bar the lightning's way ?
      Who arrest the advancing van
      Of the fiery Ottoman ?

    As the curling smoke-wreaths fly
    When fresh breezes clear the sky,
    Passed away each swelling boast
    Of the misbelieving host.
    From the Hebrus rolling far
    Came the murky cloud of war,
    And in shower and tempest dread
    Burst on Austria's fenceless head.
      But not for vaunt or threat
      Didst Thou, oh Lord, forget
The flock so dearly bought, and loved so well.
      Even in the very hour
      Of guilty pride and power
Full on the circumcised Thy vengeance fell.
      Then the fields were heaped with dead,
      Then the streams with gore were red,
And every bird of prey, and every beast,
From wood and cavern thronged to Thy great feast.
What terror seized the fiends obscene of Nile !
    How wildly, in his place of doom beneath,

Arabia's lying prophet gnashed his teeth,
And cursed his blighted hopes and wasted guile!
When, at the bidding of Thy sovereign might,
Flew on their destined path
Thy messengers of wrath,
Riding on storms and wrapped in deepest night.
The Phthian mountains saw,
And quaked with mystic awe:
The proud Sultana of the Straits bowed down
Her jewelled neck and her embattled crown.
The miscreants, as they raised their eyes
Glaring defiance on Thy skies,
Saw adverse winds and clouds display
The terrors of their black array;—
Saw each portentous star
Whose fiery aspect turned of yore to flight
The iron chariots of the Canaanite
Gird its bright harness for a deadlier war.

Beneath Thy withering look
Their limbs with palsy shook;
Scattered on earth the crescent banners lay;
Trembled with panic fear
Sabre and targe and spear,
Through the proud armies of the rising day.
Faint was each heart, unnerved each hand;
And, if they strove to charge or stand,
Their efforts were as vain
As his who, scared in feverish sleep
By evil dreams, essays to leap,
Then backward falls again.
With a crash of wild dismay,
Their ten thousand ranks gave way;
Fast they broke, and fast they fled;
Trampled, mangled, dying, dead,
Horse and horseman mingled lay;
Till the mountains of the slain
Raised the valleys to the plain.

Be all the glory to Thy name divine!
The swords were ours; the arm, O Lord, was Thine.

Therefore to Thee, beneath whose footstool wait
The powers which erring man calls Chance and Fate,
    To Thee who hast laid low
    The pride of Europe's foe,
And taught Byzantium's sullen lords to fear,
    I pour my spirit out
    In a triumphant shout,
And call all ages and all lands to hear.
    Thou who evermore endurest,
    Loftiest, mightiest, wisest, purest,
    Thou whose will destroys or saves,
    Dread of tyrants, hope of slaves,
    The wreath of glory is from Thee,
    And the red sword of victory.

    There where exulting Danube's flood
    Runs stained with Islam's noblest blood
      From that tremendous field,
    There where in mosque the tyrants met,
    And from the crier's minaret
      Unholy summons pealed,
    Pure shrines and temples now shall be
    Decked for a worship worthy Thee.
    To Thee thy whole creation pays
    With mystic sympathy its praise,
      The air, the earth, the seas:
    The day shines forth with livelier beam;
    There is a smile upon the stream,
      An anthem on the breeze.
    Glory, they cry, to Him whose might
    Hath turned the barbarous foe to flight,
    Whose arm protects with power divine
    The city of his favoured line.
The caves, the woods, the rocks, repeat the sound;
The everlasting hills roll the long echoes round.

But, if Thy rescued church may dare
Still to besiege Thy throne with prayer,
Sheathe not, we implore Thee, Lord,
Sheathe not Thy victorious sword.
Still Panonia pines away,
Vassal of a double sway:
Still Thy servants groan in chains,
Still the race which hates Thee reigns:
Part the living from the dead:
Join the members to the head:
Snatch Thine own sheep from yon fell monster's
    hold;
Let one kind shepherd rule one undivided fold.

He is the victor, only he
Who reaps the fruits of victory.
    We conquered once in vain,
When foamed the Ionian waves with gore,
And heaped Lepanto's stormy shore
    With wrecks and Moslem slain.
Yet wretched Cyprus never broke
The Syrian tyrant's iron yoke.
    Shall the twice vanquished foe
    Again repeat his blow?
Shall Europe's sword be hung to rust in peace?
    No—let the red-cross ranks
    Of the triumphant Franks
Bear swift deliverance to the shrines of Greece,
And in her inmost heart let Asia feel
The avenging plagues of Western fire and steel.

Oh God! for one short moment raise
The veil which hides those glorious days.
The flying foes I see Thee urge
Even to the river's headlong verge
Close on their rear the loud uproar
Of fierce pursuit from Ister's shore
Comes pealing on the wind;

The Rab's wild waters are before,
　The Christian sword behind.
Sons of perdition, speed your flight.
　No earthly spear is in the rest;
No earthly champion leads to fight
　The warriors of the West.
The Lord of hosts asserts his old renown,
Scatters, and smites, and slays, and tramples down.
Fast, fast, beyond what mortal tongue can say,
　Or mortal fancy dream,
He rushes on his prey:
　Till, with the terrors of the wondrous theme
Bewildered and appalled, I cease to sing,
And close my dazzled eye, and rest my wearied wing.

THE ARMADA. (1832.)

A FRAGMENT.

ATTEND, all ye who list to hear our noble England's
    praise ;
I tell of the thrice famous deeds she wrought in
    ancient days,
When that great fleet invincible against her bore in
    vain
The richest spoils of Mexico, the stoutest hearts of
    Spain.

   It was about the lovely close of a warm summer
    day,
There came a gallant merchant-ship full sail to Ply-
    mouth Bay ;
Her crew hath seen Castile's black fleet, beyond
    Aurigny's isle,
At earliest twilight, on the waves lie heaving many
    a mile.
At sunrise she escaped their van, by God's especial
    grace ;
And the tall Pinta, till the noon, had held her close
    in chase.
Forthwith a guard at every gun was placed along the
    wall ;
The beacon blazed upon the roof of Edgecumbe's lofty
    hall ;

Many a light fishing-bark put out to pry along the
  coast,
And with loose rein and bloody spur rode inland
  many a post.
With his white hair unbonneted, the stout old sheriff
  comes ;
Behind him march the halberdiers ; before him
  sound the drums ;
His yeomen round the market cross make clear an
  ample space ;
For there behoves him to set up the standard of
  Her Grace.
And haughtily the trumpets peal, and gaily dance
  the bells,
As slow upon the labouring wind the royal blazon
  swells.
Look how the Lion of the sea lifts up his ancient
  crown,
And underneath his deadly paw treads the gay lilies
  down.
So stalked he when he turned to flight, on that
  famed Picard field,
Bohemia's plume, and Genoa's bow, and Cæsar's
  eagle shield.
So glared he when at Agincourt in wrath he turned
  to bay,
And crushed and torn beneath his claws the princely
  hunters lay.
Ho ! strike the flagstaff deep, sir Knight : ho ! scat-
  ter flowers, fair maids :
Ho ! gunners, fire a loud salute : ho ! gallants, draw
  your blades :
Thou sun, shine on her joyously ; ye breezes, waft
  her wide ;
Our glorious SEMPER EADEM, the banner of our pride.
  The freshening breeze of eve unfurled that ban-
    ner's massy fold ;
The parting gleam of sunshine kissed that haughty
  scroll of gold ;

Night sank upon the dusky beach, and on the purple
    sea,
Such night in England ne'er had been, nor e'er again
    shall be.
From Eddystone to Berwick bounds, from Lynn to
    Milford Bay,
That time of slumber was as bright and busy as the day;
For swift to east and swift to west the ghastly war-
    flame spread,
High on St. Michael's Mount it shone: it shone on
    Beachy Head.
Far on the deep the Spaniard saw, along each south-
    ern shire,
Cape beyond cape, in endless range, those twinkling
    points of fire.
The fisher left his skiff to rock on Tamar's glittering
    waves:
The rugged miners poured to war from Mendip's
    sunless caves:
O'er Longleat's towers, o'er Cranbourne's oaks, the
    fiery herald flew:
He roused the shepherds of Stonehenge, the rangers
    of Beaulieu.
Right sharp and quick the bells all night rang out
    from Bristol town,
And ere the day three hundred horse had met on
    Clifton down;
The sentinel on Whitehall gate looked forth into the
    night,
And saw o'erhanging Richmond Hill the streak of
    blood-red light.
Then bugle's note and cannon's roar the death-like
    silence broke,
And with one start, and with one cry, the royal city
    woke.
At once on all her stately gates arose the answering
    fires;
At once the wild alarum clashed from all her reeling
    spires;

From all the batteries of the Tower pealed loud the
    voice of fear;
And all the thousand masts of Thames sent back a
    louder cheer:
And from the furthest wards was heard the rush of
    hurrying feet,
And the broad streams of pikes and flags rushed
    down each roaring street;
And broader still became the blaze, and louder still
    the din,
As fast from every village round the horse came
    spurring in:
And eastward straight from wild Blackheath the
    warlike errand went,
And roused in many an ancient hall the gallant
    squires of Kent.
Southward from Surrey's pleasant hills flew those
    bright couriers forth;
High on bleak Hampstead's swarthy moor they
    started for the north;
And on, and on, without a pause untired they
    bounded still:
All night from tower to tower they sprang; they
    sprang from hill to hill:
Till the proud peak unfurled the flag o'er Darwin's
    rocky dales,
Till like volcanoes flared to heaven the stormy hills
    of Wales,
Till twelve fair counties saw the blaze on Malvern's
    lonely height,
Till streamed in crimson on the wind the Wrekin's
    crest of light,
Till broad and fierce the star came forth on Ely's
    stately fane,
And tower and hamlet rose in arms o'er all the
    boundless plain;
Till Belvoir's lordly terraces the sign to Lincoln sent,
And Lincoln sped the message on o'er the wide vale
    of Trent;

Till Skiddaw saw the fire that burnt on Gaunt's em-
    battled pile,
And the red glare on Skiddaw roused the burghers
    of Carlisle.

       *   *   *   *   *

INSCRIPTION

ON THE

STATUE OF LORD WILLIAM BENTINCK.

AT CALCUTTA. (1835.)

To
WILLIAM CAVENDISH BENTINCK,
Who, during seven years, ruled India with eminent
Prudence, Integrity, and Benevolence:
Who, placed at the head of a great Empire, never
laid aside
The simplicity and moderation of a private citizen:
Who infused into Oriental despotism the spirit
of British Freedom:
Who never forgot that the end of Government is
The happiness of the Governed:
Who abolished cruel rites:
Who effaced humiliating distinctions:
Who gave liberty to the expression of public opinion:
Whose constant study it was, to elevate the intellectual
And moral character of the Nations committed to his
charge:
This Monument
Was erected by men,
Who, differing in Race, in Manners, in Language,
And in Religion,
Cherish, with equal veneration and gratitude,
The memory of his wise, upright,
And paternal Administration.

EPITAPH ON SIR BENJAMIN HEATH MALKIN.

AT CALCUTTA. (1837.)

This Monument
Is sacred to the memory
Of
SIR BENJAMIN HEATH MALKIN, Knight,
One of the Judges of the Supreme Court of
Judicature :
A man eminently distinguished
By his literary and scientific attainments,
By his professional learning and ability,
By the clearness and accuracy of his intellect,
By diligence, by patience, by firmness, by love of
truth,
By public spirit, ardent and disinterested,
Yet always under the guidance of discretion,
By rigid uprightness, by unostentatious piety,
By the serenity of his temper,
And by the benevolence of his heart.

He was born on the 29th September, 1797. He died on the
21st October, 1837.

THE LAST BUCCANEER. (1839.)

THE winds were yelling, the waves were swelling,
  The sky was black and drear,
When the crew with eyes of flame brought the ship
    without a name
  Alongside the last Buccaneer.

" Whence flies your sloop full sail before so fierce a gale,
  When all others drive bare on the seas ?
Say, come ye from the shore of the holy Salvador,
  Or the gulf of the rich Caribbees ? "

" From a shore no search hath found, from a gulf no
    line can sound,
  Without rudder or needle we steer ;
Above, below, our bark, dies the sea fowl and the shark,
  As we fly by the last Buccaneer.

" To-night there shall be heard on the rocks of Cape
    de Verde
  A loud crash, and a louder roar ;
And to-morrow shall the deep, with a heavy moaning,
    sweep
  The corpses and wreck to the shore."

The stately ship of Clyde securely now may ride
  In the breath of the citron shades ;
And Severn's towering mast securely now flies fast,
  Through the sea of the balmy Trades.

From St. Jago's wealthy port, from Havannah's royal
    fort,
  The seaman goes forth without fear ;
For since that stormy night not a mortal hath had
    sight
  Of the flag of the last Buccaneer.

EPITAPH ON A JACOBITE. (1845.)

To my true king I offered free from stain
Courage and faith ; vain faith, and courage vain.
For him, I threw lands, honours, wealth away,
And one dear hope, that was more prized than they.
For him I languished in a foreign clime,
Grey-haired with sorrow in my manhood's prime ;
Heard on Lavernia Scargill's whispering trees,
And pined by Arno for my lovelier Tees ;
Beheld each night my home in fevered sleep,
Each morning started from the dream to weep ;
Till God, who saw me tried too sorely, gave
The resting place I asked, an early grave.
Oh thou, whom chance leads to this nameless stone,
From that proud country which was once mine own,
By those white cliffs I never more must see,
By that dear language which I spake like thee,
Forget all feuds, and shed one English tear
O'er English dust.   A broken heart lies here.

EPITAPH ON LORD METCALFE. (1847.)

Near this stone is laid

CHARLES LORD METCALFE,

A statesman tried in many high offices
And difficult conjunctures,
And found equal to all.
The three greatest Dependencies of the British Crown
Were successively entrusted to his care.
In India, his fortitude, his wisdom,
His probity, and his moderation,
Are held in honourable remembrance
By men of many races, languages, and religions.
In Jamaica, still convulsed by a social revolution,
His prudence calmed the evil passions
Which long suffering had engendered in one class
And long domination in another.
In Canada, not yet recovered from the calamities of
civil war,
He reconciled contending factions
To each other, and to the Mother Country.
Costly monuments in Asiatic and American cities
Attest the gratitude of the nations which he ruled.
This tablet records the sorrow and the pride
With which his memory is cherished by his family.

TRANSLATION FROM PLAUTUS. (1850.)

[The author passed a part of the summer and autumn of 1850
at Ventnor, in the Isle of Wight. He usually, when walking alone,
had with him a book. On one occasion, as he was loitering in the
landslip near Bonchurch, reading the Rudens of Plautus, it struck
him that it might be an interesting experiment to attempt to produce
something which might be supposed to resemble passages in the lost
Greek drama of Diphilus, from which the Rudens appears to have
been taken. He selected one passage in the Rudens, of which he
then made the following version, which he afterwards copied out at
the request of a friend to whom he had repeated it.]

Act IV. Sc. vii.

DÆMONES.   O Gripe, Gripe, in ætate hominum
     plurimæ
Fiunt transennæ, ubi decipiuntur dolis ;
Atque edepol in eas plerumque esca imponitur.
Quam si quis avidus pascit escam avariter,
Decipitur in transenna avaritia sua.
Ille, qui consulte, docte, atque astute cavet,
Diutine uti bene licet partum bene.
Mi istæc videtur præda prædatum irier :
Ut cum majore dote abeat, quam advenerit.
Egone ut, quod ad me adlatum esse alienum sciam
Calem ?   Minime istuc faciet noster Dæmones.
Semper cavere hoc sapientes æquissimum est,
Ne conscii sint ipsi maleficiis suis.
Ego, mihi quum lusi, nil moror ullum lucrum.
     GRIPUS.   Spectavi ego pridem Comicos ad istum
     modum
Sapienter dicta dicere, atque iis plaudier,
Quum illos sapientis mores monstrabant poplo ;
Sed quum inde suam quisque ibant diversi domum,
Nullus erat illo pacto, ut illi jusserant.

ΔΑΙΜ. Ὦ Γρῖπε, Γρῖπε, πλεῖστα παγίδων σχήματα
ἴδοι τις ἂν πεπηγμέν᾽ ἐν θνητῶν βίῳ,
καὶ πλεῖστ᾽ ἐπ᾽ αὐτοῖς δελέαθ᾽, ὧν ἐπιθυμίᾳ
ὀρεγόμενός τις ἐν κακοῖς ἁλίσκεται·
ὅστις δ᾽ ἀπιστεῖ καὶ σοφῶς φυλάττεται,
καλῶς ἀπολαύει τῶν καλῶς πεπορισμένων.
ἅρπαγμα δ᾽ οὐχ ἅρπαγμ᾽ ὁ λάρναξ οὑτοσὶ,
ἀλλ᾽ αὐτὸς, οἶμαι, μᾶλλον ἁρπάξει τινά.
τόνδ᾽ ἄνδρα κλέπτειν τἀλλότρι᾽—εὐφήμει,
τάλαν·
ταυτήν γε μὴ μαίνοιτο μανίαν Δαιμονῆς.
τόδε γὰρ ἀεὶ σοφοῖσιν εὐλαβητέον,
μή τί ποθ᾽ ἑαυτῷ τις ἀδίκημα συννοῇ·
κέρδη δ᾽ ἔμοιγε πάνθ᾽ ὅσοις εὐφραίνομαι,
κέρδος δ᾽ ἀκερδὲς ὃ τοὐμὸν ἀλγύνει κέαρ.

ΓΡΙΠ. κἀγὼ μὲν ἤδη κωμικῶν ἀκήκοα
σεμνῶς λεγόντων τοιάδε, τοὺς δὲ θεωμένους
κροτεῖν, ματαίοις ἡδομένους σοφίσμασιν·
εἶθ᾽, ὡς ἀπῆλθ᾽ ἕκαστος οἴκαδ᾽, οὐδενὶ
οὐδὲν παρέμεινε τῶν καλῶς εἰρημένων.

VALENTINE

TO THE HON. MARY C. STANHOPE,

(DAUGHTER OF LORD AND LADY MAHON.)[1]

(1851.)

HAIL, day of Music, day of Love,
On earth below, in air above.
In air the turtle fondly moans,
The linnet pipes in joyous tones;
On earth the postman toils along,
Bent double by huge bales of song,
Where, rich with many a gorgeous dye,
Blazes all Cupid's heraldry—
Myrtles and roses, doves and sparrows,
Love-knots and altars, lamps and arrows.
What nymph without wild hopes and fears
The double rap this morning hears?
Unnumbered lasses young and fair,
From Bethnal Green to Belgrave Square,
With cheeks high flushed, and hearts loud
        beating,
Await the tender annual greeting.
The loveliest lass of all is mine—
Good morrow to my Valentine!

Good morrow, gentle Child! and then
Again good morrow, and again,

<hr/>

[1] Already published by Earl Stanhope in his *Miscellanies*, 1863.

Good morrow following still good morrow,
Without one cloud of strife or sorrow.
And when the God to whom we pay
In jest our homages to-day
Shall come to claim, no more in jest,
His rightful empire o'er thy breast,
Benignant may his aspect be,
His yoke the truest liberty :
And if a tear his power confess,
Be it a tear of happiness.
It shall be so.   The Muse displays
The future to her votary's gaze ;
Prophetic rage my bosom swells—
I taste the cake—I hear the bells !
From Conduit Street the close array
Of chariots barricades the way
To where I see with outstretched hand,
Majestic, thy great kinsman stand,[1]
And half unbend his brow of pride,
As welcoming so fair a bride.
Gay favours, thick as flakes of snow,
Brighten St. George's portico ;
Within I see the chancel's pale,
The orange flowers, the Brussels veil,
The page on which those fingers white,
Still trembling from the awful rite,
For the last time shall faintly trace
The name of Stanhope's noble race.
I see kind faces round thee pressing,
I hear kind voices whisper blessing ;
And with those voices mingles mine—
All good attend my Valentine !

T. B. MACAULAY.

St. Valentine's Day, 1851.

[1] The statue of Mr. Pitt in Hanover Square.

PARAPHRASE OF A PASSAGE IN THE CHRONICLE OF THE MONK OF ST. GALL.
(1856.)

[In the summer of 1856, the author travelled with a friend through Lombardy. As they were on the road between Novara and Milan, they were conversing on the subject of the legends relating to that country. The author remarked to his companion that Mr. Panizzi, in the Essay on the Romantic Narrative Poetry of the Italians, prefixed to his edition of Bojardo, had pointed out an instance of the conversion of ballad poetry into prose narrative which strongly confirmed the theory of Perizonius and Niebuhr, upon which "The Lays of Ancient Rome" are founded ; and, after repeating an extract which Mr. Panizzi has given from the chronicle of "The Monk of St. Gall," he proceeded to frame a metrical paraphrase. The note in Mr. Panizzi's work (vol. i. p. 123, note *b*) is here copied verbatim.]

"The monk says that Oger was with Desiderius, King of Lombardy, watching the advance of Charlemagne's army. The king often asked Oger where was Charlemagne. Quando videris, inquit, segetem campis inhorrescere, ferreum Padum et Ticinum marinis fluctibus ferro nigrantibus muros civitatis inundantes, tunc est spes Caroli venientis. His nedum expletis primum ad occasum Circino vel Borea cœpit apparere, quasi nubes tenebrosa, quæ diem clarissimam horrentes convertit in umbras. Sed propiante Imperatore, ex armorum splendore, dies omni nocte tenebrosior oborta est inclusis. Tunc visus est ipse ferreus Carolus ferrea galea cristatus, ferreis manicis armillatus, &c. &c. His igitur, quæ ego balbus et edentulus, non ut debui circuitu tardiore diutius explicare tentavi, veridicus speculator Oggerus celerrimo visu contuitus dixit ad Desiderium: Ecce, habes quem tantopere perquisisti. Et hæc dicens, pene exanimis cecidit.—MONACH. SANGAL. *de Reb. Bel. Caroli Magni*, lib. ii. § xxvi. Is this not evidently taken from poetical effusions ? "

PARAPHRASE.

To Oggier spake King Didier:
 " When cometh Charlemagne ?
We looked for him in harvest:
 We looked for him in rain.
Crops are reaped ; and floods are past ;
 And still he is not here.
Some token show, that we may know
 That Charlemagne is near."

Then to the King made answer
 Oggier, the christened Dane :
" When stands the iron harvest,
 Ripe on the Lombard plain,
That stiff harvest which is reaped
 With sword of knight and peer,
Then by that sign ye may divine
 That Charlemagne is near.

" When round the Lombard cities
 The iron flood shall flow,
A swifter flood than Ticin,
 A broader flood than Po,
Frothing white with many a plume
 Dark blue with many a spear,
Then by that sign ye may divine
 That Charlemagne is near."

LINES WRITTEN ON THE NIGHT OF THE 30TH OF JULY, 1847,

AT THE CLOSE OF AN UNSUCCESSFUL CONTEST FOR EDINBURGH.

THE day of tumult, strife, defeat, was o'er ;
    Worn out with toil, and noise, and scorn, and
        spleen,
I slumbered, and in slumber saw once more
A room in an old mansion,[1] long unseen.

That room, methought, was curtained from the
        light ;
    Yet through the curtains shone the moon's cold
        ray
Full on a cradle, where, in linen white,
    Sleeping life's first soft sleep, an infant lay.

Pale flickered on the hearth the dying flame,
    And all was silent in that ancient hall,
Save when by fits on the low night-wind came
    The murmur of the distant waterfall.

And lo ! the fairy queens who rule our birth
    Drew nigh to speak the new born baby's doom :
With noiseless step, which left no trace on earth,
    From gloom they came, and vanished into gloom.

[1] Rothley Temple, Leicestershire.

Not deigning on the boy a glance to cast
   Swept careless by the gorgeous Queen of Gain;
More scornful still, the Queen of Fashion passed,
   With mincing gait and sneer of cold disdain.

The Queen of Power tossed high her jewelled head,
   And o'er her shoulder threw a wrathful frown:
The Queen of Pleasure on the pillow shed
   Scarce one stray rose-leaf from her fragrant crown.

Still Fay in long procession followed Fay;
   And still the little couch remained unblest:
But, when those wayward sprites had passed away,
   Came One, the last, the mightiest, and the best.

Oh glorious lady, with the eyes of light,
   And laurels clustering round thy lofty brow,
Who by the cradle's side didst watch that night,
   Warbling a sweet strange music, who wast thou?

"Yes, darling; let them go;" so ran the strain:
   "Yes; let them go, gain, fashion, pleasure, power,
And all the busy elves to whose domain
   Belongs the nether sphere, the fleeting hour.

"Without one envious sigh, one anxious scheme,
   The nether sphere, the fleeting hour resign,
Mine is the world of thought, the world of dream,
   Mine all the past, and all the future mine.

"Fortune, that lays in sport the mighty low,
   Age, that to penance turns the joys of youth,
Shall leave untouched the gifts which I bestow,
   The sense of beauty and the thirst of truth.

"Of the fair brotherhood who share my grace,
   I, from thy natal day, pronounce thee free;
And, if for some I keep a nobler place,
   I keep for none a happier than for thee.

" There are who, while to vulgar eyes they seem
　Of all my bounties largely to partake,
Of me as of some rival's handmaid deem,
　And court me but for gain's, power's, fashion's
　　sake.

" To such, though deep their lore, though wide their
　　fame,
　Shall my great mysteries be all unknown :
But thou, through good and evil, praise and blame,
　Wilt not thou love me for myself alone ?

" Yes ; thou wilt love me with exceeding love ;
　And I will tenfold all that love repay,
Still smiling, though the tender may reprove,
　Still faithful, though the trusted may betray.

" For aye mine emblem was, and aye shall be,
　The ever-during plant whose bough I wear,
Brightest and greenest then, when every tree
　That blossoms in the light of Time is bare.

" In the dark hour of shame, I deigned to stand
　Before the frowning peers at Bacon's side :
On a far shore I smoothed with tender hand
　Through months of pain, the sleepless bed of
　　Hyde :

" I brought the wise and brave of ancient days
　To cheer the cell where Raleigh pined alone :
I lighted Milton's darkness with the blaze
　Of the bright ranks that guard the eternal throne.

" And even so, my child, it is my pleasure
　That thou not then alone shouldst feel me nigh,
When in domestic bliss and studious leisure,
　Thy weeks uncounted come, uncounted fly ;

"Not then alone, when myriads, closely pressed
  Around thy car, the shout of triumph raise;
Nor when, in gilded drawing rooms, thy breast
  Swells at the sweeter sound of woman's praise.

"No: when on restless night dawns cheerless
      morrow,
  When weary soul and wasting body pine,
Thine am I still, in danger, sickness, sorrow,
  In conflict, obloquy, want, exile, thine;

"Thine, where on mountain waves the snowbirds
      scream,
  Where more than Thule's winter barbs the breeze,
Where scarce, through lowering clouds, one sickly
      gleam
  Lights the drear May-day of Antarctic seas;

"Thine, when around thy litter's track all day
  White sandhills shall reflect the blinding glare;
Thine, when, through forests breathing death, thy
      way
  All night shall wind by many a tiger's lair;

"Thine most, when friends turn pale, when traitors fly,
  When, hard beset, thy spirit, justly proud,
For truth, peace, freedom, mercy, dares defy
  A sullen priesthood and a raving crowd.

"Amidst the din of all things fell and vile,
  Hate's yell, and envy's hiss, and folly's bray,
Remember me; and with an unforced smile
  See riches, baubles, flatterers, pass away.

"Yes: they will pass away; nor deem it strange:
  They come and go, as comes and goes the sea:
And let them come and go: thou, through all
      change,
  Fix thy firm gaze on virtue and on me."

INDEX.

LONDON : PRINTED BY
SPOTTISWOODE AND CO., NEW-STREET SQUARE
AND PARLIAMENT STREET